CHEERS FOR WAYNE D. DUNDEE, JOE HANNIBAL, AND
THE SKINTIGHT SHROUD

"Hannibal is the type of private investigator—tough and hard-edged, but also sexy and sensitive—that many mystery buffs will take to their hearts."　　　　　**—The Journal** (Flint, Mich.)

"Readable . . . engaging . . . an old-fashioned private eye who smokes cigarettes, drinks bourbon, beds beautiful dames and hews to an old-fashioned code of ethics."　　　　**—Publishers Weekly**

"In-depth porn facts, raunchy back talk, and steamy interludes."
—Kirkus Reviews

"Blessed with a voice as clear and pure as a Midwestern breeze, Joe Hannibal, Wayne Dundee's tough but human detective, brings a blue-collar sensibility to the genre that is as refreshing as it is real."　　　　**—Max Allan Collins**, author of *Neon Mirage*

"Wry, tough, poignant . . . Dundee writes with abiding skill and heartbreaking accuracy."
　　　　　　—Ed Gorman, author of *Murder Straight Up*

The author's previous Joe Hannibal mystery:

The Burning Season

Wayne D. Dundee

The Skintight Shroud

A DELL BOOK

Published by
Dell Publishing
a division of
Bantam Doubleday Dell Publishing Group, Inc.
666 Fifth Avenue
New York, New York 10103

ISBN: 0-440-20718-5

Published by arrangement with St. Martin's Press

Printed in the United States of America

Published simultaneously in Canada

February 1991

10 9 8 7 6 5 4 3 2 1

OPM

Pleasure is more powerful than
all fear of the penalty.

—Johann Wolfgang von Goethe

Morals are a personal affair; in the war of righteousness
every man fights for his own hand.

—Robert Louis Stevenson

At birth, you are trapped in it
At death, you are wrapped in it
Ashes to ashes, dust to dust
Hope, despair, love, hate, lust
Proving ground for Heaven, or just Hell on Earth?
God's grand design, or the Devil's twisted mirth?
Sometimes I want to scream out loud
Can't anyone see me struggling in this skintight shroud?

—Kath Howard
(a.k.a. Kat Hayward)

1

"Are you aware, Mr. Hannibal, that northern Illinois has quite a thriving adult-film industry?"

The question was posed by a silver-haired, distinguished-looking old gent of sixty or so who had introduced himself to me as Henry Foxwood, III. We were seated—each in a high-backed red leather reading chair, regarding one another over snifters of brandy held at the ready like fencing foils—in the book-lined study of his spacious and handsomely furnished apartment. It was a setting that seemed appropriate for discussing Melville or Cooper, maybe even Hammett, maybe the stock market or the trade deficit—but hardly the subject of celluloid humping.

Nevertheless, in my line of work—at least when it comes to dealing with a prospective client of obvious means—you learn to go with the flow.

"Adult films," I said, adopting my host's matter-of-fact style, "as in fuck flicks?"

He smiled. "Precisely."

I sipped some of my brandy, shrugged. "Never really gave it much thought," I said, "but with all the recent advancements in video technology, I guess these days you can shoot just about anything anywhere. Why not right here in Rockford?"

He nodded sagely. "Why not, indeed. Oh, the more ambitious productions, the full-length sound features that play what's left of the adult-theater circuit and vie for the various awards the X-rated community has created for itself, are still done primarily on the coasts. But the less pretentious fare, your basic fuck-and-suck quickies made directly for home rental and mail-order sales and the silent, 10–15-minute shorts that play in the peep booths—loops, they're called in the industry—are being churned out all across the country. Let's face it, even the *Kama Sutra* has a limited number of positions. So the name of the game becomes new faces and new bodies. It is surprisingly easy to find willing participants, even here in the Midwest. While public outcry against the availability of the product frequently assails our senses, similar attention to the actual *making* of the films—in areas such as ours, at any rate—remains minimal simply because very few people know what is taking place. And where public outcry is minimal, so, of course, is the concern of the police and various elected officials."

I took another pull of brandy, then frowned at a stray thought that wandered in from the corner of my brain mostly reserved for crazy ideas. "When you asked me here on the phone, you said you were interested in hiring my services. I naturally assumed you meant as a private detective. That *is* what you're leading up to, right?"

"As opposed to recruiting you for loop stardom, you mean?" Foxwood chuckled, appearing thoroughly amused at the prospect. "You have a very interesting face, Mr. Hannibal. The fact that it evidently has been pounded upon a number of times, the nose pushed about this way and that, gives it an intriguing amount of character. A Hawks or a Peckinpah might well have found some use for it. But I do hope you'll take no offense when I tell you that it is hardly the stuff of visual erotica." He paused and allowed half of his mouth to curve into an impish grin. "Of course, if you happen to be spectacularly endowed and can function on cue in front of a camera crew and various—"

"Like I said," I cut in, "I'm a private eye. A few other things about me are private, too. How about if we just get to the reason you sent for me?"

He put away the grin and produced some folded papers which he held out to me. "Very well. Please examine these."

What he handed me were two newspaper clippings. When I shook them open I saw they were from one of the local dailies, the most recent dated day before yesterday, the other, six days prior to that.

Both were front-page accounts of murders that had taken place in the Rockford area. As I scanned the clippings, I remembered reading and/or hearing about each death shortly after its occurrence. Rockford, striving in so many ways to be a "Big City," is still small enough to treat murder as something of a novelty.

The first victim, Jason Hobbs, twenty-seven, was stabbed to death, his body found in a ditch alongside a back road in rural Boone County. The second victim, Valerie Pine, twenty-four, was strangled and her nude corpse discovered by her roommate in their southside apartment. There appeared to be no connection between the two killings, the only similarities being the lack of any apparent motive in either case and the standard cop line about "expecting a breakthrough momentarily" that closed each article.

Without refolding them, I dropped the clippings onto the lamp stand that separated my perch from Foxwood's. I said, "If whatever you hoped to hire me for involves poking my nose into a couple of ongoing murder investigations, you may as well save your breath."

"I happen to know that you have involved yourself in murder investigations in the past."

"Uh-huh. I've also burned my rear end on hot stoves in the past. It taught me to quit leaning against them."

"But had you the proper insulation, those hot stoves would have caused you little or no discomfort. I believe I can provide you with the insulation necessary to, ah, handle this matter without getting burned."

"Insulation from the cops?"

"To a certain extent, yes."

"How about from the killer or killers?"

"Since that is an unknown factor, I obviously cannot say."

"But you *do* want me to investigate the Hobbs and Pine murders?"

"In a manner of speaking, yes. You see, I represent a, ah, group of concerned individuals who are interested in establishing not so much who *did* kill those two young people but rather who did *not.*"

I shook my head. "If that made any sense, Foxwood, it was to somebody not sitting in this chair."

He gave me a tolerant look. "If you will hear me out, I am sure I can explain it to your complete understanding. What's more, I believe I can present it palatably enough to make you reconsider your rather hasty refusal to accept the case."

I drained my glass, thoughtfully swirled its contents around inside my mouth before swallowing. Then I reached for the decanter that shared the top of the stand with the ornate lamp and the newspaper clippings I'd tossed there. The booze was good, the surroundings were warm and dry, and I hardly had a crowd of alternate clients piled up back at my office. So what harm could it do to listen to the old guy's spiel? Besides, the contrast between his cultured manner and his talk of porno films and murder had my curiosity more than a little piqued.

"Okay," I said, "I'll hear you out. But I doubt if you can change my mind."

He settled back in his chair, steepling delicate pink fingers around his drink, and waited while I poured myself some more of the brandy. After I had replaced the decanter and settled back in my own chair, he said, "In view of what has already been said, I imagine it will come as no surprise when I tell you that the two murder victims were involved in making adult films locally."

"Involved in what way?"

"In front of the cameras. Hobbs was something of a veteran, having appeared in some two dozen productions, while the Pine girl was just getting started."

My eyes flicked involuntarily to the news clippings and Foxwood read my mind. "No," he said, "there is no mention of their, ah, avocation in either of those articles. Nor in any of the follow-up articles that have appeared. And to the best of our knowledge, the police remain unaware of this potential link in the killings."

"Potential link?"

Foxwood shrugged a shoulder. "Coincidence does sometimes happen in life, Mr. Hannibal. And in death. Otherwise the word would never have been coined."

I said, "Yeah, well somebody coined the term *tooth fairy,* too. But I have it on pretty good authority that there's no such thing."

"I take it you are not a great believer in coincidence?"

"Only on the second Tuesday of every other week."

"Uhmmm. It seems you share those sentiments with the group of concerned individuals I mentioned earlier. That is why they asked me to engage your services in looking into this matter."

"But you're not at liberty to say exactly who these 'concerned individuals' are?"

"That is correct."

It didn't take a genius to figure out what group would be most concerned over the possible decimation of a thriving porn ring. That would also explain Foxwood's remark about being able to 'insulate' me from certain things. I pushed a little harder, mainly to demonstrate I was neither as docile nor dumb as might be preferred. "Could we be talking here about a bunch of rather swarthy fellows whose last names end mostly in vowels?"

"Really, Mr. Hannibal. Even if that were the case, do I look foolish enough to confirm such a question?"

I sighed, signaling I was willing to let it ride for the time being. "Okay then," I said, "where exactly do *you* fit in?"

He took his first sip of brandy since trotting out the decanter and glasses. "I fit in on a number of different levels as far as the particular enterprise we have been discussing goes. At the moment, I am merely a humble, ah, go-between. At various other times, I am everything from a recruiter to veteran performer in my own right."

I cocked one eyebrow in an expression of surprise and uncertainty.

Foxwood smiled. "Yes, yes, I realize old fogies like me are supposed to be beyond that sort of thing, supposed to be content with patting an occasional grandchild on the head, or maybe—just maybe now, on a particularly frisky day—casting longing gazes after an especially fetching member of the opposite sex. Well, for me it never quite worked out that way. For one thing, I have no grandchildren; for another, I find that mere longing gazes, without any sort of follow-through, leave one immensely unsatisfied."

"So you've continued to follow through?"

"Every blessed chance I get."

"Sometimes even in front of a camera?"

"Occasionally, yes. It is not the same experience as making love to a desirable woman in private, of course, but it can be quite pleasurable nonetheless. And more profitable, I might add."

I made a gesture, indicating the impressive study and the rest. "All of this comes from wielding your sword in minor-league porn?"

"A portion of it, to be sure, but hardly all of it. Ironically enough, considering your phraseology, most of it comes from wielding a rather different kind of sword for the cameras. Are you familiar with a television show from the midfifties entitled 'Champion of Camelot'?"

I shook my head. "Can't say as I am."

"Ah, the fleeting kiss of fame. Actually, almost no one remembers it any longer. In all likelihood, many of those responsible for perpetrating it upon the viewing public have put it out of their minds intentionally. Truth to tell, it was a dreadful black-and-white thing that ran in syndication for only two seasons. Yet for all its schlock, it was my brightest moment in the spotlight—I, who starred as noble Sir Gawaine, righting Medieval wrongs each and every week with the aide of my trusty broadsword Ironfang and my tireless steed Thunderer. After 'Champion' had swashed its last buckle, however, I was hopelessly typecast. There was a time, unfortunately, when *everyone* remembered that damned show. When I was finally able to accept the fact that I was not destined to become Hollywood's next Errol Flynn—or anything else—I returned here to Rockford, my hometown, and existed rather dismally for a while on a number of halfhearted business ventures. Until those lovely residuals began rolling in—residuals due me, I might add, not because of any astute business sense on my part but rather because in accepting the job I was desperate enough to settle for a percent of the profits and a reduced up-front salary. At any rate, the show in reruns built gradually to a giant hit overseas. The more backward the nation, the better they seem to love it. 'Champion' has been playing nonstop in various remote corners of the globe for nearly thirty years now. Recently, a couple of the smaller cable networks in this country have even started running it as a sort of 'camp' late-night feature. So it is the income from that ancient turkey—bolstered by careful investments of same—that allows me to live as you see. The recompense for my more recent on-camera swordplay and related endeavors has merely been frosting on the cake."

"Some frosting," I said. "Some cake. How does any of that qualify you for the job of go-between in this particular matter?"

"The consensus was that you would likely be more receptive if approached by someone of, ah, my station."

"Instead of some guy named Vinnie or Sal wanting to make me an offer I couldn't refuse, right?"

A wan smile. "I regret I was not apprised of your unique sense of humor."

"One of my many underappreciated virtues," I said. "But never mind that, let's get to the short hairs. Just what is it that you—the people you represent—are looking to have done in regards to these killings?"

"First of all," Foxwood replied, his expression and voice taking on the patented earnestness of a TV-news anchorman, "I want to assure you that the foremost wish of everyone I speak for is to see the killer or killers caught and punished. No matter who. No matter what. That is top priority. In addition, however, there are concerns that become considerably more complex."

"Just keep it in English and go a little slow with words over two syllables. I should be able to follow along okay."

Again the wan smile. "Yes. Of course. It shouldn't be difficult for anyone to understand that those of us acquainted with Jason and Valerie through making the kind of films I've mentioned find ourselves in rather a delicate position. For their sakes, we want very much to cooperate fully with the police investigations into their deaths. For our own sakes, we cannot help but be concerned that too much candor at this juncture will almost certainly lead to undesirable attention at some future point. Complicating the issue is the question of whether or not the murders are connected. If in fact they are, then the primary link between Jason and Valerie is the films and that means those of us who share that link could also be in danger. All the more reason to be completely open with the authorities. Conversely, if the killings are only the random, unrelated acts of violence that they appear on the surface to be, then any information we provided would likely be valueless to solving the crimes and would only serve to expose us to the kind of scrutiny we can ill afford. Do you see our predicament, Mr. Hannibal?"

I nodded. "Between the proverbial rock and a hard place."

"And then, on a less personal level, there are the concerns of the money people—the backers, if you will—who stand to lose profit if this well-established operation is thrown into disarray by paranoia or official involvement or worse. While their interest may be less personal, the problem is of no less importance to them. It was for this reason that they came up with the idea of hiring someone like you: someone who could conduct a thorough—yet discreet—investigation within our amoral little stock company to determine if its activities are in any way linked to either of the killings. If they are not, then there would be no need to bare our operation to the authorities."

"But if it should turn out otherwise?" I wanted to know.

"In that case," Foxwood said, taking a thoughtfully measured sip of his drink, "then we would have no choice but to go to the police."

"Your 'backers' are agreeable to this?"

"It is not their ideal scenario to be sure, but if it came to that, yes, they are agreeable. It is hoped that in that event your investigation might have the matter 'wrapped up' to some degree and it would become a formality of handing your findings over to the police, thus perhaps still avoiding an extensive probe on their part."

"I couldn't make any guarantees along those lines."

"No guarantees are expected."

My glass was empty again. I wanted a refill and I wanted a smoke. My mind was busy, I needed something to do with my hands. I dug out a pack of Pall Malls and held it up. "Okay?"

Foxwood nodded. "By all means."

I got one going, hung it from a corner of my mouth, poured myself some more brandy. While I was doing that, Foxwood provided a small silver ashtray. I balanced it on one knee.

The old actor's expression changed. A trace of smugness crept across his face as he settled back once again in his chair. The shrewd old bastard sensed he had me wriggling on the hook. He just wasn't sure how deeply I was impaled.

Trouble was, neither was I. There could be no denying I was intrigued by the case he was proposing. It had elements that promised to be—at the very least—infinitely more interesting and challenging than the series of surveillance jobs and till-tapper nabbings I'd been existing on for what seemed like forever. When you've got a trace of bloodhound pulsing through your veins, it's hard to resist the scent of an exciting hunt, no matter how nasty the terrain it threatens to take you through. And that was the other side of the coin: the terrain in this particular case had the potential of getting very nasty indeed. Perhaps downright unsavory.

In an apparent attempt to sink the barb a little deeper with some measure of subtlety, Foxwood said, "At no time would you be asked to compromise your principles or to violate any laws."

And then, after a moment's pause, he gave a significantly more obvious tug on the line. "Due to the urgency and delicacy of the problem, it is important that someone delve into it with all haste. I am in a position to advise you that the prompt acceptance of this case will result in generous payment and in all likelihood an equally generous bonus at its satisfactory conclusion."

I dirtied the shiny bottom of the ashtray with a tap of ash from my cigarette. Squinting through a curl of smoke, I said, "I have a standard fee."

"Yes, I am aware of that. As are my backers. But they are willing—and quite able, I might point out—to pay extraordinarily well for what they consider an extraordinary task."

"Been my experience," I said, "that when somebody is willing to pay more than the price tag calls for, then there's something fishy about the whole damn deal."

"I have outlined the circumstances to you as best I know them," Foxwood replied. "There might well be a number of 'fishy' factors involved. That is precisely the point, isn't it? That is what you are being hired to find out."

I hid a wry smile by lifting my brandy glass to it. The old swordsman was as unflappable as he was sharp, you had to hand it to him. The "backers" had no doubt sent the right man. But that still didn't make me any more comfortable with the prospect of having their hooks in me.

Foxwood set aside his drink and hitched forward slightly in his chair. Elbows resting on thickly padded red leather, fingers interlaced in lap, he tipped his head in my direction and fixed me with a Ward Cleaver-about-to-dispense-wisdom gaze.

"Mr. Hannibal," he said at length, "I sense you are vacillating on a . . . well, what you probably perceive as a point of honor. On the one hand you seem genuinely interested in the case; on the other, you are troubled by the possible identity of my anonymous backers. Is that a fair assessment of your feelings at the moment?"

"You tell me. You're the one doing the swami act."

"Very well, then I will conclude that it is. An admirable bit of reluctance on your part, I suppose. I am somewhat familiar with the symptoms, you see, as I experienced them myself not so many years ago when first approached to participate in the film enterprise we have been discussing. I will not bore you with the rationale I used to overcome my reservations. But from the vantage point of my experience, let me say that I see your indecision as being much more easily dealt with than mine. Very simply, it comes down to the fact that two lives have been taken—the lives of two young people who, regardless of questionable morals or whatever other shortcomings they may have had, did not deserve to die the way they did. You are in a position to help rectify this unfortunate wrong, to perhaps even prevent additional killings. If you don't take the job, someone else will—someone who may not be as good at it. No matter the chain of events that placed these circumstances before you, no matter how dubious the origin of the money you have been offered, it strikes me that to coldly turn your back and walk away now would, in its own fashion, also be less than honorable."

2

---

*T*he wind had picked up and was slamming over the Rock River in piercing blasts as I emerged from Henry Foxwood's building and started across the snow-packed parking lot. The December sky was overcast, the same gun-metal gray color as the water, and heavy with the threat of more snow. Already you could feel the sting from occasional chips of sleet in the air. Shoving my hands deep into my coat pockets and burrowing my head down between hunched shoulders and up-turned collar, I double-timed it toward my car.

I was driving a Honda that winter, my first foreign car. It was also the first time in memory I'd held the registration on a vehicle whose model year fell within the current decade. I'd gotten it for a song (no pun intended, inasmuch as the purchase was made from a musician) primarily because the body was so badly rust-ravaged it looked as if it had been used for howitzer practice. In spite of this and in spite of all those pro-Detroit bumper stickers you see, the little rice roadster drove out so smartly I was forced to conclude it was one of the best cars I'd ever owned. Of course, when you consider some of the heaps my budget has necessitated my laying claim to, that may not be saying a hell of a lot. At any rate, it started at the snap of a finger on even the coldest mornings and its front-wheel drive (another first for me) was a most welcome feature in what was shaping up to be the worst winter to hit the Rockford area in a dozen years.

I folded myself behind the wheel and triggered the engine now, goosed it a couple times to get it idling smoothly, then flipped the defroster and heater to HIGH. I blew on my hands until the fingers were limber enough to handle lighting a cigarette. After I had one going, I sat there smoking and waiting for heat, gunning the engine a little now and then, and mentally replaying my meeting with Foxwood.

I'd taken the job.

Partly because of the things Foxwood had said, partly because I was bored silly with the kinds of cases I'd been getting lately, mostly because right now I needed the work. Translate as money. Ironic, I guess, that one of the things that had me hung up for a while—accepting payment in "dirty" funds—ended up being the thing that tugged me over. The getting-paid part, that is. While money has never been celebrated as being a particularly noble cause, it is arguably a less disdainful one than the poets would have us believe. There's a difference between greed and need. Christmas was fast approaching, then tax time; I still had overdue notices from the electric company for running the air conditioning at their exorbitant rates during last summer's heat wave, and now the gas bill would be skyrocketing with the bitter winter . . . and so on and so forth. You know the tune.

"If you don't take the job, someone else will—someone who may not be as good at it."

So I'd soil my hands a little on some Syndicate bread—hell, we all do that much in hundreds of incidental ways every day. It's called laundering, folks. I didn't have to feel good about it, but as long as I kept my investigation clean, I could live with it.

The heater vents were kicking out warm air by the time my cigarette burned down. I tossed the butt out the window, dropped the Honda into gear. Maneuvered out of the parking lot and into the midafternoon traffic on North Main.

I crossed the river at Auburn, then headed back downtown. I pulled into the first fast-food joint I came to, a Wendy's, and went inside with my stomach demanding the lunch I'd skipped earlier. At the stainless-steel counter, I ordered a bowl of chili, a cheeseburger, and coffee from a slack-jawed youth suffering an attack of acne he'd probably outgrow and a case of sluggish indifference he maybe never would.

Although I had the place pretty much to myself, out of habit I carried my tray to a back-corner booth where I spread my feast. Before shedding my coat, I withdrew from its big inner pocket the two manila folders Foxwood had presented me with after I'd agreed to take the case. These I placed next to the food on the hastily wiped tabletop. They were a part of the menu I was equally anxious to get to. Once I had the cheeseburger unwrapped and the chili doctored to taste with a handful of crumbled saltines and some additional pepper, I flipped open the top folder and began to examine its contents as I chewed.

Each folder contained detailed copies of the various police reports connected to the two murders—initial bonuses as provided by Foxwood's "backers." I didn't question how they had been attained. Hell, I'd wangled a few unauthorized peeks at official documents before, myself. Nothing quite as elaborate as these, but it all fell under the same heading. While the thrust of my investigation was supposed to be in an area not covered by the cops, it could prove valuable to become familiar with the ground they'd already gone over, know what they'd already learned, and maybe be able to pick up on the shape and direction their investigations seemed to be taking. The latter, I knew, would require a certain amount of reading between the lines because no report, no matter how thorough, contains cops' gut feelings, their hunches, and those are the factors (along with snitch information) that often as not crack a case. Still, it was worth my time to peruse what was there and glean what I could from it.

The folder I'd randomly selected was the one on Valerie Pine. The first thing I turned to was a black-and-white 5×7 photograph of the victim, most likely reproduced from an original found among her effects or provided by a relative or friend. She was, as you would expect given her part-time career, an attractive girl, a blonde, with sensually puffy lips and one slightly crossed eye that, in life, had probably added to her attractiveness by giving her a kind of appealing vulnerability. Since the photo was a head-and-shoulders shot with the subject wearing a simple white blouse, it was hard to tell what she'd had to offer in the body department. From what I could see, I judged her to be neither especially scrawny nor zaftig, but somewhere comfortably in between.

There were several more photographs—glaringly cold and impersonal shots of Valerie Pine in death, taken from varying angles within the cluttered bedroom where her body had been found. Since the corpse was completely nude, my curiosity about her physical attributes was promptly answered and seeing her that way left me feeling cheap and dirty-minded for having wondered.

The photos didn't exactly enhance my lunch, but inasmuch as there was no blood or gore and my appetite was formidable, I continued to eat as I turned (albeit somewhat hurriedly) through them.

After the pictures came the reports: from the uniformed officers first to arrive on the scene, from the detective team assigned the case, from the county coroner's crew. There was a signed statement by one Cindy Wallace, the roommate who had discovered the body. With the murder only three days old, there wasn't much beyond that. Skimming through the jargon-laden notations, I culled out a couple of bits of information that struck me as having more than passing interest. According to the coroner's report, the Pine girl had not been sexually molested during the attack nor was there any indication that she'd had sexual intercourse for any determinable amount of time prior to her death. Not exactly what you would expect of a healthy young woman involved in fucking in front of the cameras for posterity. I learned there also was an estranged husband to consider, one Boyd Pine, age twenty-eight, whom Cindy Wallace described rather colorfully for the record as "a bitter, jealous, crazy sonofabitch who ought to be locked away somewhere." I knew the cops would be taking a hard look at old Boyd—spouses and variations thereof rate special attention in murder investigations—but I dug out my pen and spiral pad and entered his name in my personal notes anyway, along with Valerie's curious lack of sexual activity during the time preceding her death. I wanted to remind myself to be sure and give each matter some further attention as I got into the case.

I polished off my remaining chow, got up and got a refill on the coffee, sat back down, and lit a cigarette before opening the second folder. It, too, contained a number of photographs. Jason Hobbs had been a dark-haired, good-looking guy, not a pretty boy but a husky, rugged type that women would give appreciative sidelong glances to and other guys would feel at ease around, want to be beer-drinking buddies with. In death, he was diminished to a slashed, bloody pile lying in six inches of dirty slush at the bottom of a ditch with frost-coated weed stalks thrusting obscenely up between his legs and splayed fingers. The coroner's report stated he had been stabbed thirty-one times with a nonserrated blade approximately eight inches in length, possibly a standard kitchen butcher knife. The morgue shots, taken after the body had been stripped and cleaned, showed many of the wounds to be gouge-like tears, attesting to the weapon's dullness or the killer's savagery or both. It had been determined that Hobbs was killed somewhere else and then deposited in the desolate ditch, but the exact location of the murder hadn't yet been discovered. Nevertheless, this was cause enough for the official investigation to become a joint project between detective squads from Boone County (where the body was found) and Rockford (where Hobbs resided and—most likely—was killed). There were no witnesses or significant leads to either the initial crime or the dumping of the body. Complicating things further was the total lack of any apparent motive. There had been eighty-seven dollars in cash and a half dozen credit cards in the dead man's wallet when he was found. He was, from all reports, an extremely well-liked, well-adjusted individual—a hard worker who'd earned lead-man status with the construction outfit where he was employed, a considerate neighbor, a competitive sportsman, even a community Big Brother. He was survived by his mother and one sister who both lived in Arizona, where his remains had been sent for burial.

The only thing I came across in this second compilation that seemed to rate any special attention was a scribbled paragraph (one of a handful I found tucked in here and there that hadn't yet been typed into any of the formal reports) containing the information that Hobbs's live-in girlfriend at the time of his murder—Rosemary Karson, age twenty-three—had a record of two previous arrests for prostitution. I entered her name and address in my note pad, followed by a big question mark. Had Hobbs—Mr. All-Around Nice Guy on the one hand, panting porn stud on the other—known that his main squeeze was a former hooker? Or, more intriguing yet, had she perhaps still been plying her trade during their relationship? And was she, in turn, aware of her man's sexual sideline?

I clapped shut the folder, drained the last of my coffee, and emitted a satisfied sigh. It was going to be okay, I decided. I had a bellyful of food, a pocketful of retainer fee, and the juices were starting to flow. Any way you cut it, this definitely beat the shit out of watching through one-way glass for some wide-bottomed, hired-for-the-holidays store clerk to shortchange a customer and then try to stuff the difference down her dress.

* * *

It was snowing by the time I pulled to the curb in front of Wally Broznoski's Seventh Street barber shop—crisp, glistening flakes that seemed to hang dreamily in the air and then suddenly swoop and whirl in wild flight when caught by the wind gusts cutting between the buildings. Not always a welcome sight, but one that can be mesmerizingly beautiful no matter how many times you've seen it. And at least a fresh snowfall would serve to cover—for a little while anyway—the slush and the dirty gray crust that had formed over what was already on the ground.

I stamped my feet on the mat outside Wally's door and went on in.

Even in his starched, high-necked barber's smock with its front stretched taut by an ever-inflating beach ball of a stomach, Wally Broznoski always makes me think of a 1950s rock star—one gone to seed. I have no idea if he can sing a single note (which was never an absolutely essential ingredient anyway), but he sure has The Look. The dimples are still there in the smooth, round cheeks; the smile is still dazzling; and there's definitely a rakehell glint left in the eyes. But above all—literally as well as figuratively —there's the carefully maintained pompadour that, in spite of its growing number of gray flecks, would have been the envy of Bobby Rydell on his best day.

The pompadour and the eyes swung in my direction as I entered. The smile and the dimples appeared a moment later. "Hey, Joe! How they hanging?"

"In this cold weather? High and tight and damn near out of sight."

"Nothing wrong with that. Wouldn't want 'em dangling down where they could get frost-bit, right?"

He rose out of the barber's chair he'd been sitting in—the middle one of three—and put aside the newspaper he'd been reading. There was no one else in the shop. It was a long, narrow room, a functioning relic left over from a bygone era with its polished brass and soft, dark leather and sweeping mirrors and gaudy advertisements, filled by the scents of sweet hair tonics and talc and aftershave lotions and tobacco smoke. There hadn't been barbers employed to man all of the chairs since Eisenhower was in office. For a time, during the wild-haired sixties, before Wally's father handed the business down to him, the shop was only open three days a week. But it had been well and lovingly kept throughout and now a special aura about it made you think of coming here some Saturday afternoon after the monthly Social Security checks had arrived in the mail and just sitting off to one side and listening to the old-timers reminisce while they waited for their turn in the chair.

"Haven't seen you in a while," Wally said, reaching for a fresh linen coverlet. "Figured you must've decided to let the ol' pelt thicken up for the winter."

"I guess maybe I have," I said, holding out my hand to stop him from unfolding the long cloth. "At least for the time being. I'm not here to get my ears lowered, Wall, but to call on your expertise in another area."

He looked confused for a minute. Then he put away that look and replaced it with a lopsided grin. "Expertise? Me? Darn, old buddy, I hate to let you down, but I think I had vaccinations or something for that when I was about twelve."

"Uh-huh. They must have stuck the needle in the wrong cheek then. Aren't you the 'Professor of Pornography'? . . . The 'Promoter of Pulsating Pulchritude'? . . . The 'Ayatolla of Fuckyhole-a'? . . . And holder of various other titles and/or degrees too numerous and/or raunchy to mention?"

I was making reference to a seemingly endless series of joke business cards Wally has had printed up over the years. At the allusion, his eyebrows raised and his grin widened. "Oh," he said. "You mean *that* area of expertise?"

"That's the one."

The grin drooped into a mock disapproving frown. "Aw, Joe, I'm disappointed in you. I thought you had more class. . . . But you're finally interested in my fuck films, huh?"

"Praise the Lord, I saw the light."

"Well, you've come to the right place for salvation, brother. What do you need, a couple loaners? What format? Videocassettes or movies? Eight-millimeter, sixteen-millimeter, VHS, Beta— what are we talking here?"

"Whoa, whoa, hold on a minute. Jesus, you sound like a damn television commercial. I'm not interested in putting on a film festival, I just want to talk about the stuff."

He made a face. "Now I am disappointed. This shit isn't made to have discussions over, Joe. You view it. You wallow in it. If you're lucky, you get your old lady to once in a while *try* some of it. But nobody just fucking *talks* about it."

"We'll see where the talk leads, okay? What I mainly need is some information, Wall. I'm here to find out if you really know as much about smut movies as you've been claiming all these years or if you just use them for dick starch like everybody else."

"Hah! I'm ready for any test you want to put it to, pal. You are looking at a true and dedicated student of cinematic sleaze. Why, I can tell you the name of every guy who came on Vanessa Del Rio in the pig scene from *Devil in Miss Jones, Part 3* and I can tell you the exact part of her anatomy where each one of them shot his load. I can tell you—"

"I can tell this is going to be fascinating as hell," I cut in, "and I'd sure hate to have it interrupted by a last-minute customer. It's nearly five. Can't you pull the plug on the old money-maker for the day so we can go downstairs and talk in peace over a couple cold ones?"

Five minutes later—after Wally had flipped the door placard to CLOSED, locked up, killed the neon, and otherwise battened down the hatches—we were seated comfortably in the basement area directly beneath the shop, each with a frosty can of Bud in hand. The basement was a windowless bunker laid out along the same rectangular contours as the business overhead, its concrete floor covered by thin indoor/outdoor carpeting, cinderblock walls lined with bare wood bookshelves constructed of roughly finished 1×6's. Only instead of books, the shelves held cans of sixteen-, super-eight-, and eight-millimeter film and rows of videocassettes in both VHS and Beta format. At the stairs end of the room, one corner served as a small storage area for barber supplies, while in the other stood the refrigerator that housed, among other things, the cold beer we were drinking. At the opposite end, there was a large-screen TV with a pair of video players and, fastened to the ceiling above them, the long cylinder of a pull-down viewing screen. Facing these from a distance of about a dozen feet, there was a short couch, a couple of unmatched easy chairs, and a sturdy old movie projector on a rolling metal table.

Here in Wally's hobby room were his ambitious collection of blue movies and the means to enjoy them. I'd been hearing about it for years and I'd even been down here a few times before, usually with my friend the Bomber, when Wally would insist that we have a look at a particularly hot or elusive bit of footage he'd gotten his hands on. But that had been back before the video onslaught and general loosening of the public's morals combined to make X-rated fare as readily available to the average adult as a bottle of aspirin.

I saw now that little had changed since my last trip down those stairs. Except, of course, that the number of cannistered reels had stopped growing and was being overtaken by the number of plastic cassette containers.

All of this had been started by Wally's father shortly after he opened the barber shop. Strictly for his own amusement, he'd begun a collection of what back then (the post–World War II years) were whisperingly referred to as "stag movies." It wasn't long, however, before some of his regular customers learned about the steamy reels and were pestering him for a peek. He gave in without a great deal of pressure and for a time he would simply set up the projector in the basement and allow those who were interested to go down and peer at the grainy, flickering, soundless features while he and the other barbers in his employ conducted business as usual upstairs. Many times I'd heard Wally tell the story of how, within a matter of days, the crowd of men waiting to get into the basement would frequently be so large it blocked the street door, preventing haircut customers from entering. Needless to say, barber Broznoski quickly put an end to the subterranean screenings. And almost as quickly, because he still had people clamoring to see his movies, he hit on an alternate plan. He began renting out the projector and/or films. For bachelor parties, for private club smokers, for war-buddy reunions, for what have you. This kept the fare available to those who were interested, kept the congesting crowds away from the shop, and kept Broznoski's pocket lined with a little extra bread (which he used for the most part to buy more movies). Everybody was happy. And so it went for years. In some weeks during the lean period of the sixties, more profit was shown from film rental than from cutting hair.

At about the time getting your hair barbered regularly was coming back in vogue, Wally inherited the business—both of them, as it were. But this was also about the time that adult bookstores were starting to proliferate and were making "triple-X-rated" movies an over-the-counter commodity accessible to more and more people. The video boom, of course, came on the heels of that and in seemingly no time there was a rental outlet on every other street corner, 90 percent of them with an X-rated list to choose from. So these days Wally's collection, despite all his purple-prose business cards and his tendency to boast openly about his "broad selection," is pretty much a private thing. Nevertheless, his deep and abiding fascination with the subject drives him to keep it up. If you have any doubt about his seriousness when he claims to be a "true student of cinematic sleaze," he'll be happy to show you how the titles are grouped by year and then cross-indexed alphabetically in a thick three-ring binder with carefully typed notations concerning the production values, the actors' and director's real names, and various other tidbits of information.

It was this quasi-academic approach I was hoping to tap into now.

"So what's up, big guy?" Wally wanted to know. He slurped a dollop of foam off the top of his can. "What is it you want to know about that great American pastime—dirty movies?"

"I recently ran across some things," I told him, "that seem to indicate we've had a few of these masterpieces made right here in the Rockford area. What do you know about that?"

"Well, there's been a couple things, yeah. There was that priest who was slipping the holy weenie to some of his altar boys and getting it on film. You heard about that, right? Then there was the dentist who was injecting a little more than novocaine into some of his attractive female patients after he had them gassed into unconsciousness. He also had a camera set up so he could enjoy it again on instant replay and—"

I shook my head. "That's not the kind of thing I'm talking about. I'm talking about this kind of stuff"—I made a gesture with my hand, indicating the contents of the shelves. "People doing it expressly *for* the camera, with the intent of having it distributed and sold."

"You mean organized shoots, an actual porn ring?"

"That's the idea."

"Damn, that's interesting. Right here in Rockford, huh? There's been talk on and off about that kind of stuff for years, but I was never able to trace anything down. This is great. What are you onto?"

"Hey, I'm supposed to be the one asking *you* the questions, remember?"

"So what's your question? Do I have anything here on the shelf that was shot in our backyard? The answer is no, not that I know of. The way they've been cranking out some of this video slop lately, it's impossible to tell where a lot of it was made. I suppose I *could* have something here that was done locally, but, like I said, nothing I'm aware of. Shit, the idea sure is neat, though."

I lit a cigarette and sighed out a cloud of smoke. Despite Wally's enthusiasm, this looked like it was going to turn out to be a bust. I'd left the folders on Jason Hobbs and Valerie Pine locked in the Honda's glove compartment, but I'd kept out their photographs. I weighed the possible ramifications, drawing thoughtfully on my Pall Mall. Then I withdrew the pictures from my coat pocket and handed them to Wally.

"Those two people," I said. "Recognize them from any of the films you've got in your collection?"

He studied the black-and-whites intently.

"It'd be something fairly recent," I prompted. "Within the last couple years for the guy, I'd guess, and even more recent for the girl, according to what I've been told."

After several minutes, Wally looked up, frowning. "This is tough, Joe. I mean, when you see these people on the screen, they aren't exactly posed like this, you know? For one thing, they're mostly bare-assed naked, and then they've usually got their face buried in somebody's crotch or their expression is all twisty and distorted by fake ecstasy. See what I'm getting at?"

"You don't recognize them, then?"

"Well, the guy looks maybe a little familiar. Shit, I dunno. The only way I could be sure would be to try some tapes, run some footage, and compare, you know?"

I shrugged. "I'm in no hurry."

He showed me his teeth in a sheepish grin. "Yeah, but I kinda am. I promised Estelle and the kids I'd take them Christmas shopping tonight. She'll have my nuts if I don't. I been putting it off and putting it off. I don't have the faintest idea what I'm going to buy her yet and I figure she wants to get me out so she can drop some hints. I've got to go, man, or my stocking will be hanging in the dog house—with me in it."

"I understand how it is," I told him.

His expression promptly brightened with an idea. "Tell you what, though. If you could leave these pictures with me, I can come back here *after* we're done shopping and see if I can match up anything. You could check with me tomorrow, see how I made out. How's that sound?"

"Sounds fine," I replied. "I'd really appreciate it, Wall."

"Is this terrific or what? I'm helping you with a case and we're maybe going to uncover a goddamn for-real porn ring right here in Rockford. Holy shit!"

I drained my Bud, stabbed out my cigarette, and stood to leave. "Listen," I said, "if you should have any luck matching either of those mugs to a piece of film, then let's take it a step further. Make a note of the others in the cast and see if you can match any of them to anything else you've got. It stands to reason that if these two are local talent, then whoever they're performing with must be local, too. Right?"

"Sounds reasonable, yeah."

I reached out and put a hand on Wally's shoulder. "One more thing."

"What's that?"

"There's a chance that what I'm onto here could get real nasty before it's over. So you don't want to go around shooting off your mouth about it, you hear?"

"Sure, Joe. How dumb you think I am? I mean, we all know who distributes this stuff, right? Anybody can shoot a dirty movie. The swing clubs do it all the time. All you need is a camera, some film, and a few willing bodies. But try peddling copies without cutting in The Boys—if you get what I'm saying—and see how far you make it."

"The two people in those photographs are dead, Wall. Murdered. That's the kind of nasty I'm talking about. I don't know yet if their killings had anything to do with their alleged participation in porn flicks—that's what I aim to find out. In the meantime, I figure it's best if nobody but you and I are aware you know anything about anything. That clear?"

"Jesus, it's clear all right. Jesus, Joe!"

"Good. Now get a move on and go pick out such a swell Christmas present for Estelle that she'll screw you silly the minute she lays eyes on it. Then haul your butt back here and see what you can dig up for me."

3

---

*T*he snow tapered off and quit sometime during the night, accumulating to little more than an inch. Still, this was plenty to cover the brown-gray crud left over from before. The sun of the new day bounced off the fresh layer of pure white with eye-searing brilliance.

The alarm jangled me out of bed early. Early for me, anyway. I smoked a couple cigarettes and drank a couple cups of coffee while sitting in my undershorts scanning the morning paper. Then I showered, shaved, dressed, sat down over more coffee and a bowl of corn flakes, and tried to work up some enthusiasm for going out and doing something. I'm not exactly what you'd call a morning person.

After leaving Wally last night, I'd followed my standard evening routine and swung by the Bomb Shelter, the State Street bar owned and operated by my buddy, Bomber Brannigan. The Bomber is a generally genial hulk who earned his nickname as well as the various patterns of scar tissue that adorn his gloriously homely puss fighting the ring wars of both pro boxing and pro wrestling before retiring to dispense liquid good cheer instead of mat mayhem. His second-in-command at the Bomb Shelter is Liz Grimaldi, a bosomy Italian lovely who does her darnedest to keep us both in line. Since the Bomber and Liz are the closest thing I have to a family and since I suddenly had a few spare bucks to my name for a change, I'd taken a cue from Wally and had tried to feel them out as to what they might like for Christmas. We got it narrowed down to a new Oldsmobile for Liz and a robot bartender for Bomber. Swell.

Smirking around a mouthful of soggy corn flakes as I thought about it now, I decided I could maybe have some fun with the whole thing if I could find a couple of those assemble-it-yourself plastic model kits, one for each item. What the hell, nobody had specified size or practical use.

On a more somber note, I then thought about the fact that Valerie Pine's funeral was this morning. The death of an attractive young woman was bad enough, planting her in frozen earth somehow made it seem worse. The prospect chilled away the last of my lethargy and I got up and went for my coat.

Wally had struck out in his attempt to turn up some film footage of Jason Hobbs or Valerie Pine. When I stopped by his shop to check on his findings, he reported this lack of success with such a long face and such a despondent air I was sorry I'd set him up for it. I tried to explain that in the investigation racket, you're lucky if a third of your leads result in anything positive, but that didn't appear to cheer him up much. He seemed to take it as some sort of personal failure and I didn't know what else to say to him. I was grateful when his first customer of the day showed up about then. I retrieved my pictures and moved on.

My next stop was the drive-up window of my bank, where I deposited Henry Foxwood's retainer check (he was my client of record, keeping his anonymous "backers" strictly in the background all the way down the line) and held out a comfortable amount of walk-around cash. After folding the bills into my wallet, I turned my hands palms up and examined them. If it was dirty money, at least it didn't rub off.

It was pushing ten when I got to my Broadway office. I came up the back stairs with much more spring in my step than usual when making the one-flight climb. Despite the fact that the office hours as stated on the pebbled glass of the door are nine to five, it was considerably earlier for a workday than is my wont. Had I known what was waiting for me, I would have made the trip sooner and sprightlier yet.

She was a cool number, lean and poised, a shade over average height, middle twenties, with dark eyes and glossy dark hair and a wide mouth that could be either cruel or sexy. She was clad in a short-waisted fur coat (real or fake fur, I can never tell) and a short leather skirt. (Thank you, God, for bringing back minis and for giving women the courage to wear them even in the dead of winter.) She wore leather gloves and shoes that matched the skirt. A furry beret-like hat matched her coat. She sat with her left leg crossed over her right, calmly smoking a cigarette, in one of the two straight-backed chairs that are bolted to the floor in the narrow hall outside my office—my waiting room.

I approached the office door with a key drawn to unlock it, fingering back my windblown hair with my free hand. The dark eyes followed me.

"Good morning," I said as I put the key to work.

The eyes gazed up at me, measuring me. Her face was chiseled and expressionless. A trickle of smoke began to seep from a corner of her mouth. Like I said, cool.

"Are you Hannibal?" she wanted to know.

I nodded. "That's right."

Her gaze shifted to the hours painted on the glass right below where it says JOE HANNIBAL—PRIVATE INVESTIGATIONS, hung there a long moment, and then swung back to me. She didn't say anything, but her meaning was clear enough.

"Hope you haven't been waiting too long," I said.

Exhaling the last of the smoke, she stood up. "If I'd decided it was too long, I wouldn't still be here, would I?"

I let the question ride. Pushing open the door and reaching around the corner to snap on the light switch, I said, "Come in, won't you?"

"Actually, that won't be necessary. I'm only here on an errand." She withdrew a large brown envelope from her purse and held it out to me. "Henry Foxwood asked me to hand deliver this to you. He cautioned that it was too important to just push through the mail slot. My mission accomplished, there's really no need to take up any more of your time."

I took the envelope. It was a 9-by-12 manuscript size and, judging by the heft of it, filled with a substantial sheaf of papers. I knew what it must contain and found myself appreciative of Foxwood's promptness as well as his choice of delivery personnel.

"Your Mr. Foxwood seems pretty thorough," I commented.

The dark-haired girl smiled a brief smile that could have meant something or nothing at all. "Yes," she said, "Henry is nothing if not thorough."

I wanted to see more of that smile. "Look," I said, "you're out on a pretty brisk morning and you had to sit and wait in this drafty old hall. Can I at least offer you a cup of coffee or something before you leave?"

She granted my wish and showed me the brief, ambiguous smile once more before replying, "Thanks, but no. I've several more errands to run and I really must be going. I'm sure we'll be seeing each other around, though. Perhaps we can do the coffee thing another time."

I stood in the doorway and listened until the tap of her heels faded down the front stairs. I went on into the office then, carrying a faint whiff of her perfume in with me and heeling the door shut to trap it there for a while. The office was as bleak as always, colder than normal. The sheet of clear plastic I had taped over the window rustled and slapped loosely when I closed the door. On windy days it billowed and rattled and filled the room with sounds not unlike distant cannon fire. Sometimes the linoleum joined in and rose flutteringly off the floor in the corners. If a poltergeist ever decided to set up housekeeping in the building, I'd probably never notice until spring.

I dialed the thermostat up a couple of notches, plugged in Mr. Coffee, and deposited myself behind the desk. I unzipped my coat but decided to leave it on until I had things a little warmer either inside of me or out. I checked my telephone-answering machine for messages, found nothing of any importance. I pulled the Hobbs and Pine folders from my inner coat pocket and placed them off to one side on the desktop. After lighting up a cigarette, I shook open the envelope that had just been delivered and fanned its contents out in front of me.

More photographs accompanied by more reports. Only this time the latter weren't carefully typed official forms, but rather lined sheets of loose-leaf notebook paper filled with passages of neat longhand done in green ink. The script had a distinct feminine flow so I knew it hadn't been written by Foxwood himself. I wondered if it was the work of the dark-haired girl and for the first time realized I hadn't even caught her name.

I had explained to Foxwood during our meeting yesterday that it would expedite my investigation if I had some background information on the various people who had been involved with Jason and Valerie through their film-making activities, including photographs if possible and brief descriptions of how they had interrelated with the deceased. This package was the result of that request. At a rough count, I saw it covered about twenty-five people with photos for at least two-thirds of them and short histories that provided home addresses and even phone numbers. Like I said, thorough. I was impressed.

Most of the photos were candid color snapshots taken around the movie sets. Foxwood was featured in several of them and I had a feeling the snaps probably came from a personal album of his. In instances where there was more than one person in a shot, the one pertinent to the report to which the picture was stapled had been circled in green ink. One of the photos was of my mysterious dark-haired delivery girl. She was sitting on the edge of a bed, smoking a cigarette with her legs crossed in much the same way as when I'd first seen her. Her face carried a distant, bored expression and she was wearing only black panties and a bra. According to the attached report, she had appeared in a number of films with Jason Hobbs. Her name was listed only as "Tiffany" and in the spaces following "ADDRESS" and "PHONE NUMBER," it said, "That's for me to know and you to find out." So the writing *was* hers. I grinned at her coyness, but at the same time I felt that curious mixture of feelings a man sometimes experiences when he suddenly discovers that a woman he is attracted to is easily attainable. On one level, of course, it makes her more exciting; on another—residue from that good old Puritan ethic browbeaten in during adolescence, no doubt—it makes her somewhat less attractive after all. Maybe it's the trace of bloodhound in my veins again, but for me it usually works out that without the prospect of a good chase, the whole business loses much of its appeal.

I stood up, stretched, walked around and poured myself a cup of coffee. I placed the cup on a corner of the desk to cool while I shed my coat and hung it in the closet. Returning, I picked the cup back up, blew some steam off its contents, and stood gazing down at the pile of papers and snapshots. In a little while, I would begin meeting and questioning these people and in all likelihood would be spending the next few days among them. Inasmuch as today was Friday and Foxwood had informed me that there were filming sessions scheduled to take place over the weekend, I would be confronting them very much on their turf, in an environment decidedly foreign to me. I winced through a sip of scalding coffee. Looked like there was nothing to do in the meantime but sit back down and dig into my homework.

4

---

*T*he farm was located a dozen or so miles south of the city, just off Old 51 on a rugged, unplowed stretch of gravel road. The house was a huge, aging structure with dormered attic windows and faded shutters. From the road it appeared to be nearly as tall as the graying, sway-roofed barn that stood a few hundred yards behind it. The directions Henry Foxwood had given were concise and accurate, allowing me to drive straight to the place with no trouble. A final check verified that the name on the mailbox said what it was supposed to—SILAS—so I swung my Honda in across from it.

In sharp contrast to the neglected road, the driveway had been scraped clear and even lightly sanded in a few spots. It was a wide swath angling up alongside the house, where it flared to an egg-shaped parking area. A half dozen vehicles were parked at varying angles around the lot's perimeter. I slid the Honda in between a long, late-model Buick and a Chevy Luv pickup with a camper shell and smoked-glass windows.

I cut the engine, got out, flipped the butt of my cigarette into a snow bank. A fresh cloud cover had rolled in around noon, blotting out the sun that was so dazzling at day's start and turning the air raw again. I stood for several moments with my breath misting in front of me, surveying my surroundings, and thinking to myself what an unlikely spot for a porn shoot. Broad, flat pastures and fields of stubbed cornstalks stretched in every direction, checkerboarded by fence rows and lines of barren trees. Here and there, off in the distance, you could see the silo tips and barn peaks of other farms, sometimes accompanied by a wafting plume of chimney smoke. Words like *serene* and *pastoral* came to mind. It was a sight Grant Wood might have been able to get a nut over, but otherwise there wasn't anything about it you'd readily connect to prurient interests.

When calling on someone in the country, rule of thumb is to go around to the side or back door rather than knock at the front as is done in the city. I don't know the why of this, I just know that's the way it is. It's a custom I've noted over the years and one that was instilled in me personally at an early age while I was growing up in my grandparents' farm in southern Wisconsin. Whenever a salesman or stranded motorist or some other form of stranger would show up at the front door, my grandfather without fail would scowl and roll his eyes heavenward and demand rhetorically (and usually in a voice loud enough to be heard by the stranger outside), "Now what kind of infernal idiot do you suppose is out there pounding on the wrong end of our house?"

For all of these reasons—and also because that's the way a shoveled path led from the parking area—I approached the side door of the old house. A Christmas wreath tied with a bright red bow hung on the door. In its center was an old-fashioned brass door knocker. I banged the metal plate four or five times.

The door was answered by a tiny, elderly woman with soft gray curls and lovely bright eyes. She was wearing a flowered house dress and a frilly apron and stood in the opening wiping her hands on a striped dish towel. "Yes?" she said. "Can I help you?"

I was momentarily at a loss for words. I'd been prepared for (maybe hoping for?) a scantily clad, hungry-eyed amazon. Or possibly some sweaty, macho stud irritated at having his afternoon workout interrupted. Or even an albino midget with a trapeze and a can of Reddi wip. Almost anything. But not this.

"Uh," I managed once I'd regained some of my composure, "I'm looking for a man named Foxwood. I guess maybe I've got the wrong place."

"Oh, no," the woman replied with a reassuring smile. "Mr. Foxwood is here. If your name is Hannibal, he and the others are expecting you. They're inside. Won't you come in?"

I entered a spacious, high-ceilinged, brightly wallpapered kitchen filled with the warmth and mouth-watering aromas of simmering juices and roasting meat and baking bread, all overlaid with a faint cinnamon scent. It smelled exactly the way a kitchen is supposed to smell when a large family gathers together for a Christmas-season dinner. Aside from the incongruity of the situation and not that I in any way missed the clog of flush-faced shirt-tail cousins or shifty-eyed in-laws, I couldn't help being reminded of how long it had been since I'd experienced the pleasure of these particular aromas under any circumstances—the realization left me feeling momentarily saddened.

"My name is Irma Silas," the woman said. "Just call me Irma. You *are* Mr. Hannibal, right?"

I nodded. "Yes, I am. Joe Hannibal. Joe will do."

"May I take your coat, Joe?"

I shrugged out of the garment, handed it to her, and watched her carry it to a small, enclosed porch-like room off one end of the kitchen where I could see a row of hooks and other hanging wraps. Returning, Irma Silas gestured toward a door opposite where I'd come in and said, "My husband, Floyd, is through there with your Mr. Foxwood and the others. Go ahead on in. Just go slow and quiet, please, in case they're filming—excuse me, I mean taping."

The door opened onto a short hall which in turn opened onto a large, rectangularish area with a slight L-like bend at one end. The area had at one time, I guessed, been divided into a dining room, living room, and possibly a downstairs bedroom or den. All partitioning had now been torn away, however, save for a handful of reinforcing beams. The walls were stripped to evenly spaced studs with sheets of shiny insulation in between, and the windows were covered with slabs of plywood painted dull black. What had been created was a somewhat amateurish but apparently quite serviceable soundstage.

At one end of the rectangle, to my right as I stood in the mouth of the hall, were piles of lumber, furniture, various props, and leaning sections of multicolored stage backdrop. To my left, where the room jutted out wider, a set had been constructed and was awash in light considerably brighter than the general illumination provided by a scattering of bare ceiling bulbs.

No activity seemed to be taking place on the set. At its edge, a couple of guys in T-shirts—one balding and beer-bellied, the other bearded and lean—sat talking softly and drinking from sturdy mugs. Behind them, a trim woman with lustrous copper hair was pacing impatiently back and forth, streaming clouds of smoke from a lavender-colored cigarette.

Nearer my position, in the relative shadows outside the intensely lighted area, Henry Foxwood stood silently looking on beside a tall, heavyset man clad in baggy jeans and a faded blue workshirt. Contrastingly, Foxwood wore a maroon sweater vest with matching tie and slate-gray trousers with creases so sharp they looked as if they could draw blood if he brushed against you with them.

Both men turned as I walked up to them.

"Mr. Hannibal," Foxwood said. "Good to see you again. I gather you were able to follow my directions without too much difficulty?"

"No problem," I told him.

He nodded at the tall man standing next to him. "This is Floyd Silas. He and his wife, Irma, whom you've obviously already met, live upstairs and look after the property here for us. During shooting sessions, Floyd also serves as our carpenter and general handyman around the sets and Irma sees to it we do not lack for nourishment. As a matter of fact, she often sees to the latter a trifle too well"—he patted and rubbed his stomach as he said this—"but nevertheless they are both an integral part of our little team."

Floyd Silas thrust out a broad, scarred, and callused old hand and smiled briefly with tobacco-stained teeth. "Good to meet you, son. It's a damn shame what happened to them two youngsters and I hope you see to it the bastards what done it get their just deserts."

"Do my best," I assured him. I knew he'd be the type to form an impression of a man based on his handshake, so I grabbed his rough old paw in a firm grip and gave as good as I got before releasing. He reminded me vaguely of my grandfather and I felt an oddly strong urge to meet with his approval.

Henry Foxwood cleared his throat and said, "I had hoped you'd change your mind and I would see you at Valerie's funeral this morning, Hannibal. It would have been an earlier opportunity for you to meet several of the people you will be interviewing in the course of your investigation."

"Uh-huh," I replied. "And like I explained before, it also would have been an opportunity for the cops in attendance to spot me and maybe wonder what my interest in the murdered girl was. With discretion being one of our major concerns, it didn't seem like a very smart move."

"Yes. Yes, of course there was that risk, wasn't there? Pardon me if I sounded as if I was suggesting how you should conduct your business. I fear I am just overanxious to have you get started in the hopes of seeing this whole dreadful matter resolved as rapidly as possible."

"I haven't exactly been sitting on my hands since I left your place yesterday, you know."

"No, and I didn't mean to imply you had been. I trust you got the package I sent you all right?"

"Yes. I was pretty impressed with your messenger."

"And the package's contents?"

"I was impressed with those, too. Until a few minutes ago."

Foxwood looked surprised. "What do you mean?"

I made a gesture with my hand. "Mr. Silas here. His wife out in the other room. You just got done telling me they're an important part of your team. Which means they would have dealt with Jason Hobbs and Valerie Pine, right?"

"Of course. Many times."

"Yet neither of them are mentioned in any way in the package you provided."

Foxwood blinked and worked his mouth a couple of times before he found any words. "Well, I . . . I guess I . . . Jesus, man, surely you don't consider Floyd and Irma to be suspects in this?"

"At this stage of the game," I told him, "I consider everybody suspects. But that's not the point. The point is, you agreed to furnish me with a list of everyone who came in contact with Valerie and Jason through their movie making. The idea was to expedite my investigation. In order for it to work at full potential, I have to be able to trust that the list is as complete as you could make it, not edited—either consciously or subconsciously—of people you don't think matter. See what I'm getting at? If I have to backtrack every time I run across a new name and double-check your judgment, I'll be wasting time. You hired me to investigate, to sort things out. Let me do my job, okay?"

Foxwood's mouth had pulled into a tight line and some color had flared in his face. He didn't look angry, just somewhat embarrassed and properly chagrined. Silas was turned partly away, eyes downcast, looking embarrassed also, the way a man will when forced to stand by at another man's dressing down.

After several beats, Foxwood once again cleared his throat. "As before, you've made a valid point. My omission of Floyd and Irma was not purposeful, but rather, as you suggested, a bit of subconscious editing. Obviously, I knew you were going to come here today and meet them, so it was not as if I was trying to keep something from you. What I need to do now, however, is to scour my mind to make sure I did not omit any other, more obscure persons in the same manner. I will furnish an addendum if required."

I nodded. "Fair enough."

The three of us stood in uncertain silence for a minute or so. I turned my attention once again to the set. The two guys in T-shirts were still seated as before. The copper-haired woman was still pacing. I inclined my head in their direction and said, "What's going on over there?"

"Actually," Foxwood replied, "it is more a case of what *isn't* going on. They are set up to shoot a quick loop, a simple two-person story line about a college lad getting it on with an attractive female teacher who is attempting to tutor him. We were hoping to break a newcomer into our group, a fellow from Chicago who allegedly has done some live sex shows there. Here so far today, unfortunately, his equipment does not seem to be functioning very well. He is back in one of the dressing rooms now, being worked on by our fluffer."

"Fluffer?"

"Industry slang for the young woman or women hired to keep the male actors hard between shots. When you are preparing to shoot a hot fuck scene, you want the male to appear on camera erect and ready. It is usually not desirable to waste the time and talent and energy of one of your female stars to get him that way. It is their job to keep him worked up *on* camera; it is a fluffer's job to prime him when necessary *off* camera."

"Next you'll be telling me they've got job classifications and union bylaws."

"What?"

"Never mind. What about the two guys in T-shirts? They the cameramen?"

"Camera, lighting, and sound, yes. They're commercial techni-cians also out of Chicago. They moonlight for us regularly. The balding fellow is Jay Dorfman, the beard is Brad Blyth. Both of them *are* covered in the package I prepared."

I recalled seeing their names. "And the redhead?" I asked.

Foxwood suddenly looked uncomfortable, like a man with gas pains. "Her name is Belinda Davies," he said. "She will be di-recting the series of shoots this weekend. She also wrote the scripts for them, as she has a number of our previous productions. This marks her directorial debut. She is with us compliments of, ah, the backers we discussed yesterday. I know her slightly from some previous social encounters, but this is the first time she has worked with our Rockford group. So she never met Jason or Vale-rie. I therefore did not include her on my list nor do I expect she will be of much consequence to your investigation."

Which explained why I didn't recognize her name. And his careful reference to her association with the "backers" also ex-plained why she made him uncomfortable and why he'd just dropped a polite warning for me to treat her with kid gloves.

"Was I a few years younger," Floyd Silas piped up somewhat unexpectedly, "I'd damn sure include her on *my* list, and I do mean right at the top. That is one fine piece of woman. Makes the rest of those twitchy-bottomed, jiggly-boobed things Henry has been bringing around look like a bunch of dime-a-dance rejects."

Foxwood gave him a look. "Dream on, you old fool. A woman like that would turn you inside out. And Irma would feed what was left to the chickens."

Silas smiled dreamily. "Yeah, I expect you're right. But I ain't so sure it wouldn't be worth it."

"Look," I said, "while we're just standing around jacking our jaws and waiting for your new stud to get his gun, any reason I can't go over and ask some questions of Dorfman and Blyth?"

"I see no reason why not," Foxwood answered. "They, like the others, were advised that you have been engaged to look into this matter of the murders."

"Can I expect everyone's cooperation?"

"If you encounter otherwise, let me know immediately. I will see that it is taken care of."

The steeliness of his tone rang inside my head as I walked toward the two behind-the-scenes crewmen. For the first time I

wondered if my dapper client of record might be something more
than the mildly tarnished go-between he was passing himself off
as.

Dorfman and Blyth proved to be a couple of laid-back, down-
to-earth types full of dryly humorous anecdotes and observations
told with plenty of salty adjectives. Dorfman appeared to be the
senior member of the pair in more than just physical years. He'd
hooked up with the Rockford setup some three years earlier, after
pulling similar duty a few times with Chicago-based outfits. He'd
brought Blyth into it six months later and they'd been doing the
Rockford gigs exclusively ever since. Both had worked with Jason
and Valerie but had never gotten to know them on any kind of
personal basis and had no idea why anyone would want to kill
them. Both were family men who professed concern over their
own welfare as well as that of the other members of the troupe in
the event the murders turned out to be connected.

As I talked to Dorfman and Blyth, I was afforded a much better
view of Belinda Davies, the director, as she continued to prowl the
edge of the set like a hungry tigress. I saw immediately what
Floyd Silas had been referring to. There are beautiful women and
then there are beautiful women. Some make your mouth water,
some tug at your groin like a magnet; but only a special few are
capable of taking your breath away with the impact of a punch to
the solar plexus. Belinda Davies was in the latter category. Being
within ten feet of her made it hard to concentrate on what Dorfman and Blyth were saying, made it difficult even to remember
what the hell we were talking about. A part of my brain was
flashing fantasy images of the woman spread like a feast before
me, smiling seductively, that red-gold mane splayed on a silken
pillowcase; another part was triggering sweaty-palmed, adoles-
cent-nightmare anxieties at the mere thought of talking to—let
alone touching or caressing—such an exquisite creature.

When I'd decided I was about finished with the two technical
men for the time being and was working up the gumption to
approach La Davies, one of the curtained doorways that bracketed the set—marking the dressing rooms, I'd surmised earlier—
parted and a blond woman emerged. With her platinum locks and
the ample curves that were evident even in the blue sequined robe

tied loosely around her, she was attractive in a bold, flashy kind of way. Still, she ordinarily would have all but disappeared in the presence of the stunning director. What riveted my attention to her, however, was the fact that I knew her.

5

Jesus Christ," the blonde said, "isn't he ready yet?"

Belinda Davies turned to her and arched a perfectly penciled brow. "You bloody well don't see him standing about, do you?" Her cultured British accent came as something of a surprise, but only served to make her all the more intriguing.

"No," the blonde replied, "and that's just the trouble. Nobody's seen the limp little fuck *standing* since he got here."

"So what would you have me do?" the director asked. "Instruct him to dip his willy in a snow bank and freeze the damn thing erect? Or perhaps you'd like to have another go at it? Perhaps if you went in and assisted Angie, the two of you together could accomplish what you don't seem capable of getting done separately."

"I don't fluff, lady. It's not what I was hired on for. *He's* the one with the problem, not me. If you think otherwise, why don't *you* go take over for Angie and show us how it's done?"

The two women glared hotly at each other, nostrils flared, bodies rigid. You could feel the tension whipping back and forth between them, like standing near a current of electricity and having it tug at the short hairs of your arms and across the back of your neck.

Abruptly, the blonde's expression and posture shifted. She held up one hand, palm out. "Look, Belinda, I'm sorry, okay? That was uncalled for. I'm not trying to be difficult or anything but, damn it, I made it clear from the beginning I was only available for an afternoon shoot. Look at the time. It's already past four and we haven't accomplished squat."

Some fire remained in the redhead's eyes, fading only after several beats. She sighed. "I suppose you have a right to be annoyed. It has been a trying afternoon for all of us. And a decidedly unproductive one." She sighed again. "What is the absolute latest you can stay?"

"I'd figured on being out of here by five. That's obviously out of the question, even if we were able to start immediately. Damn, I don't want to see the whole thing scratched, though. I suppose I could con my baby-sitter out of a couple extra hours."

"Splendid. Why don't you go and phone her then? In the meantime, I shall see if my presence can somehow encourage the raising of our shy young lad's, ah, spirits . . . although hardly in the manner you suggest, I assure you."

The two women exchanged brief, guarded smiles. The redhead moved toward the curtained doorway to the right of the set. The blonde turned and headed in my direction.

It hadn't been clear whether either woman was aware of my nearby presence during their tiff, but as the blonde drew abreast of me now and our eyes met she didn't seem to register any surprise. She came to a halt and offered a curt nod of recognition. "Hello, Hannibal," she said. "I heard you'd be around. Can't say I've been looking forward to this."

I said, "Gee, it's really swell to see you again, too, Kath."

"Yeah, I can imagine. What's it been . . . five, six years?"

"Something like that. I have a good friend who could probably tell you to the day."

"I don't want to get into that. I understand you're here because you've got a job to do and you'll need to ask a lot of questions and stuff. But ancient history has nothing to do with it."

"It was a pretty shitty goddamned deal, Kath."

"I said I don't want to talk about it. And around here, if you don't mind, I'm known as Kat—Kat Hayward."

"Catchy."

"It's a name I started using while I was working up north, the Canadian strip circuit. I decided to keep it. It suits me better."

I had known her as Kath Howard. She'd been younger then, of course, less voluptuous (although certainly shapely enough by most standards), her makeup simpler and not as expertly applied, her hair a duller, more natural blond, her manner not as assured, not as hard. I recognized her pseudonym from the second package

Foxwood had provided. It was one of the entries not accompanied by a photo, which explained why I hadn't made the connection to an old acquaintance.

"How about this?" I said.

"How about what?"

I made a sweeping gesture with my hand. "This. Making fuck movies. Does this suit you and your new name better, too?"

"It suits me better than a lot of things I've done. Jesus Christ, Hannibal, you're not going to get moralistic on me, are you? You? Your whole life is rutting through garbage and dirty laundry. You've killed people, for God's sake."

"I never killed anybody who didn't deserve it."

"And I never fucked anybody who didn't deserve it. So what's the point? What does any of it have to do with finding out who murdered Jason and Valerie?"

I didn't have an answer for that. She was right, I *was* being moralistic. What's more, I was being something of a prick. I suddenly realized that the reason for my abrasive attitude—aside from her stunt of years gone by—was that I felt somehow affronted, offended that anyone who was a friend of mine—*had* been a friend of mine—would end up doing something like this. It might be okay for other people, I could be open-minded about that. Free country, cast the first stone, walk a mile in my moccasins, and so on. But, damn it, anybody who was a friend to the great Me was supposed to be above all that.

I dug out my cigarettes, got one going for myself, held the pack out to Kat. She shook her head. "Quit a long time ago."

"Yeah," I said. "Nasty habit."

"Don't be sarcastic, Hannibal. It doesn't become you. Can't you just knock off the shit?"

I exhaled some smoke. "All right," I said. "I guess I can knock off part of it. What you do, what you call yourself is your business. Like you said, who am I to point a finger, right? But you can't expect me to just pretend nothing happened back then. You broke my best friend's heart. You ripped out his guts and stomped on them on your way out the door. You damn near broke him completely, lady."

She let the words tumble into her, returning my gaze flatly, her face taut and expressionless. When I was through, she gave it a minute or so and then said, "So did that make you feel better? Did it help to say it out loud, to tell me all the things I already knew? Did it change anything, put any of the pieces back together?"

"Got it unloaded, got it off my chest."

"Fine. For now. This is neither the time nor the place to go into it any further. We both happen to be here on other business, remember."

"I know my job."

"And I know mine. So unless you have some questions of real importance to your investigation, you'll have to excuse me—I need to make a phone call before I go back to work."

She brushed by me and made for the short hall that led off to the kitchen. I watched her walk away, my eyes not blind to the inviting sway of her hips under the shiny robe, but my mind clouded by the old memories and old hurts that the sight of her dredged up. Not to mention the new problems.

It had been my buddy Bomber Brannigan who'd fallen so hard for her. He'd hired her as a dancer for the Bomb Shelter a few days after she arrived in town allegedly from some wheat patch out Nebraska way. That had been in late January. By Valentine's Day they were making cow eyes at each other over frilly cards and heart-shaped candy. By March he was pricing engagement rings. In the beginning it had been . . . well, kind of cute. Seeing the big bear smitten, watching him walk around wearing a sappy smile all the time, his eyes so dreamy and far-away-looking you kept waiting for him to march into a wall. But it wasn't long before some of us also started seeing something else, something not so cute: a dark, bitchy, malicious side to Kath. A side she concealed neatly from Bomber, but displayed to the rest of us with increasing frequency and intensity. She was capable of tremendous mood swings, going from up and bubbly to low and snide and vicious without warning. She was responsible for at least a half dozen other dancers quitting or being fired over the span of a handful of weeks, telling Bomber outrageous lies about them when in truth all they were guilty of was standing up to her and her high-handed tactics. And then there was the flirting, the flamboyant teasing she indulged in so often when Bomber wasn't looking or wasn't around. She'd taken aim at me and some of the other regulars on occasion, but most of the time it was greasy biker types or grungy walk-ins off the street that she came on to. It was as if she were trying to magnify the audacity of what she was doing by choosing the most undesirable elements she could find to be a part of it. And all the while there would be a kind of mad gleam in her eyes, a challenge, daring any of the rest of us to tell Bomber what she was up to.

When I finally had a bellyful, that's exactly what I did. Or tried to do. Tried to tell him she was no good for him. I got about halfway through my spiel before he let me know he didn't appreciate it. Didn't appreciate it to the point of damn near busting my jaw.

I'd steered clear of the Bomb Shelter for a time after that. It wasn't much longer, though, before the romance crashed and burned anyway. I was never sure if my attempt to open Bomber's eyes had been a factor or not. As a matter of fact, I was never sure about a lot of things concerning exactly what had transpired. I only knew my old friend had an awful rough time over it, the kind of rough that—if you're a guy like the Bomber—you pretty much have to go alone. When things fell apart, he'd shown up at my place about three o'clock one morning, looking bleached out and hollow-eyed, and announced woodenly, "It's over. You were right. That's all I got to say about it." Kath went down the street and began dancing in another go-go joint, while Bomber began moving around in a different kind of daze, this one dour and black and dangerous.

Thinking back on it now, I fast-forwarded these events as quickly as possible through my mind, not eager to dwell on any of them. But the exercise left me with a naggingly persistent question I couldn't shunt aside so easily: should I tell him I'd seen her, that she was back in town?

Foxwood moved up beside me, crowding away the tail end of my reverie. He said, "I see you are already acquainted with our Kat?"

I nodded. "From a long time ago."

"I couldn't help noticing that there seemed to be some, ah, friction between the two of you. Will that be a problem?"

"The friction between us goes back a long time, too," I told him. "It won't be a problem as far as the jobs we came to do."

Foxwood looked relieved.

"But speaking of problems," I went on, "exactly what's shaping up here as far as the shoot? What happens if your new boy can't get it on no matter what? You got some sort of understudy or something you can turn to?"

Foxwood chuckled. "I am afraid our little company is far too modest in scope to include understudies, Mr. Hannibal. Or are you perhaps offering your services in an area other than your investigative expertise?"

"Knock it off. We already covered that shit."

"Under different circumstances I myself might be persuaded to fill in—no pun intended. In this particular instance, however, I fear that even the least discriminating viewer would have trouble accepting me as a college lad."

"So what then? If Junior can't keep his flag flying, the whole thing just gets written off?"

"If worse came to worst," Foxwood said offhandedly, "the script could always be shot another day. There remain, however, a number of 'tricks of the trade' that can yet be employed to salvage this session. Belinda may appear somewhat frustrated at the moment, but she is a very bright lady who wants desperately to succeed in her directorial debut. I have confidence she will find a way to make it work."

As if on cue, Belinda Davies emerged from the dressing room and came across the set in long, purposeful strides. She was rolling a sheaf of papers in her hands—a script, I guessed, by the look of it—as she walked, her burnished hair flowing out behind her like a flame. Tapping the script a couple times against her hip, she said to Dorfman and Blyth, "It is showtime, gentlemen. We have achieved lift-off and early indication is that the craft will be capable of remaining airborne for the duration of a successful flight. I suggest you assume your positions."

Dorfman and Blyth set aside their coffee cups and obediently moved to man their equipment. Belinda lifted her face and scanned out across the minisoundstage. "Kat?" she said. "Where has Kat gotten to?"

From where he stood off to the side of Foxwood and me, Floyd Silas answered, "She's out in the kitchen, ma'am. Still using the phone, I believe."

"Would you be a dear, Floyd, and go please and tell her to return right away—we're nearly ready?"

"You bet."

Before Floyd had taken a step toward the kitchen, though,

something additional seemed to occur to the director. "Wait," she said, leaving the set and moving rather hurriedly over to him. "While you are out there, there is perhaps another small task . . ." The rest of what she had to say faded into indecipherable murmuring as the two of them pressed conspiratorially close, Belinda doing most of the talking, making animated hand gestures, with Floyd standing motionless, head bowed to catch her every word, occasionally nodding.

Beside me, Foxwood snorted in apparent disgust. "Look at that old fool," he said. "She could be asking him to jump through hoops while balancing dog droppings on the end of his nose and the silly ass would no doubt be just as agreeable."

I grunted noncommittally. My gaze was tracing the outline of the redhead's profile and my nostrils were savoring a whiff of her perfume. Made me wonder where I'd draw the line if given the opportunity to find favor in the eyes of such a stunner. Balancing dog turds, I was pretty sure, would fall out of bounds. But maybe not by much.

The conference ended abruptly with Silas heading off toward the kitchen and Belinda returning to the set. Dorfman flashed her a thumbs-up, signaling that he and Blyth were ready for their part of it. Belinda nodded and impatiently tapped the script a couple more times against her hip.

In less than a minute, Kath—excuse me, make that Kat, Kat Hayward—came scurrying out of the short hall that fed off the kitchen. At the edge of the set, she paused and began undoing her robe. "This the real deal?" she asked Belinda.

"From all appearance," the director answered. Then, not quite under her breath, she added, "It bloody well better be."

Kat removed the robe and reached for an oval hand mirror to check her hair and makeup. This left her clad only in a cream-colored push-up bra, matching garter belt, and lime-green stockings. Her body was firm and evenly tanned to a rich, dark gold. Her pubic hair was dyed—or so I suspected—the same platinum shade as the hair on her head. She used the mirror to check both high and low.

Ten feet away, Dorfman backhanded a bored yawn while at the same time his partner seemed infinitely more interested in the reading he was getting off a light meter than in the pulchritudinous display being offered as an alternative. Job indifference, I guess, can be found in any line of work.

Belinda Davies recrossed the set. Her stride and her manner were growing more assured, more aggressive by the moment. At the curtained entranceway to the dressing room she called, "Richie, Angie . . . we are ready out here. Now, please."

The curtains parted and two people emerged. The guy was of medium height and build, early twenties, with a washboard stomach, a weak chin, and an unruly shock of sand-colored hair. He was naked except for a long-sleeved white dress shirt unbuttoned at the cuffs and all down the front. His three-quarters–erect penis jutted gamely out ahead of him. The brunette at his side was a couple of years younger, half a foot shorter, slightly on the plump side. She was completely nude. The two of them were pressed tight together, hip-bumping as they walked, causing her enormous breasts to shiver and sway pendulously. The guy's left arm was draped across her shoulders, the hand dangling down, roughly squeezing her breast, thumbing the overripe tip. She, in turn, was reaching across with her left hand, fondling and pumping his organ with an expert touch. From time to time she would tilt her head forward to lick and nibble at his exposed, hair-encircled nipple.

They made their way across the set in this manner, like some shifting, shuffling, two-headed quadruped involved in self-gratification.

Belinda followed at a half step's distance, softly but persistently murmuring encouragement. "Oh, my, what a marvelous hard-on we have now. Yes, simply marvelous. So big and so rock-hard. How lucky Angie and Kat are—lucky to have such a stud to work with!"

As the procession moved into place, I took the opportunity to more closely examine the set upon which they were positioning themselves. In accordance with the story outline Foxwood had mentioned, a handful of simple props had been arranged to effectively create a classroom scene. The centerpiece was a massive, metal-sided desk positioned ostensibly at the head of the room before a green chalkboard filled with nonsensical math problems. The desk was complete with a pile of scholarly looking tomes and even a globe perched on one corner. A tiny American flag hung limply down from a rod angling out over one end of the chalkboard, with the reassuringly smiling face of our president framed close by. The classroom motif was rounded off by three or four short rows of wooden chair-desks extending out toward the camera's point of view. Like I said, simple but effective.

I watched as Richie took his mark at the end of the desk, leaning back across it, his shirt falling open wide, his bare ass flattening against the metal. Angie continued to work on him, cooing further words of encouragement. Belinda hung back now, taking in the overview. Dorfman and Blyth were poised, ready. Kat moved up.

"All right, Kat," Belinda said. "Be prepared to go in. At this point, remember, you are already very hot. We have established that. You are in the grip of unbridled lust, beyond shame, beyond good sense, beyond caring about anything else. You, Richie, on the other hand are still slightly reticent, still somewhat overwhelmed by what is taking place. As the scene builds, however, your own lust will take over. You will become more impassioned, more assertive. But let it build slowly, slowly. Let Kat drive you there. Everyone got that?"

No reply was made, but everybody seemed to know the score. After a few beats, Belinda moved around to be more in line with the camera.

"Angie dear, please step out of the scene. Kat, take your place."

Angie gave a final tug at Richie's erection and a final lick of his nipple, as if kissing it good-bye, then straightened and backed away. Kat came forward and knelt between the young man's legs. His penis seemed to wag before her face, like its slitted tip was trying to make eye contact.

"Ready camera," Belinda said, twisting the rolled script tighter in her grip. "And . . . begin!"

Kat promptly took Richie's penis in her mouth, making eager wet noises. His head rolled back, eyes shut, teeth bared in a tight grimace of pleasure. Kat's head began to bob up and down with her task, slowly at first, then gradually picking up speed.

"Perfect," Belinda said. "That is the perfect touch, Kat. You have been wanting that cock for so long—starving for it—and now it is all yours. You are torn between a desire to savor it and a desire to instantly devour it."

Watching, I, too, felt torn—torn by conflicting reactions over what I was being an audience to. That I was to a certain degree excited by it, there could be no denying. My pulse had quickened; there was a dryness at the back of my mouth, a squeezing sensation low in my gut. It was comparable to a kind of excitement you might experience when you stop to watch a building burn or see a terrier rip apart a back alley rat—there is the rush generated by some base instinct but at the same time there is the more or less guilty knowledge that, on a higher plain, you should be repulsed or at least disturbed by such things. Yeah. Right. I can't speak for anybody else, but the trouble for me has always been that these inner battles between instinct and idealism damn seldom produce a clear-cut winner.

I glanced over at Foxwood. If the circumstances were causing him to struggle inwardly with anything, it sure as hell didn't show on his face. He wore the attentive yet benignly blank expression of a minister listening to the children's choir sing slightly off-key.

I decided I needed a cigarette, only I wasn't sure if it was permissible to light up while the camera was rolling. I couldn't see exactly what the problem would be, but I conjured visions of everything screeching to a halt, all eyes whipping round to me, and Belinda Davies intoning icily, "No smoking allowed!" Not wanting to appear too much the ignorant outsider, I refrained from asking Foxwood. Hell, maybe I was just looking for an excuse to get away for a little while from what I was finding to be a more and more uncomfortable situation.

I excused myself with a sort of catch-all gesture to Foxwood, turned, and walked back toward the kitchen. Over my shoulder, I could hear Belinda saying, "All right, Richie, you should be starting to get over your uncertainty by now, starting to respond purely to the physicality of the moment. Reach down and fondle her breast . . . rougher, more eagerly. . . . Pull down the strap now . . ."

When I reentered the great-smelling room, I discovered something of a crowd already gathered there. In addition to Floyd and Irma Silas, Angie, the dutiful fluffer, was present, clad now in a fuzzy pink robe and seated precariously on the edge of a butcher-block table with a partially eaten cookie in one hand and a glass of milk in the other. And standing over near the door to the cloak-room was a tall, husky kid in his early twenties I hadn't seen earlier but who I recognized from Foxwood's files. I couldn't think of his name but I recalled he was involved in some behind-the-scenes aspect, not as a performer.

Irma Silas was handing the young fellow a cup of coffee as I came in. She turned her head and favored me with a smile. "Oh, Mr. Hannibal, you're just in time. I have a freshly brewed pot of coffee and a sheet of cookies that I took out of the oven only moments ago. Will you have some?"

"A cup of coffee would be good," I said. "I'll pass on the cookies for right now."

"You sure? These are oatmeal, made from a grand old recipe that's been in my family for years."

"I've no doubt they're terrific. But a little later, okay? Coffee, black, will be fine."

While Mrs. Silas rummaged for a cup, Angie slid down off her perch and approached me. "So you're the detective, huh?"

I said I was.

"I saw you standing out there when I brought Richie onto the set. I figured you were probably the one. Foxy told us about you."

"Foxy?"

"You know—Henry. Mr. Foxwood. The guy who hired you."

"Right," I said. "Foxy."

She giggled. "It sounds silly when you say it. But that's how most of us girls refer to him. Not necessarily to his face, although he surely has heard it a few times. I think he gets a kick out of it. After all, it's more than just a play on his name, it's a compliment. I mean, for a guy his age he really *is* is a fox."

"If you say so."

She giggled again. "By the way, my name is Angie. Angie Mullond." She extended her right hand, the hand that had been holding the cookie. When she saw it was dusted with crumbs, she jerked it away, wiped it on her robe, then reoffered it with yet another giggle.

"Joe Hannibal," I said, taking her hand. It felt warm and plump and soft, which suited her perfectly.

Irma Silas served me my coffee in a large china cup with floral decorations around the rim, resting on a sturdy saucer bearing the same design. I tried to remember the last time, outside a restaurant, I'd been served a hot beverage with cup *and* saucer. Couldn't.

I sampled some of the brew and found it, not surprisingly, delicious.

After allowing me time to take another sip or two, Floyd Silas stepped up and put one of his big paws on my shoulder, saying, "Joe, I don't believe you had a chance to meet Chuck Baines." He inclined his head to indicate the young man still standing somewhat meekly off toward the cloakroom. "Chuck has been helping me with set construction and all sorts of stuff around here. Does a heck of a fine job, too; don't know how I got along without him before. Chuck, this is Joe Hannibal, the private detective Foxwood hired to look into the deaths of Jason and Valerie."

More hand shaking, Baines and I each balancing our cups and saucers in our left hands. His grip was like having your fingers pressed between slabs of rock.

"Bad thing, those murders," he said. "Hope you get to the bottom of them real quick."

"God, so do I," Angie said emphatically. "It's awful losing two good friends that way, and what makes it worse is that I can't even grieve properly for them because every time I think about it, I end up getting scared for myself, scared that I might be next on the killer's list."

"What makes you say that?" I asked. "What makes you think there's a killing list or that you might be on it?"

Her expression changed, taking on a cornered look. "Well . . . nothing in particular. I mean, nothing except what I said—that I'm scared there *could* be such a thing. If it turns out Jason and Valerie were killed by the same person, what else did they have in common? What else but the very thing we're all here today for?"

"Really, child," Irma Silas said soothingly, "you're going to great lengths to frighten yourself. I admit there may be *some* cause for concern. That is clearly why Henry hired Mr. Hannibal—to ease our minds and to look out for our safety. But every indication at this point is that the murders were unconnected, just dreadful and unfortunate coincidences to our business here."

"I don't much care for coincidences," Chuck Baines muttered.

"Nobody does," Floyd allowed. "But that don't mean they can't happen. I believe Mother has a good point. We have to be careful not to get ate up by fear, that's all. We need to keep cool heads, for our own sakes and for everybody else's."

"Not bad advice," I said. "As long as you don't work so hard at keeping cool heads that you fail to register concern over something that really deserves it."

"What's that supposed to mean?"

"Just what I said. Go ahead and be cool, be calm . . . but above all be careful. The bottom line here is murder, never forget that. With murder you get no rehearsal, no retakes. When it happens, it's over. For somebody. Forever."

"Jeez, Hannibal," Angie groaned, "you're a real ray of sunshine."

Irma frowned disapprovingly at me.

"Look," I said, "I'm just trying to be practical. Everything Floyd and Irma said is true. At this point there is more reason to believe the two killings *weren't* connected than to believe they were. All I'm saying, though, is don't be too quick to lower your guard, don't allow yourself to feel so safe and relaxed you don't bother to question or bring attention to something that might be significant."

"Significant like what?" Floyd asked.

I shrugged. "Could be anything. No way of telling until you hold all sides of it up to the light. That's why I'm here, to sort things out, to turn over some rocks. I'm here instead of the cops because you people, due to what you're involved in, don't feel you can afford to be open with the cops. With me, you don't have that problem—the *private* part in *private detective* means I know how to keep my mouth shut."

"So what's your point?" Chuck said. "Sounds to me like you want us to snitch to you."

"That's exactly what I *don't* want—for anybody to look at it that way. What I want are direct and honest answers to my questions, that's all. Don't worry about sounding foolish with your suspicions if you have any, don't try to be overly protective of your co-workers. It's my job to separate the cream from the crap, and I'm pretty good at it. Just give me a fair shot to do my thing so we can all put this lousy business behind us."

There was an edgy quiet following my words. After a full minute and a half, Floyd said, "I guess you're making sense, son, and I'm sure that all of us here—and the others—want to cooperate with you. But you've got to remember that you're dealing with . . . well, a kind of outlaw mentality on our part. We're used to operating outside the boundaries of what most folks consider right and proper. It won't come easy for us to all of a sudden open up to a lot of questions and it'll be harder still to speak out loud any mistrust or suspicions we might have about our own."

"But you think there *are* some suspicions among you?"

"I expect you'd have that in any group this size."

"Especially if some of them started turning up dead," Angie put in.

I jerked my thumb in the direction of the soundstage. "There was an awful lot of tension and anger in there a little while ago. That sort of thing common?"

Floyd considered for a long moment. Then: "I wouldn't say so, no. It happens from time to time, but it's not common. You usually see something like that late on a Sunday, when everybody is overtired and irritable from shooting all weekend and tempers are at their shortest."

"Even then," Angie said, "it hardly ever gets as nasty as it did in there. That new guy, Richie, showed up with a chip on his shoulder and proceeded almost immediately to rub everybody the wrong way. Then, when things started not working for him, everybody was naturally quick to jump on his case right back. It came close to getting out of hand."

Irma said, "From what I saw of dear sweet Richie, I'd label him a foul-mouthed, insolent little snot who deserved to be taken down a peg or two."

"You're probably right," Floyd agreed. "But I don't figure we need to worry about it. I think it's safe to say that Foxwood and Belinda will see to it he never comes back here to work again."

I found all of this interesting enough, but it was roaming pretty far afield from where I'd been headed. In an effort to bring things back on course, I said, "How about Jason and Valerie? They ever had this kind of trouble—with each other or with anybody else?"

Looks were exchanged all around before Floyd said, "Not that I can recall, no."

"The little Pine girl was only out here a few times," Irma said.

Angie gave a firm shake of her head. "Jason never had that kind of trouble, I'm certain. You can ask anyone; Jason took all of this real serious. He was always ready with his lines and he was always ready . . . well, physically, too. Everybody liked Jason as a person and everybody liked working with him."

Floyd backed her up. "That's a fact. He was real likable, real down-to-earth. Not like some of these uppity 'studs' that come around. Heck, sometimes he'd even pitch in and help me and Chuck carry props and stuff."

"Yeah, Jason was okay," Chuck said.

I let my gaze sweep over them. Their faces all wore painfully sincere expressions. I hated to drive the pain any deeper, but I wanted to make damn sure they understood the hard realities of what we were talking about here. "Well, somebody apparently didn't think he was such a swell fella," I said. "They didn't think so about thirty-one times—that's how many times they slammed a knife into him."

The Silases both winced visibly. Angie shut her eyes suddenly, as if to hold back tears. Chuck found a spot on the floor and stared dully at it.

We were posed in more or less this fashion when the door off the short hall opened and Henry Foxwood entered the kitchen.

"Well," he said, taking stock of our glum expressions, "I obviously am not barging into the middle of a joke-telling session, am I?"

"Hardly," somebody muttered.

Foxwood cleared his throat. "The intrusion could not be helped in any event. We are once again having difficulty on the set. Floyd, I believe Belinda asked you to have a concoction prepared?"

"Right," Floyd replied. He turned to his wife. "Mother, do you have something ready?"

Irma Silas walked over to the refrigerator, withdrew a blocky, old-fashioned mug, and returned with it. As she held it out to Foxwood, I saw that it was about half-filled with a syrupy, chalky-white liquid.

"Oh, shit," Angie said. "You mean now he's having trouble getting his rocks off?"

Foxwood smiled in her direction. "Not only keenly accurate, my dear, but so eloquently put."

"Shit," Angie said again.

Foxwood was retreating back through the door, gingerly holding the mug out in front of him.

"So what's in the cup?" I asked of no one in particular.

"It's a cum cocktail," Angie said absently. "I suppose I'd better get back out there—Kat and Richie are no doubt at each other's throats and Belinda may need me to help smooth things over."

"A *what* kind of cocktail?" I wanted to know.

But if she heard me, she chose to ignore the question. She went trotting from the kitchen, her fuzzy robe flapping over her broad, bouncing rump. Floyd, his mouth a grim slash, plodded after her. Chuck, still wearing the blank expression with which he'd been staring at the spot on the floor, was at his heels.

I suddenly found myself alone in the kitchen with Mrs. Silas and feeling more than a little bewildered.

After several beats, softly, very matter-of-factly, she said, "I believe what Angie called it was a 'cum' cocktail. A pretty blunt choice of words, I'm afraid, but not really inaccurate."

I gave her a sidelong glance. Before I could say anything, she continued. "It's a preparation—in this case a mixture of corn starch and Maalox—to use as a substitute for a discharge of male semen. I'm told that the distributors of these films insist that all or most of the sex scenes end with a visible release by the male—the 'wet shot' or 'money shot,' as they are called. When that can't actually be achieved on the set, using this kind of mixture is one of the little tricks they've come up with to satisfy the requirement. The girl takes an amount of the mix in her mouth, you see, proceeds to perform fellatio on her partner, and then, with the proper histrionics, allows the mixture to spill free, giving the impression that the man has actually climaxed very successfully."

Now, I don't know about you, but, for me, receiving a dissertation on "wet shots" and phony jism and so forth from a sweet-faced, gray-haired little old lady in a flowered housedress and frilly apron ranks right up there just about as high as I ever want to get in the column headed Embarrassing Moments. It made the prospect of going back into the other room and watching Bomber's exgirlfriend blow some punk kid from Chicago seem like a walk in the park.

"Okay," I said at the conclusion of Irma's discourse. "Uh, thanks, Thanks for sharing that with me."

She smiled noncommittally, but at the same time I could have sworn I spotted a devilish little twinkle in her eyes. She knew damn well how uncomfortable she'd made me and was getting a kick out of it.

I decided not to press the issue. I put down my cup and saucer, fumbled for the door, and got out of there.

Out in the hall, I dug loose my pack of Pall Malls and finally got around to having that smoke I'd wanted. I dragged a lungful deep and held it there a long time. Jesus Christ, I told myself, for somebody who's supposed to be a two-fisted, bullet-chewing private eye you're sure spending a lot of time retreating from situations that threaten your tender sensibilities. Get in the game, wimp. You knew these people made fuck movies, what did you expect? Deal with it. Nobody's after your cherry.

I squashed the half-smoked butt underfoot and walked on around the corner.

Assuming there'd been some sort of break in the action while Foxwood went to fetch the emergency cocktail, the camera was once again rolling. Kat and Richie, both completely naked now, were positioned somewhat precariously atop the desk, sixty-nining each other. The books and globe and various other things that adorned the desktop previously had been cleared—evidently in a surge of heightened passion—and lay strewn about on the floor.

Belinda Davies monitored the action from slightly off to one side of the cameraman, her expression intense, the tightly rolled script still clutched in her hands. Foxwood stood further back, about where he'd been before, Floyd Silas again at his side. Chuck was off in a far corner, quietly sorting through some props. I didn't see Angie anywhere.

On the desk, Kat was performing her part of the act with a great deal of vigor, but it was obvious Richie was having trouble maintaining an erection no matter how fiercely she worked. At a terse signal from Belinda, Kat began releasing reverse gulps of the secreted mixture. It oozed down over Richie's testes. Dorfman zoomed in tight with his camera. He held there for what seemed like a long time. When the effect had been milked for all it was worth (no pun intended), he panned slowly back as the couple untangled and, coaxed by Belinda, engaged in a bit of decidedly unconvincing postcoital billing and cooing.

Belinda brought it to an end with a downward slash of her spindled script. "And . . . cut!"

Kat and Richie pushed instantly away from each other and slid down off the desk on opposite sides. Richie stood with his back turned, head hung somewhat, understandably chagrined by his disappointing performance. Kat, on the other hand, faced boldly outward in her tanned, sweat-slick nudity. She made a distasteful face and wiped at the stickiness around her mouth with the back of one hand. "Goddamn, I hate that shit," she announced to anyone who cared to listen.

During the final minute or so of shooting, Angie had emerged quietly from one of the dressing rooms carrying a soapy washcloth in each hand and a pair of fresh towels draped over her forearms. She proceeded to the desk area with these now and dispensed one of each to the performers. Richie, still with his back turned, began wiping himself below the waist.

Kat raised her sudsy cloth to her face. As she drew it down over her chin, she saw fit to elaborate on her earlier statement as if uninterrupted. "Rotten shit," she said. "I think I'd sooner gargle with sewer sludge."

Richie made some reply from the other side of the desk but, because Belinda and Dorfman were discussing something in the foreground, I didn't catch what it was.

Neither, apparently, did Kat. She looked partway around at him and said, "What was that?"

Richie shook his head. "Never mind."

"No. You said something. What was it?"

"Nothing. Just forget it."

"I won't forget it, you little shit. You said something, and I want to know what it was. It was something smart-ass again, wasn't it?"

Richie finally turned to face her. He'd wrapped the towel Angie provided around his waist and was cinching it tight. Having the source of his embarrassment covered seemed to shore up his courage. "Look," he said, "it's been a real bear of a day, right? Everybody's on edge, it doesn't take much for us to rub each other the wrong way. Just leave it be and let me get the hell out of here, okay?"

"I want to know what you said."

"You don't."

"I do, you limp-dicked sonofabitch."

Richie's face flushed instantly red and his mouth twisted in an ugly way. "All right, goddammit," he snarled. "When you said you'd rather gargle with sewer sludge, I said if you weren't any better at that than you are at giving head, you'd probably drown. . . . Happy now?"

Their voices had been rising steadily in volume throughout the exchange. They were almost shouting at each other by this point and had captured the attention of everyone on the soundstage.

"That will do," Belinda Davies said sharply, disengaging herself from Dorfman and taking a step toward the noisy pair.

Kat slammed her fists onto her hips and looked around incredulously. "Can you believe the nerve of this sonofabitch? He jacks everybody around all afternoon and then implies it's *my* fault? I won't stand for that."

"You give head like a knothole in a slab of wood," Richie jeered.

"I give great head, buster. I just never did it on a strand of boiled spaghetti before."

"Fuck you, cunt!"

"You tried, El Limpo. But you weren't up to it, remember?"

"Enough, I said," Belinda interjected. She looked angry and at the same time a little frightened.

"Enough is exactly what I've had," Richie fumed, throwing his wadded washcloth down on the desktop. "Drag my ass all the way out here to the boonies in the middle of fucking winter, and for what? Give me some iron-jawed, over-the-hill old broad and some lard-assed slob kid to work with, what do you expect?" He thrust a furiously trembling forefinger at Belinda. "You'd better not spread this around and try to ruin any future jobs for me, you hear? None of this is my fucking fault."

"It's for sure none of the fucking was your fault," Kat quipped.

Richie swung the rigid finger like he was aiming a gun. "And I've had all the smart-mouthing from you I intend to take!"

A disturbing shrillness had crept into his voice. All of a sudden I sensed the argument skewing in the direction of possible violence. Almost before that was a conscious thought, my feet were in motion, carrying me past Foxwood and Silas and Dorfman. As I took up a position next to Belinda Davies, hands hanging loosely at my sides, eyes locked on Richie's face, I was aware that for practically the first time since entering the old farmhouse I felt comfortable and very much at ease. It might still be their turf, but it looked like it could be turning into more my kind of game.

"Get that stinking finger out of my face." Kat said through her teeth, "or I'll break it off and shove it up your ass."

"I'm warning you," Richie told her, his voice a near shriek.

Kat laughed in his face. "Oooo, I bet the thought of having

something rammed up your ass excites you, doesn't it? That's been the trouble all along, hasn't it, faggot? Angie and I couldn't keep you hard because what you really wanted was—"

Richie lunged across the desk for her, but Kat skipped back out of reach, still laughing at him. Screaming a curse, his face purple now with rage and frustration, Richie shoved himself upright and came tearing around the end of the desk. I stepped forward and caught him, grabbing his wrist below the fist he had cocked, levering it back, slamming him down on the desktop and pinning him there with a forearm across his throat.

"At ease, Spartacus," I growled, my face pressed close to his, "before that towel slips and one of us ends up stepping on your dick."

6

I stood in the thickening dusk with a cigarette in one hand and a cup of Irma Silas's coffee—sans saucer—in the other. Both, along with intermittent gusts of my breath, streamed vaporous gray-white trails into the crisp air.

Behind me, the kitchen door opened and closed. A brief whiff of cinnamon-laced aromas teased my nostrils. Footsteps came down the shoveled path, crunching on the packed snow.

Kat Hayward walked up beside me. She was hatted and heavily bundled, hugging herself against the cold. A brightly colored tote bag hung by a white plastic handle from the crook of one arm.

"Jesus, Hannibal," she said, "you don't even have a coat on. Don't you know it's freezing out here?"

"Feels good," I told her, I motioned back toward the house with a nod of my head. "It was getting awful close in there."

She made a sound that could have meant about anything, the kind of sound people make when they're not sure just what you're driving at.

I drank some of my coffee. It was fast losing its heat.

"Speaking of 'in there,' " Kat said, "I never got around to saying thanks. For putting the stop on El Limpo Richie, I mean. He didn't have me worried until right at the last instant when he went absolutely bonkers. Don't let this come as too much of a shock, but I'm glad you were on hand."

Almost an hour had passed since the incident with Richie. After I let him up off the desk, he'd sullenly gone about getting dressed and then had departed without another word. Whatever tension or disruption the episode might have left in its wake was quickly pushed aside by the arrival of several additional performers and an ensuing mad scramble to prepare sets, costumes, makeup, camera blocking, et cetera, for shooting the next feature. My investigative role—hell, practically my entire presence—was all but lost in the shuffle. Except for having my name tossed in as part of a few fleeting introductions, my main function became abruptly relegated to standing around drinking coffee and trying to keep out of the way. When I caught myself starting to pout over the fifth-wheel status, I'd wandered outside to get some fresh air and level off.

"You know," I said to Kat now, "you needled Richie quite a ways beyond what was necessary."

"Little shit had it coming."

"Maybe. I'd say he got more than he bargained for."

"Tough. He started it. Besides, you seemed willing enough with your part."

"Yeah, maybe that's what's bugging me. I can't help thinking I might have been set up a little bit. Makes me wonder if you didn't prod him into acting the way he did in order to see if I'd act the way I did."

"What the hell is that supposed to mean? Boy, talk about paranoia."

"I don't like being used."

"God, I hate it when people say that. We all allow ourselves to be used in some way, Hannibal. Don't ever kid yourself. Everybody's a whore to something. You and me standing here right now —you want in the worst way to sneer down your nose at me, at what I'm involved in. But you can't. Know why? You can't because you know damn well we're both on the same payroll. I'm screwing for them, you're poking around at the slimy underside of things for them. All the while they stay back and keep their hands and their crotches clean. So who's being used and who isn't?"

I finished my coffee. It was as cold as tap water.

Kat shifted her stance, watching my face, waiting for me to make some reply. The snow squeaked under her.

When she'd had enough of my silence, she said, "Well? Aren't you going to say anything?"

"What do you want me to say? I'm a whore, you're a whore. . . . Hooray?"

"Oh. So that's it. I hurt your feelings."

I shook my head. "Don't flatter yourself. I don't value your opinion enough for you to hurt my feelings."

This time she was the one who got quiet.

I took a final drag off my cigarette. Snapped what was left into the piled snow, shoved my hand in my pocket. I was starting to feel the cold. The empty cup in my other hand had become a palmful of ice.

"Well," Kat sighed at length, "that was plainly enough put, wasn't it? Only a fool would fail to take a hint from that. So . . . I guess I'll go ahead and be on my way." She started across the parking area toward an old Ford with dented fenders. Over her shoulder, she said, "Thanks again, Hannibal. Thanks a bunch."

I stood there and watched her go. Watched her get in the Ford and start it, then climb back out and scrape the windows while the engine was warming up. A couple of times I felt an urge—I wasn't sure why—to go after her, to say something further, maybe try and end at least this one exchange between us on a more upbeat note.

But I didn't.

I was freezing my ass off by the time the old car clunked into gear and rolled out of the driveway. For some obscure reason it seemed important to stand my ground, not give in to the temptation of going back inside where it was warm while she was still anywhere in sight. When her taillights winked off in the distance, I turned and walked up the path, thawing my numb fingertips in the heat of my armpit.

You take your victories, no matter how small or stupid, where you find them.

7

It was pushing ten when I left the farmhouse and drove back to the city. The cloud cover had broken up partially, offering occasional glimpses of a stark white moon and ice-chip stars. At ground level there was a low, whispering wind that caused the barren trees to groan and pop as they bent under its pressure.

After my open-air encounter with Kat, I'd gone back inside, stubbornly determined to reestablish my investigative purpose, and had ended up making some measurable progress. My resolve was aided by the fact that most of the frantic preparatory activity had died down and the Betacam was ready to roll on the evening shoot.

Angie Mullond, the pudgy, dedicated fluffer, proved to be a willing and semivaluable source of information. I sat with her in one of the dressing rooms, where I'd found her tidying up behind the on-camera performers who had been called to their marks. Her duties, it seemed, covered just about anything that anybody else found undesirable or demeaning. But she was quick to assure me that was only a temporary state of affairs.

"One of these days, *I'm* going to be in front of the camera," she had said in her earnest, straightforward way. "You've heard it said that the lens puts on ten to fifteen extra pounds, right? Unfortunately it's true. And since I'm already that much overweight . . . well, you see my problem. But Belinda has taken a special interest in me. She's got me started on her very own diet-and-exercise program. Says if I can firm things up a little and lose even a dozen or so pounds for starters, she'll be able to use me in certain scenes. Wouldn't that be great?"

"Yeah, great," I'd agreed.

"I mean, I got the kind of big ol' boobs," she went on, "that men always seem to take an interest in, even if a too-wide butt comes with 'em. And I got other talents they seem to like pretty well too." She'd actually blushed a bit. "I don't mean to brag, but after so many guys tell you what a great sex partner you are, you sort of can't help it, you know? I've even had some of them—ones who were having a little trouble on-camera—tell me when I took them aside to work with them that if *I* was their partner on the set, they probably wouldn't be having no trouble to begin with." She'd produced a frown as quickly as she had the blush. "Except for that jerk Richie today. He called me a lard-assed slob kid, did you hear him?"

"Richie was a shitheel," I'd offered consolingly.

As I'd listened to her, there was a part of me that found an ineffable sadness in the thought of a vital, likable young woman whose main goal seemed to be to fuck and suck in front of the camera instead of behind the scenes. But at the same time there was something about her—her personality, her eagerness, her uncomplicated pride in what she was good at—that brought a crazy kind of wholesomeness and simplistic charm to the prospect. While my mind's eye winced so automatically at the image of Kat Hayward fellating fiercely and drooling gouts of fake semen, I was able to blink and envision, in soft focus, Angie copulating joyfully, receiving and giving pleasure in equal measure. Somehow, it seemed preferable to replays of her meekly cleaning the mess left by others or providing soapy washcloths for their postsexual ablutions.

Having loosened her up with talk of herself and her ambitions, I had then steered Angie into talking about some of the other members of the blue-movie troupe, particularly those who had come in close or frequent contact with Jason Hobbs and/or Valerie Pine. This amounted to a cross-check of the material Foxwood had already provided and I realized there was apt to be a degree of redundancy, but beyond that it would offer a personal slant that might be far more telling than flat facts and figures on a piece of paper. I learned, for instance, that Hobbs's best friend had been a black man named Barry Grainger. Grainger not only worked on the same construction crew as Hobbs and participated with him from time to time in the movie-making sideline, but he and his wife had since taken in Rosemary Karson, Hobbs's lover, and were looking out for her in the aftermath of Jason's murder. When I pressed Angie about Rosemary, she'd seemed to know nothing about the girl's background in prostitution. She described her as a small, quiet, pretty sort who had accompanied Jason to the farmhouse a time or two when he came to work. Angie recalled there had been some talk at one point of Jason and Rosemary doing a loop together, but nothing had ever come of it; she wasn't sure exactly why. She repeated her earlier stated sentiments about what "a really nice guy" Hobbs was and how hard it was for her to understand why someone had found it necessary to kill him.

As for Valerie Pine, Angie seemed to have had little contact with her. From what she knew of the attractive blonde, though, she had been competent in her cinematic endeavors and had been well enough liked as both a co-worker and a person by those who did get to know her. Angie remembered there had been rumors of a crazy exhusband lurking somewhere in the background, but she wasn't sure if that talk came before Valerie's death or only afterwards. She told me that those who had seemed closest to Valerie—aside from her roommate, Cindy Wallace, also a veteran of the movie group—were Buck and Lois Ingram, an obviously liberated married couple who happened to be among the performers working in the other room as we spoke.

I'd gotten less satisfactory results when I tried to nudge Angie in the direction of Henry Foxwood and Belinda Davies. My interest in each—although at this point anybody and everybody could be considered fair game as a suspect—was only peripherally connected to the outcome of the case. I wanted to know more about Foxwood simply because, in my mind, I was having difficulty putting a handle on him; his modestly proclaimed role of "humble go-between" was getting harder and harder to swallow as I noted the amount of water he seemed to draw in various situations. And I wanted to know more about Belinda—again, simply—because she was the kind of fascinatingly beautiful creature any red-blooded male would want to know more about; the fact that she came across as aloof and mysterious—and had been stamped "off limits" to boot—only provided seasoning for the untasted stew. But I got nothing more from Angie. Nothing that amounted to anything, anyway. It wasn't that she was unwilling to talk about the pair. Hell, she would have babbled on all night if I'd let her. The problem was that she held them both at such a high level of adulation—Belinda because she was a director, someone in a position of power who was actually taking time to pay attention to lowly little Angie; Foxwood because he had been a bona fide Hollywood star and was "so distinguished and sophisticated and everything"—it was impossible for her to be even the least bit objective about them. When she opened her mouth, all that gushed out was saccharine praise.

Leaving Angie after thanking her for her time, I'd roamed back out onto the soundstage. The atmosphere surrounding the current taping felt much different than that of this afternoon. No tension, no loosely bottled anger. The performers actually appeared to be enjoying themselves. Whenever there was a break in the action, they'd lie back in a relaxed way and talk and joke with one another.

The premise of this round of choreographed slap and tickle apparently involved two couples experimenting with group sex. The set was a reconstruction of an upper-middle-class living room where two women and two men, all quite naked, were entangled in a twisting, writhing, sporadically connecting pattern across plush carpeting and low couches. Both men were trim, tanned six-footers, one slightly older and huskier than the other. The women were in sharper contrast, a pale blonde with enormous siliconed breasts that looked as hard as ceramic lamp bases and a curvy brunette with a tan too deep and too flawless to have come strictly from the sun. I dredged up a vague recognition of each from the file Foxwood had put together for me, but was damned if I could connect any names with features, other than a pretty good hunch that the brunette was Lois Ingram. Which guy was her real-life husband would be a coin toss.

A handful of yards off the set, over against a wall and folded into one of the student desks that had been used in the previous scene, sat a gangly, thirtyish, nerdy-looking guy with mason-jar eyeglasses and an Adam's apple the size of a horse chestnut. He didn't look familiar at all, but the very out-of-placeness of his appearance had piqued my curiosity enough to cause me to wander over and strike up a conversation. It turned out his name was Tom Gilbertson and he was the husband of Bess, the pale blonde, of whom he seemed burstingly proud (not to mention uncommonly tolerant). All during our talk, he'd concentrated studiously on his wife's every move, seldom glancing my way, occasionally pausing to point out (almost always with a great deal of enthusiasm) a particular technique or act that was being performed on or by his Bess. Around these somewhat unnerving side trips, I learned that Bess had worked with Valerie Pine a couple of times and, since Tom usually accompanied his wife to her shoots, they had both gotten to know Valerie fairly well. The noteworthy capper to this was the tacked-on statement that, while they'd both liked being around Valerie okay, neither of them had felt the same about "that bitchy little dyke, Cindy, she was shacked up with." After that, he'd hummed me a few bars of the by now familiar refrain that lauded Jason Hobbs as "a peach of a guy that everybody really, really liked." The final item of note I'd gotten from my time with Gilbertson—and this had nothing to do with the case, but that didn't make it any less interesting, in a twisted kind of way—was the knowledge (accompanied by a timely demonstration, over on the set) that the rock-hard condition of his wife's breasts wasn't due to a visit to the silicone man as I'd guessed, but rather because they were packed with mother's milk. And although their son was only four months old, Gilbertson informed me, they'd already decided to keep the mammaries flowing well after he was weaned because, as any fool knew, the ability to provide a bit of lactation during foreplay or afterplay was a very salable "gimmick." "It's the extra-special little something," he'd said, eyes gleaming shrewdly behind thick lenses, Adam's apple bobbing enthusiastically, "that's going to make my Bessie a star!"

Once inside the city limits, I wasted no time finding a quiet, out-of-the-way corner in a quiet, out-of-the-way little bar where I sat alone before a pile of ice cubes wrapped in bourbon. I felt emotionally charged and at the same time weary. It had been quite an evening. I needed to sort out some things.

More often than not, as stated earlier, I wind up my day with a few drinks at the Bomb Shelter. But that was a stop I wouldn't be making tonight. I wasn't ready to face the Bomber yet, not after encountering Kat (Kath, to him) the way I had. I'd pretty much made up my mind I was going to tell him I'd run into her, that she was back in town. But how much beyond that, I wasn't sure. Would it serve any purpose, other than rubbing extra salt in the wounds, to mention what she was involved in? I couldn't see where it would. Not necessarily. But on the other hand I knew how the passage of time can affect certain people, especially those like Bomber who are prone to being sentimental saps. It might be just like him to discover his bitterness had blurred to a point where he'd want to see her again, want to reestablish contact on some cockeyed premise. And then if he found out what she was mixed up in and I hadn't bothered mentioning it, he'd end up sore at *me*. See what I mean? Round and round we go. Shit.

I ordered another bourbon on the rocks and lit a cigarette while the sleepy-eyed bartender poured. The cash register was draped in an ancient, faded Christmas wreath. Every time the barkeep punched the money drawer, the wreath would tremble and shed pine needles all over everything. Across the room, a couple of white-whiskered old drunks were loudly trying to sing along with a perverse little ditty called "Grandma Got Run Over by a Reindeer" that one of them had played on the jukebox. Under his breath, the bartender cussed the pine needles and then cussed the noisy drunks. And me, I sat there with my mind crowded by thoughts of murder and exploitive sex and sad, shallow people with X-rated dreams and brokenhearted old friends and flame-haired, untouchable mystery women. . . .

If the Christmas spirit was in town, it was playing a gig somewhere down the street.

8

*T*hey were waiting for me when I got home. Two men sitting in a dark green, late-model Pontiac sedan curbed out front with its engine running.

Home is a one-bedroom southside apartment upstairs over a TV-repair shop. Sticking to routine, I circled the block partway and then cut back through the alley so I could park facing out. I noted the Pontiac on my first pass by. In addition to not belonging there, its plume of exhaust smoke marked it distinctly. Reasoning that anyone on hand with the intent of doing me serious harm would likely make some effort to mask their presence, I nosed the Honda up alongside the building and cut the motor without undue concern. Nevertheless, before climbing out I slipped the two-shot .22 magnum derringer from the spring clip inside my boot and palmed it under the glove of my right hand. You make enemies in this racket, and I've maybe made more than my share. Doesn't hurt to be careful.

As I straightened up outside the Honda, the two guys emerged from the Pontiac. They left the car idling. The driver came around the front end and, side by side, they walked toward me over the snow-clumped ground. The driver, of medium height and build, wore a snap-brim hat pulled low across his eyes. The other guy was taller, broader, maybe running to fat; it was hard to be sure in the long, wind-flared overcoat he wore. He was hatless, with wispy tendrils of hair—the kind of wisps some guys try to keep carefully arranged over a thin spot—standing straight out beside his head.

When they got close enough, the driver said, "You Joe Hannibal?"

I nodded. "That's right."

"We been waiting awhile. Man, you put in quite a day."

"Try to give the clients their money's worth."

The big guy grunted, half his mouth curling into a sneer. "Unless that's cough syrup on your breath, it smells like you don't waste no time putting some of that client money right back into circulation at the nearest gin mill."

They'd come to a halt within the illumination thrown by the high light that bathes my outside stairway. I saw that the driver was a black guy with bright, quick eyes and a narrow, sharp-featured face that looked like it could have been chipped from a slab of obsidian. His sidekick had a pale, doughy mug piled around a big nose and eyes that were too empty and too close together. Even without the sneer and the snotty remark, you could tell by the way he carried himself and his posturing now on the edge of the light that he considered himself a real dangerous character. Maybe so. But I'd already made up my mind that if this came to anything I would take out the driver first.

I showed Dough Face a sheepish grin. "I guess you got me red-handed. Boy, you guys from MADD are really sharp."

He looked instantly confused and it didn't seem to be an expression he had much trouble fitting into. He glanced over at his partner. "What's he talking about? We're not here because we're mad at anybody . . . are we?"

The driver ignored him. He was watching me.

"You know," I said, "M-A-D-D . . . Mothers Against Drunk Drivers? You guys are a couple of their field agents, right? You sprang this trap on me because you must have heard I like to stop and have a few before coming home most nights. I figure with that nose, you're some kind of bloodhound, huh? Like a walking, talking breathalyzer test or something?"

The driver had it by then. He made a sound and looked away, but not before I picked up the hint of a smile.

Dough Face remained confused. "What the *hell* is he talking about, Crawford?" But then he saw how the driver was looking away and maybe caught a glimpse of his smile and then he started to put it together with my words. By the time he looked back over at me, he was scowling menacingly. The scowl would have worked better if the loose hair hadn't been wafting around beside his head like a swarm of gnats. "Hey! Are you being a smart guy?"

I shook my head. "Not so you could notice it. If I was smart, I would have demanded to know by now who you two clowns are and what the hell you're doing lurking around my place after midnight."

"You'd best watch who you're calling clowns, mister."

"Lurking," the driver said thoughtfully, to no one in particular. "Didn't know we knew how to do that."

Dough Face hitched his shoulders the way Cagney used to in the old black-and-white gangster movies. He was still scowling. "How about I lurk over there and rap him a couple times in his smart goddamn mouth?"

The driver—Crawford—held up his hands, palms out. "All right, all right, hold it. This is going way the hell off in a direction it never should have. Way the hell off. Let's everybody just calm down and see if we can't start all over again."

"I don't like the way he mouthed off to me," Dough Face said poutingly.

Crawford sighed. "Look, Earl, don't let this come as a rude surprise . . . but nobody really gives a rat's ass what you like and don't like, okay? We were sent here to do a job, and roughing up the merchandise wasn't part of it."

I said, "The 'merchandise' is curious to know just what it was you *were* sent here for."

"Man wants to see you," Crawford explained. "We were told to bring you along."

"What man?"

"*The* man," Earl answered. "Who the hell you think?"

I laughed. "Every piss-ant egomaniac who has a handful of chumps taking orders from him calls himself *The* Man. You'll have to do better—like a name?"

"Camicci," Earl fired back. "*That* name enough for you?"

I didn't let anything show on my face. "What if I said it means nothing to me?"

Crawford sighed again. Hard. The vapor trail of his breath shot out in a straight line, like a gout of water. "Come on, Hannibal," he said. "Let's quit dicking around. I'm freezing my balls off standing here. If you didn't figure right from the get-go that

Camicci had to be involved behind Foxwood and that business, then you've got to be the dumbest detective since the English guy who played the French guy in all those movies. And that dumb I know you ain't, so why pretend? Man wants to see you, talk to you about some things; what's the problem?"

I gave it some thought and sighed back at him. "When does 'The Man' want this summit meeting to take place?"

"Said we should bring you along whenever we caught up with you."

"Now? This late?"

Crawford shrugged. "What can I say? He puts in quite a day, too." He grinned a little. "Guess you both believe in trying to give the suckers their money's worth."

9

---

*H*eavy-metal rock music pounded from hidden speakers and two dozen steroid Rockettes with rippling, glistening, oiled gold muscles pranced to the beat in perfect unison. Arcs of silver whirled at their sides as each rhythmically arm-curled a set of chrome dumbbells.

Once past the initial shockwave of sound and imagery, I was able to determine that there was, in fact, only one gleaming lady of amazonian proportions. The multiple impressions came from a wall of full-length mirrored panels.

The three of us—Crawford, Earl, and I—were in the Olympiad, Rockford's newest and most elite health club. We'd entered through the back with the aid of a key produced and wielded by Crawford. It was well outside the club's regular business hours, of course, but the premises were clearly still open to certain parties and we seemed to be on the guest list.

Before going in, I'd stood for a quick frisk as requested by Crawford and administered by Earl. Legs spread, arms extended, I was such a cooperative lad.

They never came close to the derringer in the glove.

Once inside, we'd made our way down a short service hallway and then a longer, narrower hall lined with various doors, one of which eventually opened onto the expansive exercise room where the mirrored amazon pumped to the driving music. Only after my senses had adjusted to this dazzling display did I notice the other person in the room.

He looked to be about medium height, perhaps slightly taller than Crawford. Dark-hair and dark-complexion, with a blued jawline that said he was the type who exhibited a five o'clock shadow before the shaving lather was even dry. I put his age in the middle thirties. He was trim, but would never be called thin or slender. Too broad across the shoulders, too bulky in the arms, with a neck like a baby bull. Even when he wasn't positioned at a Universal machine doing pull-downs, as he was now, you'd spot him for somebody who worked at staying in shape.

The Camicci name and the phrase *organized crime* have been uttered in the same breath throughout the Midwest for the past forty years. The only real surprise when Earl mentioned it back at my place had been that I'd never heard it directly connected to any Rockford activity before. When the brothers Antonio and Frederico had carved (sometimes literally) their niche in the Mob ranks during the post–World War II years, they'd done so right in the heart of Mob City, USA—Chicago. And although Antonio had passed on (from natural causes, somewhat surprisingly) to that big pasta plantation in the sky a couple of winters back, from all reports Frederico was maintaining business as usual from the old territorial base. Dirty movies, apparently, had gotten included in the slice of pie the Camiccis cut for themselves. And inasmuch as tentacles of the Chicago Syndicate now reached all over the country and particularly into smaller Midwest cities like Rockford, the current problems of Foxwood and his troupe evidently fell under Camicci jurisdiction. Nevertheless, it was unexpected to actually have *a* Camicci in town handling the matter.

What I was looking at was obviously Second Generation, I told myself, measuring the guy on the Universal machine as Crawford and Earl steered me in his direction. A son possibly; maybe a nephew; maybe even a grandson. However he fit in, I pegged him as a watered-down version of what had come before. There was a ruthless twist to his mouth and a glint of meanness in his eyes, but no sign of the kind of fire it would take to battle your way to the top of the old-time Mob.

He kept us waiting while he finished his reps at the pull-down station. When he was done, he let the bar snap up out of the way and mopped sweat from his face with the ends of a towel that hung around his neck.

His gaze finally swung to us and Crawford said, "Mr. Camicci, this is Joe Hannibal, the private eye you wanted to see."

For an edgy second I thought he might offer to shake hands, but that passed quickly enough as he continued to mop sweat. "I know about you, Hannibal," he said. "You're able to keep your mouth shut, you're tough, and you're lucky, you mostly accomplish what you set out to do."

"It's because my heart is pure," I told him.

If he heard me, he let it go. We were in a shouting match with the music, and not coming off all that well.

Camicci abruptly twisted in his seat and called to the bronzed woman with the dumbbells. "Uschi! Uschi, turn that goddamned music off for a little while! Can't you see we're trying to talk here?"

The bronzed woman stopped bouncing and let the dumbbells swing idly at her side. With her lower lip thrust out poutingly, she padded over. "You know my music gives me energy, Frankie," she accused.

"Yeah, yeah, I know, doll. But just for a few minutes, okay? I can't hear myself think, let alone talk."

"Besides, you've got two more stations to do on your routine. You shouldn't be stopping now. Always the business of business comes first with you, and the business of your health and body second." She spoke with a faint Scandinavian accent.

Camicci made a tolerant sound. "You're right, doll. But this is only going to take a few minutes, I promise. And I promise I'll finish the routine with some extra zip." He reached out and stroked a glazed thigh that looked as solid as a marble pillar. "Anyway, we both know the *real* workout is going to come a little later on, right?"

Uschi chuckled throatily. "Yah, always you manage time for that kind of business, don't you?"

"That's right. So be a good girl and go kill that music for a little bit. And while you're out there, bring me back one of those little cans of O.J. from the machine, why don't you."

After setting aside her dumbbells, Uschi obediently walked off toward the lobby area, where the controls to the sound system apparently were. No, she didn't just *walk* away—she sort of rippled and glided. She was clad in a pair of very brief suspendered leotards and an even briefer tube top around her breasts. The outfit left lots of creamy gold flesh exposed. Watching her in motion made me think of seeing wildlife films run at half speed, of horses or deer or jungle cats racing and leaping and plunging, their muscles flexing and stretching beneath sleek hides.

"Go ahead, boys, take a good look," Camicci offered magnanimously, as if we weren't already doing just that. "There goes a gal who's got muscles in places other broads don't even have places. And believe me when I tell you she knows how to use every one of them . . . every *single* one of them, if you get my meaning."

Earl guffawed and snorted like an amused ape in heat. "Oh, yeah, I catch your drift, Mr. Camicci. Uh-huh, boy, do I ever."

Crawford and I exchanged glances. His expression seemed to say, "Hey, I don't pick 'em, pal, I just work with 'em."

Camicci stood up and stepped over in front of me. In gym shorts and sneakers he stood about four inches short of my six-one. I made a mental bet with myself that when he dressed for the street he wore shoes with lifts in them.

"So, Hannibal," he said, "why do you think I sent for you?"

I looked down at him. "No idea. Maybe it was to show off your girlfriend's muscles." I inclined my head toward the still leering Earl. "It damn sure wasn't to show off your hired help."

Camicci smiled. "Kind of a smart mouth. That come natural, or do you work at it so you can sound like the P.I.'s in books and on TV?"

"The only thing I work at is my job. That what this is about, Camicci? You got a job for me."

Out in the lobby, Uschi cut the music. We stood and listened to it not play for a while.

Camicci grunted. "You already got a job, dustball. You think I don't know all about the Foxwood thing, for Chrissakes? Who do you think arranged for you to have all those nice, pretty police reports? But never mind that. It's what comes next I want to talk to you about."

I shook my head. "I don't get it."

"It's real simple. Whatever you uncover, whatever you pass along to that pervert Foxwood . . . *I* want to hear it first."

"Now I really don't get it," I said. "If you're the big behind-the-scenes man for the blue-movie operation, aren't you automatically going to hear everything I report?"

"Maybe. Maybe not. Point is, I want to be sure. I want to hear it from you and I want to hear it first." He was good with his eyes. He used them to demand what he wanted.

I exhaled some air. "I don't know," I said. "Man hands me money, outlines a job for me . . . he's the one I report to. Never did it any other way. And even though there may be some extenuating circumstances here, it still doesn't feel like the right time or place to start doing any different."

Camicci used his eyes on me some more. The glints of meanness I'd noted there before flared and crackled like stoked fires. He could be dangerous with those eyes and what went on behind them. Tension buzzed in the air, replacing the music.

Whatever he might have said or done next was interrupted by the return of Uschi with his can of juice. Wordlessly, Camicci took the container, peeled back the foil seal, tipped it high, and drained it in two or three big gulps. When he lowered the can, his expression had shifted to become shrewd—which didn't necessarily mean less dangerous.

"Let me show you something, Hannibal," he said.

Turning, he handed the empty can back to Uschi and told her, "Twist this in two."

The woman took the can in one hand somewhat uncertainly, almost gingerly at first. She studied it, then studied Camicci's face, then returned her attention to the can with a sudden intensity. She lifted her other hand and held the can by its ends between her two fists. She planted her feet a step and a half wider apart, took three quick, deep breaths, held the last one and rotated her fists in opposite directions. Tore the can in two as easily as you or I would snap a soda cracker. If that doesn't sound particularly impressive, stop to think that these little juice cans aren't made from the flimsy aluminum alloy that beer and pop comes in these days, but, rather, still from the old-fashioned, sturdier grade of metal that their big brothers *used* to be in. Me, I was impressed as hell.

Smiling, Camicci took the can halves from his obedient glamazon and said, "You did good, doll." He absently tossed the ragged pieces of metal to the carpeted floor then turned to the Universal machine, leaned over, and unpinned the weighted plates from the cable end of the pull-down apparatus he'd been using earlier. Straightening back up, he indicated the now free-hanging bar to Uschi and told her, "Now that. Bend the bar. Just a little. Then put it back."

Uschi was smiling, too, now. Like a happy child enjoying her favorite game.

She stepped over to the Universal and slipped the pull-down bar behind a portion of the main frame. Bracing her knee against the frame at a lower point, she then gripped the bar near its ends with both hands and prepared to pull it toward her and simultaneously against the heavy framework. Again the quick series of breaths, holding the last one, then the concentrated explosion of power. Muscles stood out on her back and arms like a living, breathing moonscape. The bar gave. An inch, then two. Uschi relaxed and exhaled. She stood for a moment, without turning, composing herself. Then she rebraced her knee, rotated the bar, and repeated the routine, only this time straightening the chromed tube.

She stepped back from the task, breathing hard, still smiling, a sheen of perspiration on her face and shoulders.

"All right, baby, all right!" Camicci said enthusiastically. He pulled the towel from around his neck and began patting Uschi with it. "Helluva show, helluva show!"

As he continued to wipe his pet, Camicci looked around at me. "What you just saw was an object lesson, Hannibal. What you might call one of Frankie Camicci's Object Lessons for a Longer, Healthier Life. You know exactly what it was saying to you?"

"I've got a pretty good idea. But I don't want to spoil your fun. Why don't you tell me?"

Eyeflick down. "The can. It didn't give, it didn't bend, so it broke. So now it's all busted to shit and no good to nobody for nothing." Eyeflick up. "The bar. It bent, then it bent back. It's still a useful thing. Next person comes along to use that bar, he don't know it bent, he has no problem with it. Everything goes on like normal." He paused. The towel was bunched around Uschi's breasts now and Camicci's hands on it seemed to be doing more than wiping perspiration. "It's that way in life," he went on. "You bend a little, you bend back, nobody knows the difference and everything goes on just fine. You try to stand too rigid, you get broke to shit and end up no good to anybody. See how it all fits together?"

"One thing wrong with your lesson, though."

"What's that?"

"The bar bends back and forth too many times, it develops a weak spot and winds up breaking and being no good anyway."

"So?"

I smiled. "That's the difference between people like me and

people like you, Camicci—when we're willing to bend and when we're willing to break."

He shook his head, dismissing my rhetoric. "I told you how I want it. You turn up something, you tell me. First. I got my reasons for wanting it that way, no council of Fat Old Mustache Petes is going to tell me my business. Crawford'll give you a phone number that can put you in touch with me day or night. Be smart. Use it."

10

Crawford and Earl took me back to my place. The drive from the Olympiad was short and made in relative quiet. Once Earl tried to strike up a conversation about what it might be like "to make it in the sack with a wild chick like that Uschi," but Crawford's and my responding silence got the message through even his thick head that we didn't want to hear it.

They dropped me at the front curb. I didn't say good-bye, and I sure as hell didn't say thanks. I walked across the frozen ground and stomped up the outside steps to my dark apartment. I was in a foul mood. I was tired, hungry. I already had a headful of problems over this damn case, and now I'd been threatened. By a sawed-off Mafioso and his muscle-bound girlfriend, no less. Suffering H. Christ.

I let myself in, snapped on some lights. The wall clock in the living room told me it was two o'clock. Tired of the same old grind, folks? Hey, be a private eye instead! Carry a snazzy plastic badge, meet fascinating people, be your own boss, make your own exciting hours. You betcha. Send money and box tops for details.

I flopped my coat over a chair, walked into the kitchen, and dug a can of Bud out of the fridge. I stood holding the door open while I took a long pull from the can, then leaned over to peer deep inside to see what else there might be that I could turn into a late snack. Not a hell of a lot. In the meat drawer, there was a dried-up slice of baloney in one plastic wrapper and a dried crust of liver sausage in another. On a higher shelf there were some eggs I could fry, but that seemed like too much trouble. I dragged out the packages of meat and carried them over to the counter. Remorsefully, I thought of Irma Silas and her homemade cookies and of the juicy ham sandwiches she'd passed around to the cast and crew during one of the breaks back at the farmhouse. For some reason I hadn't been particularly hungry then and I'd eaten only a part of one to be polite. Now I wished to hell I'd stuffed a couple extra in my pocket.

I slapped two slices of bread into the toaster, rummaged a knife out of the silverware drawer, returned to the fridge, and pulled out a tub of margarine and a jar with a couple garlic dills bobbing around inside it. Hell, I'd make a feast out of this yet. World famous, delicately aged baloney–liver–sausage spread on toast, with sliced gourmet pickles on the side.

It was when I was turning back to the toaster that I noticed the seam of light under my closed bedroom door. I stopped turning and stood looking at it. The toast popped and the cooling coils started making their funny ticking noise. I kept watching the light.

I don't read in bed; I don't get up before daylight. I hadn't had that light on three times in five years. And I never close that door. I live alone, so who or what would I close it to? And yet there it was. Door closed; light on.

I looked around the apartment, mentally replaying events of the past five minutes. The front door had been locked okay when I'd come in, everything looked in order, nothing else disturbed or out of place. Only the bedroom door shut and the light on. Not like they should be. Had they been like that when I first came in? Probably. I was just too busy feeling sorry for myself and worrying about getting something in my stomach to notice. Had someone been here, searched the place? That didn't wash. If they were pro enough to toss the joint and leave it looking this good, they wouldn't have flubbed two such obvious things. What then? Was someone still here?

I studied the band of light under the door. No flickering shadows, no sign of movement. No sound. Putting the margarine and the jar of pickles on the countertop, I stooped and drew the derringer once again from my boot.

I walked over to the closed door and stood listening. Still no sound. But smells—a couple that didn't belong. A hint of perfume, vaguely familiar. And something else.

I took a step back, then kicked open the door and went in low with the derringer raised and ready.

She was lying on her back in the middle of my bed, blankets pulled up to just below her collar bone, one shapely bare leg thrust out, foot dangling over the edge. She held a joint of marijuana in her right hand and was nonchalantly blowing smoke rings up at the ceiling.

We regarded each other along the line of the derringer's stubby barrel.

She smiled. "Hey," she said. "Quite an entrance. I appreciate a show of eagerness in my men."

I straightened up. The kicked-open door was quivering on its hinges and so were my nerves.

"What the fuck," I said, "are you doing here?"

Tiffany, the cool, coy errand girl/secretary/starlet of such fleeting acquaintance this morning, continued to smile up at me. Her dark hair was splashed across my pillow like a mini-oilslick.

"I told you we'd be seeing each other around," she said lazily. "And you promised me a cup of coffee. Remember?"

"I remember." I jerked a thumb, indicating the kitchen back over my shoulder. "Coffee's in there."

"Had an idea it would be."

"But you're in here."

"We're both in here. Now. Coffee's for morning."

"This is morning. Two o'clock in the, to be exact."

"Coffee's for the daylight part of morning. This is the time of morning for other things."

"Like what other things?" I wanted to know.

After taking a final hit of her grass, she reached to stab out the roach in a bedside ashtray. The movement caused the blanket to slip and one of her breasts peeked out. When she lay back, both breasts were exposed. They were small and flattened by her pose, but the nipples were high and hard and flushed a bright pink. She put her hands up to the sides of her face and ran her fingers through her hair. She wasn't smiling anymore. "You're the detective," she said. "Don't you have a clue?"

11

*H*er full name was Tiffany Angelique Traver. She was twenty-three years old. She lived in a very, very monied neighborhood on the city's northeast side.

I learned these things not from the young woman herself, but rather from the contents of her purse and other belongings as I rummaged through them in the postdawn hour while she still slept. As further testimony to the wealth implied by her address, I unearthed an arm-long string of local and national credit cards as well as three or four loosely wadded clumps of large-denomination bills stuffed carelessly here and there. Every article of clothing—right down to the handful of wispy underthings she'd carelessly dropped on the floor beside the bed—carried top-of-the-line brand tags. It made me feel extra seedy, squatting to examine them in my frayed and graying Fruit of the Looms. The photo section of the billfold contained numerous shots of a beautiful collie dog romping on a well-manicured lawn. On the back of one, penciled writing identified him as "Rex." There were two professionally posed portraits facing each other as the plastic compartments unfolded: one of a long-haired, fresh-faced girl who could have been Tiffany in her senior year of high school; the other of a stiff-faced, stiff-backed elderly couple with iron-gray hair and eyes that hadn't smiled in decades. Other items of note included a set of your basic but quite serviceable lockpick probes (explaining how she'd gained entry so unobtrusively), a baggie of what looked to be good-quality grass, a second baggie of coke (the favored drug of the idle rich, further evidence of her upper-class status), and a six-pack of condoms with two missing. I happened to be in a position to know the pack had been full a few hours earlier. I guessed the fact that it had been she who came prepared with such protection was a comment on both the times and our respective generations. Hell, I'd quit carrying rubbers in my wallet back when LBJ was still in the White House.

I walked out of the bedroom feeling like something of a heel. I wondered what Ann Landers would say about a guy who screwed and then secretly snooped through his partner's personal effects. I mentally defended it as professional thoroughness, but that didn't make me feel a hell of a lot prouder of it.

In the kitchen, the pot of coffee I'd set to brewing was ready. I poured two steaming cups. These I placed—along with a creamer of milk, a bowl of sugar, and a pair of spoons—on a large plate that was the closest thing I had to a serving tray and carried the whole works back into the bedroom.

My guest stirred slightly as I settled onto the edge of the bed beside her. I pushed back the covers to reveal a smoothly rounded shoulder, gripped her there, and called her name. She mumbled-grunted something unintelligible by way of response. I shook her a second time and got the same results. The third time I got her awake. She sat up with a start, sloshing coffee and milk onto the plate balanced in my lap. Her bare breasts shook with the sudden movement; her eyes whipped around, searching, uncertain. They finally settled on me.

"Oh," she said. "You."

I showed her a rueful grin. "Gotta say I've heard more glowing testimonials from pretty ladies who spent the night after showing up nude in my bed."

"You have, huh? That sort of thing happen a lot, does it?"

"Oh, all the time. All the time. Wonder you didn't get caught in a traffic jam."

"Uh-huh. Well, don't let it burst your bubble, big guy. Not even Tom Selleck would get a glowing testimonial out of me this time of day. . . . It *is* still morning, isn't it?"

"A little past daybreak, yeah."

She groaned. "Daybreak. . . . Jesus. Don't you sleep?"

"Between cases, sometimes. A bloodhound on the scent never stops to rest."

She groaned again. "Give me a break."

I held up my makeshift serving tray. "How about I give you a cup of coffee instead. . . . Our deal, remember?"

She scowled at me. "You're not going to let me go back to sleep, are you?"

"Not likely."

She sighed. It made her breasts do interesting things. "All right, give me some fucking coffee, then."

I gave her a cup, watching her stir in three teaspoons of sugar and a splash of milk. I took the second cup for myself, black, set the plate over on the nightstand.

"Tell me," I said after we both had some coffee in us, "How is it a classy young lady like yourself knows about picking locks?"

She gave a small shrug with one shoulder. "Chalk it up to misspent youth, I guess. They don't call us the idle rich for nothing. When you're young, you burn up a lot of that idle time learning things that are mostly ill advised. The higher up the social ladder you go, the juicier the skeletons in the closets are. The ability to pick locks—figuratively as well as literally—can be very enlightening."

"Spoken like someone who's spent considerable time on the higher rungs of that social ladder."

She drilled me with a flat, wry stare. "Come on. Tell me you didn't already know that much about me, tell me you didn't go through my things before you woke me up."

I felt myself flush a little. Then part of my mouth pulled into a lopsided smile. I raised my coffee cup in a mock salute. "Touché, Tiffany Angelique Traver."

She gave the one-shoulder shrug again. "No big deal. You wouldn't be much of a detective if you didn't do that sort of thing, would you?"

"I suppose not."

"That's what I'm counting on, you know."

"What's that?"

"You being a good detective."

"Uhmm. So I can get to the bottom of the murders, you mean."

"Well . . . that, too. Of course. But along the way, for strictly selfish reasons, I'm more interested that you determine who *didn't* have anything to do with the killings."

My head buzzed for a moment with the sensation of déjà vu. This sounded suspiciously like one of the opening salvos in my initial conversation with Henry Foxwood. "You want to run that by me again?" I said to Tiffany. "A little slower this time."

"Look," she said, "it's going to take me awhile to explain this. And I've got to pee something awful. Can I go do that? Maybe splash some water on my face, freshen up a little, maybe put something on? Then we can sit down somewhere and talk, okay?"

I was going to miss the view, but I made an expansive gesture with my hand. "By all means. Help yourself. The bathroom door isn't locked, you won't need your tools. Take your time. Make yourself at home."

While she was thus occupied, I carried my cup into the kitchen, refilled it, and got a cigarette going. I heard water running in the bathroom. I went back into the bedroom, dug out clean pairs of shorts and socks, pulled them on along with slacks and a T-shirt. I went into the living room and sat down to wait. Outside, the sky was filled with slowly tumbling gray clouds that seemed to be gradually, ominously darkening. I snapped the radio on to an all-news-and-weather station. In between bouncy Christmas jingles, I was informed that a major winter storm was moving into the area and was expected to be at full force by mid to late afternoon. State and local police were advising against travel unless absolutely necessary, and various organizations and businesses were already announcing cancelations and shutdowns. I figure that's one of the reasons people remain in the Midwest, putting up with its extreme weather swings. Mother Nature provides such a convenient scapegoat for simple frustration and anger (not to mention fodder for all the variations on "crazy weather we're having, huh?" that fill the gaps in so many conversations) and then, every once in a while, she can be counted on to really switch her ass and inject some genuine chaos and excitement into the otherwise numbing daily grind.

Tiffany reappeared after about twenty minutes. She came into the living room with a refilled cup of coffee and sat on the couch next to me. She had on the same short leather skirt she'd been wearing outside my office yesterday and a black blouse with embroidered collar and cuffs, not tucked in, not completely buttoned. No stockings, no shoes. She'd brushed her hair and applied some lipstick and spritzed herself with something that smelled awfully good and probably cost more per ounce than I make in an average week. She seemed brightened, fully awake and alert now, but I suspected that had more to do with a toot of the nose candy I'd run across than it did the revitalizing effects of soap and water or fresh makeup or caffeine. That was her business. She could afford the rhinoplasty that would be necessary one day soon when her nasal cartilage turned to Swiss cheese.

She bummed a cigarette off me. I lit it for her. She tilted her head back and blew smoke at the ceiling. "God, I feel almost human," she said with a sigh. "Do you suppose it's actually possible to make it through a day that starts before noon?"

"You'll live," I told her.

She rocked her head forward, turned her face to me, and nailed me with another sudden, direct stare. "Under the circumstances, that's a pretty brash statement," she said. "Can you guarantee it?"

She had a disconcerting way of cutting through the crap when it was convenient for her, but not necessarily expected. This time it was fine by me. I was ready to get down to it too.

"I'd say odds are with you," I replied evenly. "Depending on what you haven't told me yet."

She looked away. Smoked some of her cigarette, drank some of her coffee. A full two minutes ticked by before she said, "Have you ever heard of the Rev. Timothy Concord? Or the Church of the Almighty?"

I frowned over the names. "Vaguely. Another controversial preacher heading another lunatic-fringe religious organization. Based somewhere in this area. Can't recall exactly what it is they claim sets them apart from the rest of the pack. . . . They the ones who are supposed to be ultramilitant? Accused of burning down some abortion clinics and wrecking some massage parlors, that sort of thing?"

Tiffany nodded. "That's right. Their main church and organizational center is just south of here, near a small town called Paw Paw. Rev. Concord teaches—as do most Judeo-Christian ministries—that God is a gentle and forgiving god. But only to a point. Beyond that, Rev. Concord stresses that God is capable of great anger and even vengeance. 'Offend Him to the point of His wrath,' Rev. Concord teaches—and I'm quoting here—'and ye shall be smitten down with swift and terrible righteousness.' Unquote."

"Let me guess," I said. "Concord and his Church of the Almighty have set themselves up as the instrument to dispense this righteous wrath."

"Exactly. They see the world as pretty much fucked up beyond repair. The End, they feel, is very near. Either their actions will be the salvation of mankind or, if the Big Guy goes ahead and blows this whole ball of dirt to smithereens anyway, they will have earned themselves a special place at His side for whatever comes next."

"Okay," I said. "That fills me in on the good reverend and his bunch. What does any of it have to do with you or the murders that have taken place?"

She sighed. "I don't know how much you actually know about me. . . . It doesn't matter a whole hell of a lot, I guess. You can fill in the blanks from just about any TV soap opera or juicy contemporary trash novel. Spoiled little rich bitch . . . too much too soon . . . cold, self-involved parents . . . warped values . . . very little sense of self-worth . . . and on and on. Like I said before, too much idle time filled in ways that were mostly ill advised. If I had to sum up my life's accomplishments to date, I could do so very simply with one word: kicks. You already know about the movies I made with Foxy and his friends—those certainly weren't because I needed the money. It was just something I heard about and wanted to try—like hearing about a new drug and wanting to experience it. Understand? Anyway, about a year ago, during the week between Christmas and New Year's, something happened that made me . . . well, sort of reevaluate things. My very best friend in the whole world was killed in a car accident. I wasn't with her, I didn't pull her broken body from the wreck, nothing as dramatic as that. But I'd talked to her on the phone that afternoon and she was excited about a new guy she'd met and a knock-dead outfit she'd gotten for Christmas that she was planning to wear to a New Year's Eve party we were going to together and then"—she snapped her fingers with a sharp pop— "it was over. She was gone. Just like that. Things like that make a person stop and think, you know? You ask yourself what it's all about. Do you keep trying to cram in as many kicks as you can, because life is too damn short no matter how long it lasts? . . . Or do you reach for something bigger, something maybe everlasting?"

"So you reached in the direction of Rev. Concord and the Church of the Almighty."

"Yeah," she said bitterly. "Typical me . . . ill fucking advised right down the line. I decide to get religion, I pick the biggest bunch of whackos on the planet."

"How come? I mean, what attracted you to them instead of your family's church or at least one a little less radical?"

Tiffany made a helpless gesture. "One of those stupid things. On the night of Kelly's funeral—Kelly, that's my friend who died —I was out driving by myself. Just driving around, thinking, trying to clear my head, sort things out, you know? I was stopped at a red light when I looked over and saw this poster tacked to a telephone pole. WHAT IN GOD'S NAME HAS GONE WRONG? it said in big, bold letters. And then, below that, REV. TIMOTHY CONCORD HAS THE ANSWERS. He was speaking the next night at an auditorium, the poster went on to give the details. Something there connected. The mood I was in, the questions that filled my head . . . I was at that auditorium the next night."

"And after that?"

"After that, I don't know—everything sort of snowballed. It was like Rev. Concord had a magic button he knew when to press, knew how to say all the right words, all the things I needed to hear. I was totally captivated by him. In a matter of days, I'd moved into a dorm at the Paw Paw center. In my frenzy to cleanse myself, to be worthy, I repented. I confessed all my past sins, I gave details . . . I even named names."

"Bingo," I said, finally spotting the knot that tied all of this together. "You'd already gotten your kicks appearing in some naughty films by then, so you ended up telling Concord and his people all about Foxwood and the blue-movie troupe."

Tiffany's expression was grave. "Do you see my concern? In view of what happened to Jason and Valerie and given the Church's violent reputation—their 'smite now, ask questions later' attitude—I have to wonder if they didn't take the information I gave them and turn it into a kind of hit list for God."

"To be honest," I said, "that sounds a little far-fetched. Did you see signs that they're actually capable of action that extreme?"

She rolled her eyes. "Are you kidding? They have like a military complex out behind the church proper and the community center, and then a wilderness training area further back yet, where they stage maneuvers and mock invasions and stuff. That's what eventually turned me off from their whole scene. I could buy that the world is all fucked up, I could even accept that God has every right to get really pissed—but I couldn't quite swallow that the road to salvation is paved with spent M-15 shells and bazooka blast craters."

"How long were you with this church?"

"About three months. Their militant side was exposed to me quite gradually. In other words, I opened up to them a lot sooner than they did to me."

"How about when you made the decision to leave? How did they react to that?"

"Well, they naturally tried to talk me out of it. Tried to convince me to reconsider, told me I was taking a wrong turn with my life. But there was never what I considered any undue pressure. I mean, I never felt threatened or in danger. It wasn't like those cults you hear about where people are brainwashed and practically held prisoner."

"So this was—what?—seven, eight months ago, then, when you left them?"

"About that, yeah."

"And you figure it would take them this long to make a move based on what you told them?"

"Possibly. From what I saw, they plot their actions very precisely. Look, I know this whole thing may be a screwy notion— far-fetched, like you said. Maybe I'm overreacting out of guilt for dropping names or something. But, damn it, it also *could* be possible. It at least deserves checking out. I can't go to the police for all the obvious reasons that none of the others want to deal with them. But now that you're here, now that you've been hired, I thought you should know. I'm hoping you'll make it part of your investigation."

"Do Foxwood or any of the others know about you joining the Church of the Almighty?"

"Foxy knows I spent some time with them. I don't think anyone else does."

"Does he know everything you confessed to them?"

A quick shake of her head. "No. It won't be necessary to tell him, will it?"

"I don't think so. Have you done any more movies since your break with this church?"

"No!" This denial even quicker. Too quick. Even she sensed the unmistakably false ring to it. "Well . . . once, I guess. Yes, I did one more. Somebody didn't show up. They were in a bind. I did it as a favor to Foxy."

"Did you ever work with Jason Hobbs or Valerie Pine?"

"As a matter of fact, that last shoot I did happened to be with both of them—a three-way. It was just a couple of months ago. The recentness of it only adds to my concern over what was done to them. I'd worked with Jason before. That was my first and only time with Valerie."

"Did you ever at any point hear anything in regard to either of them—any remote thing—that could possibly connect to their murders? Arguments they might have mentioned, somebody they strongly disliked or mistrusted, somebody who didn't get along with them—anything at all like that?"

"Nothing. Nothing I can think of. Except Valerie's asshole ex-husband—I expect you've heard about him by now, though."

"Yeah. He's already being looked at seven ways from Sunday."

"What about the Church of the Almighty and the things I've just told you?" she asked earnestly. "Don't you think they rate checking out at all?"

"Hell yes, I do. Don't be put off by my skepticism. Occupational hazard. I fully intend to shake Concord and his bunch through my sieve, you can count on it. And I appreciate you opening up to me the way you have."

She looked relieved. "I'm grateful to finally get it off my chest. I suppose I should have told you yesterday when I delivered that package for Foxy. I'd been wrestling with the idea of talking to him about it, but I never could get up the nerve. Then when I heard about you and saw how rugged and competent you looked, well, you seemed like a better choice."

"What exactly is your relationship with Foxwood?"

Her expression grew somewhat guarded. "What do you mean?"

"I mean I'm having a hard time getting a reading on the guy, and it bugs me. He's trying to pass himself off as a sort of second-string flunky, but there are times I get the distinct impression he wields a hell of a lot more control over things around him than he's letting on. You seem fairly close to him. What's his real story?"

"You know," she said after some deliberation, "I never really thought about it before, but you're right. Foxy is very chameleon-like. You see him in one situation, he's one thing—change circumstances and he comes across completely different. Of course, he's seldom anything but dashingly sexy as far as the ladies are concerned. He's been a friend of the family for years. He and Father met through business dealings. I had a crush on him forever. When I was seventeen, he finally let me seduce him."

"How generous of him."

"Actually, in a way it was. It took place with candlelight and soft music and intimately whispered poetic phrases and a great deal of gentleness and caressing and of course physical expertise. . . . It was exactly the way a young woman *should* lose her virginity, but so few actually do. The sexual electricity between Foxy and me cooled shortly after that initial, beautiful consummation, but we've remained close friends. In a lot of ways, especially with Kelly gone now, he's about the best friend I have. When my appetite for kicks would get me in a jam I couldn't possibly turn to my parents for help getting out of, I could always count on Foxy being in my corner."

"Was he in your corner when you decided you wanted to 'experience' making X-rated movies?"

"Yes. But only because I badgered him into it. He let it slip about the movies once when we were together. Maybe he was bragging a little. But it wasn't like he was some sort of nasty Svengali who actively encouraged me to get involved."

"Uhmm. How would you describe his status with the movie troupe—how is he viewed by the rest of them as a whole?"

"Well, I guess you'd say he's sort of the elder statesman of the group. As far as I've ever seen they all seem to respect him and look up to him. Which isn't surprising, really. He's done it all, and he's done it in style. Most of all, he was—albeit for a very brief time perhaps—a genuine Hollywood star. That can carry a tremendous amount of prestige, you know, especially with a bunch like this. To the world at large they may be just a collection of sicko exhibitionists humping for the camera, but in their own eyes —most of them, anyway, I can't say I ever had any illusions along those lines—they are performers and technicians involved in exactly the same craft as the people who turn out network TV shows or legitimate movies. They choose not to dwell on *what* they are putting on film, but rather that they *are* filming and being paid as professionals in the process. They see these X-rated outings as a potential step to the big time. And Foxy is something special— someone who's already been there."

"Only he's moving backward—*from* the big time, not *toward* it," I pointed out.

"Nevertheless, he's *been* there. That's what counts. Fueling their dreams even further is the fact that more and more people are successfully crossing over from blue to legit. Marilyn Chambers did it. Traci Lords did it. Ginger Lynn—Rockford's very own contribution to X-rated superstardom—is in the process of doing it. Any number of writers, directors, and camera people have made it. The list goes on and on. Of course, most of this crossing over is being done on the coasts, you understand. The logical sequence would be to make the move from here to the X-rated scene in either New York or L.A. and then from there on to whatever. There's a girl in this local troupe, as a matter of fact, who may be doing just that within the next few months. Have you met Sara Baines yet?"

"No, can't say as I have."

"Sexy Sara, they call her. And not without plenty of justification. I mean, this chick is *hot*. In person, on the screen—she absolutely sizzles. Makes other females want to scratch her eyes out, makes every guy she comes in contact with go all bugfuck and butter-brained, you know? Hell, she has standing offers from two or three different West Coast video outfits who are ready to sign her exclusively to a series of productions with her top-billed under their banner. That's the part that makes me laugh when I hear some of these hairy-legged feminists raging about how degrading and demeaning our films are to women. They may not like what they see on the screen, but behind the scenes the porn biz has been a hell of a lot more lucrative for—and fairer to—females than just about any other industry you can name. And I don't mean just the actresses. Writers, directors—you name it. You got the talent and the drive, you get a fair shot. Anyway, getting back to Sara, the fact that all these West Coast outfits are panting after her out here in our Midwest cornfields should give you an idea of the kind of excitement she can generate."

"So what's keeping her around?"

"Believe it or not, the kid is determined to finish her education. One more semester and she'll have her RN's license. She wants to

have that to fall back on in case the other bit doesn't work out.
Plus she still has her hands full with Chuck."

"Chuck?"

"Her brother."

"Chuck Baines . . . big husky kid who helps Floyd Silas
around his farm and with the movie sets and so on?"

"Yeah, that's him."

"I met him yesterday. He looked plenty capable of taking care
of himself. How does the sister have her 'hands full' with him?"

"Oh, yeah, Chuck *looks* fine. Hell, he's a hunk. But emotionally
he's a mess. I don't know if I know all the details, just bits and
pieces I've overheard along the way. He was a hotshot college jock
somewhere—Michigan, I think—until he got caught in one of the
bigger drug scandals. Steroids and I don't know what all else.
Anyway, it ruined his college athletic career. While he was still
tailspinning from that, his and Sara's parents died tragically in a
fire. That really wrecked him. He's been staying down here with
Sara now for over a year, and you can see he's gotten a lot better.
When he first moved in with her, he was real reclusive—stayed in
his room in the dark, wouldn't hardly talk, wouldn't show his face
to anybody but Sara. Like that. But slowly but surely he started
coming around. I think this murder business set him back some,
though. I guess it hit especially hard since he and Sara were two of
the last people to see Jason alive."

"They were?"

"Uh-huh. Jason had gone over to their place to rehearse some
dialogue with Sara for an upcoming shoot. It was some time after
he left there and before he ever made it back home that he was
killed. You can see where that could be unnerving—to anybody."

"I guess. How about Hobbs's live-in girlfriend—this Rosemary
Karson? You know her?"

"I saw her around a few times with Jason. Can't say as I ever
actually got to know her. She stayed pretty much in the background, seemed awfully meek."

"Her and Hobbs get along okay? Ever any arguments, maybe
some jealousy over what he was involved in as a sideline?"

"Not that I ever saw. Or heard of. Whenever she was around
the set, she acted totally devoted to him and . . . well, sort of
proud in her own quiet way. Proud of her man, of his being a
celebrity and a center of attention, of his being a stud who was

attractive to others. I don't think she had any trouble with it at all."

I tried going at it from a different angle. "I keep hearing about Valerie Pine's crazy exhusband," I said. "But at the time of her death she was living with a Sandy . . . er . . . Cindy . . ." I patted futilely at my empty shirt pocket. My notes were in the other room and there were simply too many names flying around in this case for me to have them all committed to memory yet.

"Cindy Wallace," Tiffany finished for me.

"Right. Cindy Wallace. Last night I heard her referred to as a 'bitchy little dyke.' Quote, unquote. The implications are obvious. Know anything about that?"

"If you mean did I know Valerie and Cindy were lovers—yes, I did. I don't think it was any big secret. Technically, I think they would both qualify as bisexuals rather than flat-out lesbians. Certainly not dykes."

"Which would explain why they participated willingly for the camera with members of the opposite sex and why, in Valerie's case, she even tried marriage."

Tiffany shrugged. "Maybe. I think a lot of people who are confused about their sexual preferences—men *and* women—try conventional marriage as a means of denying what they fear as less acceptable yearnings. I suppose sometimes they actually make it work, other times it must drive them harder in the direction they feared in the first place. Who the hell knows? One thing I do know is that trying to figure out why anybody does anything when it comes to sex is a sure way to go batty."

"Sex and money," I said, grinning a humorless grin, "the two things nobody can ever seem to get enough of. But, damn, don't we all keep chewing up the landscape going after our share?"

12

*F*ive minutes after Tiffany was out the door, I was on the phone.

The case was unraveling in enough different directions, I'd decided, to warrant calling on some help in order to start tying off a few loose ends.

The first call I put through was to the news desk of the *Rockford Bulletin*. While I held, waiting for somebody to track down Chet Mundy, I reflected a bit further on my recently departed guest and her overnight stay. When you're looking back at forty and you've got a punched-around map like mine and a wallet that usually contains more pocket lint than dollar bills, you'd think you'd consider yourself lucky to have had the opportunity to make it with a lovely young woman and be able to just let it go at that. And a part of me could—the part that connects directly from crotch to brain. But another part—the curious, analytical part that causes me to wonder about things even when I'm not getting paid to, and tries to reason right from wrong—needed something more.

Tiffany had explained her view on the matter simply enough. "I hope you don't think," she said shortly before leaving, "that I came over here and slept with you just to get you to take a special interest in my problem. I mean, I *did* come to ask for your help. But the sex part . . . well, that just sort of happened. Slipping in the way I did made me feel pretty daring, and feeling daring somehow led to feeling horny, and then I got to remembering how you were attractive in a rugged, rough-edged, brute kind of way, and I was toking some good grass that gave me a warm, fuzzy, friendly buzz. And before I knew it I was in your bed, waiting, listening for you to come home . . . and I guess you know the rest. No need to read anything special into it one way or another. Let's just chalk it up to an unexpected, mutually pleasurable experience, right? Who knows, maybe we'll get together for coffee again one of these days."

So that took care of it as far as her slant on the thing. But I wasn't able to pigeonhole it quite so easily. While I'm hardly shy and retiring when it comes to sex, I have over the years developed at least the illusion that I require something above rabbit-level stimulus to go ahead and jump a given set of bones, no matter how fetchingly packaged. Yeah. Right. So how come, then, it had taken me all of eighty or ninety seconds to make the move from the bedroom doorway to a position between Tiffany's eager thighs? Had it been the dazzling degree of insight and intellect contained in the few dozen words we'd exchanged prior to that? And why hadn't her unsanctioned (not to mention illegal) entry pissed me off or at least made me more suspicious of her motives? The answers, I somewhat grudgingly concluded, stemmed from having spent a day and a half immersed in a sexually charged atmosphere, which had evidently aroused my libido to a point of near-spontaneous combustion. When Tiffany showed up to provide the final spark, my ensuing crotch fire had blazed beyond the dampening effects of any illusion or mere common sense. In other words, I'd proceeded in a fashion painfully familiar to mankind— I led with my dick.

"Hannibal," Chet Mundy's voice cracked in my ear, ending my introspection. "Don't you have anything better to do than to bother honest people who actually work for a living?"

"Must be some misunderstanding," I replied. "Guy I'm trying to get in touch with hasn't done an honest day's work since the teacher kept him after school to clap the blackboard erasers."

"Only teacher ever kept me after school tried to give me a different kind of clap."

"How poignant. That what turned you into a bitter, disillusioned muckraker?"

"Is that what I am? Darn, I thought I was a sensitive and insightful chronicler of the human condition."

"Sure you are. And I'm a practitioner of deductive reasoning in the interests of fair play and justice for all."

We had a chuckle over this exchange before moving the conversation along. Got the been-awhiles and the how've-you-beens out of the way, then finally got around to the meat of why I'd called. Before being promoted to regional editor, Chet had been the *Bulletin*'s hustlingest nonmetro reporter. He'd covered everything from the birth of two-headed calves to the tragedy of kidnapmurders to the rivalry between small-town high-school sports teams with equal enthusiasm and flourish. The flourish had earned him his promotion, the enthusiasm had won him the respect of many, many people in the outlying areas who were convinced their problems and/or accomplishments would have gone mostly ignored by the world at large had it not been for Chet's efforts. Because of this, he's retained a host of contacts out there and an abiding interest in even the remotest corner of the paper's circulation reach. And pity any reporter under him now who's inept enough to miss being on top of a story of substance in his territory. Chet and I met through the Bomber—during the summer months we both play for him on a softball team sponsored by the Bomb Shelter. We've called on each other's talents a number of times over the years, but are good enough friends not to have to keep track of who owes a favor to whom.

"What can you tell me," I asked, "about a religious outfit called the Church of the Almighty?"

"Let's see . . . that's the bunch centered down around Paw Paw, right?"

"Right. Headed up by a Rev. Timothy Concord."

"Uh-huh. Headed up by him and a band of would-be storm troopers wearing holy crosses instead of swastikas."

"That confirmed?"

"Confirmed enough for me. Way I hear it, about all Concord and his commandos for Christ are lacking is a division of air support. Hell, they've even got a couple urban assault vehicles—for the uninitiated, that's sort of a cross between a Winnebago and a Sherman tank."

"I know. I saw *Stripes* too."

"Oh? Bill Murray fan?"

"Warren Oates."

"Figures. So what's with the interest in the Church of the Almighty? We talking a story here?"

"Maybe, but I kinda doubt it. I've got a client having some

grief. Earlier this year she was associated with Concord's bunch and now she's afraid they might be coming after her and a few of her friends because of some things she confessed to them."

"And you, of course, can't reveal the name of this client or the exact nature of her grief?"

"You got it."

"No matter. I'd say it's a pretty safe bet that whatever your client's troubles are, the Almightiers aren't behind them. Six, eight months ago it could've been a different story, but these days the church is having enough troubles from within to more than occupy its attention."

"What kind of troubles from within?"

"The Christers and the Rambos, the two factions that made it such a unique setup in the beginning, are at odds. The main rift seems to be about money, with overtones of ideology. The Christers attract most of the contributions, while the Rambos are a little too eager to spend them on military hardware and razzle-dazzle. Each side is starting to chafe the hell out of the other. The Rambos contend the church is leaning too much toward being soft; the Christers contend it's leaning too much toward militancy —and Concord is standing somewhere in the middle with a lion's tail in each hand."

"And his dream coming apart at the seams around him."

"Something like that. Been no official confirmation that any of this is going on, mind you, but that's the word filtering out mostly through former Almightiers who are splintering away in disgust over the whole mess."

"Any chance Concord can somehow pull it back together and repair the torn seams?"

"Always a chance, I guess. But from the sound of things, I wouldn't put my money on it. I think a safer bet would be that either the whole thing topples or that it breaks apart into two distinct and separate groups: one a more standard paramilitary outfit, the other a more standard religious organization—neither likely to allow Concord's affiliation. I gather that both sides are viewing him as the incompetent who misled them into their miserable alliance in the first place."

"Maybe somebody decided they needed the right cause to reunite them. Maybe the harassment of my client and her friends is a last-ditch effort along those lines."

"Maybe. Can't say without knowing more exactly what your girl's grief actually is. But I'd still bet against it. Last I heard, the Church of the Almighty sounded to be in shambles pretty much past repair."

"You got a good stringer in the area?"

"Yeah, I got a real good kid down that way. He's the one been keeping me informed on most of what I've just told you."

"How about having him aim his newshound's nose in the direction of the church and give the whole thing one more good sniff on my behalf—see if he catches a whiff of any new or unexpected rumblings, anything that could be remotely connected to the problem I got here?"

"Sure, I can do that. He's been waiting for something to break. Maybe he's sitting on more of a story than we figured."

"Maybe. Get back to me ASAP?"

"Will do. Probably be a couple days, though. Say Monday or Tuesday."

"No problem. Appreciate it, pal. Say hi to Mitzi and the kids for me."

"Right. She's always after me to invite you over to dinner, so let's make some definite plans in that direction before much longer. I personally am not anxious to watch you wolf down a batch of my hard-earned groceries, but I am anxious to get you back down in the basement and exact my revenge on the Ping-Pong table."

"In your dreams, sucker."

"What I do to you this time is going to be a nightmare. You watch. Be talking to you."

My next call was to Benny Jewel's room at the St. George Hotel. Benny is a professional gambler. Cards and horses, in that order, are his mainstays; but over the years I've known him to put money on action as diverse as how many spots on a dalmatian pup to which way a drunk would fall when he toppled off his bar stool. Due to such extremes, his living accommodations have ranged from the city's poshest penthouses to park benches and doorways. Then one night when a round of high-stakes stud came down to just him and Huey Dettbecker, the owner of the St. George, Benny combined a bit of business sense with a bit of luck and bet ten grand against a rent-free room at the hotel for as long as the building stood. Huey, who was holding sevens over tens full and looking at three threes and a jack, went for it. Benny turned over the fourth trey and the St. George has been his permanent address ever since.

I was gambling a bit myself, hoping to catch Benny in on a Saturday morning. Weekend-long marathon card games are as common in his profession as tired feet are in mine. But I was in luck. He picked up on the third ring.

"Yo. Time's money, and I ain't got enough of either. Make this worth my while."

"Time is money," I said, repeating the words slowly as if savoring each one. "Now that is special, Benny. Hurry and write it down, why don't you? I think we might be talking an immortal utterance here."

"Who is this? That you, Hannibal?"

"What if I said my initials are IRS?"

"Yeah, this is Hannibal. Gotta be. Nobody else with a sense of humor that rotten."

"So how's it going, fella?"

"Slower than a brother-in-law reaching for a bar tab. Man, you wouldn't believe how tight some of the so-called high rollers in this burg start squeezing every penny when it gets near Christmas."

"Benny, Benny . . . methinks I detect a definite lack of the holiday spirit in your tone."

"You ain't wrong there. Show me a piece of hot action, though, and watch my spirits soar right up there with Santy Fucking Claus's."

"Action I got. But it's my kind, not yours."

"No offense, but your kind of action sucks street slush. The risks are way too high and the payoffs are way too low."

"So how about helping me knock the risks down a little on this one? I need some information."

"Come on, Joe. I ain't no snitch. You know that."

"I'm not looking for a snitch. I'm just after general information—gossip, if you will. The circles you travel in, I figure you're in a position to have overheard some stuff that might be useful to me. Nobody's asking you to put your ass on the line, Benny."

It was quiet on his end for several beats. I'd never put it into words, but I was counting on him to take my "ass on the line" remark as a not-so-subtle hint. A few years back, when his luck was running through a real bad streak and he was heavily into one of the local loan sharks, I'd stepped in and put the run on a couple of goons the shark had sent around to bruise Benny, maybe break a bone or two as incentive to come up with some money. It was strictly a reflex thing—I'd been staking out a building next to the alley where the goons cornered him and had been bored enough with stakeout duty to welcome the exercise. Within the week, Benny had gotten his luck turned around and settled his accounts before there was any more trouble. The shark made some noises in my direction, but never tried to follow through with anything. And if Benny still felt indebted to me for gaining him a reprieve in that alley, well, it was a sentiment I wasn't above taking advantage of when it suited me.

Benny sighed in my ear. "All right already. What is it you're fishing for?"

"Camicci," I said. "That's the name of a less than charming individual I recently bumped into in the middle of the night. What can you tell me about him?"

"Jesus Jumped-up Christ, Hannibal!" Benny exploded. "You know the name Camicci. Anybody with anything on the ball knows the name Camicci all through the Midwest—all through the country. And the first thing you learn after you hear it is not to fuck with it. Are you crazy?"

"A lot of people figure so, yeah. But that's not news. What's news to me is that Rockford has been honored with a member of the Camicci family apparently in residence. What's the story?"

"Yeah, yeah, Jesus, talk about having your ass on the . . . okay, the charmer we're talking about here is young Frankie, right? That'd be one of Antonio's boys—his youngest—and nephew to Frederico. Way I hear it, the kid's always been a handful. Real aggressive, short-fused, not much respect for tradition or authority—that type. Guess he sees himself as a real-life Sonny Corleone or something. Anyway, like I said, he's always been a handful. And after old Antonio faded out of the picture, it only got worse."

"Frederico Camicci's reputation isn't as someone who puts up with much guff."

"That's true enough. But the thing is, see, in this case it's the baby boy of his late, beloved brother. That seems to make a difference in Frederico's flinty old eyes. One of his *own* sons he'd slam into shape damn quick. But with the nephew he keeps making allowances."

"So where does booting him out our way fit in?"

"You know about Frederico being out of the country, right?"

"No. I don't recall hearing anything about that."

"Well, he is. Back to the old country—Italy, Sicily, whatever. Been away from Chicago going on a couple months now. For the record, he's visiting what family he has left over there, mainly spending time with his mother who moved back after the father died a few years ago. She's in her nineties now and too sick to travel and not expected to live much into the new year. Strictly off the record, there are some pretty heavy rumors of one, possibly two federal investigations tightening down on the Camicci action and it's even money right now that Frederico might choose to keep viewing this part of the world from a safe distance for a time even after dear old Mom kicks."

"So who's minding the store while he's away?"

"His oldest son, Albert."

"Uhmm. Still doesn't tell me what landed Frankie in our laps."

"When Camicci started to make his overseas plans, he decided to take a . . . a . . . whatyacallit, like a retinue of some of his oldest cronies along with him. One of the first ones he invited was Tornello, who's been the Chicago Syndicate's main man in our area for years. When Tornello accepted, it was decided to send Frankie out to fill the hole his absence would make, to oversee operations while he was away. Maybe or maybe not just incidentally, this also served to get Frankie out of the immediate Chicago vicinity—where his attitude has rubbed plenty of people the wrong way and where, without Frederico around to be his buffer, he might get rubbed back."

"We aren't all that far away from Chi-town," I pointed out.

"It's more a state of mind than a matter of miles. Besides, Tornello's territory reaches all the way to the Mississippi. Through him—Frankie now, at least for the time being—the Camicci arm of the Syndicate has its finger in every adult-book store and X-rated video outlet and magazine rack and rubber-vending machine between here and East Dubuque."

"And every dirty movie being made, too," I muttered.

"What's that?"

"Nothing. Never mind. Listen, Benny, thanks for clueing me in. I appreciate it. It was important I know exactly where this Frankie was coming from."

"You steer clear of him, you hear, Hannibal? Little prick is dangerous enough all by himself, and on top of that he's connected up the gazeekus. You don't want to mess with him and his family nohow."

"When I met him, he had a couple trained mongrels with him. One a black guy named Crawford, the other a balding bag of air called Earl. Any reading on them?"

"Crawford is cool. Plenty dangerous, don't get me wrong—but in a cold, professional kind of way instead of crazy and unpredictable like Frankie. Crawford was Tornello's right-hand man for years. I figure they're probably counting on him to have a stabilizing influence over Frankie—but you can only depend on that up to a certain point. I don't know about nobody named Earl. But he sounds like one more reason to steer clear of Frankie, all the same."

"You're starting to sound like a broken record, Benny. How about humming a few bars of *them* staying out of *my* way?"

He was quiet for a few seconds, considering. Then: "That just ain't the way the tune goes, man."

13

Nine o'clock found me seated behind the desk in my drafty old office, munching the last of the two Egg McMuffins I'd picked up on the way over, washing them down with hits from a carton of Ronald McDonald's chocolate milk while I waited for a fresh pot of coffee to brew.

Considering my lack of respect for my own business hours (you can count on the fingers of one hand the number of times I show up before noon during practically any given month—even though this made two mornings in a row), I've often reflected on the question of why I even bother keeping an office. The walk-in trade it attracts is minimal, and the extra squeeze it puts on my wallet the first of every month when I have to wring out two rent payments is damn sure no bargain. I keep the office, I've concluded, because having it locks me into at least some semblance of a routine and forces me to be more organized than I otherwise likely would be. It's where I do my best thinking, where I have the most luck mentally sifting things through and rearranging events and motives until I find an order that suggests some answers.

That's what I'd come to the office for now, to try and draw matters concerning the case into sharper focus and then decide on a course of action aimed at gaining answers instead of only more questions. Yesterday's visit to the farm—although I wasn't ruling out the option of returning there—hadn't been as productive as either Foxwood or I had hoped for. Starting my investigation there, with a number of the key players who'd been involved with Jason and Valerie gathered in one place, had seemed like a good idea. But the activity level, the tension, and the minimal amount of privacy for any one-on-one discussions all had combined to create an atmosphere not very well suited to the way I operate. I was like an old lion stalking a herd of wildebeest, seeking to cut away just one or two to work on rather than hurl myself ineffectively at the whole herd.

With the McDonald wrappers cleared and a brim-full cup of coffee puffing steam at my right elbow, I returned to the files Foxwood had provided. I fanned the photos and detail sheets out in front of me. The faces and names—even of those I hadn't met yet—had become much more real, their fear more palpable, my concern more genuine. For the duration of the case, they would be a part of my world and I a part of theirs. If nothing else, my time at the farm yesterday had established that much.

I began rearranging the individuals in the file into various patterns. First I tried grouping them in a sort of natural order, putting together those who clearly or allegedly belonged together, separating those who didn't. The sheets and photos on Foxwood and Tiffany, for instance, went together in one stack; the data sheets (no photos) on Dorfman and Blyth, the two technicians, went together in another; Chuck Baines (no photo) and his sister, Sara (whose accompanying glossy was a real eye-scorcher that more than backed up her "Sexy Sara" tag), went together in a third. And so on and so forth. For those who hadn't been included in Foxwood's file but who, in my opinion, belonged in the overall scheme, I scrawled names on sheets of loose-leaf notebook paper and inserted them accordingly. Floyd and Irma Silas formed a stack by themselves. I wrote out the name of Belinda Davies, the breathtaking and mysterious director, and combined it with the file sheet and photo of Angie Mullond because of the alleged special interest shown to the aspiring fluffer. I also wrote out the names of Frankie Camicci, Crawford, Earl, and Uschi and placed them in a stack of their own.

By the time I was done, I had nine groupings arranged before me. Eight of them contained two or more individuals who interacted in some specific way outside the shared orbit of the rest. The ninth stack was a kind of leftover collection of those who didn't seem to fit with any of the others except in general relationship to the movie making. Prominent among these was the acid-tongued blonde who nowadays called herself Kat Hayward.

So what had the exercise accomplished? After refilling my coffee cup, I leaned way back in my creaky old swivel chair—carefully balancing the cup in the process—and pondered that question. My eyes shifted from one slender pile of papers to the next as I mentally ticked off each name contained in each stack. Was one of them the name of the killer? Or more than one?

My eyes swung back to the Camicci pile. It seemed a safe enough bet that Frankie had taken life in his time, even if his direct participation was only to snap his fingers and let others do the actual bloody work. Others like Crawford. Or Earl. Maybe even Uschi. Thinking about the trained amazon triggered recollections of the coroners' summary reports following the Hobbs and Pine autopsies. In each case it had been pointed out that the strength necessary to perform the murders in the manner described—strangulation and repeated deep stabbings through heavy muscle and bone—suggested a powerful individual, most likely a male of above-average size and strength. Or, I mused, a lethally muscled female freak. But intriguing as that line of thought might have been, it didn't make a lick of up-front sense. What would Camicci and/or the Syndicate stand to gain by snuffing the two performers? And if they *had* done them, they sure as hell wouldn't sanction the hiring of somebody like me to look into it and even grease my way with police reports and all the trimmings. There was, of course, some niggling uncertainty about last night's wee-hours ultimatum—but even that wasn't enough to make me bite. When professional hitters do somebody, they either do it neat and tidy or they splash it up to send a specific message. What had been done to Jason and Valerie couldn't be crammed into either category. Whatever it was, I felt reasonably sure it wasn't the work of Camicci or his crew.

I rocked forward in the chair, reached out for the Camicci stack, picked it up, and set it off to one side. I stayed hunched over the desk, pressing the coffee cup between my palms while I eyed the remaining stacks. After about a minute, I reached out again and plucked up the data sheets for Dorfman and Blyth. These I laid on top of the Camicci group. Then I did the same with the loose-leaf sheets I'd written out for Floyd and Irma Silas.

Thinning the herd.

I wasn't shutting the door completely on these individuals, merely relegating them to back-burner status. For the time being, my instincts told me they were neither likely suspects nor promising channels for any leads to the real killer(s). This whole routine was intended to narrow my focus and provide a viable alternative to the scatter-gun approach I'd employed yesterday.

All told, I pored over the desktop full of papers for a solid half hour. I set aside one more stack—the "leftovers," even though Kat was included there and I had the feeling I'd be talking with her again on one pretext or another. Whatever else she might or might not be, though, I couldn't buy her as a murderer, and her association with the rest of the movie troupe seemed a bit too distant to expect she'd have much to offer in the way of significant insight into any of the others.

Of the five stacks that remained, the two I felt held the greatest potential were the two most directly connected to the victims. Included here were Rosemary Karson, Jason Hobbs's live-in lover at the time of his death; Barry Grainger, Hobbs's co-worker both on the construction crew as well as on some of the movie sets, and who at last report was looking after the bereaved Rosemary; Cindy Wallace, Valerie Pine's roommate/lover; Buck and Lois Ingram, who reportedly had introduced Valerie to the blue-movie scene (and subsequently to Cindy) and had remained close friends with her; and, last but by no means least, Cindy's much-maligned exhusband, Boyd.

My gut feeling was that if the killings were, in fact, something other than coincidental random acts of violence, then some kind of key to the motivation behind them could be dug out of this bunch. Trouble was, while I could—based on the various situations as I knew them—conjure up a number of possible scenarios to account for either of the two murders by themselves, the thing I couldn't come up with was a common motive that might link them. The only possibility that came close to fitting that criterion so far was Tiffany Traver's suspicion that the Church of the Almighty had perhaps embarked upon some sort of lethal purging campaign. And although I had Chet Mundy and his people checking that out, I didn't really hold much hope of it amounting to anything.

Find the common denominator, I told myself, find your killer.

I spent another handful of minutes transferring necessary addresses and so forth into my pocket notebook, then drained the last swallow of cold coffee, stood, and got ready to quit the office. Before I went, though, there remained one further piece of business that needed tending to. From the bottom right-hand drawer of the desk, where it rested within the folds of a lightly oiled rag, right behind the emergency bottle of Old Crow, I lifted my trusty Government Issue .45 automatic. It felt good in my grip, heavy and solid and reassuring, like a comforting pat from the callused palm of my grandfather when I used to turn to him as a young man with what seemed like the weight of the world on my shoulders. The callused palm was no longer there, but the .45 had never let me down yet. The boot derringer was comfortable and inconspicuous, preferable to lugging the big iron around every day and adequate for close-quarters emergencies—but when I had a feeling in advance that shit was getting ready to hit the fan, it was the .45 I reached for to be my umbrella. And that's exactly the way I felt right then. With a killer's spoor wafting somewhere out ahead of my twitching snout and Syndicate hoods paying midnight visits and armed religious fanatics and crazy exhusbands lurking on the fringes, it had to be just a matter of time before I stepped in the thick of it.

I carried the piece over to the closet, where I took a shoulder holster off one of the books. I shrugged into the rig and socked home the .45 under my arm. It felt almost as good there as it had in my fist. I pulled on my coat, loaded some extra clips into the pockets. Then I headed for the door, whistling through my teeth the familiar refrain of "Jingle Bells." Only the words I sang along in my head went: "Jingle bells, shotgun shells, bullets in the air . . ."

14

Loaded with preparation and resolve and rattling with arma-
ment, I nevertheless had a personal base to touch before getting
on with the business of the day's detecting. Outside, the storm
clouds that filled the sky had grown denser and darker, but less
turbulent. They hung heavy and still and dirty gray. Made me
think of loosely packed clumps of fiberglass insulation. It was like
looking up at the underside of an old refrigerator.

I drove from my Broadway office, cut up Seventh Street, and
turned toward the river on State. At this time of morning, I had
no trouble finding an empty parking slot on the Bomb Shelter's
block.

Liz was there, as I knew she would be. She opens the doors
every morning at ten, even when she pulls extra night duty, as she
was doing all this week while Bomber's regular night bartender,
Old Charley, was away for the holidays. You never know when
the Bomber is going to show up, and even after he does he tends to
drift in and out during the daylight hours like an elusive breeze on
a hot day. Today I was hoping he wasn't around, and it looked
like I was in luck. Liz and I seemed to have the place to ourselves.

From where she stood behind the bar slicing limes, she looked
up as I entered. She had a smile for me. "Well, well, will wonders
never cease. Good morning, bright eyes."

"Morning back," I said, sliding onto my regular stool.

She made no further reply, instead leaning out to peer intently
over my shoulder toward the door.

"What's the matter?" I wanted to know.

"I figure somebody must be chasing you," she said, craning her neck, continuing to peer past me with burlesque exaggeration now. "That's the only reason I can think of that would roust you up and about so early."

I made a face at her. "Ha ha. Very funny. You just don't appreciate what a dedicated businessman I am."

She smiled again. "You said a mouthful there."

"Look, can a fella get some service around here or only verbal abuse?"

"We got service up the ying yang, mister. What'll you have—cup of coffee?"

"No, I'm coffeed up for the time being. How about a big glass of tomato juice? Splash in some Tabasco and tequila to make it more interesting."

Liz had the concoction in front of me in a jiffy. "So," she said, "nobody saw you around last night and now here you are at an unexpected hour. You in the middle of a hot case or what?"

We were speaking in somewhat hushed tones. An empty barroom in the daytime can do that to you sometimes—can take on the same sepulchral echoes and sense of awe you hear and feel in a church. Which isn't as odd as it might sound. Booze is a powerful god to a lot of people.

"I'm in the middle of something, all right," I replied to Liz's question, making my voice purposely bolder than it had been. "Something that could have some real heavy personal lines attached to it."

She leaned against the bar from her side, stacking her fists and propping her chin on the top one. Locking on mine, her eyes became very earnest. "Sounds serious," she said. "Want to talk about it?" The words caused her head to bounce on its chin rest, shaking the loose, dark curls that framed her face. For once I didn't even try to sneak a peek down her cleavage.

"Guess I do," I said. "Guess that's what I came for."

I took a hit of my laced tomato juice, then reached for a cigarette. When I had one going, I said, "You remember Kath Howard, don't you?"

Liz's mouth pulled tight. "Jesus, yes. How could I forget?"

"Yeah. Well, I ran into her yesterday."

"I thought she left town."

"So did I. I guess she did for a while. But she came back."

"She's not looking for Bomber, is she?"

"Not that I know of. . . . Think I should tell him I saw her, though?"

"What in the world for?"

"Because she *is* back. That's the whole point. She has no reason to hide out, you know. What if they run into each other somewhere—even if it's weeks or months from now—and it comes out she's been around all this time and I knew it but didn't tell him. You know how he can get."

Liz scowled. "Mmmm. Yeah. I see what you mean."

"But that's not even the worst of it."

Her eyes asked me what the worst of it was.

I took a long drag on the cigarette. "She said something about having been working the Canadian strip circuit," I said, getting rid of the words in a cloud of smoke. "I don't know if she's doing any stripping around here or not, but I do know one thing she for sure is doing around here—and that's performing in porno movies."

Liz looked puzzled. "You mean doing her strip act on video?"

"No, that's not what I said. Watch my lips. I mean she's fucking on video."

Liz straightened up so she had room to let her jaw drop. "Holy shit. Are you certain, Joe?"

"You don't even want to *know* how certain I am."

Further discussion of the matter was interrupted by the front door opening to allow entry to a couple of yuppie salesmen wearing narrow ties and glossy wingtip shoes. They swung their briefcases and blow-dry haircuts proudly and the determined set of their jaws indicated they were hell-bent on earning a matching set of alcohol ulcers by the time they were thirty. They took seats in the booth by the front window—the one that's covered by a heavy blue velvet drape at night when the dancers are on—and Liz went over to take their orders. I couldn't hear what they said, but I made a mental bet with myself that they'd each order a martini, with specific instructions as to how it should be mixed. I watched and, sure enough, when Liz went back behind the bar she reached for the gin, vermouth, and olives. You can always tell a yuppie. You just can't tell them much.

Liz returned after she'd finished serving the newcomers. She leaned conspiratorially close and said, "You mean that kind of thing—making screw movies—is actually going on right here in Rockford?"

"Sure is," I told her. "The video boom has made it an industry adaptable to just about any place—so what's the matter with Rockford? Haven't our city fathers been telling us for years that we're a thriving community of great potential and we needn't settle for a backseat in anything?"

"Somehow I don't think this is what that bunch of tight-assed conservatives had in mind."

"Tough. It's what they got. Whether they know it yet or not."

Liz smiled a nasty little smile with only half of her mouth. "Good ol' Kath. I always knew she was a slut. I just didn't realize how big of one."

Unexpectedly, I discovered that the bluntness of that remark bothered me. It put me on the defensive—not just for Kat, but for the troupe as a whole. The conclusion that anyone who participated in such a thing was automatically a slut or some kind of low life—a conclusion, I realized somewhat stingingly, I myself might not have been above reaching only a short time ago—seemed suddenly cold and narrow and unfair. I felt as if I'd gotten to know some of these people, even to like some of them a little. Don't get me wrong, I held no compassion for any of the connected jerks, the Camiccis or any of the rest from that side of it; and God knows I myself didn't have a very high opinion of Kat. What I was thinking of were the ones Tiffany had tried to explain about, the Angie Mullonds and those who were willing to try the X-rated route as a means to something bigger and better. What we're all after. Whatever their reasons for doing what they were doing, it shouldn't instantly demote them to some substrata of the society. Were they hurting anybody? Were they forcing anything on anyone? When it came right down to it, were the ones who put the dirty deeds on the screen any worse than those who watched and fantasized—either actively or passively—along with them?

This storm of reactive thoughts rolling through me must have shown on my face because Liz drew back slightly, frowning, and said, "What's the matter?"

"Nothing," I replied tightly, not meeting her gaze, not wanting to get into it right then, not even fully understanding the sudden inner spurt of liberalism. I pulled an ashtray over and stabbed out my cigarette. Hard. "Look," I said, "I don't give a rat's ass about Kat or any—"

"Who?"

"Kat. It's what Kath calls herself nowadays—Kat Hayward. It's some kind of stage name or something."

"Oh. La de dah."

"Yeah, yeah. Whatever. Look, I don't give a rat's ass what anybody calls themself or if the city fathers all have a collective shit hemorrhage if they ever hear about the porno movies or any of the rest of that. What I'm worried about is the Bomber. We all know what a tailspin he went into before over this broad. I don't know how he'd act just knowing she was back in town. Finding out she's back *and* what she's doing . . . well, I just don't know."

Liz looked grim. "I get where you're coming from. Bomber never has had a lick of sense when it comes to women. Enough time has passed that the big dumb chump might want to forget all about the heartache she caused him and just remember the good stuff. And if he learned about the movies, it'd be just like him to decide she needed saving and his forgiveness would be exactly the thing to do the trick."

I groaned. "That's one I never thought of."

"Well, you'd better try it on for size because it doesn't sound too far-fetched to me."

One of the yuppies called across the room and Liz left to serve them another pair of martinis. While she mixed, they resumed talking between themselves with lots of hand gestures and finger-pointing for emphasis. As before, I couldn't hear what they were saying, but twenty to one they were using the hell out of words like *demographics* and *market saturation* and *consumer profile.* I decided they looked like the types who'd rent X-rated videos and then whack off to them alone because their stuffy country-club wives wouldn't stay in the same room while they were playing such filth.

When Liz came back, she said, "One of us has got to tell him. Everything."

I sighed. "Yeah, that's pretty much the way I see it."

"You want to do it?"

"Hell no, I don't *want* to do it. Do you?"

She chewed her lip. "It wouldn't be something I'd look forward to. But he might take it better coming from me, don't you think?"

"Absolutely. No doubt about it. It's settled then. You handle it. Let me know how it comes out."

"Wait a minute. I didn't say I would."

"But you pointed out he'd take it better coming from you. And that's a hundred percent correct. I'm the guy who got knocked on his ass the last time I tried to tell him about that crazy chick, remember?"

"He'd never hit a girl, would he?"

"Never."

"But he might still throw a fit. Might holler the building down around us."

"Might holler the whole block down."

"You tell him."

"Hold on. How did I lose so much ground all of a sudden?"

"Your original question to me was whether or not I thought you should tell Bomber that Kath—or Kat or whatever the hell she's calling herself—was back in town. So now I'm saying yes, I think you should."

"Devious, Liz. That's what you are."

"You going to tell him?"

"Have I got a choice? What are friends for?"

"You know, he might not take it as bad as we expect. He might be all over her. Might just say, 'Who cares—to hell with that lousy bitch.' "

"Sure, Liz. And those two dildoes over there"—I jerked a thumb to indicate the guys in the booth—"might wake up tomorrow morning and say fuck it to their ties and briefcases and go down somewhere and apply for a job where they can get real honest dirt under their fingernails. Come on, give me a break. I don't know exactly what Bomber's reaction will be, but it damn sure is going to be more than 'Ho hum, who cares.' "

She showed me a sympathetic smile. "You'll be back by here later then?"

"Yeah. Sometime. Unless I get lucky and step in front of a truck. Then it falls to you."

"Like a wounded cavalryman passing on the colors, huh?"

"Something like that. You'll be around?"

"I'll be right here."

"To pick up the pieces."

"Don't I always?"

15

I had two addresses for Buck and Lois Ingram—one for their home, one for their place of business. They ran a combination exercise studio/tanning salon out on North Main. This being Saturday morning and the business address being the closer of the two from where I was, I decided I'd take a shot at finding both Ingrams at work. I drove across the river and turned up North Main. As I rolled away from downtown, with the sky threatening everything darkly from above and the shoppers on the sidewalks burrowing their faces into the warmth of their upturned collars while puffing visible gusts of breath out into the freezing air, I thought about the logic of people from the Midwest trying to maintain a tan in the middle of winter. But then I'm one of those palefaces who never seems able to work up a good tan no matter what the circumstances or time of year, so maybe it was just envy on my part.

The Trim 'n Tan shopfront was a bank of reflective goldtinted glass sectioned by flat chrome bars and framed by cream-colored fake brick. Standing between a steamy-windowed Sudsy Duds laundromat and a poster-choked Video Planet video-rental store, its gleaming facade was by far the most impressive of the half dozen businesses that shared the small shopping center about thirty blocks out. I parked my battered and splattered Honda over in front of the laundromat so as not to unbalance the visual status quo.

Inside, some sort of upbeat Muzak—what sounded like disco Henry Mancini—was playing. A pretty young woman wearing bronze skin and a sprayed-on T-shirt smiled at me from behind a blond walnut counter and said, "Good morning. How may I help you?"

I gave her my name and asked if either of the Ingrams was in. She informed me that Lois was conducting an aerobics class and that Buck was somewhere in back. Was I expected? I told her not necessarily, but that I was pretty sure they'd be interested in seeing me. I handed her one of my business cards, one of the classy embossed ones with only my name. She bade me hang on a sec, then disappeared with the card through a gold terrycloth curtain.

I stood in the waiting area and waited. There were a couple chairs to sit in, but I decided to tough it out. I took off my coat and hung it on the stainless-steel coat rack. It stirred the fronds of a potted palm that crowded close to the rack. Over on one end of the counter there was a three-foot-high ceramic Christmas tree with little lights that blinked on and off. Puddled around the bottom of it were folds of white angora sprinkled with what looked like the glittery stuff you put on cookies. I shook my head in wonderment. Blond walnut, disco Mancini, plastic palms, ceramic Christmas trees, and electric Hawaiian tans in Illinois in December. Is this a great fucking country or what?

Buck Ingram brushed aside gold terrycloth and came out smiling with his right hand extended. "Mr. Hannibal. We didn't get a chance to talk yesterday, but it's good to meet you."

I had no trouble recognizing him as the older, huskier of the two guys who'd been part of the foursome frolicking for the camera last night. He was good looking in a swaggering, lantern-jawed kind of way, with steady gray eyes, a rakish smile, and a hard grip.

After we shook, he said, "Why don't you come on back to the office? We can talk there."

I went around the counter and followed him into a narrow hallway. The smiling bronze girl with the sprayed-on T-shirt politely held aside the curtain for me. There were doors with rectangular window panels on either side of the hall. As we passed them, I saw that each opened onto a low-ceilinged exercise room with brightly colored little mats scattered about on the floor. In one of the rooms, the copper-skinned, marvelously curved Mrs. Ingram was leading her aerobics class. The pulsating music that seeped through was definitely not Mancini.

Over his shoulder, Ingram said, "I'm sure Lois will want to join us. I've left word for her to come back as soon as she's finished there."

The office was a small, square room, unpretentiously cluttered. A number of advertising brochures were tacked to the wall over the desk. On one of the chairs and on the floor beside it were stacks of health-and-fitness magazines. Most of the wall directly in back of the desk was taken up by poster-sized blowups of Buck and Lois posing in minimal amounts of swimwear.

"This interrogation bit is all new to me," Ingram said, dropping into a high-backed chair behind the desk and throwing a leg up across one of its corners. "So you're going to have to go ahead and take charge. Have a seat, have a seat. Helluva bad thing about Valerie and Jason. I'm really glad they brought somebody like you in on it."

"First of all," I said, "this isn't an interrogation, Mr. Ingram, it's—"

"Hey, hey," he interrupted. "Make it Buck, for crying out loud. Just Buck. Mr. Ingram is my father, right?"

I shrugged one of those if-you-say-so shrugs. Then, getting on with it, I said, "I understand you and your wife were good friends with Valerie Pine."

"That's right. Real good friends. Used to be good friends with ol' Boyd, too, until he went loony-tunes on all of us."

"Boyd—that would be Valerie's exhusband?"

"Uh-huh. The two of them went through a helluva nasty divorce. That's when Boyd got . . . well, the way he got. We stayed close with Val after that, but no way we could have anything to do with Boyd."

"I keep getting references to Boyd. The word *crazy* comes up a lot and now you just said he went 'loony-tunes.' But I've never really heard any of the specifics. Can you tell me what brought about their divorce, what made it so nasty?"

Ingram grunted. "Yeah, I can tell you. Matter of fact, I can tell you probably better than anybody you could've asked. You see, in a manner of speaking, Lois and I were the cause of their breakup."

He waited, apparently for dramatic effect, wanting some kind of reaction out of me. I cocked one eyebrow sharply to show my interest.

Satisfied, Ingram went on. "You've got to go back a couple,

three years, back to before Lois and I had this place. We were both holding down two jobs, squeezing pennies in order to someday be able to start something like this. Lois was teaching a phys. ed. course at one of the colleges and holding aerobics and dancercise classes four nights a week. I was working as a mechanic at Poffo Imports and giving judo and weight-training lessons on the side. We've both always been interested in our bodies, see, striving to be fit and look good. Anyway, one of the other mechanics at Poffo was Boyd Pine. Like guys sometimes do at work, we got to be sort of half-assed buddies. He was about my age, in fairly decent shape, and he showed some interest in my judo and stuff. He kept pestering me we should take our wives and the four of us do the town some night—I'd shown him one of my wallet shots of Lois in a bikini, see, and I figured he secretly had the hots to meet her in person. So we went out a time or two, the four of us, and the women hit it off good and I saw that Val wasn't exactly a bowzer —although in the beginning she needed to work a little harder with what she had—and everything was cool, right? So I got to feeling pretty relaxed around Boyd and one day somewhere in there I let out that me and Lois were into swinging. You know about swinging, don't you, Hannibal?"

"You mean as in organized mate-swapping?"

"That's the ticket. Right. You see, another thing Lois and I both believe is that an important part of looking good and feeling good and keeping your body in top shape is to give it a plenty active sex life. And we're both mature enough and reasonable enough to recognize that—considering the brain is such an important erotic tool—no two people, no matter how well suited or physically attracted they are to each other, can completely sexually satisfy one another in the long run. The mind wanders, right? You think I don't appreciate and thank my lucky stars every day that I got a dynamite-looking wife with a great body that puts tent poles in the shorts of every guy she meets? But the point is, when you're married to somebody like that, regardless of how great they look or how willing and talented they are in the sack, you reach a point where you realize *it's the same fucking person every time.* You start to wonder how a different set of titties would taste, how it would feel to slap your nuts against a different pair of ass cheeks even if they aren't as firm and perfect. You start to get sick of hearing the same little squeals and pet names when you're trying to drive home that payload stroke. And on and on. It's only natural. People trade their cars on a regular basis even when there's nothing wrong with the one they're driving, TV shows get popular and then fade away, fashions come and go, we all try different foods even though there are always a couple dishes in particular that remain our favorites. See what I mean? What isn't natural is to be attached at the groin to just one person for your whole stinking life. Even guys married to movie stars, for Chrissakes—Raquel Welch, Cybill Shepherd, whoever—you think they don't get the itch? They probably go to the supermarket and ogle the behind of the little teenybopper at the check-out counter. And I'll tell you, every bit of that works exactly the same way from a woman's end of it too."

He paused, maybe to catch his breath. His rhetoric wasn't really anything new or startling. I'd caught similar spiels everywhere from on "Oprah" to overhearing a horny barroom drunk putting the hit on somebody else's wife with closing time coming down fast.

I said, "I take it you explained all of this to Boyd Pine?"

Ingram nodded. "Yep, I did. Of course, he didn't need a lot of persuading. He'd been married long enough to have felt the itch and understand where I was coming from. He got real interested real quick in everything I could tell him about the swing scene. He was interested enough in the whole concept, I guess, but I could tell that one of the biggest attractions to him was the thought of getting a shot at my wife. But then, hell, how could you blame the guy for that, huh?"

"So Boyd and Valerie ended up joining your swing circle?"

"Uh-huh. Eventually they did. It took a while to convince Val to give it a try."

The office door opened at that point and Lois Ingram came in. She shone with perspiration and carried a short towel across the back of her neck, both fists gripping its ends. She was indeed a lovely woman, face vibrantly flushed, eyes and smile brilliant. Her generous curves were displayed by a soaked leotard of pale orange that somehow made her seem more naked and exciting than she had looked last night completely in the raw.

"Hey, babe," Ingram said. "Good session?"

She shrugged. "A session's a session. The best part is always when it's over."

A gesture in my direction. "Hon, this is Joe Hannibal, the detective we've been hearing about."

She cranked up the wattage on her smile for my benefit. "Mr. Hannibal. Didn't I see you out at the farm last night?"

"That's right," I answered. "I, uh, saw you, too. I'd hoped to have a chance to talk with you and your husband. But you were both busy and it got pretty late. I decided to come on back to the city and make it another time—this morning, as it turns out."

"Yes, the shooting did run awfully late. It was enjoyable, though, wasn't it, Buck?"

"No complaints here," Ingram said. Then his mouth curved in a smug grin. "Well, maybe one. I made such a pig out of myself on Bessie's titty milk that I'll probably have to go on a diet after this weekend."

"Don't be crude," Lois scolded. She smiled at me again. "I think he's trying to shock you. Are you easily shocked, Mr. Hannibal?"

I shook my head. "Not hardly. Surprised once in a while. But seldom shocked."

"Yes, you look rather shockproof."

"I was just telling Hannibal about the Pines," Ingram informed her. "About how we turned them on to swinging after Boyd kept pestering me."

Lois nodded, remembering. "Yes, it all seemed harmless enough in the beginning. And for a time it actually seemed to be working out well. Too bad it turned so shitty."

"That's the part we were getting to," I said. "What happened? What made it turn shitty?"

"What made it turn shitty was Boyd's attitude. His attitude was fucked right from the start, I suppose, but none of us had any way of knowing that until it was too late and he started showing he couldn't handle it."

"Couldn't handle what? The swinging?"

"That's right. Oh, he liked it fine as long as it was his idea and he was getting his jollies and Val was just sort of going through the motions for his sake. But then he had to deal with the change. She started getting into it, started liking it as much as he did—"

"Started liking it more, in my opinion," Ingram put in. "I made it with that girl the first time she swung and I made it with her plenty of times after. She was like a colt blossoming into a beautiful race horse. At first she was sort of wobbly and nervous, then before you knew it she was the hottest ride on the track."

"One of the hottest, thank you," Lois said pointedly.

"Hell, babe," Ingram replied with another easy grin. "No comparison. You ain't a race horse, you're a damn rocket ship."

I said, "So that's what broke up the Pine marriage? The fact that she got too involved in the swinging and he couldn't handle it?"

"That sure as hell put a big chink in it," Ingram said. "Ol' Boyd lit the fuse but flat wasn't prepared for the explosion."

"It was more than *just* the swinging, though," Lois added. "Val changed in a lot of ways. She became more confident in so many areas, more knowledgeable, more outspoken. She even changed her appearance. She was always a pretty girl, but after she and Boyd started hanging out with our swing crowd she put more into herself. She changed her hair and her makeup for styles that suited her better; she started attending some of my exercise classes to firm up her body. She switched to a better-paying job, as a cocktail waitress. And at one point she was checking into the possibility of taking some liberal-arts courses at one of the colleges."

"So Boyd found himself living with a Frankenstein monster he'd helped create but no longer could control."

"A very attractive Frankenstein monster, but I guess that's one way of looking at it. I suppose that's the way he saw it."

"It's been suggested," I said, "that Valerie had some lesbian tendencies. Specifically, that the girl she was living with when she was killed—Cindy Wallace—was her lover. Do you know anything about that?"

They both nodded. "Sure," Lois said. "Everybody knew Val and Cindy were lovers."

"Did Boyd?"

They exchanged questioning glances. After a hesitation, Lois said, "I'm not sure. I suppose so. They were divorced by then, of course, but he kept coming around, kept bothering her. I think he had to know what the relationship between Val and Cindy was."

"When Val's bisexual tastes became apparent, see," Ingram offered, "that was the straw that broke their marriage apart beyond any repair. It was already on awful rocky ground, no doubt about it, but me and some of the other guys were working with Boyd, talking to him a lot, trying to help him get his shit together inside his head. Only when he saw how Val was really getting into other chicks . . . well, no way could he hack that. No way at all."

"Then Valerie's bisexuality started with the swing group?"

"Oh, yeah. That's common enough. Not so much for the guys —not in any of the clubs we've been in anyway. But the whole thing about swinging is heightening your sexual awareness. What better, gentler, more thorough way for a woman to explore her feelings and her sensations than to experiment with another woman? And if you've never tried it, let me tell you, man"— Ingram spread his hands expansively—"a threesome with two chicks who've worked themselves into a frenzy and then you come in and everybody goes over the edge together—damn, there ain't nothing like it."

"I'll take your word for it," I said.

"Ooo," Lois pouted. "I'm sorry to hear that."

"Let's stick with Boyd and Valerie," I suggested. "You've indicated their divorce was messy and you also said that afterwards he kept trying to see her, kept bothering her. Did he ever physically harm her?"

Again the exchange of glances. Ingram shook his head. "No, not to amount to anything. I guess he maybe shoved her a couple times when they were still living together—you know, like she'd go to walk out of the room when they were arguing and he'd push her back away from the door. I suppose she got some bruises that way, but he never hit her or anything. His favorite thing after they were separated got to be he'd go out somewhere and get drunk and start feeling sorry for himself then go to her place and stand out front throwing shit at her house and calling her names and accusing her of filthy things until he'd roust the whole neighborhood and somebody'd finally call the cops. He took to drink awful bad, lost his job at Poffo and a half dozen more after that. Got to be a pretty sad case."

"Sad, my ass," Lois spat out. "He got what he asked for. He wanted to dip his pecker in all the pretty pussies and have all the fun he wanted, and was even willing to serve Val up as some sort of sacrificial offering to ease his conscience. But what the bastard wasn't willing to do was let her have any fun out of it. Everything would have been fine if his pitiful little ego would have been able to stand that one thing. Can anyone really blame her for turning away from men?"

"Do you think he could have killed her?" I asked.

"No," said Ingram.

"Yes," said his wife.

"I see you've discussed this calmly and rationally between you," I said.

Ingram shrugged. "Noting to discuss. She's got her opinion, I got mine. The police couldn't find anything to hold him on. If he was going to kill her, why now—why wait so long? They've been divorced almost a year. Like I said, he never even laid a finger on her."

"You also said," Lois reminded him, "how badly he took to the booze. That's what did it. That's what put him over the brink, in my opinion."

"Did Valerie ever have any trouble with anybody else that either of you know of?" I said. "Any arguments, any serious disagreements over anything?"

Twin headshakes. "No," Lois said firmly. "She was a well-liked girl, very friendly, very even disposition."

"You said she got a job as a cocktail waitress. Could anything have happened there? Trouble with one of the patrons, a drunk maybe? Maybe a flirtation—real or imagined—with another woman's husband?"

"No. Nothing like that. She only worked there a short time. Boyd came around too often, made too many scenes, got her fired."

"Did Boyd know about the movies she made?"

"No way," Ingram answered. "Nobody'd be dumb enough to trust Boyd with knowledge about the movie troupe. And damn sure not after Val got involved in it."

"Could she have told him herself? Maybe she threw it up in his face during an argument—you know, taunted him with it?"

"No, I can't see her doing anything like that. Besides, I don't think they hardly talked anymore, not even to argue—not for months. Like I said, he mostly just came around when he was drunk enough to want to cause a commotion."

"How did Valerie get started with the movie thing?"

Lois said, "Well, through us, actually. About a year or so ago, you see, Buck and I began getting a little turned off by the swing

scene—or at least not as turned on by it. I suppose the trouble
with Val and Boyd had something to do with that. And then there
was the disease issue, the growing AIDS scare. All of a sudden it
didn't seem like entirely harmless, healthy fun anymore. And yet
at the same time we both knew we wanted—needed—something
more in our relationship, some extra zing in our sex lives, some
added spice. Making movies for Foxwood and his people sounded
like a possible solution. Buck had heard bits and pieces about the
movie troupe, enough to know who to put out some feelers
through. We met with them, they liked what they saw, we found
their offer exciting, and within weeks we were before the camera.
It was great. At first we'd intended to just have sex with each
other, to get our kicks out of the exhibition angle, being on camera. But when we became more familiar with the whole setup, we
changed our minds quick enough. Attractive, sexually talented,
and energetic people to work with; regular medical checkups—
arranged and paid for by the backers—required of everyone; tremendous stimulation to our personal egos and exhibitionistic tendencies. It was a dream package. And we got *paid* for it to boot."

"That's what caused us to bring it to Val's attention," Ingram
put in. "After her separation and divorce, she was in a damn tight
squeeze financially. No decent job, no settlement because Boyd
had pissed away everything with his drinking. When we heard on
the set one day they were looking for new performers, we thought
of Val right away. She was attractive, she was uninhibited. She
worked out great."

"And it was through the movie troupe she met Cindy Wallace?"

"That's right," Lois confirmed. "Odd as it may sound, there
was a certain amount of satisfaction for us in that. Let's face it,
after being instrumental in their joining our swing club in the first
place and then having things fall apart between Val and Boyd like
they did, we felt somewhat responsible—guilty, even. So seeing at
least Val begin to make a fresh start, with Cindy . . . well, that
was nice. Their relationship might not have been one a big portion
of society would understand or approve of, but it was making Val
happy, working good for her and Cindy both."

I considered for a long moment the shiny promise of fresh starts
and the dream-smothering grayness of sudden death. Whatever
she had or had not been, Valerie Pine had at least deserved the

right to go after her own happiness. We all knew what she found instead.

I cleared my throat and said, "How about Jason Hobbs? How well did you know him?"

Ingram made a gesture with his hand. "We knew him fairly well, I guess. Nothing like Val, of course, but well enough. Worked with him maybe a half dozen times."

"Jason was a dream to work with," Lois said. "He had a really huge cock, you know. But he never used it like a battering ram, the way some guys will. Oh, he was plenty proud of it, made sure it got all the attention he felt it deserved, but he was confident enough in himself that he would always be gentle, always play to the camera *and* to the sensitivities of his partner. That was the thing about Jason, he was very professional. He wasn't only in it for the sex, he wanted what ended up on the screen to be just right, to work the way it was supposed to."

"You ever play any team sports?" Ingram asked, somewhat unexpectedly and, as it turned out, rhetorically. "You know," he went on, "how you'd have your coaches but then you'd also usually have one or two guys on the team who were so damn dedicated and sincere—maybe not even your best players, but so fucking intense—they'd drive everybody else to play harder and better? Well, that's how Hobbs was, how he came across. Like an on-field captain. Christ, he'd help with the sets, he'd help lug lights and shit around, he'd let you rehearse your lines off him. When you worked around Hobbs, you went in sharper and better prepared than you might otherwise. You took it more seriously when he was around."

"So did any of this come off as pushy or irritating? Did he get along with everybody okay?"

"Oh, hell yeah. Couldn't help but like the guy. He was real popular."

"He and Valerie must have worked together, right?"

"Sure. I can't say exactly how often, but I knew they did some things together, yeah."

"And they got along okay?"

"Just fine as far as we ever heard."

"Can you think of anything out of the ordinary they might have shared? Something that might have happened while they were together, or at least both in the same general vicinity?"

Exchanged glances, then headshakes. No, nothing.

"Either of them do drugs?"

Lois shrugged. "Some grass, I suppose. I know Val did. More so after she hooked up with Cindy. I can't say for positive about Jason, but I'd guess about the same. Neither of them could have been into anything hard or it would have shown up on their tests. Foxwood and his backers won't allow heavy druggies in the troupe."

"What exactly is Foxwood's capacity in all this?"

They both appeared to give the question serious thought. "Well," Ingram said at length, "to go back to my team-sports example, if Hobbs was the on-field captain, then Foxwood would be like a player-coach. Sometimes he's in front of the camera, sometimes he directs, sometimes he dabbles in the writing. Sometimes he's just . . . *around,* you know? Overseeing things for the backers, I guess."

"And who do you figure the backers are?"

Ingram chuckled. "Come on, man, who do *you* figure the backers are? You're taking their money, too."

I sighed. "This whole thing keeps going round and round like a roulette wheel and the little silver ball keeps showing up in the slot that says Valerie and Jason were friendly, likable kids that nobody had a grudge against. Yet they're dead. Murdered. That isn't supposed to happen to the kind of people they've been painted as being. Either somebody isn't leveling with me or it's beginning to look more and more like they were both wasted in exactly the kind of coincidental, unconnected acts of random violence that nobody wants to accept."

"So what's your point?" Lois wanted to know. "*We* aren't holding out on you. Why would we?"

"We don't want to accept their deaths *period,* man," Ingram said. "They were two free spirits, living life to the hilt."

"Why—because they fucked a lot?"

"It was more than that. Don't make it sound cheap and dirty. You had to know them. If they were killed randomly, then that's bad in one way and we have to deal with it. If their deaths were connected, then that's bad in another way and we have to deal with it, but we also have to deal with the fact that there could be danger out there for the rest of us in the movie troupe."

"So what's your gut feeling? Which one are you instinctively dealing with?"

"I already told you," Lois said, "that I think Boyd might have had something to do with what happened to Val. But I don't see how any of that could connect to Jason's death."

Ingram shook his head. "I still can't buy Boyd Pine as a killer, leastways not of Val. With or without him, though, I agree as far as not seeing any link in the two killings."

"Have either of you ever heard of the Church of the Almighty?" I asked, really scraping the bottom in my bag of questions. "Has anyone representing that organization recently been around to your home or place of business or maybe paid a visit to some other member of the movie troupe that you heard about?"

Lois frowned. "What is it, some kind of religious outfit?"

"Well of course it is," Buck said. "The Church of the—whatya think?" He made a disgusted, phlegm-clearing sound in the back of his throat. "No, Hannibal, none of them Bible-thumping, goody-goods has been anywhere near me in a long damn time. I think they got some kind of grapevine among themselves and word has spread to steer clear of Ol' Buck. Last time any *did* come around, see—and this was years ago—me and Lois was in the middle of a marathon fuck session. I'm talking a real rip-snortin', upside down, inside out, all-weekender. So, anyway, I took time out to throw something on and answer the door and when I saw who was there and what they wanted, I whipped open my robe and waggled my red, drippy, half-hard schlong in their faces and told them if they could please bless that sonofabitch and keep it stiff for one more charge down the valley, I'd buy a whole case of their Bibles and be singing their praises in church next Sunday. They left me the Bibles okay, but they never did come back and they never even sent me a bill. Last I saw of them, they were on a dead run like the Devil himself was biting at their asses."

Lois was laughing out loud by the time he finished. "He did that," she affirmed. "The crazy fool really did."

I stood to leave, out of questions and suddenly very weary of the company I was in. I told them I could find my own way out, then paused at the door, and added, "I'll be around. You have my card. If you think of anything that might be helpful, I'd appreciate it if you got in touch."

But they were scarcely paying me any attention. They looked like they wanted to get in touch all right. With each other. Lois was still laughing, leaning back against her husband, who was beaming down at her, his chest swelled arrogantly, proud of his retelling and prouder still of the initial incident and proudest of all that his wife found the whole thing so delightful. I had the feeling they were about to replay the "marathon fuck session" part as soon as I was out the door. Maybe sooner, if I didn't hurry. Charming couple. They made me think of simple-minded, self-indulgent children who saw nothing wrong with publicly scratching their private parts or belching or farting or even evacuating themselves—no matter the circumstances, as long as it made them feel better to do so.

16

Number 1031 Arthur was a small, cottage-type house in a fringe neighborhood on the city's northwest side. It sat a ways off the street in the lowest point of a large, bowl-like lot. A half dozen huge, bare old elm trees surrounded it in a ragged circle, shading it (from nothing on this overcast day) and making the cottage seem even smaller by their hovering presence. A restlessly prowling German shepherd was chained to a doghouse out back. He watched me cross the snow-crusted front lawn, but didn't bark until I raised my right fist and rapped on the door.

The woman who answered my knock was short, middle thirties, with closely clipped brown hair, unfriendly eyes, and a cold, thin-lipped mouth. Through the frost-caked glass of a storm door that remained closed (and, presumably, locked), she said, "If you're selling, I ain't buying. If you're collecting, I ain't paying. If you're polling, I ain't got an opinion. What else?"

"I'm looking for somebody."

"That's different, at least. Who?"

"Young lady by the name of Cindy Wallace. I was given this address, told she was staying here." I held up one of my business cards. "I'm a licensed private detective. I believe Miss Wallace has been advised I'd probably be around."

Behind the glass, the brown-haired woman looked like she'd bitten into something sour. "Shit," she said. "This is about that little Pine cunt who got herself offed, isn't it?"

"Is Cindy here?" I asked patiently.

"She's staying here, yeah. But she's not in right now."

"Could you tell me when you expect her back?"

"I could. Not saying I will."

"Why not?"

"I don't want you bothering her."

"My intent is not to bother her. I only want to ask her a few questions about Valerie Pine. Cindy might know something that could help my investigation."

"If she knew anything she would have told the police by now."

"Maybe she knows something she doesn't realize she knows."

"That doesn't make any sense. You implying Cindy's some kind of idiot?"

"That's not what I said."

"It's what you implied."

We glared at each other through the fogged storm glass. "You're going to make this as tough as you can, aren't you?" I said.

She smiled. "That's the idea."

"I suppose stepping inside for a minute is out of the question?"

"You suppose right."

In the backyard, the German shepherd was still going at it, a monotonous, deep-throated growling bark accompanied by the slap of the chain he dragged back and forth. He seemed to be expressing a sentiment toward me that echoed his mistress's attitude.

I said, "Lady, is there some particular reason you feel you have to treat me like dirt?"

"I don't like you."

"You don't even know me."

"I don't like the look of you all the same. Most of all, I don't want you bothering Cindy. Like I already said."

"With Valerie's killer still on the loose, did it ever occur to you that Cindy may be in some degree of danger?"

"Nobody needs to worry about Cindy. I'll take good care of her."

We regarded each other through the glass some more. "So," I said, "that's the way it is."

Her eyes were a challenge. "That's exactly the way it is."

"If I decide I want to talk to her badly enough, I will. One way or another."

"Maybe. But I'm still not going to make it easy for you."

"You've already accomplished that much."

I turned and walked back across the lawn toward my Honda. The dog continued to bark.

I heard the creak of the storm door opening, and the brown-haired woman called to my back: "Come around here again and I'll sic the fucking dog on you."

17

*F*reshly deflated by the encounter with Cindy Wallace's house-mate (I never even caught the brown-haired woman's name) and already wrung out from my session with the hedonistic Ingrams, I found myself feeling suddenly very tired, feeling every minute of lost sleep from the night before.

I swung onto Kilburn and headed back downtown. The noon hour traffic was heavy with weekend workers on their lunch breaks, scrambling to squeeze in a burger and a beer and maybe a quick stop at the market or dry cleaners before returning to their six-days-a-week grinds. I spotted a Kentucky Fried outlet and got in line in the drive-thru lane. At the little window, I paid for a pile of nuggets, a side order of fries, and a jumbo Coke, then pulled around and parked in a far corner of the lot. I left the engine idle, its breath warming the interior of the Honda. Outside, a wind was starting to gust, nudging at my little car, rattling the bare branches of the trees that edged the parking lot. I spread my fare on the passenger seat beside me and began tossing down chicken nuggets. Every other one I dipped in mustard sauce. I worked intermittent handfuls of fries and hits of Coke into the routine.

While I ate in solitude, my grogginess deepened. The whisper of the heater vents and rocking motion of the car only served to lull me along. A couple times I caught myself chewing with my eyes closed. I tried not to think about the case, tried not to think about anything. The result was a crazy, totally disconnected mishmash of remembrances and imaginings staggering in and out of my fuzzy consciousness, the reassemblage of which probably would have scared the Freudian crap out of any right-thinking psychoanalyst as well as myself. When the meal was done, I shoved the empty containers back into the sack they'd come in and wadded the whole works into a handy throwaway ball. Then I dropped the back of my seat down (another of the Honda's convenient features), laced my fingers across my stomach, and lay back with my eyes closed.

If I were a more complex or pretentious person, I might try to pawn off what I was about to do as a form of meditation or modified yoga or some such. What it was, folks, was a catnap. Given the kind of screwy schedule I keep, this wasn't the first time I'd been hit by an attack of the drowsies at a low point in the middle of the day. I learned a long time ago that, rather than attempt to slug on through, I was better off when at all possible to give in, grab some quick, concentrated shut-eye, and climb up out of that low point the easy way. It's amazing what forty winks— almost literally—can do. The trick is to go after them in a spot where you can totally relax for a brief time but not be comfortable enough or segregated enough to risk it stretching into prolonged slumber.

Whatever the physiological or psychological particulars, it usually works for me. It has in the past and this storm-threatened Saturday was no exception. At about the nine-minute mark, I was roused by an old pickup running straight pipes that tore into the parking lot with all the unobtrusiveness of a freight train. I snapped awake, sat up, reached to readjust the seat. After a second or two of disorientation, I came back on line, only refreshed and more alert.

I cut the Honda's engine and got out. The cold bit into me. Carried the throwaway bundle over, dropped it in a trash can alongside the building. Went in, used the Colonel's facilities, washed my hands, splashed water on my face, ran a comb through my hair. Bought a cup of black coffee at the counter and took it back to the car, feeling like a new man.

Onward.

The game is afoot, Watson, and all that jazz. . . .

The first light flakes of snow were drifting down by the time I pulled up in front of Barry Grainger's duplex. It was centered in an upper-middle-class block of Twentieth Street, just off Charles. Lots of half-brick housefronts, wood trim painted soothing pastel colors, strings of Christmas lights draped across hedges and front-lawn fir trees.

Parked in the Grainger driveway was a year-old, powder-blue Cadillac with gleaming whitewalls, chrome spoked wheels, whip antenna, and vanity plates that read STEEL DREEMZ. A 747 grounded in the same spot would have been only slightly more conspicuous. Look up *pimpmobile* in the dictionary and it might very well show a picture of this car.

I left my Honda at the curb and walked up a neatly shoveled sidewalk becoming powdered by the new snow. At the front door, I thumbed the bell button and stood waiting, not able to keep my eyes off the Cadillac. Its being there bothered me. No way it belonged. And yet I knew Rosemary Karson, Jason Hobbs's girl-friend, had a history of prostitution and I knew she was supposed to be staying here—the chance to talk to her being one of my main objectives in coming over. But that still didn't answer the question of why the pimpmobile was on hand. Did its presence indicate Rosemary was considering returning to The Life? And, if so, what skin would that be off my nose, why did I find the prospect so troubling?

I punched the button a second time. There was more than snow flakes in the air. Something was causing me to feel restless and edgy. The house seemed strangely quiet, unresponsive.

I checked the storm door. Finding it unlocked, I pulled it open and knocked hard on the inner door. Maybe the bell was broken.

I gave it a full minute. Still no answer. Swearing under my breath, left with little choice but to accept that there was no one at home, I was starting to turn away when the noise came from inside: two brief outcries—one of sharp pain, one of desperation—followed instantly by the rattling crash of what sounded like light furniture and glass being broken. One of the cries, the desperate one, was distinctly female.

Some decisions make themselves. Without conscious thought, without any choice, really, we sometimes suddenly find ourselves in the middle of something—reacting—and no one is more surprised by what we're doing than we ourselves are. It's a kind of instinct, I guess, but not necessarily one of self-preservation, not necessarily one that is at all healthy.

What I found myself in the middle of doing—reacting to what

I'd heard, minus any deserved deliberation—was throwing the storm door wide and ramming my shoulder full-force against the inner door behind it. The door gave with a loud splintering pop and my momentum carried me through, stumbling, skidding to one knee, left hand outstretched to maintain balance, right cocked into a fist.

The scene in the Grainger living room looked like something posed for the cover of one of those gaudy true-crime magazines. Not counting me, there were four people in the room: two men, two women. Off to my right stood a huge Oriental-looking slob with a drooping mustache, a mouth curled into a sneer, and dangerous slits for eyes. In his grasp—one arm wrenched up behind her back in a hammerlock, her throat clutched by a bearlike paw—was a stunning ebony-skinned woman. Her own eyes blazed with equal parts fury and fear. At their feet were an overturned wooden stand and the shattered remains of a small aquarium. Gasping fish flopped on the floor amid glass shards and broken bits of pink porcelain sand castles. Straight ahead, sprawled on her back half-on and half-off an overstuffed maroon couch, lay a dark-haired young woman in jeans and a black blouse that had been ripped open to reveal full breasts heaving within lacy bra cups. Hovering over her—left foot planted on the floor, right knee driven between the girl's legs, one hand pinning her at the collarbone and driving her head and shoulders deep into the maroon cushions—was a lanky man clad all in studded black leather. His bone white hair jutted away from his scalp in sharp spikes. Ruddy, pock-marked flesh pulled tight across a gaunt face. Inverted crosses and pentagrams dangled from his pierced ears.

The tableau seemed frozen obligingly before me for several beats. In truth, my sweeping gaze took it all in in a fraction of a second. The only sound was the thud of my pulse and the frantic wet slaps of the scattered fish on the floor.

And then the spike-haired one spoke. "I don't know who the hell you are, mister, but you picked a *real* bad time to come calling."

I stayed on one knee but straightened my upper body, recentering my balance. In the same motion, smooth and easy, I reached my right hand across my chest and hauled the .45 out from under my coat. "That's right, porcupine," I said, "real bad for you."

The Oriental grunted and said something that sounded like "Fuck."

A disdainful grin split the lower half of Spike Hair's narrow face. He beamed it at me. "That some kind of magic gun that can shoot two different directions at once? It better be. You start that kind of shit, man, me and Ho gonna both be all over you like stink on shit."

"Nothing magic about the piece. It only shoots where I aim it." As I said this, I angled the barrel of the .45 in the general direction of his face. "In case you're interested, I believe in taking off the head and letting the asshole void itself."

The grin stayed in place. "Hear that, Ho? I think he just called you an asshole."

The Oriental grunted again and this time he definitely said "Fuck."

"I suggest you let go of the ladies and back off," I said.

It was Spike Hair's turn to grunt. "Shit, these two bitches ain't ladies. They never even been in the same room with a real lady."

"Back off all the same."

The grin went away. The expression it left was cold and blank. No fear of my gun, no emotion showing at all. "Or else what? You gonna start blazing away, hero?" The hand that had been hanging unseen, blocked by his torso, suddenly slid into view and pressed the gleaming blade of a straight razor against the throat of the girl underneath him. "Go ahead, hero. Pull that fucking trigger. Maybe you can take me out, but you willing to risk I can't split this bitch's pipe before I go?"

Everything went into freeze-frame again. Once more the only movement came from the fish on the floor, the only sound that of their tiny struggles. The glint of the razor's lethal edge taunted me, dared me to make a move.

"What about it, hero?" Spike Hair demanded. "You came busting in here to save the day. . . . Go for it, man. Get the job done, why don't you?"

"Do it," the black woman hissed vehemently, unexpectedly. "Shoot the sonofabitch!"

I kept my eyes and my gun muzzle locked on Spike Hair. I was counting on my peripheral vision to keep track of the Oriental. By that means, I saw his massive shoulders roll. The black woman jerked back against him. From the strangled sucking noises she began to make, it was clear he had tightened his grasp on her throat.

"Go ahead, Ho," Spike Hair urged. "Do that bitch. Throttle her. That sassy mouth of hers been a pain in my ass since we walked in here."

The black woman's feet left the ground. The sucking noises grew higher pitched, more desperate. She kicked frantically, toes slapping the floor in a kind of spastic tap dance.

Spike Hair laughed a throaty laugh and his eyes flashed wild as he said to me, "Oooo, this is getting tense, ain't it, hero? I'd say you're losing ground, man. You still got one here under the blade, now you got that one over there on her way to the Big Gone. Shit, is this exciting or what? I can't wait to see how you're going to pull it off. Clock's ticking, man. . . . You got about thirty seconds before that's one dead nigger."

"Then you got about thirty-one seconds before you're just as dead."

"Fuck you. That's movie shit. If you're gonna do it, do it. You come in here waving a piece and talking Clint Eastwood and you think we're all gonna piss our pants and just roll over for you?"

"Let go of the women and back off. We can all walk away from this. You and I can look each other up another day."

"No. I see it different. You put down the piece, then I tell the Chink to put down Miss Sassy Mouth. We go from there."

His eyes stayed wild, the size of twenty-five-cent pieces. I couldn't be sure if he was high on something or just plain crazy. Either way, it was obvious he was as thoroughly unpredictable as he was dangerous.

The black woman had quit making noises. Her kicks were growing feeble.

My nerves thrummed like high voltage pouring through a transformer. Under my skin, a thousand tiny muscles were flexing and twitching in apprehension. A drop of sweat rolled from the hinge of my jaw and made its way down inside my collar.

It was beginning to look like I'd botched this royally. Spike Hair was right—if you're going to do it, do it. The first rule of gunplay is never draw your weapon unless you're ready to use it. With the razor at the dark-haired girl's throat, the time for shooting was past. Unless I was willing to sacrifice her. Which I wasn't, at least not at this point. Hell, I didn't even know for certain who she was. I was assuming that she was Rosemary Karson and, inasmuch as I knew Barry Grainger was black, that the black woman was Grainger's wife. Excuse me if that logic sounds prejudiced. In these more racially tolerant times, of course, it could be completely the reverse. Or the women could be two visiting neighbors for all I knew. At any rate, I'd barged in on the sound of someone in trouble and it would be decidedly poor form to proceed in a manner that provoked worse trouble instead of rescue. With the distances and positioning involved, I had little doubt I could blow away Spike Hair and Ho before they could cause me any harm. But I had substantially greater doubt I could manage it without getting one—maybe both—of the women seriously injured or killed.

Damn.

Some rescuer I was. Some hero.

Damn it to fucking hell.

Slowly, never taking my eyes off Spike Hair, I leaned forward and placed the .45 on the floor in front of me.

When I started to lift my hand, he said, "Shove it away."

I shook my head. "Not until Godzilla lets her breathe."

Spike Hair flicked a glance in Ho's direction, nodded once.

The black woman's feet returned to the floor. I heard long, hungry intakes of air.

"Now the gun," Spike Hair said to me.

I pushed the .45 hard to my left, away from all of us, aiming to skid it under the bottom shelf of the TV stand where it wouldn't be too easily retrievable by the wrong hands. It came to rest with only a sliver of the butt sticking out.

Before I had any chance to savor this bit of cleverness, however, Ho—whether on his own initiative or at some unseen signal from Spike Hair, I was never sure—literally threw a whole new problem my way. With a sudden straightening motion of his arms he hurled the black woman away from him and directly at me. She covered the eight feet that had separated us in a kind of galloping stutter step, eyes and mouth wide, hands instinctively outflung to catch herself. Still kneeling, I managed to get a shoulder turned and one arm partly raised in a fending-off gesture before she crashed into me. Knees and thighs and hip bones pounded me like a flurry of punches. Her upper body dropped across my head and shoulders as her momentum took both of us down in a thudding, sprawling tangle.

Anticipating what would come next, I struggled frantically to get clear of her.

Ho was waiting when I did. He lashed out a little too eagerly with a savage kick that only managed to graze my forehead but sent pain rocketing down through my face and chest and knocked me back. I twisted away, scrambling, trying to make it to my feet. My legs became tangled with those of the black woman once more and I heard her cry out as my heels pummeled her. I made it briefly to my hands and knees. A second kick tore into my side, just below the ribs, driving me against the wall.

I was vaguely aware of Spike Hair shouting excitedly in the background.

I tried to climb the wall. Slashing, edge-of-the-hand chops ripped across my kidneys and the back of my neck. My face bounced off the wall. Gritty plaster dust mixed with blood inside my mouth.

In a rage of desperation, I pushed away hard, lunging up and back, bringing my elbow around in a sickle-like arc. I caught Ho leaning in, his hand raised to deliver another blow. I drilled the point of my elbow into his mouth and felt the teeth give. It backed him up a step and a half, allowing me room enough and time enough to get turned the rest of the way around.

Spitting blood, Ho charged back into me, pinning me against the wall. His hands clawed at my throat. I slammed in some body shots; it was like pounding on the fender of a GMC. Both of us were pumping our knees high, practically running in place, trying to rip into each other's groin or guts.

The hands closed around my throat and he began lifting me off the ground exactly as he had the black woman. At 230-odd pounds, I am not accustomed to being hoisted into the air. No grown man is. As we develop in size and maturity, the very thing we found so comforting as a child—being picked up and held—becomes extremely disorienting and frightening. It was that for me now. I had several seconds of blind panic, my feet and hands wildly digging air like an amok marionette.

Spike Hair's face was a blur off to one side, a blur highlighted by a broad, mocking smile. "You got him, Ho," he cheered. "You got him now. Hold that motherfucker and I'll slice him up like a loaf of store-bought bread."

Beneath the smiling blur, I saw the gleam and twinkle of the straight razor.

The words and the threat of the blade galvanized me, taking me beyond my panic. I worked my hands and forearms up in between Ho's, levering away some of the pressure, digging into his face, my fingers slipping on sweat and blood. I sank my nails deep, drawing more blood, wanting to peel the flesh from his skull. A growl of pain and anger rumbled from deep within him.

"You're losing him, man," Spike Hair cautioned. "Don't do that. Break on away, let me take the fucker."

If Ho heard, he wasn't having any. Our eyes were only inches apart and I'd seen the look in his before—the killing look. He wanted me all for himself. But the one thing I had on the big bastard was reach. As we dug into each other, bending one another over backward, arms extending, my advantage increased in direct proportion to his decreasing. When I felt the instant was right, I gave a final fierce gouge at his eyes, my thumbs hooked like talons, and as he jerked his head reflexively I slammed my arms out, breaking his grip on my throat. My feet returned to earth. When he blindly lunged back at me, attempting to regain some kind of hold, I met him with a head butt, ramming my forehead into his already mangled mouth. Teeth sawed my scalp, blood splashed down over my face.

I'd hoped to put him down with that, but the massive Oriental was nothing if not durable. He staggered back, weaving unsteadily. Damned, though, if he didn't stay on his feet.

I wasn't entirely clear-headed or steady on my own feet. So intent was I on the anticipated tumble of the big man, I forgot for a second about his partner. In that unguarded moment, Spike Hair danced in, blade flashing, and cut a Z pattern across me. My heavy winter coat took a lot of it, but he still managed to lay open a track the length of my collarbone, only a couple inches lower, and another slash half the distance from elbow to wrist. A mist of blood sprayed from my arm, chasing him as he danced away.

I spun, cursing, and kicked out, trying to crush a kneecap. I didn't do the damage I wanted to do, but I got enough of his leg to trip him and knock him down. The blade stayed high, thrust out at me, keeping me at bay while he scrabbled crab-like to safety.

The brief interruption was all the time Ho needed to get set for another turn. The two of them were working me like picadors wearing down a bloodied bull.

Ho got the bull's attention with a chop to the kidneys. When my body went rigid from the shock of the blow, he stepped in close, wrapped his arms around me in a bear hug, whirled me a half turn, and slammed me to the floor. I had so many individual aches and bruises by then I was like one raw wound, numbed to the pain of these fresh blasts. I rolled over twice, sucking hard for air, then tucked myself into a fetal ball and began digging at my ankle.

As a series of stomping kicks rocked me, I deeply regretted not having shot somebody while I'd had the big .45 in my fist. The derringer slapping into my palm from the spring rig in the boot offered considerable consolation. I wouldn't make the same mistake twice.

I picked the next kick and rolled with it, twisting around with all the strength and speed I had left. When Ho moved in, foot raised for more stomping, I was coiled and ready. I sprang to meet his attack, swinging the hand with the derringer in a scooping uppercut, jamming the muzzle of the little gun solidly into his crotch and emptying both chambers.

The near-simultaneous shots, muffled by his body, were flat, dull pops. My hand was scorched by the back blast, then instantly bathed in a wash of blood. A single puff of smoke rolled up past Ho's belt buckle. His body stiffened, teetered precariously over me for a long two seconds, and then toppled straight back like a falling tree.

Eight feet away, in the fading echo of the gunfire and Ho's crashing fall, Spike Hair stood watching with an awe-struck expression. His face had turned as pale as his hair, his mouth hung agape. He seemed unable to take his eyes off his fallen comrade. When he finally was able to, he swung them in my direction. I can only guess at the image I must have presented, battered and torn and bloody, clutching the gore-splattered derringer, crouching beside the leaking body of the Oriental.

"Jesus," Spike Hair said in a hoarse whisper. "Jesus Christ . . . is he dead?"

"He's singing soprano in Hell," I answered. I stood up. "I expect you'll be there soon to hear him."

Spike Hair's eyes shifted, becoming fearful. They bounced back and forth between my face and the derringer in my hand. He evidently didn't realize the little gun was only a two-shot piece.

"Oh no, man," he said. "You got no need to kill me too."

I stepped over Ho and began walking toward him. "Why not?" I wanted to know. "You think you deserve any better—you were the one who was going to slice me like a loaf of cheap bread, remember?"

As I moved toward him, I became reattuned to the other things around us. The stink of blood and sweat and shit and cordite that hung in the air. The sobs of the dark-haired girl, who still lay on the couch, her eyes shut tight, her hands covering her ears, trying to block out the horrors that were coming down so close. The excited, nostril-flared expression on the face of the black woman. Pressed against the wall near where she and I had fallen in a tangle, she seemed to see not horror but satisfaction in the turn things had taken.

Most of all I was aware of the fear emanating from Spike Hair. It fueled me. It pumped me up. It was like a drug for my aches, blurring the memory of my own fear of death that had coursed so recently through me. I liked the feel of someone else's terror better. I wanted more.

"The razor thing?" Spike Hair said. "That was just a bluff, man. All a big bluff."

"You cut me."

"But I wasn't trying to kill you. Jesus!" He held the razor up in front of him, as if suddenly realizing he still had it in his hand. "See?" he said, flinging it down and away. "See? All just a big bluff, man."

I walked up to him and stood with my nose only an inch from his. His chin trembled, his eyes kept sliding away. The smell of his fear was strong. I filled my lungs with it, relishing it.

"Please don't kill me," he begged. "Please don't."

I pressed the derringer against the zipper flap of his trousers.

"Go ahead," the black woman urged. "Blow his goddamn balls off."

"Jesus," Spike Hair pleaded. "Jesus, please."

"You beg good," I told him. "You know a lot about begging,

don't you? Bullying women and weaklings, you've probably listened to all kinds of it in your time, haven't you?"

"Sweet Jesus, don't shoot me there. Don't shoot me. I never killed anybody."

I pulled the trigger and even though the hammer fell on an empty chamber his entire body jerked. I smiled at him and pulled the trigger several more times. Clickety, clickety, clickety, clickety. He jumped every time and I began to laugh in his face, a deep, throaty laugh, the way he'd laughed at me while Ho had held the black woman by the throat and I'd been forced to lay aside the .45.

His face changed. Realization. Humiliation. Then anger. His eyes slid off me, past and down to where he'd tossed the straight razor. Nothing like telegraphing your intentions. Spitting a curse, he was fool enough to try for it. I let him get part way around me, let him think he might have a chance, then pounded him to his knees and kicked him the rest of the way down. I dropped onto him, one leg pressed across the side of his neck, forcing him flat, my out-stretched left foot pinning the hand he'd been reaching for the razor with.

It was I who picked up the razor. I held it before me, turning it this way and that, for the first time enjoying the way the light played off the blade. "Razor man, razor man," I said. "You really like getting up close and personal with this baby, huh?"

"You're a dead motherfucker!" he managed to squeeze out through the pressure applied by my leg. "I'll gut you like a skinned otter."

"Ah, the different songs you sing. I think I liked it better when you were humble."

"Fuck you!"

I reached down and wrapped my fingers around the inverted cross and pentagram and the other doodads dangling from his left ear. "Since the loss of faithful old Ho over there apparently didn't instill any lasting humility in you," I said, my voice tight, my chest heaving with blood lust, "maybe the loss of something a little more personal will."

Before he could make any reply, I stretched the lobe taut by the ornaments in my grasp, then whipped the blade in a backhanded swipe and took the lower part of his ear off clean.

The dark-haired girl, who apparently had opened her eyes at some recent point, screamed.

The black woman said, "Right fucking on!"

Spike Hair fainted.

18

Crawford was waiting when the doctor was finished with me.

Together we walked down the narrow hall and out the back door of the clinic, the way we'd come in. Behind us, the doc, a nut-brown little Pakistani whose name I never caught, proceeded brusquely in the opposite direction, toward the other examining rooms and the paying patients who had been kept waiting, without so much as a further glance our way. From his sullen manner and expression throughout the time spent administering to me, I had gotten the impression he was somewhat resentful of whatever it was he'd done to place himself in the Syndicate's pocket. Regardless, he was smart enough not to let it show in his work. The shots and stitches and patches and pills I'd received seemed to be doing the trick and had me feeling about as functional as could be reasonably expected.

Outside, Crawford held the door while I eased myself creakily into the passenger seat of his car. Today's vehicle was a sporty, wine-colored Mazda rather than the Pontiac sedan he and Earl had transported me in last night. I guessed this was Crawford's personal set of wheels and I had a feeling lunk-headed Earl probably wasn't allowed to set foot in it.

The snow was coming down harder—bigger flakes whipped by more and more frequent gusts of wind. Over an inch had already accumulated in the couple hours since it had started, with—according to the weather bulletins that kept interrupting various local broadcasts—the worst yet to come. About 50 percent of the afternoon drivers had their headlights snapped on and a predictable number of idiots and cowboys were beginning to fishtail their starts and skew half-sideways on their stops, as if they'd never seen a flake of snow before. By evening, side streets and secondary roads would be closing not so much because the crews couldn't keep up with Mother Nature, but because clowns like these would have the plow routes blocked with smashed and/or stalled vehicles.

Crawford rolled the Mazda through the storm and around the fools.

"So how you feeling?" It was the first he'd spoken since the doctor had ushered me into the examining room.

I shrugged, forgetting about the line of stitches running below my collarbone. They reminded me in a hurry they were there. "I'll make it," I replied through gritted teeth.

"So will Steel, in case you're interested."

"Not especially. Didn't figure he'd die from a cut ear, though."

"Steel" was Bo Steel—my spike-haired pal with the razor fetish (although there was a good chance I'd cured him of that particular malady). Bo Steel possibly wasn't his real name, but it was how he was known on the street. He'd been Rosemary Karson's pimp for a number of months before she had left him to go straight with Jason Hobbs. Steel's visit to the Grainger place, in the wake of Jason's death and carefully timed to coincide with the absence of Barry Grainger, had been a bald attempt to recruit Rosemary back into his stable with his sharp-edged toy threateningly wielded as a bit of "or-else" inducement. Not to mention Ho's hulking presence. My unexpected arrival at the scene had, of course, queered the recruiting party and after Bo passed out upon sampling my party-crashing techniques, the two women—Rosemary (the dark-haired one) and Grainger's wife, Freda (the black) —were able to fill me in on exactly what I'd busted up.

"How are the ladies?" I asked Crawford.

He nodded. "They'll be okay. I made a phone check while you were being patched up. They've got some bruises, but nothing more serious. No cuts or fractures or internal injuries. The Karson chick is still a little shaken, but calmed down considerable from what she was. A sedative's been prescribed if she needs it later on. Freda Grainger's main pain seems to be a case of serious disappointment that you didn't kill both of those sleazeballs while you were at it. That's one feisty lady."

I nodded. "She's something all right. She was the one who

managed to get my attention in the first place, when I was on the verge of deciding there was no one at home and walking away. She apparently took a bite out of the big Oriental's hand and then managed to call out and kick over the fish tank."

"Feisty and foxy," Crawford said. "Dangerous mix."

"What about the big Oriental, the guy I *did* kill?"

"Name was Phuoc Dak Ho. Pretty murky background, not even clear if he was Vietnamese or Chinese or just what kind gook-ese he was. Came to Rockford a couple, three years ago by way of Chicago's Chinatown. Typical strong-arm type—long on muscle, short on brains. Apparently Steel used him from time to time, when he figured he needed some extra brawn to back his play. Ho's been disposed of in a way that shouldn't raise any embarrassing questions. I think it's safe to say he won't be greatly missed. You did the smart thing, calling us."

I tapped out a cigarette and lit it. Dragged the smoke deep. Sat silently, watching the snow and the fools slide by. As the background shifted and I caught fleeting glimpses of my reflection thrown by the glass, I wondered if I was looking at the biggest fool of all.

The decision to contact Camicci's people had been another of those that more or less made itself. When things had started to wind down at the Grainger place, after I'd crashed from my adrenaline high and been given the bare bones of an explanation as to what was going on, the bottom line was that I still had one dead man, one badly damaged one, two traumatized women, and my own unignorable injuries to deal with. The right and proper thing to do would have been to call the police. But none of us in that room—dead or alive—were completely proper people. As far as what had just happened went, there was no crime left unsolved, a kind of justice had already been meted out (one more satisfactory to the majority present than would probably be delivered by any court)—all that was left for the cops would be to hassle me over the shooting, no matter how justified, and to dig around routinely until they maybe picked loose the ends of some thread that could lead off in directions where official interest was definitely not desirable. Had there been no alternative, that course might have been necessary, risks and all. But in my wallet I carried the phone number Frankie Camicci had provided for me to get in touch with him "day or night" if and when I had anything of note concerning the movie-troupe murders. Since that delicate situation was high on the list of things a police probe into this new can of worms might unbalance, it didn't seem to be stretching the point too far to conclude that a quicker, tidier resolution of the whole pimp incident would be in Frankie's best interest as much as anyone's.

So I'd made the phone call. Not to the proper authorities like a good little chin-up citizen, but to the local arm of the Syndicate like a politician in the night. Covering my own ass and, just incidentally, those of my constituents.

It had been Crawford who came on the line and Crawford who ended up handling matters, making all the necessary arrangements. It went without saying that he'd had to get Camicci's sanction somewhere along the way, but at no point since the previous night had I talked directly to The Man himself. I figured I still had that to look forward to. I guess that was the part that was getting to me. I felt no remorse about what I'd done to Ho or Steel, even though I recognized I'd gone a little crazy, skidding off the deep end for a while back there with the razor and all. But I could live with covering up Ho's death from the cops and knowing his body was disintegrating inside a coffin of lime in an unmarked grave somewhere. The part I didn't know whether or not I could hack was having another little piece of me in the Syndicate's pocket. And that was damn sure the way Camicci would see it. No matter how mutually beneficial things worked out, in his eyes I would be that much deeper into him. First I'd accepted Syndicate money and fringe benefits for the job, now I'd sought out and accepted additional assistance. Sooner or later he was going to expect something in return.

I thought about the bitter expression on the face of the pocketed little Pakistani doctor I had just visited and then I thought back on what Kat had told me in the cold outside the farmhouse last night: "We all allow ourselves to be used in some way, Hannibal. Don't ever kid yourself. Everybody's a whore to something."

Yeah. Don't ever kid yourself. Who the hell did I think I was, anyway—somebody with principles or something?

"Hey," Crawford said beside me. "You okay?"

I dragged my Pall Mall down to a half-inch butt, reached to stab it out in the dashboard ashtray. "Yeah," I replied, expelling smoke. "I'm okay. I'm swell."

"You were starting to look a little green around the gills."

"Must be the shot or something the doc gave me. Where is it we're headed, by the way?"

"I'm taking you home. After what you've been through, it seemed reasonable to expect you'd need some R&R. I already had your car driven there."

"Pretty damn thorough, aren't you?"

"We try. Barry Grainger was gotten hold of and is now with his wife and the Karson girl. Arrangements have been made for them to spend the night at friends'. I've got a crew cleaning up the Grainger pad in the meantime, putting everything back in order right down to a new fish tank with the right kind of fish in it. By this time tomorrow, nobody will ever be able to tell there was any kind of disturbance there."

"Now you're showing off. How about Spike Hair—Bo Steel, the pimp? Has he been put in order?"

"His ear, you mean? Fuck him. You play with the buzzsaw, sooner or later you get buzzed."

"Will he go along with whitewashing everything that happened?"

"He will if he knows what's good for him."

I smiled grimly, wondering how long it would be before Crawford or somebody else in his circle might be saying the same about me.

We rode the rest of the way without talking much, save for a comment or two on the worsening storm.

When we pulled up in front of my place, Crawford said, "Looks like this blizzard's going to have everything bottled up for a day or so anyway, so take advantage of it. Lay low, get in some sack time, lick your wounds. It's what you need. You lost plenty of blood and you got banged around pretty good back there."

"I know," I told him. "I was there."

I levered open my door and started to get out. Crawford reached over and put a hand on my arm.

"One thing more, Hannibal."

"What's that?"

"When you *are* up and about, Mr. Camicci will be expecting to hear from you."

We regarded one another across the distance of his outstretched arm. Wind and snow blew in over my right shoulder and dotted the dark skin of his exposed wrist with glistening white flecks. I nodded at length and said, "I know that too."

"Do I tell him he can count on you?"

I sighed. "Tell him anything you want, Crawford. Right now your guess is as good as mine as far as what I'm going to do."

I got the rest of the way out, closed the door, turned and walked toward my stairs without looking back.

Up in my apartment, I shed my coat and frowningly examined it for damage. It appeared bloodied and slashed beyond reasonable repair. I swore. It had been my best winter wrap, scarcely two years old.

I emptied the pockets, spreading their contents on the kitchen table, then balled up the rag and shoved it in the garbage. I peeled off my shirt and did the same with it

While a partial pot of leftover coffee was reheating, I walked into the bathroom and started some water running. In the steam-streaked mirror, I studied my own visible damage. It could have been worse, I guess. The stitches across my forehead where I'd head-butted Ho were in a neat row covered by a single, long, flesh-toned bandage. There were bruises and some puffiness around my mouth, from being mashed against the wall, but nothing too ghastly. At least I hadn't had any teeth knocked out or even loosened as far as I could tell. The abraded skin on my throat where Ho had tried to throttle me looked not much worse than a moderate case of razor burn. Except for the additional stitches below my collarbone and down my arm, my remaining battle scars consisted of various scrapes and bruises to the body, concentrated mostly in the rib and kidney areas. Yeah, it could have been a lot worse. There had been a couple of points where it came close to going the way of someone else tallying these wounds off a morgue slab.

I washed my face and hands, brushed my teeth, combed my hair, dressed in clean clothes from the skin out.

Back in the kitchen, from the cabinet under the sink I pulled a shoebox filled with rags and brushes and cans of oil. These I carried over to the table where, after I'd poured myself a cup of coffee and lit a cigarette, I sat down and began cleaning my guns. A gun is like any tool. Take care of it after you've used it, it will be ready to do the job for you when you need it again. And spare me any lectures or tired statistics or grievous tales of woe concerning gun control or lack thereof. Please. All I know is that as long as the assholes out there are armed—and they are, in ever-increasing numbers—then I intend to be too. It's as simple as that.

In addition to its practical benefits, the task of servicing my weapons was also meant to occupy my hands and my attention. I needed that. I needed to focus, however loosely, on some mundane activity for a while, to let my mind coast, to let my thoughts float on calm waters for a change.

But it wasn't working. The chore was too simple, the moves too automatic. My mind cartwheeled off in a dozen different directions, most of them pot-holed by jarring question marks. Could Bo Steel have killed Jason Hobbs for the purpose of removing him as an obstacle to luring Rosemary Karson back into his stable? If so, why wait a full week to make his follow-up play? And even if any of that held water, how could it possibly connect to Valerie Pine's murder? But what about the surly brown-haired woman with the equally surly dog who was so protectively "consoling" Valerie's surviving lover, Cindy Wallace? What if her protective/possessive attitude had been in development while Valerie was still alive and the elimination of the younger, prettier woman was perceived as necessary to make way for a new relationship? Jealousy is the oldest motive for murder. And murderous jealousy, these days, comes in all shapes, sizes . . . and sexes.

Questions. Always more questions, more possibilities. But no damn answers. The deeper I dug, the more tangled the handful of roots I was trying to yank free.

When my guns were clean and shiny and pristinely lethal once again, I got up and put the shoebox away back under the sink. I stood leaning there for a long time, gazing out at the stormy afternoon through the little window above the faucets, watching the snow come down. Feeling as restless as the wind gusts that rattled the glass. I thought some more about the events at the Grainger place, specifically my actions there. No remorse, like I said earlier; never, not for the likes of scum such as Steel or Ho. The troubling thing was the part of me—the dark, psychotic side —which had emerged to wield that razor no longer in self-defense but purely for the sake of inflicting pain and humiliation. It wasn't the first time I'd had to look at that side of myself and probably wouldn't be the last, but that didn't make it any prettier. It's there in all of us, somewhere down inside. The trick is to recognize it, learn to deal with it, but never be comfortable with it—never allow it to take over. The ability to keep that dark side turned away more often than not is, in the final analysis, the only thing that separates us from the Bo Steels of the world.

I pushed from the sink still feeling restless and edgy. Despite my wounds and the limited amount of sleep I was operating on, despite the wisdom of Crawford's advice to lay low and get some R&R, I was wired, running high on some kind of charge, a need to be in motion, to be doing something. Maybe I was too aware that the clock was ticking on the case, too aware of all its complexities; maybe it was anticipation of being bottled up by the storm; maybe it was my discomfort at having again faced that dark side of myself; maybe frustration over not knowing how I was going to handle Camicci if and when the time came. Whatever it was, it seemed a safe bet I wasn't going to be able to relax or get any decent rest until I did something to work off at least part of it.

19

This time the driveway leading back to the Silas farmhouse was as choked with snow as the gravel road it branched off from. Out here in the country, out in the open, the wind was steadier, fiercer, whiting out vision at nerve-scraping intervals and at ground level sweeping broad, obscuring drifts of white across everything. The Honda and I negotiated the route with a minimum of difficulty. Nevertheless, as I swung into the egg-shaped parking area and spotted the expected assemblage of vehicles, I questioned my own sanity as well as everyone else's for being out in such weather.

I covered the distance to the back door in a kind of stumbling trot, hands jammed hard into pockets, shoulders hunched, the hood of the old parka I'd dug out of the storage closet flipped over my head. The snow I churned through swirled up to sting my face. The cold drew my stitches tighter, the biting wind drove the aches around my kidneys and ribs wincingly deeper. This was shaping up to be the kind of blizzard that spawned stories of farmers who grew hopelessly disoriented between house and barn and ended up freezing to death only yards from the warmth of their own home; of motorists who foolishly tried to walk away from stranded vehicles and met the same fate; of unsuspecting little kids who snuck outdoors to play in the mesmerizingly beautiful white stuff and became faces smiling hauntingly back at us from photographs supplied to the news media. Hard to imagine, perhaps, if you've never experienced the fury of a Midwest winter storm. But it only takes a few minutes out in one to make a believer of the biggest skeptic.

It was Irma Silas who once again answered my knock, her eyes widening with surprise at the sight of me. "My goodness gracious, Mr. Hannibal," she said, ushering me in along with a blast of icy air, "what on earth brings you out on an afternoon like this?"

"Just trying to prove I've got a crazy streak as wide as the next guy's, I guess. Although judging from the number of cars parked out there, there's plenty of competition."

"Only difference being most of them have been here since early this morning and are preparing to leave soon—not arriving smack in the middle of the worst blizzard to hit us in ten years."

I grinned. "So that makes me the craziest kid on the block."

"You'll get no argument here. Let me take your coat. Then I'll pour you a cup of coffee. The others are all inside, completing a shoot. They've decided to wrap up early because of the storm."

I shook snow off the old parka and handed it to her. While she was still in the cloakroom hanging it up, the door that led off to the soundstage opened and Floyd Silas came in. He began talking before he noticed me.

"They'll be through in there shortly, Mother. Chuck should be able to handle any more set adjustments they might need, so I'm going to go ahead on out and—" He stopped when he spotted me.

I smiled and inclined my head in a nod of greeting.

"Well, good Christ almighty, Hannibal," he blurted, "I surely didn't expect you to show up anymore today."

Emerging from the cloakroom, his wife said, "Mr. Hannibal has come out to make sure there's really going to be that winter storm they're predicting."

Silas grinned. "I see. Must be the detective in him." To me he said, "What have you been able to decide from the evidence so far then? Think we're in for it?"

I chuckled at their good-natured chiding. "It's a little too early to go on record, but I'd say there's a darn good chance, yeah."

Silas waved a hand dismissingly. "Aw, but this is nothing. You think this is a blizzard? Why, I've seen the times, back in the thirties and forties—back when they didn't have a smidgen of the fancy equipment they're supposed to have nowadays, mind you—"

"Now, Floyd," Irma said sharply, cutting him off. "If I let you get started telling tales, none of us will have to worry about the blizzard because the spring thaw will be here by the time you run out of gas. Besides, I'm sure Mr. Hannibal didn't struggle all the way out here to listen to your overblown memories of the winter of '37. And if I heard you right, you were saying as to how you were on the way to get something or other done yourself, weren't you?"

Silas gave me one of those "what are you gonna do?" looks. "When the little woman's right, she's right," he said. "No matter how blasted regular that gets to be." Sighing and hitching at his belt, he walked in the direction of the cloakroom. Over his shoulder, he said, "The thing I was on my way to do was go plow out the driveway some for those who'll be leaving soon. How bad was it when you came in, Hannibal?"

"Manageable," I told him. "But drifting in fast. Wouldn't pay to do it very far in advance of when they'll need to get out."

From inside the cloakroom, he said, "Should only be a half hour or so. I've got a plow blade rigged to my old Farmall that ain't the handiest thing in the world to work with. It'll take me that long to get it cleared."

He reappeared wearing a heavy plaid coat and matching cap with the earflaps down. He was pulling on big leather mittens. "Foxwood's on inside there," he said to me. "I expect he's the main one you came to see. He got a phone call about an hour ago, just before the storm took the lines out. Said there'd been some kind of disturbance in town, some trouble involving Jason Hobbs's girlfriend. You know about that?"

I nodded. "I know about it, yeah."

"That what happened to your face?"

"Uh-huh."

"Anybody else get hurt?"

"Nobody important."

"Things getting rough, are they?"

"They were rough before I ever started. Doesn't get any rougher than murder. Maybe they're just tightening down."

Silas started to say something further, but his wife cut him off again. "I declare, Floyd Silas," she said, "you are a rude and nosy man. Mr. Hannibal didn't come here owing you a report. You have no right to . . . to . . . grill him, for heaven's sake."

Silas smiled down at her and reached out to pat her cheek with a mittened hand. "Mother, if you didn't have me to scold three or four times a day, I swear I think you'd blow up and bust."

"Well," she huffed, "the way you carry on, that surely will never be a problem we'll have to worry about, will it?"

"Not as long as I'm around," he said, his smile broadening. He stepped past her and made for the door. "While I'm out," he told her, "I'm going to go ahead and tend to the livestock. When I come in, then, I'll be able to settle for the night."

Irma nodded. "Fine. I'll plan an early supper."

"See you, Hannibal," Silas said to me before stepping out into the mean air. "You take care."

"If you get too cold," Irma called after him, "come in and get warmed up before you finish." Then, turning away from the door as it closed, she murmured, "Old fool. Still thinks he can go at everything like he did when he was twenty."

"Probably healthier than sitting back and developing rocking-chair calluses," I offered.

She shrugged fatalistically. "There's no changing him, regardless." Then, with sudden realization: "Gracious, I promised you a cup of coffee, didn't I?"

A few minutes later, balancing one of Irma Silas's excellent cups of coffee on one of her unfailingly provided saucers, I emerged from the short hall onto the soundstage. Henry Foxwood was straight ahead, standing at his usual spot, arms loosely folded, face expressionless, eyes following the activity taking place on and around the set. I walked over and stood beside him.

The script being shot this afternoon was apparently a period piece dated to the time of our Pilgrim fathers. I gathered this readily enough from the set (a representation of the interior of a stark old Plymouth colony church) and from some key props—a blunderbuss-type musket leaning against the roughwood pulpit plus various articles of discarded clothing, including somber black tunics with starched white collars and cuffs, and a high-crowned hat and a pair of shoes with prominent square buckles. The participants performing in the center of all this, however, were displaying a hearty disregard for any Puritan attitudes I'd ever heard of. There were three of them—two males and a female. All were nude at this stage of events. The female lay on her back on one of the pew benches, enthusiastically taking on both partners, one at each end. I didn't recognize the two guys, possibly because of the square-cut wigs they wore. But I had no trouble placing the girl, even in her somewhat unflattering position. The flaring hips, the upthrust pneumatic breasts, the wheat-colored mane of hair spilling down, the superheated sexual energy—I was watching the much-vaunted "Sexy Sara" Baines in action, and she definitely was *hot*. Even the normally unflappable team of Dorfman and Blyth seemed hunched over their equipment with extra intensity.

And Belinda Davies, from her directorial position, also appeared to have an added flash of excitement in her eyes. Not the excitement of sexual attraction, I judged, but rather the simple excitement of recognizing the extraordinary in something—or, in this case, someone.

Indeed the only one present outwardly unaffected by the antics of the luscious Miss Baines seemed to be my urbane client of record. Nor did my arrival on the scene cause any noticeable ripple in his detached coolness. After several beats, he acknowledged my presence with a shift of his eyes. "From all reports, Mr. Hannibal," he said, "you have had a very eventful day. I must say I find it commendable that you are carrying on with such immediacy."

"We need to talk, Foxwood," I told him.

He regarded me as if considering the request.

"Now," I demanded.

I turned and walked toward the far end of the soundstage. After a half step's hesitation, Foxwood followed. Behind us, the moans of Sara Baines and the guttural noises of her partners sounded like the roadside wailings of car-crash victims.

As I neared the back-wall area, with its poorer lighting and long shadows cast by stacked boxes of props and leaning piles of backdrop, I almost stumbled over Chuck Baines before I saw him. He sat on the floor, Indian-style, his back against an old-fashioned steamer trunk, a paperback novel held open before him in a narrow patch of light. He looked up suddenly, as startled to see me as I was him.

"Oh," he said, blinking. "Hullo there, Mr. Hannibal . . . Mr. Foxwood." He stood up. "Do they need me for something with the set?"

"Uh, no," I answered. "No, not that I know of."

"Actually, we did not realize you were back here," Foxwood explained. "Pardon the intrusion, but it appears Hannibal and I need to discuss a matter with some degree of privacy. Would you mind terribly?"

The kid blinked a time or two more before he fully comprehended what Foxwood was asking. "Oh," he said then. "Okay. No problem."

He folded the page of the book he'd been reading—an entry in a popular juvenile sports series—before closing it and shoving it in his hip pocket. That done, he brushed between Foxwood and me and moved away, leaving us to the privacy of the cramped corner. As he walked off, I noted a reluctant drag to his feet and a sort of hang-dog slouch in his posture. At first I thought he might be sulking because we'd rousted him from his spot. But then, glancing beyond him to the activity on the set, I better understood the reason for his slumping body language.

"Jesus," I muttered, "that's gotta be more than a little rough."

"What does?" Foxwood asked.

"That," I said, nodding after Chuck Baines as he angled toward the short hall, head hanging, eyes averted. "Being around, seeing your own sister going at it the way his is right now."

"I see no shackles on him," Foxwood responded. "No one dragged him here, no one is forcing him to stay. If the circumstances bothered young Baines as much as you suggest, I should think he would simply not avail himself to be present."

I gave him a look. "Under all those ten-dollar words, you're a cynical old bastard, you know that?"

His expression remained calm. "Perhaps I am," he said at length. "In your line of work is it common—say nothing of advisable—to point out such character flaws in your employer?"

"*Are* you my employer?" I said.

"Really, Hannibal. I thought we covered that sufficiently at our initial—"

"Let's cut the bullshit. The only thing you and I covered sufficiently was your well-rehearsed song and dance to convince me you were nothing but a quasi-legitimate go-between with a letch for young tail and some obscure Syndicate connections. But we both know there's a hell of a lot more to it than that, don't we, Foxy?"

"Do we?"

"Late last night I was summoned for a little visit with Frankie Camicci and a handful of his goons. Are you going to pretend you don't know who Frankie Camicci is?"

Foxwood got a little tight around the mouth before replying, "I know Frankie. What is your point?"

"My point is that the gist of last night's visit was to provide Frankie the opportunity to tell me that he expected me to report directly to him—specifically ahead of you—with any substantial information I gathered during my investigation. Now that's a pretty flat contradiction to all the fancy logic you laid on me as to why I was contacted through you in the first place, wouldn't you say?"

"If you are seeking an explanation for Frankie Camicci's logic and/or actions, may I make the observation that you are asking the wrong person?"

"I'm asking *you*. And I don't have the time or patience for any more cat-and-mouse games about it."

"Very well. Frankie is known to be frequently paranoid, to on occasion allow his own impatience or his volatile temper to trigger irrational acts. I would surmise his allegedly contradictory demands of you last night stemmed from one of those traits. Is that what you want to hear?"

I dug out my Pall Malls, got one going, and hung a cloud of smoke between us. "How much do you know about what happened at the Grainger place earlier today?" I asked.

"I was informed there was an, ah, altercation which threatened Mrs. Grainger and Jason Hobbs's former girlfriend, Rosemary, but that your timely intervention saved them from any serious harm."

"Who told you this? And why?"

He frowned. "What difference does that make?"

"Just answer the questions."

"Look here, Hannibal, I resent your tone and attitude. I am, after all, the one who—"

"Right now all I see is that you're the one who's holding out on me."

"How preposterous. Why would I do that?"

"That's what I'm trying to find out. Do you expect me to believe that Frankie—after going to all the trouble last night of threatening me to keep you in the dark and then having things work out today so he ended up with a big chunk of me tucked neatly in his pocket—turned around and promptly provided you with an update of everything that had gone down? That doesn't wash worth shit, Foxwood."

"What are you implying as an alternative—that perhaps the ruffians who invaded the Grainger apartment were the ones who contacted me with an appraisal of what had happened?"

"I figure it was Crawford," I answered flatly. "I think you and him are in bed together in a way that involves the Syndicate but not necessarily crazy little Frankie. Am I right?"

His face bunched into an expression that told me immediately I was, no matter how hard he might want to deny it.

As it turned out, he didn't even try. The bunched expression slid away after a few seconds and was replaced by a rueful smile. Sighing heavily, Foxwood said, "I find it difficult to decide, Hannibal, whether you are a good deal brighter than your rough-hewn exterior would suggest, or if it is simply your unfailing tenacity which wears down everything and everyone until you eventually expose what you are after. At any rate, it is becoming increasingly clear that we chose the right man for the job."

"Yeah, I'm downright amazing. I do even better when I'm not hamstrung by half-truths and flat-out lies."

Foxwood shook his head. "For my part, I plead guilty only to a few half-truths."

"So now are you willing to level with me all the way?"

He shrugged. "You seem quite capable of reaching the bottom line, as they say, regardless."

"I'm on target, then, about you and Crawford being teamed to baby-sit Frankie Camicci for the Chicago front office?"

"Bluntly put, but accurate enough I suppose."

"Based on what I heard through my sources and from some of the remarks you've made here, Frankie is apparently a loose cannon, a cause of considerable concern and embarrassment to the rest of the Camicci clan. It would appear he was sent out here to the boonies where things are supposedly tamer and where there was less likelihood of him stirring up any big commotion while old Frederico wasn't around to smooth it over. So as not to ruffle his ego, he was placed 'in charge' of a string of ongoing operations —but with you and Crawford on hand to walk him through his moves. That about the size of it?"

"Once again, accurate enough."

"The last thing anybody expected was for people connected to one of those operations to start turning up murdered."

"To be sure."

"Let me guess—is that where you and Frankie came to a parting of the ways?"

"We had distinctly differing views of how best to approach the problem. Frankie thought it vastly preferable to allow his thugs an opportunity to strong-arm their way to the bottom of things before ever considering calling in someone such as yourself. His primary motive was to impress upon Uncle Frederico and the rest of the Syndicate hierarchy how autonomously capable he was. This, above any genuine concern for the safety of the troupe or even the actual truth of the matter."

"So how'd you get around him?"

"By appealing to the better sense of his cousin, Albert, Frederico's oldest son, who was left to helm the various Camicci interests during his father's absence. Albert conferred with a number of his father's closest advisors and they quickly agreed to sanctioning a discreet investigation by a trained professional."

"The 'council of Fat Old Mustache Petes,' " I mused aloud.

"Beg your pardon?"

I shook my head. "Never mind. Just something Frankie said last night when he had me hauled in for our little chat." I dragged my cigarette down next to nothing, dropped the butt on the floor and pressed it out under my heel. "It's pretty clear at this point," I said to Foxwood, "that you're a lot tighter with the Syndicate than you let me believe at the get-go. Just how tight are you?"

He smiled wistfully. "I am not a 'made' individual, if that is your question. My association with the Syndicate, as you choose to call it, is quite simple, really. I attended high school with Frederico and Antonio Camicci. We played on the same sports teams, we went to the same school dances, we discovered we had a number of shared interests, we became quite good friends. Frederico and I are the same age, Antonio was a year behind us. My parents moved here to Rockford during the last half of my senior term and I did not see my Chicago friends again until years later, after I had returned to Illinois from my bittersweet Hollywood experiences. We became reacquainted through some overlapping business ventures. I had, of course, heard many stories about them but that mattered not. To me, they were still Rico and Tony from the sandlots and from all those painfully unrewarding Saturday-night mixers in the St. Basil gymnasium."

"And when your old buddies got ready to start their local blue-movie enterprise, they naturally thought of you and your big-time film-making expertise, right?"

"Quite. Both my background in legitimate film and my reputation with the ladies, I was told, were important qualities they were willing to pay very well for. At first I was offended. Terribly so. But in the end, their instincts and their business sense proved indisputably sound."

As he related this last bit, a change seemed to settle over Foxwood, draining away much of his aloofness, and self-assuredness. A grim expression pulled at his face, erasing any residue of the dashing swashbuckler he had been in his brightest moment and leaving him looking like nothing but the troubled old man he was after all.

"Which brings to bear," he said somberly, "a very personal slant on all of this for me. You see, Hannibal, I feel a tremendous responsibility for the involvement of everyone who has gone before these cameras. My name, my mystique, the glossed-over account of my Hollywood screen 'career,' is used as an inducement, a pry bar if you will, at every opportunity. And although most of these youngsters never heard of—let alone *saw*— even a glimpse of 'Champion of Camelot,' they are nevertheless drawn like moths to the flickering flame of a celebrity aura. In other words, if there exists a threat to the troupe as a whole, if there are—God forbid—more murders planned, then it is I who have placed so many in the path of that danger."

"That's pretty damn ridiculous," I said. "It's greed and lust and exhibitionism that places people like the Ingrams and Bess Gilbertson and Sexy Sara Baines over there in front of those cameras."

Foxwood smiled sadly. "Those traits may be what *keeps* them in front of the cameras, but the fact remains that in far too many instances the first step might never have been taken without the lure of my name."

"You're a grown man," I conceded. "If you're bound and determined to heap blame on yourself, then I guess I can't stop you. But as long as you've got your personal side opened up, how about providing me with some insight or at least a gut feeling on a few questions? Back when you were pretending to be only peripherally involved, we never got around to that."

So we went through the drill. No, he knew of no enemies either Jason or Valerie had had, nor of any recent disputes that might have left someone holding a grudge; they were both such popular kids. Yes, he'd known Valerie and Cindy Wallace had formed a lesbian relationship, they seemed very happy. No, he'd never met Valerie's exhusband but he'd heard plenty about him; he sounded like the kind of lowlife who was certainly capable of resorting to murder, only hadn't the police already checked him out thoroughly? Yes, Cindy Wallace had had a lesbian lover before Valerie —her name was Inez something—and from my description of the brown-haired woman, it could be the same person; in fact, now that I mentioned it, it seemed that he had heard something along those lines, about Cindy moving back in with Inez following Valerie's murder, apparently for solace. No, he hadn't known that Rosemary Karson was a former prostitute or that there was a possessive pimp in her background, not until the events of earlier today had been relayed to him; it certainly seemed to him that said pimp rated closer scrutiny as a prime suspect for at least Jason's killing. Yes, he recalled Tiffany Traver having spent some time with the Church of the Almighty, but knew of no overtures made to any other members of the troupe by that organization— and what on earth did that have to do with this, anyway?

The words bounced back and forth between us, basically echoing the other question-and-answer sessions I'd already conducted regarding this case, gaining me little except perhaps an improved vocabulary from listening to Foxwood's precise English.

"All right," I said, snapping flame to a fresh cigarette. "Let's try something from way, way out in left field. What if Frankie, realizing he'd been sent here because he was perceived as a fuck-up in the big city and therefore anxious to make a more positive impression on his uncle and the rest of the Syndicate wiseguys, arranged these murders with the intent of setting up some chump for them when the time was exactly right so that he—Frankie— could emerge from the whole thing looking cool and competent for having handled a major problem?"

Foxwood stared at me as if I'd asked permission to wipe my ass on his coat sleeve. "Good God, man," he sputtered, "wherever did you get such an outlandish notion?"

"It's not a notion. It's not anything, necessarily. I'm just spitballing, just tossing out random thoughts to see how hard they get thrown back. You were the one who said Frankie's main concern seemed to be making a good impression on the Chicago string-pullers. Besides—outlandish or not—it's one of the few scenarios I've been able to come up with to link the two killings."

"Your job is to uncover the truth, not tie matters up in a preconceived fashion. It may be that the two killings are *not* linked."

"Is that what you believe?"

He scowled at me and at the question.

"Well?" I pushed.

"No," he said finally. "I, too, remain highly skeptical of that great a coincidence."

"And my spitball conjecture about Frankie—that totally outside the realm of possibility?"

"Well . . . not totally, no." He scowled some more. "Damn it all, I suppose that is the truly disturbing part. It sounds just bizarre enough to be something Frankie might consider. But surely Crawford would have advised us if anything like that was taking place."

"Come on. Frankie might be crazy, but he's not stupid. He's wild-animal clever and instinctive. You think he doesn't suspect Chicago has some kind of tag on him? He may already have Crawford pinpointed. At any rate, if he *did* have something this hairy underway, you can damn well bet he'd be playing it real close to the vest, probably using strictly wild cards and nothing from the Syndicate deck."

"You sound as if you are attaching more and more credence to the idea."

I shrugged. "So far it's just a new angle to check out, that's all. One I hadn't thought of before."

Over on the set, the taping had apparently concluded. The Betacam had been rolled back and cast and crew were milling about, talking, stretching cramped muscles, winding down. Sara Baines remained the center of attention. Nude, shiny with perspiration and expended semen from the obligatory "money shots," she was laughing and talking animatedly as she waved an unlit cigarette held between two fingers. Dorfman and Blyth hovered close, hands poised over shirt pockets, both ready to quick-draw their lighters at Sara's convenience. Had her two co-stars any pockets available, they likely would have been prepared to participate in the dueling-lighters competition as well. Angie Mullond materialized once again with towels and soapy washcloths. These she distributed, and the performers began wiping themselves. Belinda Davies stood watching from a distance of several paces, half of her mouth curved in an enigmatic smile as she thoughtfully smoked one of her long, lavender cigarettes—which she had lighted herself.

"Speaking of angles still to be checked out," I said to Foxwood, "how about your director, the redhead over there? Back when you were admittedly masking certain things from me, you dropped a couple of none-too-subtle hints that I was to steer plenty clear of her."

"My reasoning, as I believe I explained at the time, was simply that, inasmuch as Miss Davies had no real contact with the troupe prior to this weekend, your time would be ill spent questioning her in regards to matters with which she could not possibly be familiar."

"Uh-huh. But there's something more, isn't there?"

His lips pursed sourly. "A short time ago I stated what an admirable trait I found your tenacity to be. Did I also mention that there are times when it can be tremendously annoying?"

"I don't believe you did, no. But if it makes you feel any better, that's a sentiment that has been expressed by a whole bunch of different people over the years, usually in far less polite terms. So what's the rest of the scoop on La Davies?"

He had to chew it over a while longer before he finally gave in. "If you absolutely must know, she is the current mistress of Frederico Camicci."

I emitted a low whistle. "Now that definitely makes the cheese more binding. I'm surprised the old boy would allow his personal bed-warmer anywhere near this bunch, what with the possibility of a crazed killer stalking them and all."

"Mmm. That is but one aspect of the matter that makes it, ah, more binding, as you put it. At this point, you see, Frederico knows nothing of the events that have taken place here. When he departed for the old country, he left everything in the capable hands of Albert, along with adamant instructions that he was not to be bothered with business affairs except in the most extreme emergency."

I nodded. "He was covering his ass there. If the feds are really closing in on him, as rumor has it, they'd like nothing better than to be able to sink their teeth into a few overseas communiques full of juicy details about Camicci business dealings. It could even give them an extradition edge they might otherwise be lacking if old Frederico decides not to return to these shores for a while."

Foxwood made a dismissive gesture with one hand. "In any event, Albert so far—and rightfully enough, I must admit—has not deemed our situation here as being one of emergency status. Although he tried his best to dissuade Belinda from assuming any directorial chores for the time being, she wouldn't hear of it. The chance for her to direct was a promise Frederico had firmly committed to before he left, in order to pacify her and to occupy her time during his absence. As a graduate of some very prestigious film courses, she is eminently qualified and has, as I mentioned earlier, already written several scripts for our productions. As long as she was willing to accept whatever risk there might be, there was really no justification for breaking the promise that had been made to her."

My gaze lingered on Belinda Davies. Beauty, poise, talent—and guts. She was one hell of a package of womanhood. I reflected briefly on the difference between her kind of beauty and that of Sara Baines. The difference between smoldering sensuality and blazing sexuality. The difference between, say, a Garbo and a Monroe. The difference that makes men stand back in awe of one and throw themselves outrageously after the other. The difference between the searing intensity of a white-hot coal and the superficial crackle of an open flame.

Foxwood turned and let his gaze follow mine in the general direction of the set. "They will be preparing to depart soon," he said. "We decided earlier not even to take time to strike the set this afternoon, but rather to leave it for another day and make all haste in getting out of here before the storm worsens." His eyes swung back to me. "I trust you and I have settled whatever uncertainties there were between us?"

"Seems so," I agreed. "For the time being, anyway."

"Let me again compliment you on the job you are doing for us and extend my regrets over the recent events that left you wounded. You seem to have unearthed a number of, ah, 'leads' worth pursuing. For my part, I shall in the meantime do everything I can to implement your investigation, particularly in the area of clearing up the question of Frankie's possible culpability."

"Just don't get your tit caught in the wringer in the process. That won't do either of us any good."

He smiled wanly. "To be sure."

I inclined my head, indicating Sara Baines. "I just remembered something I was told about Sexy Sara over there. Is it true she and her brother were the last ones to see Jason Hobbs alive?"

Foxwood considered briefly before answering. "Well, yes. Yes, I believe that was the case. As far as anyone has been able to determine. Why?"

"Seems to warrant a few questions, wouldn't you say? How about an introduction, maybe run some interference for me to clear that gaggle of wolves out of my way?"

20

So you're the detective," Sara Baines said after Foxwood had made the introductions. She'd gotten her cigarette lighted—I hadn't noticed by who—and now she blew a cloud of smoke over my head. Smiling and pointing her formidable bare breasts straight at me, she asked, "Are you one of those hard-boiled dicks I've heard so much about?"

Dorfman, Blyth, and the others chuckled dutifully at the worn-out double entendre.

"Lady," I replied, irritated by her teasing manner and by being the brunt of her attempted humor, "I'm old and aching and operating on about two hours' sleep. So far today I've been given the runaround, I've been treated rudely and probably lied to, I've had a dog sicced on me, I've been beaten and kicked and sliced with a razor, and I've had to dish out bodily harm in return. Right now my dick is about as hard as a bowl of vanilla pudding. Does that answer your question? If so, I'd appreciate getting past the lame humor and asking you a few questions of my own."

Splotches of color crept up Sara's neck and flared brightly high on her cheeks.

One of the guys who'd been in the scene with her, still wearing his goofy Pilgrim wig and with a towel wrapped loosely around his waist, started forward and said, "Now look here, fella, there's no need to—"

I stopped him with one look. "Sonny," I told him, "I suggest you attend to wiping off your pee-pee and just butt the hell out."

"It's all right, Roger," Sara said quickly. "We need to finish getting cleaned up and dressed anyway. Mr. Hannibal can come with me to the dressing room. He can ask his questions there. Then we can all get out of here."

Roger looked petulant and wouldn't meet anyone's eyes.

"That is," Sara went on, addressing me directly again, "if that suits you?"

"Fine," I answered, "Lead on."

She turned and proceeded back to the dressing room off the left of the set. I followed. A part of me was aware of Belinda Davies watching, still thoughtfully puffing her cigarette. The rest of me—particularly the part below the belt, no matter what I'd said before—was only aware of Sara's high, proud, golden-skinned rump twitching enticingly in front of me. It made me think of the way Kat had walked off the set yesterday and that, in turn, made me think about the talk I was supposed to have with Bomber later on. The whole process had the same effect as a cold shower, but without the fuss.

The dressing room was laid out almost exactly like the one on the other side, where I'd talked with Angie Mullond last night, except that this one had a tall make-up mirror ringed by bright lights with articles of feminine clothing and other doodads scattered about. This side was obviously the "Girls'," the other side evidently the "Boys'." Considering what the boys and girls who used these dressing rooms went out on the set and did together, it struck me as darkly amusing that they required separate facilities at all.

Sara ground out her cigarette in an ashtray beside the mirror and said, "You're an awful testy guy, aren't you? What happened, you get up on the wrong side of the bed this morning?"

I shrugged. "My bed's against the wall. Only one side I can get up on."

"You almost made Roger crap his pants, you know, the way you barked at him."

"Roger wasn't wearing any pants," I pointed out.

She laughed at that. "No, I guess he wasn't, was he?"

She turned from snuffing her cigarette and leaned back against the vanity table in front of the mirror, palms pressed down on the tabletop alongside each hip, breasts and still-damp pubic mound thrust out at me. "So, what's on your mind, Mr. Detective?" she wanted to know.

I drank in a good long gape of all her goodies, then shook my

head, grinning, and said, "If you don't put some of that stuff away
and quit aiming it at me all the time, we both know damn well
that there's only going to be one thing on my mind."

She blinked innocently. "Oh, but I thought you were so old and
tired and beat-up that you couldn't possibly . . ."

"Give it a rest, why don't you? You got all the ego feed off me
you're going to get. If you don't know by now you're capable of
boning up anything male that isn't already dead and buried, then
you've got bigger problems than I can help you with. The problem
I'm here to talk about is murder."

Bludgeoning her with the word seemed to snap her out of it, get
her past the notion, for the time being at least, that she needed to
play sex-tease games with every man she met. Pressing her pouty
full lips into a straight, somber line, she reached for a robe and
pulled it on.

"Better?" she asked, cinching the belt tight around her waist.

I nodded. "It's a start."

I lit fresh cigarettes for both of us then and we talked. We
covered the familiar ground—how everybody liked Jason and Valerie, how Sara knew of no enemies either of them had had, what a
dirty rotten shame it was what had happened to them, and so on.
She was able to confirm that Inez Corby, the brown-haired
woman with the dog who was looking after Cindy Wallace so
protectively, had been Cindy's lover before Valerie came into the
picture. And yes, there had been some bitterness and nasty scenes
when Inez got dumped, but surely I didn't think she could be the
killer, did I? For one thing, wasn't all the news coverage indicating that the savagery of the two attacks, related or not, pointed to
someone—most likely a male—of above-average strength? Opening antics aside, it became quickly evident that this chick had
more on the ball than just her X-rated talents.

Having done enough polite waltzing, I decided she was ready
for some rock and roll. "I understand," I said, "that you were the
last person to see Jason Hobbs alive. That right?"

She looked extremely glum. "I guess I probably was, yeah. The
last one, that is, except whoever killed him."

"How did he seem that night?"

"What do you mean?"

"Well, did he act upset or anything? Worried, maybe—or preoc-
cupied about something?"

She shook her head. "No, he acted the same as he always did."

"Did he mention anything—a name, a place—where he might be going afterward?"

Another headshake. "No, as far as I knew he was going straight home."

"Take your time. Think about it. This could be very important."

"Don't you think I know that? Jesus, do you think I've thought about anything else?"

I took a long drag off my cigarette and sighed out some smoke. "All right. He came to your place that night for—what?—to rehearse some lines or something?"

"Uh-huh. We were going over dialogue for a shoot we had coming up in . . . well, it would have been this weekend."

"Isn't that a little unusual? I mean, no offense, but what you people do here is hardly Shakespeare."

She flashed a wry smile. "That's true enough. And you're right, it is unusual to have to rehearse much for the stuff we shoot. But this was a really special script, one Belinda had written specifically for Jason and me and it deserved the extra consideration. Are you familiar with the TV show 'Moonlighting'—you know, the one with all the snappy dialogue and the overlapping lines? Well, Belinda came up with a terrific take-off on that—not a lousy rip-off like so many X-rated productions do to try and cash in on whatever big-time show or movie happens to be hot, but a genuinely clever parody as good as most of what they put on ABC every week. Belinda called it 'Poonlighting' instead of 'Moonlighting,' and we were going to be Hattie and Darwin instead of Maddie and David, and our detective agency was going to be the Blue Poon Detective Agency instead of the Blue Moon, and so on like that. But what really gave it its pizzazz was the dialogue Belinda had written, and that's why Jason and I decided we had to put forth the extra effort. It was a chance to make Belinda look good in her directorial debut and a chance to show that we could do something on screen besides take off our clothes and fuck."

"But it was still X-rated—still had hard-core sex, right?"

"Oh, sure. No way of getting around that. But in between the screw scenes was the chance to do some real acting and to deliver some intelligent lines for a change. You said we don't do Shakespeare here, but 'Poonlighting' would have been at least some kind of small step in that direction, believe me.''

"You're not going ahead with it now?"

"No. It's shelved for the time being. I couldn't bring myself to do it with anybody else for a while. Besides, we don't really have anybody else in the company right now who could do Jason's part.''

Scratch the idea of a jealous understudy that was starting to niggle around in the back of my brain. I said, "Did the, uh, re-hearsal go pretty well that night?"

"Yeah. Not bad. I had most of my lines memorized and Jason had all of his, naturally. He was such a dream to work with in so many ways. We would have needed a few more run-throughs to get the timing just right, but it was already starting to click, al-ready starting to feel pretty darn good. I remember what a terrific rush we both got from it . . .'' She developed a peculiar kind of faraway look in her eyes and her voice sort of trailed off on those last few words. And then, after about a half minute, damned if a couple of silvery tears didn't leak out of the corner of one of her lovely eyes.

I said, "I'm sorry to put you through this."

"Don't be. It was a good night. It was a hell of a night. I'm glad I had it to remember him by." She wiped at her eyes, snuffling a few times, then said, "Did you know we made love that night? I guess you couldn't, could you? I don't think I ever told anybody." She pulled some tissues from a box on the vanity table and blew her nose hard before continuing. "I suppose it sounds strange for me to say it that way, like it was some big deal. I mean, Christ, Jason and I must have screwed twenty-five times in front of the cameras, right? And we'd made it off the set, too, back when we first met. God that seems like so long ago. But this last time, that night . . . I don't know, something about it seemed special. I think I felt it even then. Saying it now sounds awfully corny, but it was almost as if we somehow knew it was going to be our last time together.''

"What made it seem that way?"

"Hell, I don't know. Maybe I'm just being maudlin, overly ro-manticizing a simple fuck session because Jason's gone now.''

"Did either of you have in mind at the outset that the rehearsal would end up with you having sex?"

She flashed a brief but wicked little smile. "The kind of life I lead, the possibility of sex is never very far away, mister. But I don't think either of us were figuring on it that night. That's the thing, it just sort of happened. You know, the way it does in mushy books and old-time movies. Jeez, Chuck was there in the beginning—Chuck, that's my brother who stays with me, you've met him, right? Anyway, there couldn't have been very much premeditated in the sex department because Jason and I both knew he was going to be home. As it turned out, Chuck left because he couldn't concentrate on the TV or anything with us doing our lines right there at the kitchen table. After he was gone, when we were through rehearsing and were relaxing with some smoke and a couple drinks, well, one thing led to another and . . ."

"Did you know Jason's girlfriend—Rosemary Karson?"

"Oh, sure. We met. Jason brought her along to the set sometimes. I think he was trying to get her to do some loops with him. She was cute. She probably would have worked out real good."

"So she was able to handle okay what Jason was involved in? No problem with jealousy?"

"Apparently not."

"How about what happened between you and Jason the night you rehearsed—how do you think she might have reacted to that?"

"I don't imagine she would've been too thrilled if she'd known. I mean, screwing for the camera and screwing for your own pleasure are two entirely different things. But even so, it wasn't like Jason and I pledged our undying love to each other that night or made plans to announce our engagement or anything. It was something that happened, something a little special. But it was just sex. It ended there. It never would have been a threat to their relationship, not even if Jason hadn't . . . well, you know."

"Uhmm. How did Jason and your brother get along?"

She gave a one-shoulder shrug. "Okay. I suppose you've heard that Chuck is going through some emotional problems, so he doesn't relate particularly well with anybody right now. Jason was no exception, no better or no worse. Chuck and I are still close and he's warmed nicely to Mr. and Mrs. Silas. Helping Floyd out around the farm here has been a real positive experience for him."

"I don't know exactly what the nature of Chuck's trouble is, but I've got to say it surprises me that you bring him out here to see what you do. He's able to handle this okay?"

"Chuck and I are close, like I said. We always have been. A couple years ago, back before he got all messed up and before our folks died in that fire, when we were all together on summer holiday—the last summer we ever could all be together—I told him what I was getting involved in here. I was contemplating telling my parents, too, and I guess I was using Chuck as a sort of guinea pig. I never got around to telling Mom and Dad, but Chuck was really cool about it, supportive even. That was before the AIDS thing had become such a big concern. Anyway, he said as long as nobody was getting hurt, as long as I wasn't being forced to do anything I didn't really want to do, to go for it. So after things turned to shit the way they did and he had to move to Rockford last year to live with me, well, there was no big secret about it or anything. He was so reclusive, having so much trouble facing people and dealing with them, that at one point I finally decided it might actually be good for him to come here, to experience the openness and the interaction of the regulars in the troupe. It turned out it *was* good for him, getting the chance to work with Floyd and everything, even if it was in a different way than I expected."

"Chuck ever expressed any interest in going in front of the cameras?"

"No. One of his primary problems is still—" Sara stopped abruptly, her mouth pulling into a hard frown. "Look, I'm willing to cooperate, but aren't we getting a little far away from what you're supposed to be asking questions about? My brother has his troubles, that's no huge secret, but it's not something I want to talk about with anybody and everybody who comes along."

I nodded. "Understandable enough. Didn't mean to pry unduly. Just my inquisitive nature, I guess. Would it be all right, though, if I asked Chuck a few quick questions about that night Jason was there? Maybe he picked up on something you missed or might have forgotten."

Her frown stayed very much in place. "I really wish you wouldn't. This whole business has been so rough on Chuck, I hate to see him made to think about it any more than he already has. He's been having bad dreams again, sometimes several a night. My parents' deaths disturbed him deeply and now, within the one group of people he's been able to feel halfway comfortable around, suddenly there's terrible death again. Do you see my concern? I can't believe he knows anything that could be of value to you—he surely would have told Floyd or me."

"Okay," I said. "We can leave it go for now. Look, I'd better let you get dressed. If that storm is still kicking up out there the way it was, we'd best all of us be on our way or no one is going to make it out."

At the curtained doorway, she said my name.

I looked back at her over my shoulder.

"I've read about you in the papers," she said, "the things you've done to creeps who had it coming. I hope it's you, not the cops, who catches the rotten bastard that killed Jason. I hope you rip his guts out."

I shook my head. "I'm no vigilante, kid. No matter what the papers have said. I only do what I have to do, when I don't have any other choice."

"Then I hope the bastard doesn't give you one."

21

We arranged to head out in a kind of loosely grouped caravan, with Dorfman and Blyth in the lead, breaking trail in their big old sturdy Travelall, then the others falling in behind in no particular order. I volunteered to bring up the rear.

Inasmuch as I'd driven my Honda within the hour, I had an advantage over everybody else in the window-scraping and engine-warming departments. I used the extra slice of time this gave me to duck into the barn where Floyd Silas was tending his livestock. Spotting the lights on in there had aroused a bit of nostalgic curiosity in the old farmboy in me. The snow whipped fiercely at my face and body as I made my way from the car to the hulking structure of the barn.

I located Silas by the sound of silage tumbling down the chute of the silo and thumping into a pile on the concrete floor of the blocky connecting shed that jutted off the main part of the barn. The mound of steaming, sour-smelling, fermenting chopped corn was already nearly four feet high, indicating he likely didn't have much more to throw down. Beside the pile was a boxlike four-wheeled cart which I knew would have to be filled and then rolled to the feed bunk. Almost automatically, I picked up one of the wide, eight-tined silage forks leaning against the wall and began filling the cart. Before I was done, Silas was climbing down the ladder inside the chute and slid off one side of the aromatic heap.

"Hey there," he said, "darned if you don't swing that fork like an old pro."

"I should," I told him. "I've done enough of it in my time."

"The hell you say?"

"My grandfather had a dairy farm not too far up into Wisconsin," I explained. "He and Gram raised me from the time I was nine, after my folks were killed in a car wreck. So I've slung my share of shit and silage and grain and hay and just about anything else you can name."

Silas laughed. "That's the way of it, all right." He lifted his cap, mopping at the sweat he'd worked up throwing down the silage. In the cold air of the empty barn, steam rose off his damp scalp. "I had me a dairy herd here for a lot of years," he said, gesturing at the long stretch of dusty gutters and unused, cobweb-streaked stanchions. "Back in the seventies, when milk prices weren't spit and hadn't been for what seemed like forever, I got rid of 'em like a lot of others around here did. Wouldn't you know, now milk prices are high and steady and the only small farmers still making it with any degree of comfort are the ones who kept their dairy herds."

"The luck and lot of a farmer," I said.

"Boy, ain't that the truth. I got forty-some head of beef steers in the heifer barn off the back end there. They're about all I monkey with anymore. Keep a hundred or so chickens year-round, take the eggs to a place in Schaumburg three times a week. That and tilling a few acres of land is plenty to keep me busy."

"You've had this place a long time then?"

"All my life, son. Took it over from my father before me. Woulda been more than happy to hand it down to one of my boys, but they wouldn't have any of it, neither of them. The oldest one, he went into insurance selling, does real well down in the Fort Myers, Florida, area. The youngest, he's an electrician up in Minneapolis. Expect you passed up a chance to take over your grand-dad's spread, too, am I right?"

"Yeah, I did," I answered, feeling a twinge of the old guilt.

"How'd a Wisconsin farmboy turn out to be a big-city private eye?"

"Long, long story. First big step, I guess, was a decision early on that whatever I ended up doing, I didn't intend to be tied down to some stubborn, uncooperative piece of land and a herd of even more stubborn, more uncooperative damn bovines whose main goals in life seemed to be to step on your feet or smack you alongside the face with tails dipped in fresh manure."

"Yup. That's the way of it. My generation, it was just sort of understood that a fella mostly stayed in whatever line his pa was in. After the wars, seemed like youngsters—guys and gals both—got some kind of taste of independence and everybody's been going every which way ever since. Ain't saying it's good or bad, mind you—just different than it used to be, that's all."

Outside, above the howl of the wind, I could hear engines revving, indicating the others must be getting ready to leave. The old man had touched a nerve, though, and had piqued some fresh curiosity on my part.

"How is it," I asked, "you came to put your farm at the disposal of this blue-movie bunch?"

He smiled, a trifle sadly I thought. "Wish I had a real flashy story to tell on that. You'd think a situation like this would deserve one, wouldn't you? But, in fact, it was all pretty simple. About five years back, see, I'd finally reached the end of my rope. This old place, farm prices and inflation and everything had ground me down, wore me out. It came to making a choice between selling and trying to salvage at least a little something, or having the bank take it all away in another year or two anyway. So I put 'er on the block. One of the hardest things I ever done in my life. A real heartbreaker, like having to shoot a favorite old dog or something. Worse. Anyway, after just only a couple days, these two sharpie lawyer types out of Chicago showed up. They had a proposition for me. They represented people who were willing to subsidize—that was their word—my farming, if I'd lease out the use of the bottom of the old house to them. They'd bring in a remodeling crew to fix me and the missus proper living quarters upstairs and make the necessary alterations down, everything would stay in my name, all I had to do was sign a binding agreement to allow them use of their half whenever they wanted it. Now I might be just an old country gaffer, but I didn't fresh fall off the turnip truck either. I smelled a rat, I don't mind telling you. First thing I figured was that they wanted to make or store drugs or some such down there. No way I woulda stood for that. I guess when everything boiled out and I finally found what they really wanted it for, well, that somehow made it easier to swallow. So we went for it, Mother and me. We talked it half to death and worried it up one side and down the other and finally agreed it sounded better than bailing out and moving to some damn retirement village some damn where. Things have changed a lot since the beginning, what with me and her helping out like we do. They ain't really bad folks once you get to know them. A lot of them come back again and again and after you've seen them do their thing a few times, heck, it don't seem like such of a much—not all that different than turning the old bull loose in the barnyard to take care of business."

"Hey," I said, "you adapted. You did what you had to do to keep your farm."

He sighed, the vapor of his breath puffing out in front of him. "Yeah, that's what I'm able to tell myself most days. But every once in a while there's this voice down inside that wants to know what the hell kind of farmer has nekkid people running around in his parlor getting their picture took screwing while his wife is out in the kitchen mixing up batches of phony spunk for them to splash around on each other? On those days, I ain't able to feel very good about it at all."

22

The others had started out without me. Down on the road, through the blowing snow and rapidly descending dusk, I could see the receding reddish dots of the last set of taillights.

I trudged from the barn to the warmth of my idling Honda. I cocooned myself therein and sat a minute, feeling blue for Floyd Silas, for the compromises the old man had had to make with his life, regretting somewhat that I'd asked him to talk about them. While I was at it, I felt a little blue for myself, too, and for every other poor schmuck who'd had their dreams kicked out of shape by the hard edges of reality. Which, when you thought about it, amounted to just about everybody every damned where.

On a more immediate front, shoveling that cartload of silage was proving to be far from the smartest thing I could have done for my various bruises and stitches. The bodyful of aches throbbing through me now were making that point very clear and reminding me how long it had been since I'd popped any of the little doc's painkillers. I dug a couple of the capsules from my pocket. After finding the glove-compartment flask empty as a means to wash them down, I cracked the driver's door and reached out to scoop a handful of clean new snow. This I held in my mouth until it melted, then threw in the capsules and swallowed them down. Primitive perhaps, but whatever works, works. Just watch out the snow isn't yellow, that's all, if you ever go to try it.

With the new dose of painkillers on the attack in my system and a freshly lit cigarette hung from a corner of my mouth, I dropped the Honda into gear and rolled out into the teeth of the storm.

It was a pisser every foot of the way. The stretch of side road that carried me back to the highway wasn't too bad because I was driving with the wind. But immediately upon turning onto Old 51, the Honda started bucking drifts as high as its headlights. The tracks of the preceding vehicles, even when I could find them, were of little value due to the narrower wheel base of my smaller car. The Honda plugged doggedly on, though, engine growling confidently, windshield wipers slogging away fist-sized spatters of snow.

Over the radio, a somber-voiced announcer was repeating at regular intervals the information that all county road crews would be pulled within the hour, before the onset of full dark. As far as I could see, the plows had already given up on this outlying portion of the county.

On the other side of New Milford, a wide-spot-in-the-road community that bumps up against Rockford's southern limits, the highway widened to four lanes. The plow work through here was more recent and, although the open areas were drifting back in fast, the going much easier. Ahead, the lower edge of the storm-slashed sky was stained by subdued streaks of color from the city lights. I pressed the foot feed a little harder, anxious for the security of my home turf, even—make that especially—in the grip of the blizzard.

She hadn't made the Bypass 20 turnoff. She'd apparently been part way into the turn when the Olds's rear end had lost it and begun to slide. Whether she'd panicked and locked the brakes or fought the wheel the way she should have and simply couldn't control the fishtail, the big car had skewed sideways into the V created by the branching lanes and ended up hung there in the piled snow, as helpless as a turtle on its back. That's where it remained as I approached, its back tires whirring to no avail, a plume of exhaust smoke streaming out in the wind. I had no trouble recognizing it as the Oldsmobile I'd seen Belinda Davies get behind the wheel of back at the farm.

I snapped on my emergency flashers (strictly force of habit— there was no other traffic anywhere in sight) and eased to the side of the road, careful to avoid getting sucked too deeply into the ridge of slush there. Once again flipping up the hood of the old parka for protection against the bite of the storm, I piled out and high-stepped through the clinging snow over to the passenger side of the Olds. I pulled open the door and stuck my head in.

"You all right?" I wanted to know.

Belinda Davies, swathed in sleek fur, looked sullen and eerily beautiful in the glow of dashboard lights. "As all right as one can be, I suspect," she replied, "in such a bloody ineffective beast as this."

"You're hung up pretty good," I said. "Not likely to be able to break free without the help of proper equipment. There's a string of service stations just ahead. One of them is bound to have a tow truck. Why don't you ride in with me? We'll make arrangements for somebody to come back and winch it out."

"Can't you give me a push or something?"

"No way. Even if we could get you rocking back and forth, there's higher snow both in front and behind you. No place to go."

Defiantly, she gunned the engine. The tires revved uselessly, spinning to high-pitched screams in their pockets of glazed ice.

"Forget it," I told her. "The deeper you dig it in, the harder it's going to be for anybody to get out. Another plow comes along, they'll have it socked in solid. Let's go for a tow truck."

"Shit," she said distinctly.

Finally, with frustrated resignation, she gave the ignition key an angry twist and cut the engine. Clutching the keys and her handbag, she skimmed across the seat toward me. I assisted her out and, gripping her by one fur-encased arm, guided her back to my car. Around us, the wind heightened to a conquering howl and hurled snow and ice particles at us like thousands of tiny daggers.

Inside the Honda, I leaned back to catch my breath. Beside me, Belinda Davies was breathing hard also. Under the same conditions, most women would have looked bedraggled or at least somewhat windblown. For her, it was only an enhancement. The droplets of melting snow caught in her hair and on the fur of her coat, shining like miniature pearls. She smelled damply of some intoxicating perfume. God, she was gorgeous. Being that close to her was in no way conducive to catching your breath.

I snapped off the flashers, shoved the Honda in gear, spun out of the slush, and eased on into Rockford.

Old 51 becomes Eleventh Street at the city line. Eleventh Street, right from the start, is lined by a wide variety of businesses. There are a handful of motels and a pair of big implement dealers, then your K-mart, then your Eagle supermarket, then your Denny's and your Ponderosa, then dozens of other fast-food joints representing just about every chain known to man, then a proliferation of nonchain restaurants, then doughnut shops and bait and ammo shops and video-rental stores and beauty parlors and hardware stores and barber shops and bicycle-repair places, a sprinkling of small used-car lots, a church or two, and even the city's biggest year-round indoor flea market. Scattered among these are a goodly number of full-service gas stations.

We tried four of them. All four had tow trucks operating and all four had the same sad story: their trucks were out, they were radio-dispatched, but each and every one was already backlogged by fifteen to twenty calls. No way of telling how soon they could get to Belinda's car and no way of moving her up on the waiting list.

Plopping dejectedly back into the Honda for the fourth time, Belinda said, "Have you ever seen so many revoltingly honest clods in all your life? What does one have to do in this city of yours to get a bit of extra consideration? God knows I displayed a roll of bills large enough to choke a goat—surely I made my intentions clear enough. What hope can there be for civilization when you can no longer find a trace of solid, dependable greed?"

I grinned. "On a night like this, if you own a tow truck or a snow plow you don't need greed—everything comes your way anyway."

She grinned back. "Perhaps next time I should try opening my coat and undoing the top few buttons of my blouse—appear to be offering more than the possibility of just cash payment?"

"Might work. Cold weather can have an adverse effect on a guy that way, though, too. Besides, if you've been paying attention, half of these places have had the wives or daughters left handling the station while the old man was out with the truck. Out there in the field, so to speak, an open blouse or an open pair of thighs would probably do you more good."

She withdrew one of her lavender cigarettes. I flicked my Bic for her. After she'd inhaled and exhaled some smoke—she even made the act of smoking look glamorous, the way it used to in old black-and-white movies and on TV commercials—she said, "Well? What do you suggest now?"

I shrugged. "The only thing I can see is to leave your keys and a deposit of some kind, have them pick up your car as soon as they're able and deliver it to you."

"You'll take me on to my lodgings then?"

"Naturally."

So she went back in at the last place we'd stopped and made arrangements along those lines. Returning to the car, she informed me she was staying at the Clock Tower Inn on the city's east side. No surprise there—it's long been Rockford's finest hostelry. We proceeded in that direction.

The storm had by no means lessened, but its ferocity here in town was buffered by the buildings, its streaking winds chopped for the most part to erratically swirling gusts. Still, getting around was no picnic, not even on the main routes such as Eleventh Street. The snow kept coming, pelting everything with fat, wet flakes that stuck like gobs of Elmer's Glue-all and accumulated at a smotheringly intense rate.

I worked my way north and then east, staying with main arteries, timing it carefully not to hit any red lights, avoiding any inclined turns. In this manner, it took the better part of an hour to make it across town and out to the Clock Tower. By the time the hotel's distinctive silhouette rose into view, its lighted clock faces beaming from some fifty feet in the air, it was full dark.

All through town, there had been very few other vehicles moving. Out here, out on the fringes once again, in the vicinity of many of the city's busiest shopping centers, not to mention its controversially popular OTB, traffic was heavier but nevertheless decidedly sparse for a Saturday evening. Up on the interstate, I could see strings of headlights creeping along like funeral processions.

As I turned into the entrance drive of the motor inn, Belinda said, "Bear to the right. My suite is down near the far end, well past the registration area. There is a door at the end of the building where I can let myself in. You may drop me there, please."

I maneuvered between rows of parked vehicles, following her directions. Not surprisingly, on a night like this, the place appeared to be packed. I knew the layout of the Clock Tower complex after a fashion—not that I'd ever had occasion to stay there, and certainly not because I'd ever felt flush enough to visit any of its shops or eateries. But in keeping with its name and overall motif, the place also houses the Time Museum, a unique collection of time-telling devices from throughout history and throughout the world. It's quite a setup, justifiably renowned as one of the most complete in the world. I manage to kill one or two Sunday afternoons a year there and always come away mildly amazed, either at something new or something I hadn't noticed before.

As we rolled through the parking lot, Belinda continued to talk. "I can't tell you how grateful I am for all the trouble you've gone to. I insisted on being near the end of the caravan when it left the farm, because I was so sure my big car would do all right, even under these conditions. You can bet the others won't let me forget it when they find out I got no farther than I did. Your coming along was bloody lucky for me."

"No problem," I told her.

"In your line of work, I suppose rescuing damsels in distress is commonplace?"

"Sure. Don't I wish."

"Under different circumstances, I would of course suggest you come in for a drink. But given the weather . . . How far have you to drive back?"

"About half the distance we just traveled. I live on the south side, a ways off Broadway. That your door there?"

"Yes. If you like, you may—" She stopped suddenly, in mid-sentence, and just as suddenly her hand flashed across in the shadows and grabbed me above the wrist of my right arm. Grabbed me hard. "Don't stop," she said, her voice tight and insistent. "Please. Not here. Keep on going, drive around the building."

Something in her voice and in the way her eyes gleamed panicky in the half-light made me pause only the briefest second before obeying her. I held the gas pedal steady, left the clutch and brake alone, and let the Honda carry us unhurriedly around the building.

Once we were away from the brighter lighting out front and into the more stingily lighted auxiliary parking lot on the back side of the complex, Belinda released my arm and sat back in her seat. "Damn," she said, only partly under her breath. "Damn that recklessly spoiled brat!"

"What's the routine?" I said. "Stop now? Keep on going? What?"

"Keep on going."

"Where?"

"I . . . don't know."

"Come on, lady."

"I'm not sure."

"Look, I'm probably willing to stick with you on this. But I've got to know what's going on. What the hell happened back there?"

She didn't answer for several beats. Snow crunched under the tires. Wind shook the Honda, rattling shards of ice against it. I watched Belinda Davies out of the corner of my eye. She kept tucking her lower lip between her perfect white teeth and then drawing it slowly back out, unconsciously, anxiously. It gave her a new dimension: vulnerability. Made me want to help her no matter what was wrong, made me want to fix it so nothing would ever cause her to do that again.

"I saw something back there," she replied at length. "Something that alarmed me."

"Uh-huh. Something like a green Pontiac sedan maybe?"

Her head snapped around and her eyes went wide. "How could you know?"

"Because I saw it, too. The same car—or one just like it—was waiting for me at my place when I got home last night."

The Pontiac had been parked three slots down from the door she'd been going to enter through. It was almost certainly the same one that had been dispatched for me the previous night. As then, its engine was idling, producing a cloud of exhaust smoke that marked it like a banner. It apparently had been parked there for some time. The windows were clear and the heat of the motor had warmed the hood to the point that all snow had melted from it. This in sharp contrast to the surrounding cars upon which the white stuff was piled several inches thick. I'd spotted the Pontiac just as I was about to loop around for Belinda's drop-off, but before I could react to it in any way her hand had clamped my arm.

I was running out of parking lot now, waiting for Belinda to make up her mind about what she wanted to say or do. I steered over and braked at the end of the row of cars.

"Look," I said again, "we both know who sent the Pontiac. And your affiliation with the Camiccis is no secret, at least not from me. I guess that's why I'm having trouble understanding why the sight of the car was so upsetting to you."

She dug out a cigarette and got it going quickly on her own. Exhaling smoke hard through her nostrils, she said, "You obviously do not know darling little Frankie very well, do you?"

"You don't have to know Frankie well at all to know he's a jerk. So what? Your beef is with Frankie? I thought you were Frederico's . . ." I let it trail off.

"Frederico's what?" she wanted to know. "His 'woman'? His 'whore,' perhaps?"

"Hey, don't jump on my shit, okay? I'm the one trying to help you here. I was told you were Frederico's mistress. If that's wrong, tell me otherwise."

She exhaled some more smoke. "No, that's not wrong," she said in a more subdued voice. "I am Frederico Camicci's mistress. I have been for a number of years."

"So what's the problem with Frankie?" I asked it, but I already had a pretty good idea I knew.

Smiling sardonically, Belinda said, "The problem with Frankie is that he is here and I am here and Uncle Frederico is away across the ocean. Frankie apparently feels he has a certain obligation—a right, perhaps, putting it more accurately—to 'care' for me in a certain way in his uncle's stead."

"I get the picture," I said, tasting a splash of bile at the back of my mouth. "Is Frankie in that car?"

"Not likely. He'll have sent a team of his underlings . . . to fetch me like a take-out order from a restaurant."

"Then send the delivery boys packing. Tell them to go back and tell their boss no dice, this restaurant reserves the right to refuse service."

"That worked last night. I have the feeling it won't tonight. I have the feeling Frankie instructed them to be much more insistent."

"Then tell the creep to his face. Make it clear in no uncertain terms that you're not interested."

She laughed out some smoke. "You think it would be that simple?"

"All right, then threaten to tell Uncle Frederico what a naughty boy his nephew is being."

Her face in the dimness took on stark lines of concern, perhaps a touch of sadness. "My contact with Frederico has become very limited. Frankie knows this. Frederico is traveling with his wife, he is visiting his mother. There are other complications. Besides, Camicci blood is very thick. Frederico has already shown a distinct blindness a number of times in the past where Frankie was concerned. There is the risk he would choose not to believe me."

23

Like I keep saying, some decisions make themselves. The decision to take Belinda Davies back to my place was yet another one of those. Like the one at the Graingers' earlier in the day that netted me a rainbow of bruises and enough stitches to sew a new pair of pants, it maybe wasn't the smartest thing in the world—I realized that much going in. But it was a way to get her through the night, at least, a chance for her to sort things out in her head and decide how she wanted to handle it from here on out. How much of the idea stemmed from leftover teenaged lust fantasies on my part—the opportunity to spend a stormed-in night with a beautiful mystery woman—I didn't want to think about.

Remembering how pitifully low my supplies were at home, I had to make a stop at the twenty-four-hour Magna on State Street. Belinda came in with me and showed a surprising amount of interest in this bit of emergency stocking up, asking questions about my cooking facilities, offering suggestions, making some valuable comparison-pricing observations. When we were pushing the loaded cart back out to the car, she excused herself to duck briefly into the Osco drugstore next door "for a few personals."

It was going on seven when we climbed the outside steps to my apartment, each puffing under our burden of shopping bags.

Now I'll admit to being something of a slob, but I also take a certain degree of pride in being a rather neat one. Which is to say that while I may not be much for scrubbing and polishing and the like, I can be creative as hell when it comes to tidying the outer layers of the clutter so things look reasonably presentable. The towel in the bathroom might be a week old, for instance, but it is folded and hung neatly on the bar. The pile of dirty dishes in the kitchen sink might sit there two or three days, but they will be scraped and neatly stacked (or, better yet, tucked out of sight in a roaster pan in the oven). You get the idea. Luckily, I have a cleaning woman who comes in twice a month to keep the less superficial crud from reaching bacteriological-warfare status. By and large, though, you can visit my place most any time and not come away feeling like you need to be steam-Lysoled. Just watch out you don't open the wrong drawer or closet, that's all.

Anyway, for all of these reasons, I was able to unlock the front door and usher Belinda in ahead of me with no major apprehensions. The cleaning woman had been by in the middle of the week and, as far as I could remember, I'd left things in decent order. No roaches scattered visibly when I snapped on the lights. No trapped mice rattled in death throes from inside any of the cupboards. Everything was cool. I did wish, though, that the cinder block that held up one end of the couch didn't peek out from under the slipcover as much as it did.

I took Belinda's coat and hung it along with mine in the little nook off the kitchen. I removed my shoulder-holstered .45 and left it there as well. That out of the way, the next order of business as far as I was concerned was some hot coffee. But it occurred to me —somewhat belatedly—that my English guest might expect tea.

"I could use a cup or two of coffee," I told her. "I'm afraid I don't have much else in the way of a hot drink to offer you. I don't use tea and I never thought to get any while we were at the store. I maybe have some packets of cocoa mix around somewhere, if you'd prefer."

She smiled. "Coffee will be fine. I've become Americanized to the point of craving all its bloody caffeine as much as you Yanks. Besides, the myth of us English and our tea is vastly exaggerated in the first place."

So coffee it was. While I set some to brewing, she began unpacking the groceries. By the time we'd finished putting away the supplies and disposing of the emptied bags, the percolating pot was filling the room with its one-of-a-kind aroma.

This bit of domesticity—coming on the heels of the shopping, the haggling at the various service stations, and the vulnerability she'd displayed in the parking lot outside the Clock Tower— served to humanize Belinda through one more stage in my eyes, taking me a little further past her stunning beauty and removing another chunk of the pedestal that beauty had caused me to place her upon. Nevertheless, the loveliness of her and the nearness of her kept my pulse thudding double-time most of the evening. I couldn't help staring—unobtrusively, I hoped—at how her hair rippled, at the translucent flawlessness of her skin, at the way she'd smile that enigmatic half-smile of hers, sometimes with her brown-gold eyes truly caught up in it, other times with them mysteriously vacant or sad-looking. I'd been around beautiful women before—and have since—but I never came across one who at the outset made me feel like such a sweaty-palmed nerd. When I wasn't busy surreptitiously ogling her, I was inwardly cursing myself for reacting the way I was.

Over coffee and cigarettes, we sat at the kitchen table and talked. Foremost on Belinda's mind was concern about exactly what we might have let ourselves in for. "Surely you realize," she said, "that Frankie is not going to take this lightly—not for either of our sakes. And an upset Frankie can be a highly unpredictable and potentially dangerous force to reckon with."

"We covered all that in the car," I reminded her. "Like I told you then, Frankie and I are already on a collision course. If we're going to butt heads, it might as well be over something of my choosing as opposed to waiting for his convenience."

"You are either a very brave man or a very foolish one."

I shook my head. "Nothing brave about getting yourself backed into a corner and deciding to try and fight your way out. Foolish, on the other hand? That one I can't argue so good."

"I don't believe that for an instant. If I thought you a truly foolish man, I wouldn't feel as safe and as confident with you as I do."

"Yeah. Well, we'll see."

"What you said about backing yourself into a corner," she went on thoughtfully, "is intriguing. When you actually stop and think about it, we spend a great deal of our lives fighting our way out of the various corners we've allowed ourselves to be backed into, don't we? Much as we all like to believe we are in control of our individual destinies, in fact we're more like little laboratory mice in a maze—and we twist and turn often off-course instead of following the more direct routes we would choose if we really had any substantial degree of control."

I blew some steam off my coffee. "You're going a little deep for this ol' country boy, lady. What you're suggesting sure as hell doesn't sound like it's going to win this year's Pollyanna Award, but maybe you've got something."

"So those most in control," she went on, "are those most skilled at fighting back out of corners. You strike me as such, Mr. Hanni-bal."

"Uh-huh. But maybe there's another way you should look at it. Maybe I'm so good at bouncing out of the corners because I've had a lot of practice—which means I'm dumb enough to keep blundering in in the first place."

"I choose not to see it that way."

"Let's hope you're right. But how about you? You're obviously bright, intelligent. Getting tangled up with the Camiccis—*any* Camicci—should have read DEAD-END STREET in big, flashing letters right from the get-go. How did you manage to take that particular turn in the maze?"

"You're presuming, in light of this current mess with Frankie, that I am not deeply in love with Frederico."

"You're right. I'm presuming that much. Am I wrong?"

She gazed down into her coffee cup for a long time, as if the answer could be found there. "No," she said eventually, "I am not in love with Frederico. I may have thought I was. For a long time. I have always . . . appreciated him."

"That's a strange choice of words."

"Only if you don't understand what came before. What Frede-rico took me away from, what he has helped me to become."

I didn't know if I wanted to pursue that. I got up to refill our cups. As I replaced the pot on the stove, she went ahead with it anyway.

"When Frederico first took an interest in me," she said, "I was a five-hundred-dollar-a-night call girl with a drug habit taller than the Sears Tower and self-esteem lower than the leavings of a tene-ment rat. In three years I'd gone from being the blushing bride of an American serviceman who stopped off in Britain just long enough to claim my heart and whisk me away, to becoming one of the highest-priced specialty tricks in the city of Chicago. But I was skidding, and skidding fast. In another three years, if I'd been unlucky enough to live that long, I probably would have been rough-trade bait on some waterfront stroll. Along the way, of course, I gained ample experience as a battered and betrayed young wife, as a bitter divorcee, as a disillusioned nine-to-fiver trying to get by in any number of secretarial pools without lifting my skirt for every junior executive who had fifteen minutes to spare, and so on and so forth. At no point did the possibility of returning home to the UK seem desirable or feasible. I had burned those bridges behind me. My family had disapproved wholeheartedly of my marriage. And even in the event they would have been willing to forgive my folly and attempt to help me, there wouldn't have been sufficient money for it."

"So you were on your own," I said. "Backed into a corner."

"Very much so. In the end, I fought my way out by taking advantage of the best weapons at my disposal, the very things, ironically, I had refused so many times to let others use when they wanted them—my looks, my body. It began innocently enough with some modeling and then some dancing. Before long, I was allowing certain wealthy and influential men to 'see' me after my sessions or shows."

"And this is how you met Frederico Camicci?"

"Eventually, yes. By then I had for all intents and purposes given up the modeling and the dancing. I had established a regular clientele and had developed a reputation as a dominatrix of some renown. You Yanks, when you are of such bent, seem for some reason to prefer your degradation to be dished out by foreigners. In the fifties and sixties, I'm told, tastes ran toward buxom Teutonic types. More recently, the greatest demand has been for seemingly icy, aristocratic Brits like me. I'll let you ponder whatever psychological ramifications that suggests. At any rate, I became very popular, very 'in' in certain circles. Every third executive of any consequence throughout the city, it seemed, was waiting in line to have me squat over his face and piss down his mouth while admonishing him for being such a disgustingly naughty little boy. I never went in for the truly rough stuff—broken teeth and deep bruises and bloody welts and the like. My forte was providing precise verbal abuse augmented by the wearing of drop-dead leathers, the application of straps and paddle-spankings and the like to create mild physical discomfort, and humiliating demands such as the ever popular boot-licking and the aforementioned feeding of bodily excrements. Everything is relative, you must understand. If all that sounds terribly revolting, please remember that to me it seemed vastly preferable to allowing these same men to slobber and sweat all over me and to fill me with their jabbing little members and their pent-up loads of frustration."

"Yet you had to do drugs to get through it," I pointed out.

"True enough. At the time, of course, I would have argued that the drugs were a benefit, a luxury afforded me by the life I was living, rather than a habit that life made necessary. It was Frederico who came along and helped me to see the difference."

"He became one of your clients?"

"For a time. I did three brief movies for the B&D crowd. I was billed as Belinda the Boss Brit. Most of the routines were those I had developed with my clients—there were a few new ones the scripters came up with. They paid me marvelously and I saw it as a chance to advertise to a much wider untapped audience. Naturally, it was Frederico's people who distributed the films, and through them I came to his attention. Before long, he contacted me."

I smiled a shark's smile. "You'll have to pardon me if I find a bit of perverse pleasure in the thought of the Godfather kneeling to lick your boots."

She regarded me under one sharply arched brow. "Is that your only perverse pleasure, Mr. Hannibal? Have you no kinks, no secret little thing trips your lever to high voltage more automatically than any other?"

"Matter of fact, I do," I told her. "I have this recurring wet dream that involves a hot air balloon, a school of porpoises, and two dozen female Russian cosmonauts. Want to hear about it?"

She laughed in spite of herself. "You are an ass. I bare my soul, you make jokes."

This time the gold flecks in her brown eyes danced more brightly than I had ever seen them. I liked watching her laugh. I liked watching her do anything, even talk about a past that was by almost any standards decidedly checkered. With those eyes and that face and that laugh, she could confess to every foul deed from being a registered Republican to preferring the taste of New Coke over the old, and you'd still consider forgiving her.

Abstaining from further cracks and interrupting with only a handful of questions, I let her tell the rest of it. How, after only two visits, Frederico had approached her to become his mistress, to be set up in an elegant apartment, to receive a handsome monthly cash allowance plus an array of prestigious credit cards plus access to the finest services and entertainments the city had to offer—all in exchange for availing herself exclusively to him. How, because she was equal parts fascinated and frightened by him, by his reputation, she had accepted. How a genuine fondness had quickly developed between them, diminishing the importance and the frequency of the kinky sex. How he had recognized the signs of her drug abuse and had helped her beat it by putting her through the most reputable program in the country and then making sure he was there for her during the roughest parts of the maintenance. How he had encouraged her interest in cinema and writing and had prodded her into taking college courses in those and other areas. How he had displayed sincere pride in her academic achievements and had demonstrated his belief in her by allowing her to submit scripts to Foxwood's troupe without sanction of the Camicci name, not until a number of her works had already been accepted.

"In my eight years with Frederico," she concluded, "I have seen things and experienced things and grown in ways that never, never could have been possible otherwise. Do you see now why I say I 'appreciate' him?"

"But given all that," I said, "why do you think he might turn against you at this stage, if advised of the situation between you and Frankie?"

"As I said, Camicci blood runs very deep."

I shook my head. "Sooner or later Frederico is going to have to face the fact that his nephew is a putz and deal with it. You might be one of the few people who can get away with pointing that out to him."

"Perhaps. Then again, perhaps not. At the moment, it strikes me as a moot point. As I also said, my contact with Frederico these days is quite limited. I'm the one who is going to have to deal with Frankie and this current problem long before I could ever hope to get word to Frederico."

"That's what the little prick is counting on."

"To be sure."

"What he isn't counting on," I reminded her, "is me."

* * *

The conversation got considerably lighter after that. Touched on the blizzard that was still raging outside, worked around to a discussion of winter in general and her remembrances of winters in England and other parts of the world she'd visited, then trickled into talk of Christmas and the like. It was at this point that she noticed I had no tree or decorations of any kind in the apartment. After ascertaining I was not Jewish or any other nonparticipating religion (so as not to offend me, I guessed), she scolded my apparent lack of support for the grand old Christmas traditions. I pointed to a couple of brightly colored cards that had arrived in the mail that morning and were dropped on one of the end tables next to the couch. "If it'll make you feel any better," I told her, "I promise to leave those lying around until after New Year's. They'll be my Christmas decorations."

By then my stomach was growling so loudly and so frequently that it threatened to drown out whatever subject might have come up next. So I made sure that subject was supper.

With the broiler pan wetted down and the grill preheating over a low flame, I dug out the two sirloins I'd purchased especially, spread them on the counter, tenderized and seasoned them. The slabs of meat hit the grill with a satisfying sizzle. While I was thus occupied, Belinda assembled the lettuce, tomatoes, olives, and other ingredients we'd selected and tossed the works into a crisp, glistening salad.

When the steaks had been probed and flipped, I excused myself for a few minutes and ducked into the bathroom, where I gulped down two more of the little doc's pain pills. Even with a gorgeous redhead on hand to keep all the juices pumping, I was starting to feel the effects of the long, hard day. Wouldn't do to fold up now, wouldn't do at all. I splashed some cold water on my face and the back of my neck, ran a comb through my hair. Before going back out, I couldn't resist slapping on a hit of Old Spice.

The steaks were perfect, the salad appropriately zesty. The bargain-priced Cold Duck culled from Magna's sparse liquor department was palatable enough, certainly up to the standards of the Smurf jelly glasses in which it was served. I'm sure I must have eaten better meals in my day, but on that particular night I would have been damned hard put to name one. Belinda displayed a healthy appetite with no evidence of the dainty pickiness I'd sort of expected. Instead, hers was a no-nonsense, dig-in approach that made me suspect she hadn't been an only child back in England. I also suspected that in a different setting, in different company—a posh restaurant, say, on the arm of Camicci—she would have gone about it with a great deal more reserve. In other words, me and my humble environs brought out the best in her.

The meal completed, the table cleared, and the dishes soaking in the sink, we retired to the living room with the last of the Cold Duck in our glasses. The small talk had started to lose its zing. There wasn't much on the tube and my collection of dusty old albums seemed to interest Belinda only as a historical curiosity. In my stack of prerecorded movies—mostly old Westerns and the Roger Corman/Sam Arkoff-type sleaze-and-cheese grade-Z thrillers I've been hopelessly addicted to since I was a kid—she found a print of *The Quiet Man*. So we plugged that in. Belinda curled up in the big easy chair, I hooked the couch. On the TV screen, John Ford's lush Irish countryside and Maureen O'Hara's chiseled beauty seemed to roll on forever. As much as I always enjoy that movie—*dump-dump, dump-dump, dump-dump, deedle-deedle dump-dump*— I couldn't seem to stop yawning. The Duke had his redhead, I had mine; only I had the feeling one of us was going to make out a hell of a lot better than the other, even if he had to wade through Victor McLaglen to do it.

I made it as far as where Wayne sends Barry Fitzgerald to see if O'Hara "goes for it" and that's the last I remember.

24

I awoke in a Marshall Field's display window. Or so it seemed. A row of Santa's reindeer smiled at me. Christmas lights blinked on and off around them. Tinsel glittered. Bing Crosby or Perry Como or one of those types was warbling some nonsense about "let it snow, let it snow, let it snow." The air was sprinkled with the scent of pine needles, mixed with a strengthening aroma of bacon and eggs frying. Wait a minute—bacon and eggs?

I sat up, remembering to favor my wounded arm, but wincing sharply as my chest muscles flexed against the row of stitches there, while the hundred other aches and bruises scattered throughout my body clamored to make sure they weren't forgotten.

I'd been sprawled on my living-room couch. My boots had been removed, a light blanket had been spread over me. On the nearest edge of the coffee table in front of the couch were arranged plastic replicas of Santa Claus in his loaded sleigh being pulled by eight tiny reindeer. They continued to smile at me. Behind them, centered on the tabletop, stood a two-foot ceramic Christmas tree (almost identical to the one I'd smirked at in the reception area of Buck and Lois Ingram's Trim 'n Tan) with blinking lights. Streamers of tinsel were woven around its base. The bright cards I'd received in the mail were fanned neatly across the tinsel. Over against the wall, my boxlike, single-speakered little record player had been flipped open and plugged in and the Crosby/Como/whoever record was revolving scratchily on its turntable. By now it had switched to "Deck the Halls." Atop the TV stood a tall aerosol can whose partly turned label read something like WILD

PINE. While I'd slept, the demons of Christmas Commercialized had invaded my home.

I groaned to my feet and shuffled out to the kitchen.

"Good morning," she said over her shoulder, somehow sensing I was there. "I had an idea the smell of breakfast cooking might bring you around."

Belinda Davies stood at the stove, stirring a pan of scrambled eggs. She wore one of my old sweatshirts, the bulky sleeves shoved up past her elbows, the bottom pulled down to midthigh. She was bare-legged and barefooted. Her long copper hair had been pulled into a loose pony tail that swung behind her head and struck sparks off the sunshine pouring in through the window.

I took a Pall Mall from the pack on the table, snapped a flame to it.

"My, my," I said. "Looks like somebody has been awfully busy this morning."

"And someone else has been zonked to the world," she replied. "For about twelve hours."

I grinned a little sheepishly, even though she wasn't looking at me. "Sorry about that. A lot of things caught up with me. I guess I leave plenty to be desired as a host."

She turned from the stove. "Nonsense. You gave up your bed, didn't you?"

I grunted. "I've slept in that bed for a lot of years. It's no big treat, I know."

I walked over to the window and looked out at the day. It was clear and bright, the way it often is after a storm. The sunshine was blinding off the new snow. The sky was a cloudless cobalt blue. The trees were bending under what appeared to be a fairly stiff and steady wind. Mists of glittery loose flakes swirled from the crests of some of the bigger drifts.

"It's about ten degrees out there right now," Belinda said. "The radio says we should only see a high of eighteen. Eighteen is also the number of inches of new snow we received."

I craned my neck so I could see part of the street. No plow had been through for hours. Down below, my Honda was wrapped in a drift that obscured all four tires and both bumpers. It looked like a rusting tin cup turned upsidedown on the snow.

"Also according to the radio," Belinda went on, "most of the main arteries in the city have been cleared, and crews have started on the side streets. They hope to have most neighborhoods dug out by late afternoon. There is another storm system headed our way which should reach us sometime tomorrow."

"Swell," I muttered.

"I have a fresh pot of coffee made. Would you like some?"

"Definitely. But first I'd better go, uh, wash my hands."

I ambled into the bathroom. I did get around to washing my hands, but first order of business was unloading all the Cold Duck and coffee from last night that had been building up pressure in my bladder for over a dozen hours. That taken care of, I felt about fifty percent better. I knocked back a couple of painkillers to go after the other fifty percent. I was chasing a bar of soap around in a basin of sudsy water when Belinda rapped on the door. "Hurry along, please. Breakfast is nearly ready."

We sat down at the table over mounds of scrambled eggs, a platter of bacon, hot buttered toast, and coffee. After sampling some of each and finding everything fairly delicious and stating same, I jabbed a thumb over my shoulder to indicate the living room. "So where did all the Christmasy paraphernalia come from?" I wanted to know. "You some kind of magician as well as a good cook?"

"I was beginning to wonder if you had even noticed."

"Of course I noticed. I notice everything. I'm a trained detective."

"You didn't seem to be noticing much while I was arranging it all around you. I believe I could have started a bloody chainsaw in the middle of the living room and gone out to fell a real tree and you would have slept through it. Of course, your snoring would have effectively countered the noise of most chainsaws, I suppose."

"Protective camouflage," I said defensively. "But that still doesn't tell me where all the stuff came from."

She smiled mischievously. "I finally found someone in this fair city of yours who was bribable."

"Bribable?"

"As we were driving here last night, I noticed one of those round-the-clock little convenience markets a few blocks away. When I awoke this morning, for some reason all I could think about was that you had absolutely no Christmas decorations. It seemed so sad and empty. And then I remembered the little store.

So I bundled in this sweatshirt and your big parka and tucked my pants into my boots and hiked there."

"You walked in all that cold and snow?"

"Actually, it was exhilarating. On the way, I helped some children lift the head onto a perfectly smashing snowman. At the store, I bought them a great long carrot for his nose. They were delighted. But more to the point, I was also able to get these decorations there. They had only a very limited selection that was for sale, but when I looked sad for the little man behind the counter and told him of my poor invalid mother who didn't have a single colored bulb to brighten her season and how I couldn't make it downtown because of the snow and everything and especially when I let him glimpse some of the money I was willing to part with in order to cheer her up, it turned out he was willing to sell just about anything. Strictly out of compassion for the poor old bedridden soul, mind you. The tree and everything came straightaway out of his front window. He even sold me the Christmas albums he was piping over his PA system."

I shook my head. "You're something. You know that?"

She was still smiling. Beaming would be more like it. "Why do you say that?"

"Look at you. You look like a duchess who fell off the royal carriage in the wrong part of town. You're miles from everything you know, all the comfort you're used to. You've got the Godfather's crazy nephew after your lily white ass. You're snowbound with a beat-up stitched-up retread like me. Yet through it all, you're worried about Christmas decorations and a carrot for a snowman's nose."

Her smile was gone. Her gaze on me was steady. The gold flecks had faded from her eyes, leaving them pools of deeper, richer brown. She said, "In these past few hours—last night, this morning—I have felt more relaxed, more at ease, more *at home* than I have at any other time in years."

I gave a little laugh. "Come on. You can't mean that." I had a kind of lump in my throat. It wasn't the eggs, it wasn't anything I could seem to get swallowed down.

"My only regret," she said softly, "was when I awoke in the middle of the night and found myself alone."

* * *

I carried her into the bedroom and we made love. Slowly. Gently. Endlessly. Her body was supple and splendid. I explored every centimeter of it—its sweetness, its pungency, its heat. When I entered the molten moisture between her legs, it was like being drawn into the searing brilliance of an atomic flash.

Afterwards, we lay back and smoked and laughed a little and talked. And then we made love again, this time more fiercely, more frenzied. Blood leaked from the stitches on my chest, smearing her breasts and stomach. We licked it from each other.

For the first time since we'd been together, we got around to talking about the case I was on, about the murders of Jason Hobbs and Valerie Pine and the possible consequences for the rest of the troupe.

"Everyone seems to have the utmost faith in you," Belinda was saying. "One could physically feel the tension lift after it was announced you had been retained. Kat Hayward says you are one of the best there is at what you do and if anyone can satisfactorily see this through, then you can."

"Kat said that?" I grunted. "I'm surprised she could find it in that ice-cube heart of hers to say anything flattering about me."

I was lying across the bed on my stomach, still naked, watching Belinda. She, fresh out of the shower, wrapped in a barely adequate towel that kept peeking open in interesting ways all up and down the seam below where she had it knotted, was combing out her long hair in front of the full-length mirror on the back of the bedroom door.

"Because of the hard feelings between you two over the way she treated your friend, you mean?"

"She told you about that?"

"Mmm. We had a rather interesting tête-à-tête out at the farm yesterday morning during which she opened up to me about a number of things. She had arrived early for a scheduled girl–girl shoot involving herself and Sara Baines, but Sara, as usual, was running late. So, while we were waiting, Kat and I chatted. Mostly she talked. I suspect that a number of recent stress factors —the murders, the trouble on the set Friday with Richie, your arrival on the scene, and God knows what else—had built up pressure in her to the point where she had to release some of it. I happened to be on hand to listen."

"My heart bleeds for poor Kat and her stress factors."

"How cruel."

"She's a cold-blooded bitch who ripped out my best friend's heart and kicked it into the middle of the street for everybody to see."

"Did you ever think that she must have had her reasons?"

"I just told you the reason."

"She said you would never understand, that you were too much like him."

"Like who?"

"Your friend—the Basher."

"Bomber," I corrected somewhat testily.

"Bomber, then. She said the two of you are relics, throwbacks to a more colorful time when men tried always to act in a certain way, to be men, to be stoic, to shoulder the responsibility for every task and never accept defeat or failure."

"So what? That some kind of fancy way of saying she blames Bomber for the way things turned out? It was his fault she was a tramp who did all the shit she did behind his back?"

"Their relationship went too far too fast. Before she knew it, she was in the middle of a thing that everyone around her—not just the Bomber—interpreted as serious and lasting. What she could see but no one else seemed able to was that they were no good for each other—not in any long-term sense. When she tried to tell your friend that, talk to him about it, he either would not listen or would reassure her with platitudes. Her only recourse, as she saw it, was to end it and end it with such ugly finality that no one would be encouraged to cling, to try and work it out."

"My, wasn't she being a regular little Mother Teresa, putting him out of his misery that way?"

Belinda frowned. "You seem dreadfully bitter. Especially about something that happened to someone else."

"Yeah, well, maybe I'm showing Bomber's pain and bitterness for him. Because he has to be stoic and can't for himself. I guess that's the way it is with us throwback relics."

"Obviously this was an unfortunate subject to get onto. I just want to add that I've known people in the kind of relationship Kat described. No one gets out of them without pain. Which means she must be carrying around her share, too."

"Tough."

"After talking to her yesterday, listening to her, I am convinced that her cynicism and the coarseness she sometimes descends to are just masks to hide her pain. She hasn't led a particularly easy life, you know. She admits that many of the difficulties are her own doing, but she's trying desperately to get back on track."

"Sure. Anybody can see that. Doing fuck movies is a real positive step in that direction."

Reflexive anger flared on Belinda's face. But she kept it in check. "Her main concern is for her two-and-a-half-year-old son, the product, as she so poignantly puts it, of 'a roll in the hay with some damned lumberjack up there in Canada who must have been using brand X.' For whatever reason, she decided to keep the child when she could have easily gotten rid of him. At least give her credit for that. But you can imagine the problems of trying to raise a child while working the strip circuit—shaking your bum on stage in a different town every other week, sometimes every other night. It was for the boy's sake that she came back here to settle in Rockford, to live with her divorced sister—who also has a child. The X-rated work and an occasional stripping gig when she can find one close enough to home are done strictly to make ends meet. Every extra cent is poured into the sister's business, a small chain of beauty salons salvaged from her divorce. Once the struggling business is solidly in the black, the plan is for Kat to retire from this kind of dubious but temporarily necessary moonlighting and learn whatever new skills she needs to become a full partner in running the business."

Belinda's flash of offended anger and her talk of Kat's baby son, neither of which I was prepared to deal with, took most of the remaining steam out of me. My crack about "fuck movies" being "a real positive step" had been harsh and dumb under the circumstances—priggish at best—and I regretted the hell out of saying it. But it was one of those things that, once said or done, it's better to leave alone rather than go back and try to fix. And while Kat's mention of a baby-sitter on the set Friday obviously had implied a child, the fact for some reason never really sank home in my thick skull. Now that it had, I suddenly found it difficult to dredge up all the old hard feelings, the bitterness and contempt I felt for her, to channel all that toward the mother of a two-and-a-half-year-old little boy.

I sighed wearily. "I guess it's like you said, that was an unfortunate subject for us to have gotten onto. Let's forget it."

"There is nothing else to say, anyway," Belinda replied a bit coolly. "By the time we'd discussed that much, Sara arrived on the set and there wasn't any more time for idle chitchat."

Eager for something—anything—else to talk about, I grabbed at that. "Sara Baines," I said, "now, there's a young lady who ought to be stamped 'X-rated' just to be allowed to walk around out in public. Does she really cook in real life as hot as she comes across on screen?"

"She does indeed. Sexy Sara lives up to her billing every minute of every day." Belinda switched to a soft-bristled brush and continued to work on her lustrous hair. Her strokes, which had grown sharp and choppy during the height of her ill-concealed anger, now began to smooth out again into long, flowing motions.

I said, "I saw how the crew and everyone was acting during the shoot yesterday, and then afterwards, even the two guys who's just done the scene with her. She obviously has whatever it takes to strike the responsive chord."

"Sara is what every X-rated star ought to be, what all the viewers probably fantasize they are. One could accurately say she is obsessed by sex, that it is the driving force in her life. The reason she comes across so intensely, both on screen and off, is that none of it is forced or faked. She seems literally to be in heat twenty-four hours a day—a veritable nympho—and she exudes this to everyone who comes in contact with her. There are stories of her doing two or three complex and lengthy shoots in an afternoon and then, before wrapping up for the day, being willing—eager, even—to take on all present who weren't lucky enough to be in a scene with her."

I shook my head. "Christ. She carries on like that even with her kid brother around?"

Belinda shrugged one shoulder. "They seem to have an understanding. Apparently young Chuck is able to accept Sara's appetites."

"Uh-uh. That's what everybody keeps telling me, but I don't buy it. I saw the way he looked—or rather wouldn't look—on the set yesterday when she was playing pump-the-Pilgrim with those two clowns in wigs. I know everything is supposed to be up-front and open with you people—husbands, wives, girlfriends, boyfriends, what have you. Maybe I'm more of a prude than I ever thought, but when you get into blood relatives, too . . . well, there's a place you have to draw the line."

"Good lord. You make it sound as if we're promoting incest or some such. I assure you that is not the case, and you can rest doubly assured that it could never be the case with Chuck Baines. From all reports, the lad is totally impotent. In addition to his substance-abuse problem, he is suffering emotionally from a tremendous guilt trip over his parents' death. It was while they were visiting him for the weekend at the rehab center, you see, that the motel in which they were staying caught fire and they died. Chuck withdrew from everything and everyone after that—all but Sara. That was one of the reasons she insists on bringing him around the set. As I said, she is obsessed by sex. Apparently she felt that exposing him to all the lascivious goings-on that surround a blue-movie troupe might somehow stimulate him, help him past his sexual hang-ups, and then open the floodgates to help clear away his other problems. She encouraged many of the actresses to play up to him, attempt to seduce him. Angie Mullond, Cindy Wallace, Kat . . . a number of them tried. None were successful."

"A sort of sexual cure-all that didn't cut it, huh?"

"Something like that."

"I guess I've heard weirder rationales, especially in the past few days. You hit the nail smack on the head about one thing, that's for sure—Sexy Sara certainly lives up to her billing."

Belinda turned and eyed me appraisingly. "You had better not be lying there letting our talk about Sara Baines give you a hard-on, luv, or I shall be forced to come over and apply the back of this hairbrush to your member until it is but a bloody wee stump."

I grinned at her. "I was wondering when we were going to get to the kinky stuff."

"You want kinky? I shall show you kinky."

"You'd punish a fella purely on circumstantial evidence?"

"Most assuredly."

"Well, you'd better do something about the way that towel you're almost wearing keeps falling open then, or you might discover more circumstantial evidence than you're ready to deal with."

Putting aside the hairbrush, she undid the knot that was holding up the towel with a flip of one thumb. The towel fell at her feet. She placed her hands on her hips. "Is that better? Now it can't fall open and distract you."

"No, it sure can't," I agreed.

"So how is your circumstantial evidence now?"

"I refuse to answer on the grounds I might incriminate myself. Guess you'll just have to come over here and frisk me."

She did. And she was able to deal just fine with everything she found.

25

At three o'clock that afternoon, the plows finally made it to clear my street. Fifteen minutes later, as I was dressing to go down and shovel out the Honda, there was a knock at the front door.

Crawford stood on the landing, his dark face wearing a grim expression. "Jeez, man. Don't you answer your damn phone?"

"It's been out of order," I lied. "The storm." In truth, I had switched it off shortly after returning with Belinda last night, not wanting any interruptions while she was there trying to sort things out. I hadn't thought to turn it back on.

"You've got bigger problems than a broke phone," Crawford said. "There's been another murder."

My teeth ground together way at the back of my mouth and I felt my stomach muscles yank into a hard knot. "Who?" I wanted to know. "When?"

He shook his head. "Ain't for me to say. Camicci and Foxwood are both waiting to see you, talk to you about it. Together. I'm to bring you straightaway."

"Right," I told him. "Give me a couple minutes. I'll be down."

I closed the door and turned slowly from it. A clammy film of sweat was threatening to bead up across the back of my neck.

Belinda emerged from the bedroom and stood in the middle of the kitchen. Her face was drawn, slightly pale. She'd heard every word.

"Well, that blows everything to hell and gone," I said. "Can't run around sticking our heads in the sand and pretending the murders might not be connected any longer. Damn it, anyway."

"What will you do?"

"What I hired on to do. For openers, I'll have to go see Camicci and Foxwood, hear what they have to say. I'll decide my next step after that. They may not like one of the options open to me, though."

"What do you mean?"

I made a catch-all gesture with one hand. "The cops. I may have to bring them the rest of the way in on this—all the way in. I don't want to risk somebody else turning up dead while I'm conducting a one-man show on this side of the fence and the blues are going at it on their side half-blindfolded. It's getting too big, too messy for that. Right now all I have is a bellyful of questions, a few dim possibilities. Loose ends that go off in every which direction. The cops have the wherewithal to run down those loose ends in a matter of hours. Me, it could take days. The next victim might not have that long."

Belinda said nothing. Muscles fluttered around the fine curve of her jaw.

I walked through the kitchen and took my shoulder-holstered .45 from the little nook back there. As I shrugged into the rig, I said, "For the time being, there's at least one positive aspect to this. Under the circumstances, Frankie won't be able to concentrate on your disappearing act over the past twenty-some hours as tightly as he otherwise would have. You should be able to put him off with a simple story: you got stranded, couldn't make it back to your hotel, had to spend the night somewhere where the phones were out. He'll have to buy it. There obviously won't be any more taping this weekend, so you can go on back to Chi-town where he isn't as likely to bother you. That doesn't solve anything for next time, of course, but it gives you a chance to work on it. In the meantime, maybe you'll make contact with Frederico."

She gave a small nod. "Yes. Perhaps."

I pulled on the big parka. In the living room, I switched the phone back on. "You can call for a cab whenever you're ready, have them take you to the Clock Tower. You own car should be there waiting for you by now."

She walked me to the door and leaned close. "What about us?"

I put my hands on her shoulders. "I don't know. I wasn't sure there was an 'us.' Can there be?"

"These past hours, the time we've been together . . . wasn't that something special?" She put her hands over mine.

"It was for me," I answered truthfully. "But it's easy to make a few hours, a few days something special. What about what comes next? What about all the comforts, all the high living and fine things you're used to?"

She withdrew her hands. "You believe I'm that shallow? You think that's what I care about?"

"I think it might be more important to you than you want to admit. Look around you, for crying out loud. My guns are the only expensive things I own. I don't remember planning it that way, but that's the way it is. And what about my job, what I do?"

"You could do something else."

"Uh-huh. I could have done something else a long time ago. But I never did. Just like you never did. Neither of us ever got around to it, did we? That's the thing."

She took a step back. "You are a cold man."

I started to argue with her, but I stopped myself. "Look," I said, "this isn't the time to get into this. You know I have to go. If you want to be here when I get back, we can talk then."

"And if I'm gone?"

Over my shoulder, as I went out the door, I snapped, "Then I'll find you. I'm a goddamned detective, remember?"

Wispy-haired Earl answered the door of Henry Foxwood's apartment. He looked stiff and uncomfortable in the posh setting. After ushering Crawford and me in and making sure the door behind us was closed and locked, he led us back toward the book-lined study where I had been hired. But before reaching it, he turned into a different room, this one brighter, less somber, its walls lined not with bookshelves but with gaudy movie posters and framed photographs and hung with all sorts of Medieval fighting paraphernalia such as crested shields and gleaming broadswords and battle axes and savagely spiked maces. At the far end, in sharp, ultramodern contrast, stood a giant-screen television bracketed by polished slotted shelving filled with row after row of videocassettes. This, then, was Foxwood's movie room, his entertainment center, overlapping as a quasi shrine to his "Champion of Camelot" days, his brief shining moment of glory and immortality. A closer glance at the posters revealed them to be blown-up, colorized ads for the old TV shows, and the photos showed a young Foxwood rubbing elbows with various Hollywood greats and near-greats of thirty years gone by.

Today's Foxwood was seated on a low, furry-looking couch situated at a forty-five degree angle to the broad, blank screen. Across from him, on an identical couch, sat Frankie Camicci and Uschi, her steel-edged curves wrapped in a short skirt and tailored blazer.

All eyes fell on me as I entered the room.

Foxwood got up and walked over. "This is a hell of a thing, Hannibal," he said, his voice shaken. "A hell of a bad thing."

Camicci remained seated, watching. His face was expressionless.

"Who got it?" I asked Foxwood. "What happened?"

His eyes went darting around, then came back, and got caught by mine. Licking his lips, he said, "Kat. Kat Hayward. They found her early this morning, just after the storm broke."

It was as if a giant fist reached out from somewhere and wrapped around me, squeezing me like a tube of paste, crushing the air out of me, making me feel tiny and trapped and insignificant. I wanted to strike something or someone, to crush back in retaliation.

"How was she killed?" I said. My voice sounded far away.

Foxwood blinked a couple times. "Strangled. Very similar to what was done to Valerie Pine."

"Who found her? Where?"

"Her sister found her. In the garage of the house they shared. Kat went out for a few groceries early last evening, while the storm was still building. When she did not return, the sister was naturally worried. But she convinced herself that Kat must have gotten stranded somewhere and could not make it back—somewhere where she was unable to use a telephone either because they did not have one or because the storm put it out of order. The sister's concern had increased only slightly by this morning as she made her way out to the garage to get a shovel and a bag of salt for the sidewalk. That was when she found Kat. She had made it back after all and apparently was attacked the moment she got out of her car. She lay dead beside it, the bag of groceries scattered around her."

On a glossy coffee table that separated the two furry couches sat an oval serving tray arranged with glasses and a decanter of the excellent brandy I remembered from my first visit. I walked over and helped myself. Poured three meaty fingers, knocked them back, poured three more.

I looked down at Camicci. "What are the cops saying?"

He spread his hands. "What do the cops always say? 'We're investigating a number of leads. . . . We expect a breakthrough within the next 24 hours. . . . Blah blah blah.'"

"What's the straight dope?"

"Far as anybody can tell, they don't know dick."

"What about the sister? She must have known what Kat was doing, about the screw movies, the troupe."

"No," Foxwood said. "Kat and I had occasion to discuss that very thing a short time back. The sister—her name is Louise—knew Kat was a dancer, a stripper, that she did club dates and sometimes smokers and stag parties to bring in the extra income. She could accept that all right. But Kat never told her about the videos, she never felt Louise would have been able to handle it."

I looked around the room. Everybody looked back.

"Well, there's no two ways about it," I said. "The cops have got to be told."

Camicci shot to his feet. "The fuck anybody's going to the cops!"

I stood nose to nose with him. It was like I figured, the twerp wore lifts in his street shoes. "Wake up and smell the coffee, mister," I said. "Somebody is changing the rules of your ballgame. They're bumping off your players and as long as you're stupid enough to freeze out all the umpires, they're going to keep bumping them off."

"What the hell are we paying you for?" Camicci demanded. "I thought you were the hotshot who was going to figure all this out for us."

He backed me up a little with that one. "I can get the job done," I conceded. "But I'm one man. The cops are a hundred—a thousand if need be. You willing to risk more lives for the extra time it's going to take me?"

"Read my lips—no fucking cops. No way."

I turned to Foxwood. "I made it clear from the beginning," I reminded him, "that there were certain lines I wouldn't cross. I was cutting it thin enough the way it was. There's no longer any doubt the killings are somehow tied to your movie troupe. To not let the authorities in on that amounts to withholding evidence in a felony. That's my license and the whole nine yards."

Foxwood looked appealingly at Camicci. "He has a point. The understanding we had was—"

Camicci cut him off with a chopping motion of his hand. "I don't care about no candy-ass understanding. Like Hannibal just said himself, the rules are changing."

I shook my head. "Not mine."

On the couch behind Camicci, Uschi went tense. Out of the corner of my eye I thought I saw Earl shift his stance. I had to laugh.

"If you're planning on siccing Fred and Ginger on me," I said to Camicci, "I don't think they're good enough. And even if they are, that leaves you no investigator, no umpires, no nothing. What's the percentage in that?"

Camicci's eyes whipped around, flashing dark and dangerous. I felt myself tensing, going on full alert. Crawford was the main one I was worried about; he was somewhere behind me, back where I couldn't see him at all.

Camicci's eyes continued to burn threateningly, but suddenly there was a smile beneath them. "Nobody's going to try and stop you, hotshot. Go ahead, walk out the door. Run to the cops. Spill your guts. But then you might as well hang around right there. Because in just a little while, a body is going to turn up—the body of a big ugly Chink with a couple bullets where his balls used to be. Even the dumb-fuck cops shouldn't have any trouble matching those slugs because they already got a pile of yours on file from other shootings you've done. Those shootings went down as justifiable. Only this time it's going to be obvious that somebody tried to sweep this one under a rug. How do you think your buddies in blue are going to feel about that, hotshot?"

26

The cop said I should call him Al. It might even have been his name, but I doubted it. He looked to be in his late twenties, medium height and build. Wore a stocking cap pulled down low over his ears to a point even with the tops of his brows, leaving me no hint as to the cut or color of his hair. He also wore a mustache. I couldn't decide if it was real or not, but given the paranoia he was displaying I had a feeling it could be fake.

Al didn't much like the idea of having to spend time with me. I wasn't real crazy about his company either. But when you're damn fool enough to allow yourself to get tucked into the Syndicate's pocket, you don't get to pick the lint you end up rolling around with.

Frankie Camicci had me by the balls. I knew it, and his little spiel there in Foxwood's apartment had been designed to show me and everybody else that *he* knew it. Once that was established, it came down to deciding where we went from that point. I had no choice but to continue my investigation and to go along with keeping the cops out of it for as much longer as we could. It was crazy to think they wouldn't trip to the blue-movie tie-in sooner or later, even if you had as much contempt for them as Camicci did. My job, as he saw it, was to solve the case before they found out too much. Just incidentally, it would be nice if that also happened to be before anybody else turned up dead. When he said he'd get copies of the police reports on Kat's killing to me ASAP, I'd pounced on that. I was working too cold, I explained, too far removed. Pictures and professional analyses are okay, but they can never give you the complete first-hand feel and smell and juice of a thing the way actually being there and being able to touch or grab hold can. I told him I wanted to visit the latest murder scene and I wanted to be accompanied there by whatever cop-on-the-take was feeding him the reports.

Camicci had seen the logic in my request; I'll give him that. So arrangements were made for me to get together with Al. Al, like I said, wasn't very happy with any of this, but he was just as stuck with it as I was.

We met that evening in a greasy spoon a ways out on Kiswaukee. We drove in my car from there to the address where Kat had lived and died. "When we get there," Al said as we pulled out, "drive around the block once. If everything looks okay, park across the street." He gave me those instructions twice more during the drive over, as if saying them out loud enough times would somehow help ensure everything going all right.

He sat hunched in the seat beside me, clasping and unclasping his gloved hands, shifting his feet, sighing frequently, writhing with nervous energy. It was like sitting next to a crate of snakes. Once he said, "Boy, I hate this shit. Sometimes they keep an eye on these places, you know? Like 'return to the scene of the crime' and all that shit, you know?" The rest of the time, except for repeating the instructions on how I should proceed once we got there, he was quiet.

The house was a single-storied wood frame job in a solid middle-class neighborhood on the northwest side. We circled the block without spotting any signs of a trap waiting to be sprung, not that this seemed to do much to relieve Al's anxieties. I then pulled to the curb on the opposite side of the street—well, as close to the curb as I could get given the ridge of snow left by the plows —and cut my engine.

It was full dark by now. The night was as clear as the day had been. In the light of a fat moon and a skyful of stars bouncing off the new snow, it seemed almost as bright. I wasn't carrying anywhere near the load of apprehension my accomplice was, but even I could have gone for a nice, convenient cloud cover.

With our breath chugging vapor trails into the crisp air, we piled out of the Honda. Crossing the street, our feet crunched on the cold, packed snow like the crack of Nazi jackboots goose-stepping through Berlin Square.

The garage was unattached, standing about ten yards off to the right of the house. A very basic, one-car facility painted a matching white-with-black-trim. Somewhere under the snow there was probably a sidewalk connecting the two structures, but no one had ever gotten around to using the shovel Louise had gone out for that morning just before she found her sister's body. Instead, the front yard was pockmarked by a thousand footprints, some of them combining to form stomped-out trails, all of them converging on the garage.

Al and I followed one of these trails to the garage's side door, where he produced a key (attained from exactly where, I didn't ask) and inserted it in the lock. There was no police seal, the detectives and the lab crew apparently having decided they'd already gotten everything in the way of pertinent evidence they were going to find. While Al fumbled with the key, I glanced over at the house. It was appropriately dark. Foxwood had ascertained for us that Kat's sister and the children would be staying with friends for a few days, until they felt composed enough to attempt returning here to pick up the pieces of their lives. It looked like a nice home, I thought, the kind of place that isn't supposed to be visited by the disruptive shock of murder. Now it would be stained by that forever. I hoped Louise and the kids wouldn't be.

Al led the way into the garage and closed the door again behind us. Inside, naturally, it was much darker. There were only two small windows, one on each side, none in the roll-down bay door. I swung the beam of my pencil flash, locating a wall switch, and reached to snap on some lights.

"Jesus Christ, turn that off," Al hissed excitedly. "Turn that the fuck off!"

"Will you relax," I told him. "If anybody noticed us coming in here, it will look a lot more suspicious if they see us poking around with flashlights than if we pop on the overheads and act like we've got every right in the world to be here. Just cool your jets."

"Screw you and your cool jets. All I want to do is get this the hell over with and get out of here."

"It won't take long, not if you stay out of my face."

He muttered something under his breath that I didn't catch. I didn't push it because I wanted to get the hell out of there, too.

The garage was empty of any vehicles, but muddy tire tracks and clumps of dirty snow that had dropped from inside wheel wells clearly marked where one had been parked. And beside those tracks, scratched onto the gritty concrete floor, was the chalk outline of where Kat's body had lain. The bag of groceries was still there, ruptured from being dropped, its contents scattered recklessly.

I walked over and knelt beside the chalk marks, careful not to place my knee in the yellowish slush that leaked from an upside-down egg carton. I reached down and touched the outline, first at its edges, then further into the shape it formed. For some reason I did this with a gentleness, as if there could be something there I might disturb.

Goddamn your miserable heart, Kath or Kat or whoever you were trying to be. I never liked you alive and now you went and got yourself killed and sucked me even deeper into a mess that already had me by the short ones. I bet you're laughing in Hell, aren't you?

"You can see where she put up a bit of a fight," Al said, gesturing. He'd moved over to stand beside where I knelt. His voice and manner had shifted slightly, the cop in him showing through in spite of himself.

What he indicated with his hand gesture was a section of metal shelving that had been fastened to the wall on what would be the driver's side of any car pulled forward into the garage. Part of the shelves had been knocked down, their contents—stacks of old *Cosmopolitan* magazines, two or three dozen romance paperbacks, some rusting cans of auto-related gunk, a collection of peanut-butter jars that had been washed and refilled with nuts and bolts and screws and nails and the like—strewn about with items from the broken grocery sack.

"It wasn't much of a struggle, though," Al went on. "She didn't suffer very long or anything. The big door there had no kind of remote device, see, so it would have been standing open after she pulled her car in. She might even have left it open while she was gone; the sister never noticed. So the killer could have already been in here waiting or he could have walked in behind her as she drove in. No way of finding any tracks with all the new snow that fell. At any rate, he was standing behind her as she got out of the car. He swung something around her neck, probably a long scarf, and throttled her. She dropped the groceries and managed to knock down those shelves in the few minutes of fight she had in her."

I remained kneeling. "Any guess on the time of death?"

Al shook his head. "The coroner couldn't pin it, not with the cold and all. If the sister had her times straight, though, it most likely was around six, no later than seven. Nobody was anxious to go out in the storm so they kept putting it off, the way the sister tells it. But when it became obvious it wasn't going to let up and they probably weren't going to be able to get out at all in the morning, they decided they had better stock a few staples—you know, milk, bread, like that. The victim was only going as far as the Eagle over on North Main. Figure forty-five minutes tops for the round-trip, allowing shopping time and the weather, so if she left before six like the sister said, then she should have been back before seven."

"And dead within a matter of minutes."

"The way it looks, yeah."

I straightened up. "Anybody take away anything in the way of evidence?"

"Not that I know of. You're looking at all there was. Except the body, of course. And it looks like the sister or somebody got her purse. No cigarette butts, no conveniently dropped matchbooks with the name of some bizarre nightclub or a phone number penciled inside, nothing like that. I guess the coroner found some fibers on the victim's throat that didn't match any of the clothes she was wearing when she died. That's what led to the theory she was strangled with a scarf of some kind. They're working on those fibers now, but everybody expects they'll turn out to match something sold in K-mart or Venture by the hundreds, so what good will that be?"

I looked all around at the inside of the garage. It was an okay little garage, fine for its intended use, maybe a little cramped. But it was a lousy place to die. I wondered what had been the last thing Kat had seen, what had she focused on in her final seconds? It couldn't have been any part of the killer, not if he was positioned behind her the way the cops had reconstructed. I wondered if she had any idea who it was back there choking the life out of her? Did it make any difference? Would it be any harder to die not knowing the who or the why of it?

I looked down again at the stuff scattered on the floor around the chalk outline. The broken eggs, the badly dented carton of Cocoa Pebbles cereal. The cans of gunk that promised to do everything from fine-tune the roughest-running engine to restore mirror-like lustre to even the most thoroughly rusted old beater. The half dozen years' worth of *Cosmo*s. The paperback romances that bore titles like *Wild Flowing Love, Storm Winds of Passion,* and *Uninhibited Conquest,* with an entry in the "Skip Steamer, Sports Star" series mixed incongruously among them. Ill-fitting bits of refuse marking the end of a life, like the discharges of a sunken ship bobbing on the surface of the ocean. I'd never known Kat to be much of a reader, other than maybe a weekly dose of *National Enquirer* and *People,* and I would have figured her to be too cynical to be snared by the tinny promises of the auto-supply sharks. All of those things must have belonged to her sister. But that possibility didn't suit my mood right then, didn't fit my need to fuel my sadness and my bitterness, to twist in a little guilt.

Turning away, I said the words Al had been wanting to hear since before we'd even arrived. "Let's get the hell out of here."

27

It started bugging me after I'd dropped Al back at the greasy spoon and was on my way over to the Bomber's. So far the case had been a long series of questions and disjointed possibilities, complicated by personal entanglements and a miscue or two that had all combined to drag me too fast, too far into a thing I wanted out of but didn't dare let go of. It was like trying to assemble the pieces to a jigsaw puzzle on a windswept table, knowing you needed to step back once in a while to get the overall view, but also knowing that the minute you did, the pieces would blow away. Only now, unexpectedly, there came the briefest lull in the wind. Something, somewhere—either recently or a ways back, I couldn't be sure—had clicked in my subconscious, had connected two or more dots that suggested themselves to be instrumental in shaping the whole. And now that something was trying to scratch and dig its way out. The conscious part of my brain sensed it, knew it was back there, but couldn't quite reach through to pull it free.

It was the kind of thing that only becomes more obscure the harder you try to bring it into focus. So I made an effort to block it out, leave it alone for a while, let it swim around in the background until it was ready to edge forward some more. In the meantime, I had plenty of other things to think about.

When I left Foxwood's earlier, waiting for the meeting with Al the cop to be set up, I'd had Crawford return me to my place. It was no big surprise that Belinda wasn't there. On the kitchen table she'd left a piece of paper with a Chicago phone number. Under it, she'd scrawled simply, "Call me—B." There was no way she could have made it back to Chicago by then, but I dialed the number anyway. I got an answering machine with a recording of her elegantly modulated voice, "This is Belinda. I will be out of town for a number of days. If your business can wait, leave your name and number and I shall return your call as soon as I can. If your business is more urgent, then you should know how else to reach me." I hung up on the beep, leaving no message. Hearing her disembodied voice left me feeling emptier than if I hadn't gotten an answer at all.

Next I'd called Liz Grimaldi at home. The news about Kat's murder had been on the radio and TV and, yeah, she'd heard about it. What the hell was going on, she wanted to know? Did Kat's killing have something to do with the case I'd said I was in the middle of? I told her I'd tell her more about that later. What about the Bomber? She'd been in touch with him and he'd heard about the killing, too. He seemed to be taking it all right, a little blue, naturally. She hadn't mentioned anything of our talk yesterday. Damn it, Joe, why didn't you come around last night like you were supposed to? I got a little sore with her on that, telling her to quit badgering me with questions. What the hell difference would it have made to Kat if I'd gone to see Bomber anyway? She was already dead by the time I'd figured on talking to him about her. Liz got sore right back, telling me if I had all the stinking answers, why was I bothering her in the first place? We calmed it down a little after that, but when we broke the connection a few minutes later there was still a definite chill on her end. And who could blame her? She'd had every right to express her concern and I'd had none to snap back at her the way I did. I can be a genuine louse sometimes and, like so many of us, I too often dump on those who least deserve it.

After the phone call to Liz, I'd gone down and worked off some of my pent-up hostility shoveling out the Honda and clearing a path to the street. I was back upstairs, just climbing out of the shower, when the phone rang and Camicci came on to tell me that the meet with Al had been set up.

So now all that had come and gone and here I was still a roiling mass of questions and uncertainties and aimless anger. On my way to see my best friend, to tell him I wasn't even sure what. Something that wasn't going to be easy for either of us, I knew that much.

Bomber's big old brickpile of a house had only a couple of lights visible from the street. But his Buick was parked out front—the replacement for another Buick that had been destroyed a while back when a vengeance-crazed killer from my past had returned for me and had tried to go through Bomber to get the job done. I thought fleetingly of that incident and a handful of others as I curbed my own car and strode up the shoveled walk and the steps of the front porch. Sometimes it's hell what friends put friends through.

I thumbed the door buzzer and waited. There were Christmas lights wound around the porch railing and a wreath hung on the door. My big buddy displayed a lot more Christmas spirit than I did. At least the front of his house did. I doubted he himself felt very festive right now.

The door opened and Bomber stood there, all six and a half feet, three-hundred-plus pounds of him. He had on a T-shirt, slacks, socks, no shoes. His expression was glum, but not extremely so. He held a can of beer in one oversized paw.

"Hey, Joe."

I nodded. "Bomber. Mind if I come in for a while?"

" 'Course not. Come ahead."

I knew the way well enough. Went in and helped myself to a beer from the fridge. When Bomber didn't join me in the kitchen, I roamed back out, expecting to find him in the living room. Instead he was seated at the dining-room table. I'd never seen him do that before. I'd been there plenty of times—for backyard barbecues, for poker parties, for pay-per-view sporting events, what have you—and whenever we'd been in the house, it had always been in either the kitchen or the living room. It was disconcerting to see him break the routine after all these years. But the dining-room table was where he was at, so that's where I joined him.

The TV was on in the other room, an ESPN recap of the day's NFL games.

"Bears win?" I asked.

"Yeah. Big. Dent had four sacks, Singletary kicked ass all afternoon in the secondary. Offense was able to do pretty much what it wanted to on the ground so that's what they stayed with. You know Ditka—solid old grind-it-out football whenever he can get away with it."

"Uhmm. Sounds like it would have been a good one. Sorry I missed it."

On the table between us sat a shoebox filled with papers and photographs. Some photos were out of the box, spread in front of Bomber. At his elbow was a sheet of typing paper containing several short lines of typescript. I didn't have to ask what the memorabilia pertained to.

I drank some of my beer. "I heard about Kat," I said.

"Kath," he replied quickly, firmly. "The news reports said she was calling herself by that other name. I didn't even know who the hell they were talking about at first, until they flashed a picture of her on the TV."

"It's a bitch the way things go sometimes."

He shuffled the pictures in front of him. "A long time back, back when I was first starting to get it through my thick skull that it was no good between us . . . you know how many times a day I'd wish she was dead?"

"You didn't really mean it, though."

"Didn't I? I used to think that if she was dead, that if it ended between us like that, then it would be something I could understand, accept. The way it was, I could never quite figure out why we couldn't sit down and iron out our differences, fall back in love like we were in the beginning."

"The way it *seemed* like you were. It couldn't have been real love, not the way it fell apart."

"What are you? A fucking expert on the subject?"

"Let's just say I'm able to be a hell of a lot more objective about this particular episode than you ever can be. Dammit, man, she nearly wrecked you. *You* almost got yourself killed over the whole deal—when you went off on that trip to get away from it all and got involved in that mess overseas, remember?"

"Of course I remember. But I only *almost* got killed. The real thing happened to her."

"She was dead for you a long time ago. Or she at least should have been."

He smiled ruefully and gave a sort of grunt. "Sure she was. That's what I tried to tell myself. So why'd I keep this box of shit around, huh?"

He shoved the shoebox toward me. I ignored it. It contained personal stuff, stuff that meant something to him and maybe to

Kat at one time. Things that were none of my business, things one of us might later regret my having poked through.

Bomber got up and lumbered into the kitchen. He returned with two fresh cans of beer. As he sat back down, handing one over to me, he said, "On the news they were saying she had a kid."

"A two-and-a-half-year-old boy," I said. I said it too quickly.

Bomber's eyes snapped to mine. "How'd you know that?"

I killed my first beer, set the empty aside. Popped the new one. "A couple days ago," I said, "I happened to bump into Kat— Kath. Ran across her in the course of a thing I've been working on."

"And this is the first I'm hearing about it—that she was even back in town?"

"I'd been meaning to tell you. I was, uh, trying to decide on the best way to go about it."

"What do you mean 'the best way to go about it'? I'm some kind of idiot or moron who has to be approached in a certain way about things?"

He got under my skin a little with that. "Yeah, goddamn it," I fired back, "when it comes to this particular chick, your track record hasn't exactly been that of a well-balanced person."

He glared balefully at me. His empty hand was balled into a fist.

"You going to punch me again?" I asked. When he didn't say anything for several beats, I said, "That's exactly the kind of thing I mean. You see?"

He continued to glare at me, but the fire in his eyes had begun to cool. After a while, the fist relaxed.

"I guess maybe you're right," he said in a voice that sounded tired where it hadn't before. "I've made a fool out of myself over that woman more times than I can count."

"It's a club with a mighty big membership, pal. Making fools out of ourselves over the opposite sex is practically a national pastime."

We sat there sipping our beers, not saying anything more for a time. The TV droned on in the living room. Bomber's forefinger plucked absently at the edges of the photos fanned in front of him.

Inside my head, whatever was trying to come to the fore, trying to tell me something, kept plucking at the back of my brain in much the same way.

Every few minutes, Bomber would clear his throat. About the fourth time, he used this as a preamble to ask, "When you saw her, Joe, did she seem okay? I mean, was she . . . well, how was she?"

"Doing just fine," I lied. I hadn't known until right at that moment that I wasn't going to tell him about the X-rated movies. If that came out later, well, I'd find a way to deal with it then. Right now, he had all the load he could carry. "She was still doing some dancing," I went on. "Stripping. But not a lot of it. She was winding it down, getting ready to settle into business with her sister. They had a small chain of beauty parlors getting off the ground in pretty good shape."

"The sister—that would be Louise, the one she was living with?"

"Uh-huh."

"Good kid, Louise. She moved here to Rockford shortly before things went really to hell with Kath and me. I talked to her a few times after, not for two or three years, though. I think she felt a little bad about some of the shit Kath pulled on me. But she was still loyal to her sister, you know?"

"Can't fault her for that."

Bomber eyed me closely. "This thing you were working on when you first bumped into Kath—her getting killed got anything to do with that?"

"I don't think so," I lied again. "You can bet it's a possibility I'll keep my eyes open for, though."

He accepted that okay. "The little boy, Kath's son—you know what his name is?"

I shook my head. "Sorry, never heard."

"No husband?"

"I don't think so."

Bomber smiled wryly. "Hard to picture Kath a mother."

"I think she worked at it real hard. I think she was a good one."

"Yeah. There always was more to her than . . . well, than most people ever realized. I guess that's why it was so hard for the rest of you to understand why I went so nuts over her. In the beginning, when it was still good for us . . . God, she was something. She even wrote poetry, did you know that?"

I shook my head again. "No. I never knew."

He reached for the typed sheet at his elbow. "This was always one of my favorites. It touched something in me, even if I was never sure why. I used to ask her what it meant, and she'd say, 'It means whatever it means to whoever is reading it.' It's the only thing out of that box I've looked at in the past three years until tonight. And she was right, you can go back to it in different moods and at different times and it can mean totally different things."

He handed me the poem. There was no title, just eight neatly typed lines signed in red ink with "Kath" underlined. It read:

> At birth you are trapped in it
> At death you are wrapped in it
> Ashes to ashes, dust to dust
> Hope, despair, love, hate, lust
> Proving ground for Heaven, or just Hell on Earth?
> God's grand design, or the Devil's twisted mirth?
> Sometimes I want to scream out loud
> Can't anyone see me struggling in this skintight shroud?

I read it through twice before putting the paper down.

"Well, what do you think?" Bomber said.

"You mean what do I think it means?"

"Uh-huh."

"Hell, I don't know. I was never any good at that shit."

"Come on, give it a try. I'd like to know what you see there. Really."

Sighing, I picked the paper back up, skimmed it again. "All right," I said after a minute, "I don't know how much of this is actually here on the page and how much i'm reading in because I knew her a little, knew some things about her. But it sounds to me like the lamentations of a beautiful woman who feels a little trapped by her beauty, feels disappointed and confused by some of the choices she's made, feels like maybe she wouldn't have had to make those choices if she'd been seen differently by others."

I put the paper down for a second time.

Bomber was looking at me in a strange way, the way you might look at a pup who licks the scratch on your hand. "That was beautiful," he said. "That was fucking beautiful."

"Come on."

"No. Really. I never saw any of that in there before, but I think you might have just given it the exact right interpretation."

"Listen, if you don't quit looking at me like that and don't get that sappy tone out of your voice, I think I'm going to throw up. I'm sorry Kath's gone. I'm sorry for her. I'm sorry for you. Let's drink a toast to her memory or something, but let's not eulogize her way beyond what she was."

His eyes shifted and went somewhere far away. "She used to have a favorite toast. 'To lost chances and lost friends,' she'd say. She said those were the two saddest things in the world."

I raised my can of beer. "Sounds appropriate enough."

Bomber raised his too. "Yeah," he said huskily. "To lost chances and lost friends."

We touched our cans together with a tinny clink.

"And lost causes," I added softly.

28

I spent another hour or so with the Bomber. Long enough to polish off another brace of beers and to get him unstuck from the subject of Kat, get him smiling a little and talking about some other things.

He said at one point that he hadn't made up his mind whether or not to attend the funeral. By the time I left, I felt convinced he could handle it okay whatever he decided.

I drove home to wrestle with my own demons. The nagging feeling rode with me—something I'd seen but not seen, or heard but not heard—its significance now trying to register, to scratch through from my subconscious, to make the more prominent impression it had failed to make in the first place.

As I climbed the stairs to my apartment, I could see through the window the silhouette of the little Christmas tree in the living room. I naturally thought of Belinda (not that she had been very far out of my thoughts all day). I vividly recalled the taste and smell and sound and feel of her—the way she made *me* feel. My mind's eye saw the sunlight spraying through her hair the way it had that morning at breakfast and the gold flecks dancing in her eyes when she laughed and then those same eyes closed in that special dreamy way above a slackened mouth as she shuddered to a climax. Yeah, those had been special moments, and they would forever be great memories. But the flip side was the stark contrasts between us. I was clipped from the pages of a Sears *Big and Tall* catalogue, she from *Vogue* or *Harper's Bazaar*. I was baloney on Wonder Bread, she was caviar on a Ritz. Her boots got licked by the Godfather; mine were scuffed and scarred from trying to walk the line. Man'd have to be a damn fool to ignore all those differences, to think they could somehow be overcome. What had happened between us had been a fluke, a quirk of fate. The thing to do was to roll with it, to savor the memories, to tuck them away for blue Mondays and honky-tonk lonely nights. To pursue it in hopes of expanding it into anything more would only be asking for trouble.

So the first thing I did when I got inside, after taking off my coat and hanging it up, was to dial the Chicago number she had left. I listened to her recording again, listened to the beep again, hung up again without leaving a message.

Damn.

I cursed her for not being there, cursed myself for being chump enough to make the call and get set up for the disappointment.

To hell with her.

I banged a frying pan onto the stove, cracked some eggs into it, toasted some bread, and put together a couple of fried-egg sandwiches. These I ate standing at the kitchen counter, washing down the steamy mouthfuls with hits from a tall glass of milk.

The stitches in my arm and forehead were slightly inflamed and starting to itch. The ones across my chest ached dully, but not too badly. I hadn't taken any painkillers for several hours and decided I would try to make it through the night without any. My most immediate concerns were mental, not physical.

My mind churned. I thought about Kat Hayward, aka Kath Howard. Her death had been pivotal to a number of things. Her murder made it clear beyond any reasonable doubt that a killer was methodically stalking the movie troupe; her murder marked an escalation of sorts from popular, unsuspecting "kids" to a more seasoned, more guarded victim; her murder served as the catalyst to cause the Syndicate to reel in the noose I had so obligingly stuck my neck through; and, last but not least, her murder brought a whole new element to the case for me—a personal angle. Number one, she had been killed after I was on the job. Number two, she had been someone I knew. Not somebody I liked—I wouldn't be hypocritical enough to claim that—but somebody I knew and had an interest in nevertheless. Where I come from, that's enough to make a difference.

I considered the common thread that ran through it all, at least the only one I could be certain of—the X-rated movies. Every few months, it seems, we in the Rockford area are assailed by some new or resurrected pack of civic-minded darlings (invariably backed by one or more churches, usually operating under a banner proclaiming their cause to be in the interest of "decency"—as if there is anything decent about imposing your will on others through means of extortion and public ridicule) who are hellbent on saving us from the insidious evils of pornography. Whether we want it or not. Could it be that one of these groups had had its own kind of insidious effect, had caused some loosely wrapped Christer to declare a *literal* war on pornography? Such a possibility bounced back to Tiffany Traver's fears about the Church of the Almighty. But, as then, I couldn't get too cranked up over anything along those lines as the motivation in this matter. Zealots—religious or otherwise—cut too wide a swath, cast too long a shadow, are too full of what they are trying to accomplish in the name of their beliefs to go about it with so much anonymity. These killings bore the mark of someone killing for a more calculated, more personal reason.

I contemplated the whole pornography thing further. I had become more deeply involved with it than I was prepared for. If I completed my job successfully, then I would be responsible for preserving at least a portion of what many well-intentioned people saw as a dangerous evil, a very real threat. I wasn't sure how that made me feel. Not particularly proud, I knew that much. But at the same time, I also knew I wouldn't feel any less uncomfortable pulling comparable duty for the do-gooders' camp. There is a renegade streak in me that balks violently at the prospect of somebody—anybody, no matter how lofty their position or ideals—deciding for me what I should read or view or enjoy in the privacy of my own home or any place where neither the law nor the rights of others who may be offended are infringed upon.

I don't buy the statistics that point an accusing finger at pornography as the root cause of everything from serial killings to ring around the collar. If you want to play the statistics game, how many atrocities through the ages have been committed in the name of God and/or the Bible? The thing is, anyone unhinged enough to commit these acts is going to be triggered by *something* —an overdraft notice from the bank, an unwelcome visit from the in-laws, the ketchup not coming out of the bottle fast enough, you name it—no matter what. Certainly no one in the erotica biz can lay claim to a noble purpose, and there can be no denying that the pursuit and purchase of porn lines the pockets of a decidedly unsavory element of our society. But many of the extremists on the other side of the issue maintain pretty well-lined pockets, too, and in their own way are equally unsavory. The way I see it, that's the trade-off you have to be willing to make for the right to have the choice. It is, after all, the extreme—not the ordinary—that truly tests our freedoms and our common sense to use them. The bottom line on pornography is that it is largely a state of mind. For those who require it, either to rail against or to revel in, it will always be there. Take away the hard-core videos and the raunch magazines, porn will then be perceived in the bra and girdle ads in mail-order catalogues. Get rid of those, it will be back to the jungle maidens in old *National Geographic*s with dinner plates in their lips and nipples drooping down to mid-thigh. And so on. You get the idea. Whatever was in the cards as far as any of that went, I decided, was already there; and no matter how I played what had been dealt me this particular time around, it was just one hand in a game that was a hell of a lot bigger than me any way you looked at it.

Weary from so much profound pondering, I shoved away from the kitchen counter, stacked the dirty dishes in the sink, roamed into the living room to tune in the late news, and put my brain on INPUT for a while.

The top story locally, no surprise, was Kat's murder. An appropriately somber-faced anchorwoman set it up and then cut to a videotape of a field reporter at the scene. The latter, backgrounded by the garage where the body had been found, grimacing under cold, stiff tendrils of hair that had once been blow-dried and sprayed to perfection now poking out at various unflattering angles, spoke intensely of "the tragedy that struck here last night, leaving a young mother dead, brutally murdered, her body left to be ravaged further by the bitter cold of a fierce winter storm." He then called on camera a detective spokesman for the police department. Yes, the detective assured him, the department was tracking down a number of leads and expected a breakthrough on the case very soon. When the reporter asked if there might be any connection between this killing and the murder by strangulation of another young woman (a certain Valerie Pine) five days before, the detective further assured him that there was no reason to think so at this time. Having thus informed and comforted the masses, the reported signed off and no doubt raced to the nearest mirror to get his hair back in order.

When the rest of the news, weather, and sports had wrapped up, I shut off the tube and got ready for bed. A slow, hot shower; a generous blast of bourbon by way of a nightcap. I paused for a long moment in the bedroom doorway, looking back at the telephone. It seemed to be urging me, tempting me like one of those devil-on-your-shoulder routines you used to see in old movies and cartoons. *Come on, man, call her. Do it. You know you want to.* But this time I managed to shrug the devil off. Killed the lights, burrowed between the covers, tried to convince myself I couldn't really smell her perfume on the sheets, that it was just my imagination.

Sleep came easily enough. With it came dreams. Lots of them. Bumping together, overlapping, splintering into weird mutant offsprings, falling away in crazy bits and pieces that would pile up around the edges of my memory for when I awoke in the morning.

I dreamed I was on a date with Belinda Davies. We were both much younger. I had a duck's-ass haircut; she wore bobby socks and a yellow skirt with big black polka dots and a lot of petticoats underneath. I took her to a drive-in movie. I had a '57 Chevy convertible. We watched Frankie and Annette cavort on the big screen. When they necked, so did we. I wanted to feel her up, but didn't dare. At intermission, I went to get us some popcorn and Cokes. As I was walking back from the concession stand, in that strange, sudden way that everyone seems so casually to accept in dreams, I noticed that things had turned back into the present again, that I was the way I am now, complete with a thinning spot in my hair several inches above where the duck's ass used to be. When I got to the car, it had changed into a long, sleek, silver-gray limousine. A uniformed chauffeur who looked suspiciously like Floyd Silas got out and held open one of the rear doors, saying, "You should have allowed me to get your refreshments, sir." "It's okay," I told him. As I ducked into the cavernous back seat, I saw Belinda there waiting for me. She was now clad in a black leather corset embroidered with silver studs and with holes cut out for her sharply erect nipples to poke through. In addition, she wore glossy black boots with seven-inch stiletto heels, black fishnet stockings, and full-length black patent-leather gloves. Her hair was pulled back, her eyes were heavily made up, her mouth painted the color of fresh blood. She was smoking one of her lavender cigarettes from a long ebony holder. She blew smoke in my face and said, "The servant was right, you *should* have allowed him to fetch the refreshments." "I'm sorry," I said. She took the popcorn from me and dumped it on the floor at her feet. "For being such a naughty, thoughtless boy, you must eat your popcorn from there," she ordered. I got down on my hands and knees on the broad floorboard of the back seat and put my face down and began eating the popcorn. Belinda produced a riding crop from somewhere and began swatting me across the butt as I ate, continuing to tell me what a naughty boy I was. This seemed to go on for a long time. When I had eaten all the popcorn, I straightened up. Looking over the back of the driver's seat, I could see the chauffeur's face in the rearview mirror. Only now it had turned into the face of Henry Foxwood. He was looking back, smiling lewdly. "Fuck you," I told him. "No, fuck me," said the woman on the seat behind me. It was no longer the voice of Belinda and, turning, I saw that the woman was no longer Belinda, either, but rather Kat Hayward. She wore the same leather outfit, her exposed nipples glowing like red-hot coals. She had the handle of the riding crop between her legs, working it back and forth through a slit in the leather crotch. "That's the real reason you never liked me," she said. "You never wanted me to be Bomber's girl because you wanted me for yourself. *You* wanted to fuck me." "No, that's not true," I told her. "Yes, it is," she insisted, smiling, continuing to work the riding crop back and forth. "No." I protested, but all the while I was leaning toward her. She withdrew the riding crop handle, raised it with one hand and put it in my mouth. With her other hand, she deftly unzipped me and pulled me free. I was rock-hard and ready. I lunged into her, slammed into her, causing the whole limousine to shudder. I bit the handle of the riding crop off with a loud crack. "Yes," she urged. "Yes! Yes!" And then there came an ominous kind of rumbling sound and the car shuddered with a new movement. "So, you sonofabitch, she was right!" This was Bomber's voice, bellowing. "You wanted her for yourself all that time." I jerked away from Kat's clutching arms and legs, turning at the sound of glass shattering, watching in confused horror as the Bomber, dressed in the chauffeur's uniform, punched away the glass partition and reached over the back of the driver's seat, grasping for me with massive hands. "No," I shouted, "none of it is true." I scrambled away, fell hard against the door, worked the lever and tumbled out onto the rough gravel of the parking lot. My still-exposed penis swung around, whacking painfully against the rough stones. Imploring, leather-clad arms reached immediately after me, hands beckoning. "Please come back. Come back and fuck me." "No!" I said. "No more!" A face and a body followed the hands out. Sara Baines stood there, naked except for the gloves and stiletto-heeled boots. She placed her hands on her hips and explained patiently, "Everybody wants to fuck *me.* It's all right that you do, too. Come back and take your turn." All I could do was shake my head, partly in denial, partly in total bewilderment. I managed to get my pants zipped back up. And then the chauffeur came skidding around the end of the car. Now the uniform and cap were on Chuck Baines. He pointed an accusing finger at me. "See? You're just like all the rest. All you're after is my sister." "That's not true," I tried to tell him. "I came here with somebody else." "That's a dirty lie!" As he shouted this, he came running at me with both fists drawn back. I surged to my feet in order to defend myself. I let him take a big roundhouse swing, ducked in under it, stuck my foot between his legs, and shoved, knocking him down. I stood over him with my own fists balled. "Take it easy now," I told him. "I don't want to hurt you." On his hands and knees, the chauffeur rolled his head and looked up at me. The face that sneered into mine was the face of the brown-haired woman—Inez Corby—who wouldn't allow me to see her reclaimed lover, Cindy Wallace. "Well, I want to hurt *you,*" chauffeur Inez hissed. *"We* intend to hurt you." That "we" caused me to look back around at the car. Beside it, just outside the open rear door where Sara had been standing, squatted the big German shepherd from Inez's backyard. Around its neck was a collar of black leather with silver studs. It bared its teeth and growled menacingly at me. "Sic him!" the chauffeur commanded. "Bite his fucking balls off!" The dog launched itself at me and I was off on a dead run, the beast gnashing at my heels. Across the theater parking lot—now eerily empty—we raced. Weaving around the speaker poles, thudding over the graveled mounds. At last, nearly out of breath, my lungs on fire, I reached the high wooden fence that surrounded the grounds to keep out nonpaying viewers. With my last ounce of strength, I hoisted myself up and scaled the scraping wall, falling to the other side just as the dog tore into the spot where I'd been. From his side, he howled and growled and clawed and chewed at the weathered wood like a demon. When I had regained just a fraction of my breath, I began running again, still frightened, wanting to put more distance between us—between me and that nightmarish drive-in. Abruptly, it seemed, I found myself running along a riverbank. Layers of fog hung in the air. Everything was quiet, the only sounds that of my heavy breathing and the thump of my footfalls. As I was considering working my way inland and finding some warm, dry place to rest, I stumbled and fell face first onto damp and crumbling earth. I tried to get to my feet, but the ground clung to me, held me down. I struggled harder. And then, with a horrid sucking, crunching sound, the ground heaved up as if the world was vomiting and it disgorged the form of a large man. Muddy fingers reached for me, digging into my throat. The creature shoved its face close to mine and glowered at me with fiery Oriental eyes—the eyes of Phuoc Dak Ho, the man I had killed. I opened my mouth to scream, but never got it out. That's when I finally woke up.

29

I crawled out of bed feeling a little shaken and disoriented. Pulled back the curtain to look out at an overcast morning, a sky gray with the threat of a new storm as predicted. With hands less steady than usual, I lit my first cigarette of the day.

They say that the average dream takes only a few seconds and that dreams occur only during a certain cycle of your sleep pattern. They also claim that when you think you have awakened directly from a dream, it actually has been a matter of hours. I suppose "they" know what they're talking about, but it sure as hell didn't feel like it. Not this morning, for sure. It seemed so vivid, so recent. When I padded into the bathroom to take a leak, I leaned out in front of the medicine-cabinet mirror half expecting to see muddy finger marks around my throat. There weren't any. Nor, upon further examination, were there any gravel scrapes on the part of me I was dangling over the toilet bowl. I was able to relax some.

I go in spurts when I dream almost every night; then other times, I go for weeks, it seems, without dreaming at all. Of course, "they" claim we always dream, it's just that sometimes we remember, sometimes we don't. At any rate, when I do remember my dreams, they often are pretty screwy. Seldom as screwy as last night's mental meltdown, but screwy all the same. When I take time to think about it, I can usually figure them out. But it's not something I spend a lot of time on. And I had the feeling I'd probably be better off not understanding all of last night's trip anyway. Parts of it were obvious enough, other parts could be troubling. *Had* I had the hots for my best friend's girl, for crying out loud? And what of the jealousy bit concerning Chuck and Sara Baines, what had that been all about?

Just forget it, I told myself. Haven't you got enough to worry over already, you dumb ass?

It was while I was rummaging through my underwear drawer for a clean pair of socks, shoving aside the faded hankies and the tattered old jock strap I wear when I play softball and stuff, that it came to me. The elusive something that had been nagging at me on and off plopped out of my subconscious like a big, fat ball bearing and rolled smoothly to the center of my brain pan.

Just like that.

It was the book—the goddamned Skip Steamer, Sports Star book I had seen lying with the *Cosmo*s and paperback romance novels scattered beside the chalk outline of Kat's body on that cold garage floor. It had struck me as incongruous even then, but only mildly so. Now I realized the greater significance of it; not only that it didn't belong there, didn't fit that scene at all, but the recollection of where I had seen that exact title—*Skip Steamer and the Skateboard Raiders*—only a short time before.

Practically no boy born in this country since World War II has passed through his preteen or early-teen years without reading at least a few titles in the Skip Steamer series. After forty years, they're still publishing them to the tune of four new titles a year, plus some of the more popular older ones, updated to keep them current with the times. In the early sixties there was even a Skip Steamer TV series, with the logo at the lower-right-hand corner of the book covers incorporating the face of the young actor who played Skip. After the series was canceled, the logo returned to the familiar illustration of the square-jawed, all-American boy with a shock of carrot-colored hair poking out from under the bill of his ball cap. I myself had been a huge Skip Steamer fan, gobbling up everything in the series *(Skip Steamer and the Battling Batters, Skip Steamer and the Football Phantom, Skip Steamer's Boxing Brigade,* and on and on) from the time I was ten until I was well into my teens.

And now, after all these years, damned if it didn't look like Ol' Skip was going to come through for me again. . . .

30

Sara Baines answered my knock at her apartment door. A segment of her face gazed out at me from the opening allowed by a sturdy-looking security chain.

She blinked a couple of times, then smiled. "Mr. Hannibal. This is a surprise."

I nodded. "Morning, Sara. Sorry to drop by without calling first or anything. Can you spare me a few minutes?"

"Of course. No problem."

She closed the door long enough to undo the chain, then reopened it and ushered me inside. She wore faded blue jeans, a tight, fuzzy pink sweater, no shoes or stockings. Her toenails were painted to match her fingernails and her lipstick. She smelled faintly of some fresh, flowery scent.

The apartment was a third-floor walk-up on East State above a medical-supply shop at ground level which displayed wheelchairs and bedpans and prostheses in its front window. The building was old but solid. Hardwood floors and real walnut trim. She had the apartment fixed up nicely—clean and bright with obvious touches of femininity but nothing too overpowering. The heavily decorated Christmas tree in the living room looked real and, in my Scroogish way, I wondered how many fire codes it was violating.

Sara held her hand out for my coat. Indicating the pattern of wet spots across the shoulders and sleeves, she asked, "Is it snowing out already?"

"Afraid it is," I told her. "Coming down pretty good."

"They kept saying we were in for more snow," she said as she hung the big parka in a closet off the kitchen, "but I kept hoping they were wrong."

"Only supposed to be about six more inches. Piece of cake."

"Boy, the one thing I'm for sure not going to miss when I get to the West Coast is these Midwest winters."

"Oh? Headed for the coast are you?"

"Damn right." She twisted her mouth wryly. "Maybe a lot sooner than I figured on."

I shook my head. "I guess I'm not sure what you mean."

She gave me a look. "God. You heard about Kat, didn't you?"

"Naturally."

"Well, what do you think that does to the rest of us? How do you think that makes us feel? It's got everybody scared shitless, that's how. Not just me—my brother, Buck and Lois Ingram, Barry Grainger, everybody. Buck was determined that somebody had to go to the cops, tell them everything. He was ready to do it, too, until Foxy managed to talk him out of it. I'm not sure Buck wasn't right."

"He might very well have been," I conceded.

Sara made an abrupt gesture with one of her hands. "Boy, I'm some kind of lousy hostess, aren't I? I haven't even invited you to take a seat. Can I get you a cup of coffee or something?"

"No, that's all right. Really. I came here to talk about . . . well, exactly what we were talking about. I'd like to continue."

She regarded me solemnly. "We all have a lot of faith in you, Hannibal. Haven't you been able to come up with anything that can help us?"

"As a matter of fact, I just might have something," I told her. "Is your brother at home, Sara?"

She looked a little startled. "Chuck? Why, no. Not right now. He left a little bit ago to get something for the car. He should be back before long. Why?"

"Does Chuck do much reading? When I saw him out at the farm the other day, he had a paperback stuck in his back pocket. Some sports book."

"Oh, God, yes. He's reading all the time. Sometimes he gets into science fiction a little. But mostly it's, like you said, sports stuff. Either true-life biographies or those adventures of, uh . . . Sandy . . . no, Skip. That's it, Skip Steamer. Skip Steamer, Sports Star. He's been reading those since he was a kid. Chuck was a fantastic athlete, you know, all through high school and college. Until his troubles. When he was little, he said he wanted to grow up to be just like Skip Steamer and he darn near did."

"Can I see Chuck's room?" I asked.

She swallowed, then moistened her lips with the tip of her tongue. "You'll have to give me some idea . . . tell me why, what this is all about."

I took her hands in mine and held them gently but firmly. "You've got to bear with me a little on this, Sara. I'm going to ask some things, maybe imply some things you aren't going to want to hear. In fact, you're going to hate hearing them and probably hate me for saying them. I may be way the hell off base. But you've got to help me see this through in order to be sure."

She shook her head slowly back and forth. "You can't possibly be thinking that Chuck . . ."

"Can we take a look at his room? Please?"

She led the way back silently. Pushed open the door, snapped on the ceiling light, let me go in ahead of her. It was a large room, filled to capacity, maybe even a little crowded, but reasonably neat. The bed was made. It had a foot locker with extra blankets folded on top of it. There were a number of pennants on the walls, along with two or three *Playboy* centerfolds. Along the walls on either side of the bed were moderate-sized bookcases whose tops were filled with sporting trophies; the lower shelves held rows of books, mostly paperbacks. There was a stack of magazines at the end of one of them. A stereo bracketed by record racks had been arranged diagonally across one corner. In the opposite corner there stood an exercise bike with a pair of free-weight dumbbells on the floor in front of it.

I went over to the nearest bookcase and knelt to examine its contents. I found an entire row of Skip Steamer titles, more than thirty of them. I scanned the spines quickly but thoroughly until I'd determined that *Skip Steamer and the Skateboard Raiders* was not among them. I walked around the end of the bed and examined the other bookcase. There were no Skip Steamer books there at all.

As I straightened up in front of the second bookcase, Sara said from the doorway, "For God sake, say something. What are you looking for?"

"When Chuck left a little while ago." I said, "did he have a book shoved in his hip pocket like he had before?"

"I—I'm nor sure. Maybe. But I don't think so. Hell, I don't know."

I let that one ride for the time being. I said, "When you drove back from the farm yesterday evening, what did the two of you do after you got home?"

She thought about it a minute. "Well, we were both pooped out. It had been a long day, and then fighting the storm and everything, you know? Neither of us felt much like making supper so we ordered a pizza."

"You had it delivered?"

She shook her head. "No. They wouldn't send out any drivers in the blizzard. Chuck had to go after it."

"Which pizza place?"

"Pizza Boy. It's our favorite."

"What time was that?"

"Well, let's see, it would have been right after we got home. About six, six-thirty, I guess."

The nearest Pizza Boy was over on North Main—in the same shopping center as the Eagle Foods where Kat had gone last evening at approximately that same time to get her groceries. Click. Another piece had fallen into place. I wasn't crazy about the picture that was starting to form, but that's the way the blurred edges were coming into focus regardless. My job wasn't to like what I found out, just to find it out.

I already knew Chuck had been out on the night Jason Hobbs was killed; we had covered that much before. That only left the timing of one more murder to account for.

"Think back to last Wednesday, the afternoon Valerie Pine was killed," I said to Sara. "Do you remember where you were, what you were doing? More to the point, do you know where Chuck was?"

Her eyes looked at me in a hard, despising stare. "On Wednesday afternoons," she said flatly, "I attend training classes at Rockford Memorial."

"And Chuck?"

"When Chuck isn't helping out at the farm, he just sort of hangs out. He doesn't venture very far from home. He has his room here, his books, his stereo. I've never pressured him to get a job because he still has problems to sort out."

"So as far as you know, Chuck was here, but you can't be sure. You had no reason to call him or get in touch with him any time that afternoon?"

"No." She got the word out, then she blurted a sort of sobbing sound. "You sonofabitch, you're accusing my baby brother of murder! Why, I'd like to know? Based on what? Even if he does have a lot of free time, even if he *could* have been there when those people were killed—*why*? Why in God's name would he do anything like that? What makes you even suspect such a thing?"

I told her about the Skip Steamer book, told her the specific title. How I'd seen it beside where Kat's body was found, how it hadn't belonged there. How I'd seen that same title in Chuck's possession earlier out at the farm, how it no longer seemed to be a part of his collection.

"So what?" she demanded. "They publish a million of those fucking books. That one in the garage could have come from anywhere. You still haven't come up with any *reason* for Chuck to be a killer."

Maybe not, but I'd come up with at least an idea along those lines. I tried it on her. "Kat Hayward was one of the women you talked into trying to seduce your brother, wasn't she? How about Valerie? Did you get her to take a turn at it, too?"

"Hell no. Not Valerie. She was suffering her own hang-ups over little dyke-twatted Cindy. What the hell kind of theory is that, anyway? He killed everybody he failed to make it with? You think I talked Jason into trying it with him, too?"

"Did you?"

"Fuck you."

"Maybe Jason teased him, made some kind of remark about Chuck not being able to cut it. Maybe Valerie said something, too."

"They never would have done anything like that. Besides, there was no longer any reason to. Chuck was able to make it just fine— I saw to that."

It took a full minute for the realization of what she'd just admitted to completely sink in. When it did, I don't know what showed on my face, but whatever Sara saw there caused her to flush deeply.

"Don't look at me like that," she said. "Fucking is what I do, remember? I'm the best there is. When the rest of those tired cunts couldn't help Chuck, I finally decided I had to take care of it myself."

"You seduced your own brother?" I said, still somewhat stunned by the notion, even more so at her blasé attitude.

"A fuck is a fuck," she replied coolly. "There are a number of cultures on this planet where it is considered permissible—even desirable—for the father or the brothers in a family to take the maidenhead of the girls when they reach a certain age in order to ensure that the act is done with a degree of gentleness and loving that might be lacking at the hands of a stranger."

I said, "That's real educational, sweetheart, but it's a bunch of hogwash as far as I'm concerned."

She thrust her chin out defiantly. "Chuck didn't think it was hogwash. He thought it was a great idea, couldn't get enough."

"You sick bitch. You think you were *helping* him by doing that?"

A shadow fell across the doorway and suddenly Chuck was standing there behind Sara. He put his hands protectively on her shoulders. "You leave my sister alone," he said, eyes hot and angry. "I won't allow you to talk to her that way."

He might be some kind of victim in all this himself, but that didn't make him any less dangerous. "Two days ago, Charlie," I said to him, "I saw you shove a copy of *Skip Steamer and the Skateboard Raiders* in your pants pocket. Where is that book now?"

He frowned. "What the hell are you talking about?"

"Show me the fucking book," I growled, "or I show you the inside of a cop station."

Sara laughed nervously. "Hannibal has this crazy idea you killed three people. Jason and Valerie, and now Kat. He has this crazy idea you could do something like that."

The heat of Chuck's gaze never left me. "I had the feeling right from the start you might be good enough to cause me trouble. I figured I'd probably end up having to kill you, too."

I caught that "too" right away, but Sara took a little longer. She slowly turned her head and torso so that she was looking up and back at her brother. "What do you mean?" she asked, her voice breaking into a hoarse whisper. "What are you saying?"

Chuck's hands patted her shoulders comfortingly. "It'll be all right. We'll still make it out west like you wanted. Maybe not California, maybe Arizona or somewhere. Somewhere we can start brand new, just the two of us. Nobody around here will think anything of us leaving. They'll figure we were scared off by the killings."

"I *am* frightened by the killings."

"Everything will be all right," he told her. His eyes stayed on me.

"But California is where I need to go. I have opportunities there. I want—"

"No," he said sharply. "You need to stay away from those people. You need to be with me. Bad things happen around those kind of people. That's what I've been trying to show you, to make you see."

"How have you been trying to show her?" I said. "By killing 'those kind of people' in order to frighten her away from them?"

"No!" Sara protested, not wanting to hear it.

"It was the only way," Chuck said. "We're in love, we want to be together. But we could never have a life together as long as she was around them, as long as they could keep luring her away from me."

"God!" Sara jerked free and stumbled to the middle of the room. She spun to face her brother, emitting a great hiccupping sob. "How could you? They were my friends."

For the first time since he'd appeared in the doorway, Chuck's eyes left me. Knots of muscle bounced at the hinges of his jaw, his teeth flashed in a snarl that aimed at Sara. "Jason was no friend! I know what happened the night he came here to rehearse. I came back and saw the two of you, heard you . . . in your bed. The same bed where *we* made love. Where you told me how special I was, how much you cared for me."

"Of course I care for you—you're my brother."

He made a gesture with his hands. "But don't you see? It's more than that with us. Didn't you ever wonder, when we were kids growing up, why we didn't fight and squabble like other kids in the same families did? It was because there was an *extra* kind of feeling between us. You revealed the truth to me—to both of us— when we had sex. Physical love. You showed me—"

"Stop!" Sara cried. "Stop!"

"Is that why you killed Jason Hobbs?" I asked Chuck. "Because you caught him in bed with your sister—your lover?" I was standing flat-footed, arms at my sides, in full view. I wanted to edge my right hand closer to the .45 in the shoulder rig under my sweater, but at the same time I didn't want to do anything too overt, didn't want him to clam up or to turn rabbit on me before I got more information out of him.

Chuck's eyes snapped back to me. "Yes, that's why I killed Jason," he said. "He was a greedy pig. He had sex with her all the time on the set. Why did he have to come here—to our place, our bed—for still more? I hated him for that. There was a butcher knife on the drainboard of the sink. I saw it when I went running out and took it with me. I waited for him. When he came down, I stabbed him in the back and pushed him to the ground. Then I fell on him and stabbed him some more. I stabbed and stabbed and stabbed. I pretended I was fucking him, sticking my knife in him for all the times he'd stuck his thing in my sister."

Sara sank to her knees and leaned heavily against the edge of the bed, groaning, pressing her face against the bedspread, digging her fingers into it like claws.

I kept at him. "Why Valerie then? What did she ever do to you?"

Chuck looked at me the way you might look at somebody who'd asked a ridiculously simple question. "That was the plan that came to me," he said. "Don't you get it? When I saw how upset everybody got over Jason's murder, how shook up and scared they were, afraid some crazy might be stalking the whole movie troupe, I realized a way I could get Sara away from them, make her *want* to get away from them, away from the danger. I had to arrange more killings, make the danger more real. Valerie was always friendly to me, sitting down to talk with me, inviting me over sometimes. She thought I was safe, see? She'd heard I couldn't get it up no more. She was going through her lez thing and I was no threat as a male. So I stopped over to her place one day like she asked. She was alone. . . ."

Still with her face pressed into the bedspread, Sara moaned, "Oh, God, what have I done? What have I done to everybody?"

I said, "And Kat the same way, huh? Just to pile up the bodies."

"It was like an omen, man, seeing her out in that blizzard that night. I knew I was going to have to kill somebody else. At least one more. And there she was. So I followed her back to her place and did her there in the garage."

Sara pushed herself away from the bed, swiveling on one hip "Goddamn you," she shouted at her brother. "God-fucking-*damn* you! After everything I tried to do to help you, after what Mom and Dad went through . . . how could you be so awful? So insane?"

Chuck held out a hand to her. "I did it for us."

Sara lunged to her feet. "You *ruined* everything for us. For me! Everything! Ruined!"

She ran at him with fists flailing, raining punches onto his broad chest. The blows sounded like the thuds of a distant bass drum. Harder and faster she punched, screeching like a banshee from some guttural place deep inside.

Chuck held his ground, bracing himself by gripping the sides of the door frame. He looked down at Sara, frowning, taking the blows, letting the sound of her rage wash over him. And in one heartbeat of time, amid that flurry of whitened knuckles and saliva-spraying wails of frustration, I saw a kind of realization descend over his face. A realization of everything he had done. Everything he had become. Everything he had lost.

When his eyes swung to me this time, all the heat was gone. In its place was emptiness, sadness maybe. And tremendous loneliness. The eyes followed my hand reaching for the .45 and for a second his expression told me he hoped I'd use it. But then something stronger took over, a survival instinct. He hurled Sara away with a double-palmed slam to her chest, reeled and sprang from the doorway in a single fluid motion.

I heard him go pounding out through the apartment and then the bedroom was rushing by me as I broke into a run after him.

Out of the apartment and down the main corridor and down the flights of stairs we thundered, kicking up dust motes that swirled in our wake like snowflakes. Outside, it was the real thing. Nearly a full inch of new snow had accumulated already, greasing the streets and sidewalks like shortening on a giant concrete griddle. This proved to be my equalizer, the only chance in hell I had of keeping pace with Chuck. On dry ground, his youth and fitness would have eaten me alive.

I skidded out of the street-level door, head whipping back and forth, eyes scanning for my quarry. I spotted him three quarters of a block down, heading west along State Street, toward the river, proceeding at a kind of slipping, stuttering gallop on the treacherous sidewalk.

I went after him. I'd never gotten the .45 drawn. Its weight in the underarm holster slapped against my ribs as I ran, urging me on like a boot heel in a stirrup.

When I hit the State Street bridge, I could feel chips of sleet blowing up off the water, stinging the side of my face. The midmorning vehicular traffic on State was very light. There were no other pedestrians in sight. The only sounds I was aware of were the scraping slap of my feet on the sidewalk and the *huff-huffing* of my own labored breathing.

Ahead of me, Chuck began to angle across the street, cutting toward the landscaped front courtyard of the United Bank complex. I followed. As he reached the opposite curb, his foot slipped and he pitched forward. But he turned it into a tumbling roll and bound back up, agile as a cat. I gained not a fraction of an inch on him.

In fact, I was starting to lose ground. Not even the lousy footing was enough of a hindrance to his athletic prowess to drag him down to my league.

In desperation I called out for him to stop. Of course he paid no heed.

He made his way across the courtyard, weaving in and out among the stone benches and barren shrubbery. Up on Wyman Street, he turned south. I lost sight of him for several seconds behind the high plane of a retaining wall. I struggled up the slight incline on the far side of the courtyard, my lungs and legs aching, the vapor of my breath gusting ahead of me like miniature cannon blasts.

I slipped and fell as I made the turn and started along Wyman. Belly flopped with all the grace of a whale on sand. My teeth clicked together hard and most of what little air there was left in me whistled out between them.

A block and a half ahead of me now, Chuck appeared to have really gotten the feel of the slick track and was running in long, heel-kicking strides, head low, arms pumping. Grunting, I clambered to my feet in what seemed like slow motion, leaned forward, and tottered stubbornly after him once again.

Chestnut Street runs one-way east, paralleling State from a distance of two blocks, intersecting Wyman. This, along with Jefferson Street, running one-way west parallel to State on the opposite side, was designed as an express route around the city's busy downtown hub. With the growth of the outlying malls, of course, the city's downtown congestion has been greatly reduced, but this does nothing to deter drivers from using the four-lane expresses as originally intended. Which is to say, if you're on a streak, hitting the lights right, go like hell.

The point of all this being that the intersection Chuck was approaching was Chestnut. The light on Wyman was red. From his angle, however, Chuck must have seen Chestnut's green turn to yellow. Figuring to have the right-of-way in a matter of seconds, he did nothing to alter his course or speed. What he didn't figure on—or see, apparently—was the city plow coming down Chestnut, emerging from the shadow of the block-wide Metro Center, and flattening out of the shallow curve that swept around it. In the early stages of a storm, street plows go along at a pretty good clip in order to throw the snow back as far as possible to make room for the continuing accumulation. This plow was coming at just such a clip, charging the yellow, hugging the edge of the street with blade low, skimming sporadic sparks from the pavement along with the first inch of white. Chuck couldn't beat it. One second he was there, then the plow, then a swirling mist of snow, then nothing.

By the time I made it to the intersection, the plow had gotten stopped, three-quarters of the way across the bridge with its rear end skewed out at a forty-five-degree angle. In between were scattered scraps of clothing, one torn shoe, and a half dozen piles of stained, shredded meat, steaming in the December air. I leaned against a lamppost, feeling exhausted and weak and sick and stunned. When I couldn't take my eyes off the streaks of gore, I shut them tight. The only sounds were the icy lap of the waves below and the retching of the city driver who had climbed down from his cab and looked back.

31

I got away from there before the cops showed up. I had little to offer as far as anything pertinent to the accident itself, and there was damn sure nothing I could say or do to help Chuck Baines. It probably would have eased the grief and guilt of the plow driver to know the whole story behind the emotional state of the kid who'd raced into his path, but that wasn't a story I was ready to tell. Not right then, anyway. Maybe never.

I went back to Sara Baines's apartment and broke it to her. She was already in a bad way, still reeling from Chuck's confession and trying to deal with her own role as his motivation for the killings. Telling her that her brother was dead on top of it was like delivering the third blow of a Mike Tyson combination. She had every right to go down, but she managed to hang on. I talked her through it, got her past the initial shockwaves, tried to prepare her for the impending visit from the authorities bearing official notification of the accident. When I had her somewhat stable, I put a call through to Foxwood, gave him a quick rundown on the situation, and told him I thought I could get Sara through the notification visit okay but that he'd better have some professional help ready for her after that.

A pair of somber-faced officers arrived within the half hour. With a fair mix of compassion and detachment, they informed Sara of the Chestnut Street fatality involving her brother. She met them with an appropriately blank expression at the outset then went appropriately to pieces after they had delivered their news. I told the officers I was a friend of the family, thanked them for their consideration, and assured them I would look after Miss

Baines. When they were gone, I got back on the horn to Foxwood and told him he'd better get some damned body over there right away.

It was past noon before I arrived back home. The snow seemed to be tapering off, giving indication of the storm system moving through considerably quicker than forecast. Climbing the outside steps to my apartment, I felt like an ancient and aching remnant of the gung-ho hotshot who had descended them only a few hours earlier. The case was completed—very satisfactorily, as far as those who hired me were concerned. You'd think I would have had more positive feelings about that, some sense of accomplishment or at least relief that it was over. I suppose all of that was there somewhere inside me, but for the time being it was dulled by the images that kept reeling through my mind's eye: the expression on Chuck Baines's face as his sister pounded his chest and called him names, then flashing to the ground-up pieces of him scattered across the Chestnut Street bridge. He was, admittedly, a crazed and cold-blooded killer, and I'm hardly renowned for my compassion over that breed; there are dozens and dozens of them on Death Row and elsewhere I would happily pull a trigger or a lever or drop a handful of pellets on. But I'm not sure anybody deserves to go the way Chuck did. And even if they do, I know I don't want to witness it.

Inside the apartment, I shed my coat and stood for a minute leaning against the kitchen counter, trying to decide my next move. The case had consumed practically my every thought and deed for the past four days and now, with it so suddenly over, I was feeling a little disoriented and aimless. The chase and the tumble hadn't done my wounds any good, I was sure of that much. A handful of painkillers seemed to be in order, no matter what else. I washed them down with a glass of tap water, then sent a slug of Old Crow along to keep them company.

I thought about going in and stretching across the bed and closing my eyes and letting the world spin on without me for a while. The thought of lying down made me think about sleep, and the thought of sleep made me think about dreams, and the thought of dreams made me think about Belinda Davies.

I looked over at the phone.

Damn her.

My hand dragged me over there, my fingers punched out the numbers of their own volition. Three rings, then a poppity-click to the recording. Only this time a new one. "This is Belinda. I am unable to come to the phone at the moment. Please leave your name and number at the tone and I shall return your call as soon as I am able."

When the beep sounded in my ear, I shouted into the mouthpiece, "Pick up, goddamn it!"

But if she was there to hear, she didn't respond. I waited for what seemed like a long time, listening to the whispery scratch of the recorder. In the end, I slammed down the handset like a pouting teenager.

I prowled a caged cat's prowl for a time, trying to work off the edge of my frustration. I carried the bottle of Old Crow around with me, taking frequent hits. At some point I wound up lying across the bed anyway, on my stomach, chin propped on my fists, bottle of Old Crow nearby on the nightstand. I must have fallen asleep that way.

The phone had the same effect as a gun going off beside my head. I nearly leaped off the bed and through the wall.

When I came back down to earth and realized what was actually going on, I picked up the receiver a little out of breath. "Hannibal here."

I wanted so bad for it to be Belinda that I felt disgusted with myself for having such a strong need, like it was some dirty addiction.

I recognized the voice on the other end of the line, but it wasn't one I wanted to hear. "Hannibal," he said. "This is Henry Foxwood. We seem to have a problem." His voice sounded strained.

"I'm through with you and your problems," I told him.

"Perhaps. But this particular one may not be through with you. I fear we may both be in grave danger."

"Yeah, well, it's a dangerous old world, Foxy. What with cancer caused by everything known to man and the fucked-up ozone and the nuclear threat and all those crazed druggies out there looking for a fix, it's a bitch. I appreciate your concern, though. Thanks for the tip."

"Damn it, man, this is serious. He may be coming after us next."

" 'He' who? What the hell are you talking about?"

"Haven't you heard? The radio and television have been full of it all afternoon."

"The radio and television are full of it most of the time. I'll say it once more—what are you talking about?"

"Frankie Camicci is dead. Have you truly not heard? He and Crawford and Earl and Uschi, all of them. Their automobile blown to smithereens outside Laguna's restaurant just past noon today."

I gripped the handset a little tighter. "That's a real loss to the community," I said. "But what specifically does it have to do with you and me—why does it put us in danger?"

"The description of a man seen fleeing the scene of the explosion. It sounded alarmingly like Bo Steel, the pimp you fought with at the Graingers' and then turned over to Frankie's people to sit on. He apparently has embarked upon some sort of all-out campaign of retribution. My name may or may not have entered into it. I cannot be sure. But certainly he has reason to look you up."

"Steel? Are you sure?"

"I cannot be one hundred percent sure, no. To be that may mean to be dead. I know only that I have this tremendous sense of . . . dread. I fear to be alone this evening. Your presence here would be most reassuring, Hannibal. At least until I am able to make other arrangements. Will you come? Please?"

"Jesus Christ, Foxwood. Grow up."

"Please. I will beg if I must. All this death and murder is most unnerving. I am not a hardened man such as yourself. I take no shame in that; we are what we are. I will make it worth your while to act in the interest of my safety. If Steel is indeed running amok, you will have to face him sooner or later regardless. Why not be paid for it?"

It wasn't his offer of money that caused me to go. Not this time. Nor was it the desperation in his voice, although that held more sway than the other. Mostly it was what he said about having to face Steel—if it really *was* Steel out there—eventually. I was the one who'd wounded the leopard and left the job unfinished in the first place. It should be up to me to go into the bush after him, before he killed in his wounded frenzy again.

On the drive over to Foxwood's, I dialed around on the car

radio and, sure enough, the local stations, while completely ignoring Chuck Baines's unseemly death—after all, it was just another traffic accident to them—were riddled with news bulletins and discussions concerning the explosion at Laguna's only a few hours before. One commentator identified Frankie Camicci as "a reputed racketeer with heavy ties to the Chicago Mafia" and another started his broadcast by saying, "Gangland warfare hit Rockford today in a most explosive manner." And so it went.

Dusk was settling as I parked in the lot beside Foxwood's building. The gloom matched my mood.

He answered his door practically before I'd lifted my finger off the buzzer. He looked like hell, his face ashen, his perfect silver hair disarrayed.

"Jeez, old timer," I said, stepping in and past him, "you look—"

I never got any more out. The hard rectangle of a gun butt slamming into my solar plexus saw to that. I folded, expelling air with a great *hooompf!,* and hit the carpet skidding. I lay in a kind of fetal position for what seemed like a long time, snot and saliva dripping from my nose and mouth onto Foxwood's expensive carpet, tears running from my eyes, mewling noises emerging from my throat as I tried to suck some breath back in.

When my eyes had quit watering and I was breathing more or less evenly again, I rolled back on one shoulder and looked up.

Foxwood and Bo Steel stood over me, the former looking pasty-faced and horrified, the latter smug with a crazy, dangerous gleam in his eyes. His spiky hair was partly flattened out and the ear I had cut was bandaged to a white lump. He was dressed all in leather as before, zippers in every conceivable place, sparkling like jewelry. In one hand he held a big automatic pistol—some foreign job by the look of it—with a metallic cigar silencer stuck in the end.

"Greetings and salutations, motherfucker," Steel said to me.

Foxwood swallowed hard and gazed down with mournful eyes. "I deeply regret my part in this, Hannibal. He held a gun on me, forced me to make that phone call to you. I—I tried to think of something clever, some way to tip you off, but I was too frightened to think of anything except what he told me to say."

I gave a little shake of my head. "Never mind," I told him.

"Yeah, never mind, you fancified little fruitcake," Steel mocked.

"Tell you what you do next, though, is get down on your knees—that's a position you're used to, I bet—and strip the big guy of his guns. There's one in the shoulder holster, one in one of his boots for sure. If he's got any more, you'd better find those, too, if you know what's good for you. Don't get all boned up while you're down there and start humpin' his leg or somethin', neither."

Trembling, Foxwood knelt beside me and began removing my weapons. His eyes wouldn't meet mine. At this closer distance, I could see red welts across the side of his face and neck.

I looked back up at Steel. "You've had a real busy day, haven't you, pimp?"

He smiled broadly. "Real busy and real satisfying. Wish I could have sold tickets to me blowing up the Godfather Junior and his crew. Man, that was beautiful. Every day he had lunch at that same restaurant, every day he parked in his special spot right next to their big sign. I plastiqued the fuck out to that sign—a little trick Uncle Sam and his army boys taught me, thank you very much—and remoted it from a parking garage across the street. Tripped it just as they got their doors open and were starting to get out. Big Syndicate hot shit thought he could shove a little pimp around with no problem, right? Well, I dropped a turd before breakfast this morning that was bigger than the biggest part of him that was left when I got done."

"And now it's my turn, huh?"

"Bet your ass, big man. Only you I ain't going to do so fast."

"Why here? Why drag Foxwood into it?"

"Because here is where I followed you the other night. I was getting ready to whack you then. But when I saw Camicci and his people coming and going out of here, too, I decided to change my plan a little. Took some doin' to pinpoint this apartment, but I finally narrowed it down. Instead of just you, I'd get all the sonsabitches who tried to shove me around. Fuck it if they were Syndicate. I decided to show everybody who not to mess with. After I whacked those four at noon, I figured you'd be on your guard, alerted. Forcing Foxwood to call you seemed like a good way around that, a way to get you here unprepared and to finish it."

Foxwood stood, having stripped me of the .45 and the derringer. He held these meekly out to Steel, who took them in his free hand. "Remember your promise," the old actor said softly.

"You mean not to hurt you anymore it you cooperated?" Steel

said earnestly. "Hey, not to worry, little man. I never forget a promise." His mouth split into a taunting smile. "The thing is, though . . . I'm a fuck of a liar."

And he shot Foxwood right there. The silencer went *phrrt* two times and Foxwood fell back and down, careening off the end of the couch with blood spraying from a black-rimmed hole high on his chest and another at the base of his throat.

It was all so fast and so unexpected I had no chance to react. Even if I had, Steel would have been ready for me. He immediately fired a third shot, punching a slug through my left thigh where I lay. I bridged and bucked, bellowing in pain, and tried to roll away. He came after me, aiming kicks at my head, smiling maniacally all the while. It wasn't long before the pain and the whirling black leather engulfed me and I dropped into unconsciousness.

I don't know how long I was out, but when I came to I was sitting upright in a straight-backed chair, lashed securely in place, my hands and arms pulled hard behind my back, my ankles and calves bound to the chair legs. My head pounded, the left hinge of my jaw felt gritty and swollen. As far as I could see, my bonds were plastic-coated electrical cords.

Steel's face, wearing that fatally taunting smile, swam into view.

"Hey, tough guy, finally coming around, huh?"

We were in a medium-sized dining room, where I'd apparently been dragged and placed in the chair. Through the doorway, past Steel, I could see a section of the living room where I'd been shot and where, presumably, Foxwood's body still lay. Beside us was an oval, glossy-topped table overhung by an ornate chandelier pouring hot, bright light down onto us. High-backed, beautifully carved wooden chairs were arranged around the table. I assumed it was one of those I was bound to. Steel sat in another directly in front of me.

He continued to smile. "Now the real fun starts. Bet you're excited, ain't you? I know I sure am." He raised his right hand from where it hung at his side. He no longer had a gun in it. Instead he held up the wickedly glinting blade of a straight razor. "And looky, looky at the old friend I brought along to play with us."

"Carve away, you cocksucker," I snarled. "I hope you drown in my blood."

He held the blade in front of my face for a long minute, smiling all the while, then slowly began to lower his hand. Slowly. Until it came to rest on my thigh. Until the handle of the razor jutting from the bottom of his fist pressed into the bullet hole there. Pressed hard, gradually harder. He twisted it back and forth, as if working a corkscrew into a neck of fine red wine. The fresh wound made wet sounds, like a washcloth getting the last few drops of water wrung from it. Blood ran off the edge of the chair seat and down the back of my leg. Pain radiated up through me, making a million beads of sweat pop out on my face and neck, squeezing my eyes and my teeth shut tight, straining me not to let a sound out.

"Talk tough to me some more," Steel urged. "You're going to be screaming like a woman before I'm through with you, so make it good, motherfucker, get it out while you can."

"Eat shit," I grunted.

He threw back his head and howled with laughter, releasing the pressure on my leg. "That's the best you can do?" he crowed. " 'Eat shit,' that's as original as you can get? Jesus-fucking-Christ, man, we're talking your very last words here. Can't you do any better than that?"

"Inspire me, maggot."

"Oh, I will. I'll do my part, you can count on that. Let's see, should I stay below the waist or go upstairs for a while? You got a preference, tough guy? Never mind, I'm saving the downstairs stuff for dessert. I think maybe we'll have a look at what I was able to get done the first time, how about that?"

After slicing open my shirt and sweater, he tore strips of them back between the cords that crisscrossed my chest, exposing my bare torso.

"Hey," he said admiringly at the sight of the long cut below my collarbone. "Got you a good one there, didn't I? But some damn fool went and sewed it all shut, undid all my hard work. Don't worry, though, I can fix it back." He reached out with the tip of the razor and—*bink, bink*—cut through two of the stitches. The pain was quick and sharp, like needle bites. "See? Easy as pie. But you're a good healer there, big guy, everything all wanting to grow back together and everything. Going to make me work for it all over again, ain't you?" With that, he ran the razor the full length of the old cut, reopening it, gouging it to make sure the flaps of healing skin peeled back.

This pain was searing, like a branding iron raked across my hide. I threw my head back and clapped my teeth together tight, but couldn't completely hold in a sort of gargling cry of agony.

"Wheee," Steel giggled. "Now this is really getting fun, just like I promised. But look at how selfish I'm being, working you all on the one side. Here, let me balance things out a little."

He whisked the razor the other way, cutting a diagonal track down across my chest, splitting my right nipple. It didn't feel all that deep, but sonofabitch did it hurt. I tossed my head back and forth, like a dog shaking water, and made the chair I was in bounce on the floor.

Steel sat back, laughing, waiting for me to quit thrashing. When I did, I let my head hang forward, chin resting on chest. I was puffing hard, dripping sweat and blood.

There was a squirming sensation deep in the pit of my stomach. It was the snake of fear, getting bigger, blowing its icy breath into my veins, numbing me, freezing my will and my resistance, threatening to take over. I'd been afraid before, faced danger and even what seemed like sure death. But never like this. Never so slow and so tortuous—and never so fucking certain. Who knew I was here? Who cared? Who knew about Bo Steel? What chance in hell did I have of getting out of this? The crazy bastard was going to kill me and he was going to love every slow, terrible second of it. Would I break? Would I beg and plead and slobber, like he wanted me to? If I did, at what point would I crack? And what the hell difference did it make anyway? Maybe I should start right away, right now. Maybe I'd disappoint him, piss him off, make him kill me quicker.

Sometimes I want to scream out loud . . .

I raised my head and looked at Steel. "What's the matter, you puny fucker?" I said. "That spaghetti strand arm of yours tired already? We done slicing and dicing for the night? I thought we came here to get down, to rock and roll, man. The sight of a little blood make you queasy or something?"

Steel straightened in his chair. I'd managed to wipe the smile off his face. "You want slice and dice, motherfucker?" he snarled. "You want fucking *blood*?"

Can't anyone see me struggling in this skintight shroud?

"Yeah, I want blood. I told you I want to see you drown in it. I want everything you can dish out, you cheap whore wrangler. Let's see who's got the strongest stomach for it."

Steel hitched forward and began undoing the front of my pants. "Now you're big and brave again, since I made the mistake of letting you catch your breath. We'll see how long you stay that way. We'll see how bad you want slice and dice when your cock is laying over there on the table like a pile of cubed carrots."

Over his shoulder, in the doorway, Henry Foxwood appeared. He teetered unsteadily on his feet. The front of him was wet and shiny red from his wounds. His face was bleached out as pale as his hair. In his hands he carried—dragged, to be more accurate—a huge Medieval broadsword like the ones I'd seen on the walls of his trophy room. Could it be that the old celluloid swordsman, pumped full of lead and left for dead, had, while Steel was so occupied with me, crawled off to that room and pulled down one of the ancient weapons? Wherever and however he'd gotten hold of it, it seemed clear he was of mind to use it. Lurching, using the sword almost like a cane, he started across the room toward Steel's back.

In the meantime, Steel had my pants undone. He was panting from a rush of blood lust. "Looks like some parts of you ain't as brave as that big, fat mouth of yours, Hannibal. Look at it, all shriveled up and hiding back in the fur. Or is that nubbin as big as you got?"

I sneered at him. "Why don't you put it between your lips and see if you can make it big enough to suit you, you smiling sonofa-bitch?"

He backhanded me across the mouth. "I ain't no goddamn switch-hitter!"

"Tell that to somebody whose crotch you aren't digging in."

He backhanded me again. "Knock that shit off." With his other hand, the one clutching the razor, he hacked at my exposed stomach, slashing at the corner of my navel. "There's some slicing for you, motherfucker. That the way you like it, huh? That make you happy?"

My stomach muscles jerked in and my upper body snapped rigid, causing the chair to hop back again. Blood trickled down into my pubic hair and my bunched undershorts.

"Don't back away," Steel cooed. "Hold still and get some more of the slicing you pretend to like so much."

Foxwood was immediately behind him now, trying to raise the huge old sword for a two-fisted strike. It threatened to overbalance him. From the doorway to where he stood wavering there was a trail of blood on the carpet. I tried not to look at him, tried not to give anything away with my eyes. Every muscle I had was straining along with his. Inside, I was screaming: *Come on, you glorious old bastard, get it up there. Get it up. Do it. Do it, for God's sake!*

The sword arced through the air, flashing brilliantly. Steel never had an inkling anyone was there. The great blade sank three quarters of the way through his neck. Take the sound of a shovel shooting into wet sand and the juicy pop of biting into a crisp apple, mix them, and you'd have a simulation of the blow landing. Blood flew all over me, the table, the chandelier, everywhere. It felt good.

Steel slid off the side of his chair and fell to the floor and was still, the sword remaining lodged deep.

Foxwood stood teetering over his victim, looking balefully down at him. In a surprisingly bold and strong voice, he announced, "Vanquished . . . by the champion of Camelot!"

And then he toppled to the floor himself and was dead.

EPILOGUE

I eventually learned that "vanquished by the champion of Camelot" was the catch phrase from Foxwood's old TV series. In almost every episode, usually near the close, after Sir Gawaine and Ironfang had saved the day, some grateful beneficiary of their heroism would intone those words as an epitaph for whatever villainy had been dispatched. They became, then, enduring words from the brightest moments as well as the final moments of his life.

I learned this, among other things, during my stay in the hospital. After Foxwood had died saving my life, I had been able to kick over the chair in which I was bound and, with patient and exhaustive struggles, had maneuvered into a position where I could rub my bonds against the edge of the sword still through Steel's neck, finally severing the cords that held me. Drained by the ordeal, from my loss of blood and the beating and the stress, I was nearly done in by the time I was free. I made it to the phone, though, punched out an emergency number, and got a rescue squad on the way.

There had been no way to keep the cops out of it this time, not entirely anyway. I glossed it over as best I could, claiming that Foxwood had called me for bodyguard work, citing some obscure danger he felt he was in. When I'd gotten to his place, I found Bo Steel already there with the drop on him and then on me, too. I related the rest of it pretty much the way it had gone down, maintaining I never knew the exact relationship between Foxwood and Steel or what their animosity stemmed from.

I got away with it, but just barely. The authorities didn't want to buy the bill of goods I had to sell and weren't very damned happy about getting it crammed down their throats.

Lieutenant of Detectives Ed Terry, my almost-friend on the RPD, stopped by on the second day of my hospital stay to tell me as much. Part of what he said went like this: "There are a lot of loose ends flapping around out there in the breeze, Hannibal. Some of them seem to keep wanting to get tangled together—like the deaths of Steel and Camicci and an ex-stripper named Kat and now this Foxwood guy who had some very interesting tapes in his video library which I, of course, had no cause to officially view. Makes a fella wonder. Makes me personally wonder like a sonofabitch. How many times, I'm curious, were you able to eel in and out of that tangle before you finally got your ass skinned but not so bad you can't still lie there now looking as smug as the cat who gulped the prize goldfish? Most of the ones who bought it were no tremendous loss to the world, so it don't matter so much, I guess. Losing some of them was a downright bonus, in fact. So it looks like you're probably going to get away with it. I just want *you* to know that *I* know the fucking difference. That's all."

Bomber and Liz came to see me, too, of course. Plenty of times. The first time Liz cried over me and called me "baby" and "poor thing." Bomber had to play it stoic, naturally. But when he went to leave that first night, he took my hand and held it considerably longer than a handshake is supposed to last.

On the third day, Belinda Davies showed up. She was sitting there when I opened my eyes from a nap. I smelled her before I saw her. That's how I knew it wasn't a dream. She smelled great and looked better.

"Hello," she said softly.

"You didn't have to come," I said. "You could have sent a recording, had the nurses play it for me."

"Please. Don't be cruel."

"Elvis. About 1958."

"What?"

"Never mind."

She smoothed the fur folded across her lap. "How are you feeling?"

"Peachy. Want to go slam dancing later on tonight?"

"You look as if you have been slam-danced quite enough."

"Yeah, but I just can't make my feet behave."

She smoothed her fur some more. "I—I wanted to see you one last time. To say good-bye."

"I thought I'd already gotten that message."

"Frederico returned for Frankie's funeral. He wants me to go back with him. He says he wants me closer by. He has promised to get me work in the Italian cinema—legitimate films."

"Well, I hope you'll all be real happy. You and Frederico and Mama and his wife and a cast of thousands."

"Please. No need to be bitter. The time we spent together was—"

"The time we spent together was great. Some of the best fucking I've had in years. I'm much obliged. Who's bitter?"

Holding her body very rigid, she leaned forward and placed a fat envelope on the bed beside me. "Frederico and Albert want you to have that. Your discretion and your thoroughness are greatly appreciated."

I slapped savagely at the envelope, knocking it off the bed, sending it skidding across the hard, polished hospital floor.

"I don't want any more of their stinking money," I said. "And I damn sure don't want it from you."

She stood. "I am sorry. Coming here was a mistake."

She moved around the end of the bed, her heels cracking on the floor like whip lashes across my heart. At the door she paused and looked back. Her eyes were shiny and her hair, backlit from the hallway, glowed like molten copper. "I shan't soon forget you, Joe Hannibal," she said.

And then she was gone.

I lay there for a long time with my eyes squeezed tightly shut, trying not to smell her or think about her or ache over her.

Sometime in the middle of the night, I got out of bed and retrieved the envelope off the floor. I dropped it in the wastebasket beside my bed, stuffing it deep into the used tissues and crumpled paper cups.

When I awoke in the morning, the wastebasket had been emptied. I'd never looked to see how much the envelope contained. That way I never knew just how big a fool I was.

Robert B. PARKER

"The toughest, funniest, wisest private-eye in the field."*

☐ A CATSKILL EAGLE	11132-3	$4.95
☐ CEREMONY	10993-0	$4.50
☐ CRIMSON JOY	20343-0	$4.95
☐ EARLY AUTUMN	12214-7	$4.95
☐ GOD SAVE THE CHILD	12899-4	$4.95
☐ THE GODWULF MANUSCRIPT	12961-3	$4.95
☐ THE JUDAS GOAT	14196-6	$4.95
☐ LOOKING FOR RACHEL WALLACE	15316-6	$4.50
☐ LOVE AND GLORY	14629-1	$4.50
☐ MORTAL STAKES	15758-7	$4.95
☐ PALE KINGS AND PRINCES	20004-0	$4.50
☐ PROMISED LAND	17197-0	$4.95
☐ A SAVAGE PLACE	18095-3	$4.95
☐ TAMING A SEAHORSE	18841-5	$4.95
☐ VALEDICTION	19246-3	$4.95
☐ THE WIDENING GYRE	19535-7	$4.95
☐ WILDERNESS	19328-1	$4.50

The Houston Post

FREE FROM DELL

with purchase plus postage and handling

Congratulations! You have just purchased one or more
titles featured in Dell's Mystery Promotion. Our goal is to
provide you with quality reading and entertainment, so we
are pleased to extend to you a limited offer to receive a
selected Dell mystery title(s) *free* (plus $1.00 postage and
handling per title) for each mystery title purchased. Please
read and follow all instructions carefully to avoid delays in
your order.

1) Fill in your name and address on the coupon printed below. No facsimiles or
copies of the coupon allowed.

2) The Dell Mystery books are the only books featured in Dell's Mystery
Promotion. No other Dell titles are eligible for this offer.

3) Enclose your original cash register receipt with the price of the book(s)
circled plus $1.00 **per book** for postage and handling, payable in check or
money order to: Dell Mystery Offer. Please do not send cash in the mail.
Canadian customers: Enclose your original cash register receipt with the
price of the book(s) circled plus $1.00 **per book** for postage and handling in
U.S. funds.

4) This offer is only in effect until April 29, 1991. Free Dell Mystery requests
postmarked after April 22, 1991 will not be honored, but your check for
postage and handling will be returned.

5) Please allow 6-8 weeks for processing. Void where taxed or prohibited.

**Mail to: Dell Mystery Offer
            P.O. Box 2081
            Young America, MN 55399-2081**

NAME_____

ADDRESS_____

CITY_____STATE_____ZIP_____

BOOKS PURCHASED AT_____

AGE_____

(Continued)

Book(s) purchased:_____

_____

_____

I understand I may choose one free book for each Dell Mystery book purchased (plus applicable postage and handling). Please send me the following:

(Write the number of copies of each title selected next to that title.)

BLOOD SHOT
Sara Paretsky
V.I. Warshawski is back—this time a missing person assignment turns into a murder investigation that puts her more than knee-deep in a deadly mixture of big business corruption and chemical waste.

FIRE LAKE
Jonathan Valin
In this Harry Stoner mystery, the Cincinnati private eye enters the seamy and dangerous world of drugs when a figure from his past involves him in a plot that forces him to come to terms with himself.

THE HIT MAN COMETH
Robert J. Ray
When a professional hit man who has his sights set on a TV evangelist wounds Detective Branko's partner instead, Newport Beach's hottest detective finds himself with a list of suspects that is as bizarre as it is long.

THE NANTUCKET DIET MURDERS
Virginia Rich
A handsome new diet doctor has won over Nantucket's richest widows with his weight-loss secrets—and very personal attention. But when murder becomes part of the menu, Mrs. Potter stirs the pot to come up with a clever culinary killer.

A NOVENA FOR MURDER
Sister Carol Anne O'Marie
"Move over, Miss Marple, here comes supersleuth Sister Mary Helen, a nun with an unusual habit of solving murders."
—*San Francisco Sunday Examiner & Chronicle*

SHATTERED MOON
Kate Green
When a young woman gets involved with the L.A.P.D. and a missing person case, her most precious gift—her healing vision—becomes her most dangerous enemy, filling every moment with mounting menace. . . and turning the secrets of her past murderously against her.

TOO CLOSE TO THE EDGE
Susan Dunlap
Jill Smith, a street-smart, savvy detective, finds herself trapped within a murder victim's intricate network of perilous connections.

A NICE CLASS OF CORPSE
Simon Brett
When the sixty-seven-year-old Mrs. Pargeter checks into a seaside hotel for some peace and quiet, what she finds instead is a corpse in the lobby and a murder to snoop into on the dark side of the upper crust.

POLITICAL SUICIDE
Robert Barnard
A member of Parliament meets an untimely—and suspicious—demise.

THE OLD FOX DECEIV'D
Martha Grimes
When the body of a mysterious woman is found murdered, Inspector Richard Jury of Scotland Yard finds himself tracking a very foxy killer.

DEATH OF A PERFECT MOTHER
Robert Barnard
Everyone had a motive to kill her. . . so Chief Inspector Dominic McHale finds himself stumped on his very first homicide case—puzzled by a lengthy list of suspects and a very clever killer.

THE DIRTY DUCK
Martha Grimes
In addition to the murders being staged nightly at the Royal Shakespeare Theatre, a real one has been committed not too far away, and the killer has left a fragment of Elizabethan verse behind as a clue.

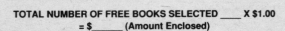

TOTAL NUMBER OF FREE BOOKS SELECTED _____ **X $1.00**
= $_____ (Amount Enclosed)

Dell has other great books in print by these authors. If you enjoy them, check your local book outlets for other titles.